# Musings of a Madwoman

# Also by Jazzy Mitchell

*Leveling Up*

*Undertow*

*You Matter*

*Lost Treasures*

# Musings of a Madwoman

Jazzy Mitchell

# Musings of a Madwoman

By Jazzy Mitchell
©2018 Jazzy Mitchell

ISBN (trade)  9781633040489
ISBN (eBook)  9781633040465

Launch Point Press
4804 NW Bethany Blvd, Suite I-2 #148
Portland, OR 97229

Editor:  Kellie Doherty
Cover Design:  Michelle Brodeur

# Blurb

Three women's lives interweave as they struggle to navigate life and love. And the effects of a meteorite.

Patricia Steitz, a successful romance writer, is flabbergasted when Rudi Singlewood shows up at one of her book signings and initiates a summer romance. She worries that the fantasies she's harbored regarding the world-renown Broadway actress may prevent her from accepting who Rudi really is. She relates her fears to her best friend, Marcia Struthers, a successful Manhattan litigator.

Knowing that Patricia has dreamed of Rudi for years, Marcia urges her to give the actress a chance by getting to know who she is behind her public persona. While working a high-profile case, Marcia must confront her resurging feelings for lead opposing counsel, Lexie Yamin, and the appearance of an unrequited love. All is not as it seems, however, as Marcia deals with unexpected physical changes and developing mental abilities after an encounter with a meteorite. Marcia's not the only one dealing with changes induced by an extraterrestrial rock, though.

Kiernan Connelly, who has received intriguing letters over several months, begins to question her lifestyle. Her casual sexual relationship with Rudi and passable acting career no longer fulfill her. As Kiernan makes changes in her life, she finds herself dealing with the strange reality of being able to hear others' thoughts. Could it be related to her close encounter with a meteorite?

# Acknowledgments

Many people ask me how I came up with this idea. It is a deceptively complex question for an author to answer. How do we come up with ideas? What spurs our imagination? How do we get from here to there? I began by writing bits and pieces of this book years ago. Eventually, I began to see a storyline immersed within all the scribbles and false starts. And I got excited. Because, I know others think about these things. I know others want to explore these roads. I know others are exploring and seeking, and wanting more. More from their lives, from their daily grind, from their struggles and triumphs, failures and successes. We are on Earth to experience and to love that experience. Yet, sometimes within this mad, wonderful world, we get lost, lose focus, question, and disconnect. So, let's reconnect, rebuild, love, and accept.

Of course, no acknowledgment page would be complete without thanking the phenomenal, enlightened being in the form of my wife, Peggy—I could not have gotten this far without her constant support and faith in my abilities. I am thankful for the many late-night debates and the help she provided to propel me toward clarity and succinctness. More importantly, her unconditional love and belief in me mean everything.

I would be remiss if I did not mention my beautiful children, Jacqui, Drake, and Kat. Every day I see reality through their pure perspective. It is uplifting and renewing. It reminds me that experiences shape our interpretation of everyday events.

And of course I want to thank Ashley for her tough love, Sara for her helpful ideas, and Rosemary for her staunch support. Most writers will agree that it's hard to slash and burn the written word, no matter when it is best for the story. They pushed me, cajoled me, and let me know in comforting terms it was okay to remove the words which did not further the story. Similarly, I am grateful to Kellie, CK, Mich, Lee, and Desert Palm Press for working with me to polish this rough stone into a shiny gem. I appreciate being the recipient of their guidance, talent, and patience.

# Chapter One

"WE INTERRUPT THIS REGULARLY scheduled program to bring you this late-breaking news. We have our lead reporter, Amy Craft, live at the scene. Amy, can you tell us what's happening?"

"Yes, thanks, Greg. I'm at Sunny Horizon Resort where an unidentified object blazed across the sky moments ago, lighting up the entire area before punching into the ground. Excuse me," Amy said with a slightly raised voice as she walked to the left. "Excuse me, sir, but did you see what caused the sky to light up?" She placed her microphone in front of a young man's face.

A blond-haired man in his twenties looked startled, glancing down at the microphone in confusion and clearing his throat. "Um, yeah. I was in my room when I saw a flash of light through the curtains and ran outside to see what was happening."

Amy pulled the microphone back. "And what did you see once you ran outside?"

The man leaned in to speak into the microphone. She held it steady, a fake smile pasted across her face.

"Yeah, I saw a white plume of smoke across the sky. You know, like when a plane sky-writes? It was huge. I saw an area where the trees looked mowed down. I tried to get closer to see what happened, like whether a plane crashed or something, but a bunch of government types wouldn't let me get close."

Greg interjected, "Amy, were you able to see what caused the damage to the trees?"

"No, Greg. The area was cordoned off. In fact, we were unable to get close enough to even confirm something hit the ground, although the surrounding trees obviously were flattened by a concussive force."

"Thank you, Amy," Greg said.

Amy kept a smile while she listened to Greg finish the segment. "Well, there you have it, folks. We'll be sure to keep you updated on this developing story."

As soon as the feed stopped, Amy stepped away from the camera. She watched several government officials pile out of a black SUV and head to a side trail. She wouldn't be able to get anywhere near the impact point. Although she was tempted to try again, she decided to pack up and go home. She doubted it would be interesting to anyone other than science nerds. *No one cares.* Including her.

# Chapter Two

STANDING IN FRONT OF a rapt audience, Patricia Steitz concentrated on reading, enunciating each word and using her voice to convey her character's emotions. She could hardly believe she was in front of so many people while reading a passage from her best-selling romance, *Star Light, Star Bright (Make My Wish Come True Tonight)*. The first and only book she'd ever written. She felt as if she were in a dream—a damn awesome dream.

Taking a steadying breath, Patricia glanced at the page. "A flurry of activity caught Jenny's eye. Turning, she froze in amazement, not daring to believe the object of her affection stood not six feet away. Rooted to the spot as a wave of awareness roared through her, Jenny concentrated on her breathing. The handsome man strolled toward her. Once he reached Jenny, her eyes widened, mouth opening and closing several times before her eyes rolled back and, as if a Victorian heroine, she fainted."

Patricia finished with a grin, gratified to find some people chuckled and clapped. She answered a few questions before moving to a table where several novels were stacked. As she signed books and handed them to her visitors, she tried to contain the broad smile fighting to surface, thrilled so many people came to the event. Astounded, even.

"Thank you for coming by," Patricia said to a little old lady. *Mary*, she thought, handing back the signed book. She watched Mary clutch the book to her chest, bow slightly, and scurry away. Turning to the next person, Patricia sucked in her breath. Blinking, she sat up straight, her visitor delivering a brilliant smile. *Stunning*.

"Will you sign my book?" Rudi Singlewood asked.

Patricia took it automatically and lifted the book cover. "Well, this is a switch," she mused. Pausing before she wrote an inscription, she gazed at the woman through lowered lashes. "Do you remember me?"

"Of course. You gave me those wonderful roses."

Thinking for a moment, Patricia scribbled, "Life is short—take chances! Patricia M. Steitz."

Looking at the words, the actress laughed. "I wish I had taken a chance."

Patricia smiled. "There are no mistakes, and no need to regret any decisions you've made. You did what felt best for you at that time. Thank you for coming by."

Rudi reacted to the polite dismissal by nodding, then she leaned toward Patricia in an intimate pose. "Would you consent to joining me for dinner tonight? I may have wasted time, but I intend to make up for it, if you'll allow me."

Patricia's stomach dropped at the offer while heat raced through her veins. It was one thing to fantasize how Rudi would waltz into her life and sweep her off her feet, and quite another for it to actually happen. She wasn't ready. *I still need to learn how to walk gracefully in high heels for fuck's sake.* She knew she was doomed. Ready or not, she needed to give an answer, and she refused to let her insecurities get the better of her. Slipping into the star-struck haze she often felt regarding Rudi, Patricia swept her eyes toward the line of people patiently waiting for her autograph before studying the woman before her. Short, spiky, chestnut-colored hair framed delicate features and mesmerizing gray eyes. Blinking, Patricia stuttered her consent, and they arranged to meet in front of the restaurant located at Patricia's hotel that night.

Patricia allowed herself to sit, flabbergasted, for all of five seconds before focusing on the rest of her visitors, her hand tingling where Rudi squeezed it before departing. After another hour of autographing, the signing ended, and Patricia took a last look around the posh bookstore on the Upper West Side of the bustling city. In the back corner a barista prepared coffee, the mouth-watering aroma permeating the area. Several chairs surrounded small tables, and when a book reading occurred, it was easy enough for everyone to find space to listen. Walking through the bookstore to the exit, Patricia noticed how the displays focused on summer reading lists. Several of the books included those she loved reading when she was in school. She wondered whether one day students would read a book she wrote. *Not if all I write are silly romances.* She sighed and began to process that somehow she was going to be dining with the most beautiful, passionate, and enigmatic woman on Earth. *Good lord, what am I going to wear?*

She only had a few hours to figure it out before she attended the most important dinner of her life. It amazed her that Rudi remembered her at all. *All because I gave her some flowers at her show.* Well, now that she had Rudi's attention, she needed to keep it. *Not that I have any clue on how to do that.* Such a well-known celebrity probably had people flinging themselves at her feet all the time. She'd have to wing it. Hurrying back to her hotel room, she stared at each article of clothing with critical eyes. Finally, she decided to wear the little black cocktail dress. It would have to do.

Seated in the restaurant two hours later, Patricia sought to calm her nerves while listening to Rudi's story. Her face heated, chastising herself once more for her klutziness when she arrived at the restaurant. Patricia didn't pay attention while she walked toward her date. One moment she had eyes only for Rudi, and the next she was on her backside, wishing the floor would swallow her up. *Those damn stilettos.* Patricia even practiced walking in them, but she was like a drunk on stilts, teetering with each step and losing her balance as if she were the headliner in a comedy skit. Rudi quickly kneeled beside her, face radiating concern. She helped Patricia rise, and then regaled her with several stories of how she'd tripped while walking on the stage, off the stage, upstage, downstage, until Patricia had tears of laughter running down her flushed face, her mortification diminishing with each story. Coming back to the present, she listened to a tale of how one night a mob of fans camped outside Rudi's theater, waiting for her in the pouring rain after a show.

"I didn't leave immediately due to a surprise visit from some friends I hadn't seen in years. We reminisced on past events, discussed our projects, and talked about what we were hoping to do next. After finally bidding adieu, I was dismayed to find a group of people huddled in the rain near the backstage exit. While one person held an umbrella, I signed autographs and took pictures with them."

"That was so nice of you," Patricia gushed, imagining how happy she would have felt if she were one of the soaked fans.

"It took nearly two hours, but everyone was happy. It was the least I could do after what they endured," she ended with a chuckle. Taking a sip of chardonnay, Rudi glanced at Patricia, eyes bright and teeth gleaming.

"I'm sure they were grateful for your willingness to spend time with them. They'll probably always remember that day."

"Oh, no." Rudi waved the comment away with a flick of the wrist. "I doubt it."

Patricia was quick to heap on more praise. "No, really. I was thinking that if I were one of those people, I would have felt so grateful. It's a great example of how you don't take your admirers for granted. You care about them."

"Of course I do. I wouldn't be doing what I love if not for people like them. They go to my shows. Write letters to me. Support my projects."

"Well, you are good at what you do. Tell me," Patricia leaned forward, "did you always want to be an actress? Have you thought about starring in any of the classics like Ibsen or Williams or Shakespeare?"

Rudi's eyebrows pulled down, a crinkle forming between them. "My show is doing so well I haven't really thought about the next project. Anything's possible." Her eyes flittered around the room.

*Way to kill a conversation and a perfect date. Better get this back on track.* "I read about your play. It sounds like it was made for you. The reviews talk about how effortlessly you inhabit the role. I can't wait to see it."

"Are you still in town tomorrow night? I can leave a ticket for you at the box office."

"Unfortunately, I have to get back to Boston, and my flight's tomorrow, early evening. Definitely the next time I'm in town, though."

Once Rudi paid the bill, they stalled outside the entrance to the restaurant, and Patricia felt a wave of heat move through her, anticipation and fear warring within her. *What if Rudi never wants to see me again? Am I about to get the practiced brush off?* She waited for the worst.

"I have enjoyed this evening. When will I see you again?" Rudi asked.

Patricia stared at Rudi, slack-jawed. This was a surprise. A fucking amazing surprise. For years she had imagined spending time with Rudi, and now here she was, offering that dream on a silver platter. She took note of the older woman's defined cheekbones, flawless skin, toned body, and sinfully long legs. She wore black tailored slacks showcasing her tight ass, and a burgundy-colored silk blouse with the top three buttons undone. The hint of cleavage made Patricia dizzy. *Well, one more meeting won't hurt.*

"I don't have any great plans for tomorrow before I fly back to Boston."

"Let's meet for lunch then."

After arranging the details, Rudi insisted on walking Patricia to her room. The look in her eyes made Patricia feel weak, but she was determined not to swoon again. She needed to calm the hell down. Once they reached her hotel room, Patricia turned to say goodbye. "I'm so glad you came to the book signing."

"Me, too. I knew I couldn't let another opportunity slip by." Rudi stepped forward, laser eyes holding Patricia in place, and ran long fingers down her cheek before cupping her jaw. "There's something about you. I felt it when you gave me those flowers. I felt it when I read your book. And I felt it when I heard your voice at the bookstore. You are quite mesmerizing."

Blinking, Patricia found it hard to believe. *I have this effect on her?* Before Patricia could string together enough words to reply, Rudi leaned in and brushed their lips together. She was slow and soft and teasing, ripping a low moan from Patricia's lips when they parted. Rudi took the invitation, swooping back in. Their tongues met for the first time, and Patricia's breath stuttered. She trembled, moans escaping with every stroke of Rudi's talented tongue. She clutched on to Rudi's back for dear life.

*This is not cool. This is not me acting cool. At all.* Forcing herself to loosen her grasp, she ran her hands up Rudi's spine and rested them on her shoulders.

Rudi delivered one last devastating kiss, which somehow managed to remove all the bones from Patricia's body. It was that good. Patricia kept her eyes closed even after Rudi pulled back, taking a moment to revel in the euphoric high and trying to catch her breath.

"I'll see you tomorrow," Rudi murmured.

Opening her eyes, Patricia nodded. She turned toward the door and fumbled with the cardkey several times before getting it open. Glancing at Rudi, she felt her face flush at the amused look she saw. "Good night," she whispered, stepping in to the room and closing the door before leaning against it with a sigh. *Real smooth.* Getting ready for bed in a haze, she slipped under the sheets and replayed the evening in her mind with a giddy smile. She was nearly delirious with happiness. Tomorrow couldn't come quickly enough.

*** 

After a restful sleep, one filled with dreams of Rudi kissing her and whispering in her ear, Patricia felt invincible. Walking over to the window to view the bustling metropolis and blushing as her thoughts traveled a well-worn path through her fantasies, she realized they had nothing on the truth. She had devoted much time—*too much time,* she thought wryly—toward possible first encounters. Patricia shook her head in amusement. And those kisses—so full of promise. Whatever her future with Rudi Singlewood, she intended to enjoy every moment.

Hurrying through her ablutions, Patricia found herself walking toward the deli where she was meeting Marcia Struthers, her former college roommate at Boston University. She thought her friend would be excited to hear about Rudi but an hour later, Marcia's face displayed a myriad of emotions. Marcia was as much a fan as Patricia was. In fact they had gone to the play together where Patricia had offered two dozen coral roses to Rudi during the standing ovation. Rudi made a great display of trying to give the roses to the other leading ladies. They had shaken their heads, shielding themselves playfully with their hands. Rudi then bowed toward Patricia with a full-fledged smile aimed her way. The next few seconds were a bit fuzzy for Patricia. She only remembered feeling heat rush through her body and suffusing her face as a roaring sound filled her ears. Then Rudi winked and disappeared.

About six weeks later, Patricia received a hand-written letter thanking her for the roses. Patricia had stuck her business card in the bouquet with the hope she might receive a response, but she never expected one. Once she received the note, her hopes of something more drove her to write to the actress with the request to become pen pals. She wrote at the end of the letter, "Take a chance!" Of course, she received nothing. How could she suppose that a celebrity would take the time to write to her? Eventually Patricia released her unrealistic expectations and moved on.

Yet, here it was merely a year later, and she had enjoyed dinner and several goodnight kisses with this woman who haunted her dreams. Patricia snorted at the thought of Rudi seeing all the collector memorabilia she had accumulated regarding her. Pictures, books, magazines, interviews, T-shirts— she had them all.

Marcia, a willowy blonde with washed-out blue eyes, demanded every detail. "Oh, my God! And you didn't just pull her into your hotel room and ravage her? Are you nuts?"

Patricia smiled. "Nope. Although I must be mad for even contemplating seeing her again. Last night was nerve-racking and exhilarating. I'm surprised I didn't have a heart attack. But we're meeting for lunch today."

"Is it me, or did it get hot in here?" Marcia joked, fanning herself with her hand.

Patricia shot a mock glare Marcia's way and laughed.

"So, what's your schedule like once you return to Boston?"

"Actually, I'm taking a summer course at B.U. It sounds fascinating. The name of the course is  Enlightenment 101: Musings of a Madwoman. The professor teaching it is Thea Corelli." Patricia bit into her onion bagel loaded with extra cream cheese, and moaned at how good it tasted.

"What's the course covering, besides enlightenment that is?" Marcia hummed as she polished off her chocolate croissant.

"As far as I can tell, it covers self-awareness and self-actualization in the modern world, but this woman seems as normal as they come. She's taught high school and college classes for about ten years and received great reviews." Patricia took a sip of her orange juice. "This is the first year she's offering it, and there are over a hundred people signed up."

"Wow. You'll have to let me know how it goes. Is she a philosophy professor?"

"No. I believe she's a part-time English professor. Maybe she's basing the class on literary classics." Patricia shrugged. "I don't know. Since there's no reading assignment for the first class, I have no idea what to expect." She took another bite and waved her hand. "Enough about that. Tell me about that team-building retreat you're going on next weekend. What's it for?"

"Oh, you know." Marcia rolled her eyes. "A bunch of lawyers pretending to get along for three days. I'm surprised they're making us go when it will cut into our time for cranking out those billable hours."

Patricia chuckled. "No kidding. Then again, isn't that what first-year associates are for?"

"True. Perhaps I'll be surprised, and it will be interesting. I doubt it'll be anything close to the excitement in your life."

Patricia scoffed.

"Hey, I'm not the one who made out with Rudi Singlewood."

Thinking of how it felt to kiss Rudi, Patricia had to agree. "There is that."

***

### TUESDAY, JUNE 6, 2017 10:33 A.M.

Looking at her reflection in the mirror, Kiernan Connelly frowned. "Honestly, is it too much to ask for someone to powder my nose?"

A young intern dabbed her face with some powder as assistants helped others get ready for the celebrity auction. Several stars sat in neighboring chairs while they had their hair shaped and cosmetics applied.

Satisfied the shine was gone, Kiernan shooed the young lady away and called to her assistant hovering in the background. "Get me some Evian." Kiernan framed her dark brown hair with her hands. "Call the hairstylist back over," Kiernan directed her assistant after she received the bottle of water. "Look at how flat my hair is. I can't go on television like this."

"I'm so sorry, Miss Connelly. Let me just…" the stylist didn't finish her sentence, instead opting to flitter around her, using her comb and hairspray while Kiernan read her emails off her phone.

Kiernan rose a few minutes later to take her turn auctioning items for the event. Her hair actually looked presentable. Smiling at herself before turning away from the mirror, she murmured, "This will do." The stylist grinned. They both knew her outbursts were legendary. Her favorite description was that they could be compared to summer storms—extreme, furious, dangerous—and over as suddenly as they began.

Taking the stage to a cacophony of sounds, Kiernan basked in the audience's admiration. This was what she loved the best. The bantering and flirting, laughing with the crowd.

"I am so glad to be here with you today. When I was asked to participate, I didn't hesitate. And why would I? Having the opportunity to spend time with you while raising money for such a great charity is irresistible." Kiernan led a round of clapping, a practiced smile pulling her lips. "So, let's get to it!"

For the next twenty minutes, Kiernan attached stories to the items, calling each winner up to the stage to deliver a hug of thanks. Her body buzzed with pleasure. After auctioning the last item, Kiernan received the audience's roar of approval and waved her way off the stage. Her assistant met her backstage.

"They love you, Kiernan. In ten minutes you'll have lunch, where you'll be joined by several people who've donated to sit near to you. After that you'll be autographing pictures for about an hour. Once that ends you'll have about twenty minutes for a snack before taking photos with people. Last is the television interview."

"Right. Let me use the bathroom before you bring me to lunch," Kiernan said.

It was a long day, but her agent told her these events fed her popularity. So, bracing herself to deal with the goofy smiles, maudlin emotional displays, and obsequious charity workers, Kiernan gazed at herself in the mirror as she washed her hands, calling up several comments she could use while greeting each person she met. It felt like telling the same jokes over and over again, but none of her fans knew the difference.

Much later, Kiernan sat in a chair sipping some tea, wondering how many photographs she'd have to endure. About to call over her assistant for the answer, she spied Rudi chatting up some young, pretty girls. And, by Kiernan's standards, they were only girls. Smirking, she unraveled herself from the chair, glided over to Rudi, and placed a possessive arm around her waist. They were nearly the same height and made a striking pair. Rudi beamed as she leaned in to kiss Kiernan on the cheek.

"Darling, how wonderful to see you. You look ravishing." Her eyes swept up and down Kiernan's body as potently as her hands had many times in the past.

Smiling at the girls, Kiernan turned to Rudi, effectively dismissing them. "Dinner tonight?"

"Of course. Let's go to Carvallo. I know you love their food. I'll meet you there after our shows?"

"Perfect." Sealing the date with a heated kiss, Kiernan winked before walking away. The day was looking up.

An hour later, Kiernan sat before a live camera, focused on the interviewer's words. Karin Donagel was a well-known news anchor who had interviewed Kiernan several times. Kiernan felt comfortable with her. Karin was a petite blonde with bright green eyes. Her bob framed her oval-shaped face, emphasizing her nymph-like appearance, as did the mulberry-colored, knee-length dress she wore. *Not many people can pull off that color.*

"How great that you are helping to raise money for such a worthy cause. What got you interested in donating your time for this particular charity?"

Kiernan nodded, focusing on Karin. "Our nation is filled with contrasts, whether that refers to people or landscapes, weather or perspectives, and that amalgamation makes us unique. Special. It also makes us susceptible to certain challenges. Sometimes, people need help."

"And I'm sure your participation is helping many of those who don't have the money or resources to fight stomach cancer." She looked down at her notes. "I see every dollar is used for treatment and research."

"Yes, and that's exactly where the money should go. It's heartening to be a part of this organization. I must admit, my priorities have changed over the years. Life's too short to squander. Rather than giving in to fear of how others will interpret my every word and deed, I've decided to spend time pursuing what fulfills me." Kiernan turned to look into the camera, trying to look sincere. "Like this charity, for instance. I'm fortunate to find myself at a point in my life where I can help others. After all, what good is it to be well known if I don't use my popularity to educate others on the struggles so many face? I'm extremely thankful to see all the wonderful people donating their time and money toward finding a cure. Thank you."

"And thank you for being here. I am sure that your presence here today encouraged others to donate."

Kiernan grinned. "That is my hope."

As soon as the segment ended, Kiernan gathered her belongings. She felt vaguely dissatisfied with the day, and she couldn't understand why, a gnawing sense of ennui filling her. Lately, everything she did felt so empty. It was as if she were missing some important factor, some essential piece of the puzzle. *I should be happy. I'm successful. I have a wonderful home, a sexy lover, and enough money to never have to work another day, if I so desired.* Yet, she felt incomplete. She thirsted for something more meaningful.

Kiernan had many celebrity friends who donated their time toward charities, using their elevated status to help the less fortunate. For Kiernan, such activities didn't seem to slake her thirst. Perhaps she needed to pick a new charity. Kiernan rejoined her assistant to leave the venue. Such thoughts would have to be revisited later.

Several hours later Kiernan glided into the upscale restaurant on Rudi's arm. She knew she looked gorgeous in a dark blue stretch of silk that left little to the imagination. Feeling eyes track her progress, Kiernan swished her hips. Smiling at her date, Kiernan purred, "Darling, I adore this place. Thank you for bringing me here."

Rudi ogled Kiernan's attributes, which nearly burst forth as Kiernan leaned forward. "Think nothing of it."

Biting her lower lip, Kiernan sat back in her chair. While Rudi ordered wine for them, she allowed her eyes to travel over her date. She wore a cool gray pantsuit obviously tailored to emphasize her feminine curves. The color made her eyes pop— shades of gray and blue coalescing into an irresistible mixture. Instead of a blouse, Rudi wore a lacy black camisole underneath her jacket, and Kiernan wanted nothing more than to see it up close. Their chemistry was undeniable, and the sex was divine.

Relaxing into the well-acted roles they assumed when together, they discussed how their shows went earlier. Nothing of import occurred. Kiernan said her lines, made her marks, and bowed during the ovation like every other night.

As they sipped port after finishing their dinner, Kiernan's mind wandered, but she refocused on Rudi's words. She was talking about herself again, something about how she felt bad not being about to sign autographs tonight when so many people waited for her. Irritated, Kiernan opened her mouth to utter some cutting remark about how good Rudi was at wrapping her care for her fans in a blanket of self-absorption, but she decided against it.

*Why am I irritated with her? Tonight is no different than any other time we've spent together. Aren't I just as egocentric?* Kiernan nodded, smiled, and laughed when it seemed appropriate, as all the while her mind tried to make sense of her sudden impatience with Rudi's shallowness.

Kiernan didn't like her life. She didn't like having to present herself in a certain way to the fawning crowds. She could never let down her guard and felt like she was losing herself. She no longer knew who she really was or what she really wanted. *Kind of late to be having doubts about my career.* She couldn't shake the feeling she was missing the point that so many celebrities seemed to understand. People would do anything to live her life. *Why aren't I satisfied?* Feeling Rudi's hand cover hers, she looked up to see Rudi staring.

"Are you all right?"

*I must have missed my cue to laugh.* Grinning at her snide thought, Kiernan replied, "I'm merely worn out from all the pandering to the masses today. Let's get out of here."

"Come over?" Rudi asked. It was understood they wouldn't return to Kiernan's home. She didn't care to have Rudi within her sanctuary. As it were, Rudi had visited Kiernan's home only a handful of times over the years.

Acquiescing with studied coyness, Kiernan allowed herself to shelve her turbulent thoughts until she was alone. She was determined to enjoy the debauchery Rudi promised. Now wasn't the time to grapple with life-changing thoughts. It was too hard, anyway. Better to leave it to the thinkers, those who had nothing better to do than to wonder at the meaning of life. She had a sexy lady offering herself without reserve. *Who am I to refuse such a proposition?*

Much later, lying by Rudi's side, sleep eluded Kiernan. The lovemaking—*no, the sex,* Kiernan corrected herself—was fantastic. Rudi was attentive and inventive. Kiernan grinned, but her grin faded as she realized that although her body was satiated, she was not.

Finally giving in, Kiernan got up, wrapped Rudi's robe around her, and walked into the den. Sitting on the leather sofa, Kiernan leaned against the arm with chin in hand, taking inventory of her life. She came to New York fresh out of high school, determined to become a star. After a couple of years pounding the pavement, she got her first break. A friend of a friend of a friend allowed her to audition for a small off-Broadway role. She got the part. In those early years, every day felt like school for her, so hard did she study the other actors, the machinations of the stage world, and the politics for getting, and more importantly, staying in the business.

A television producer caught her show and offered her the lead in his new drama series. That show made her a star. Everything flowed. She got parts in movies, leading to bigger parts in better movies, and when she had enough, she returned to the theater, which received her with open arms. The syndication of the television show and repeated airings of the movies made her rich. That enabled her to choose the roles she accepted. Always on Broadway, always her in the main role. Plays were especially created with her in mind. All in all, she lived a glorious life. She frowned. *So, why isn't it enough anymore? What's changed?*

When she started out, she believed she would change the world through her craft, but she'd allowed that goal to die a quiet death while she reaped the benefits of fame. Once upon a time, she felt loved, cherished, and respected. Now she felt that others viewed her as a prima donna. The sad truth was that she acted horribly for no other reason than that she could. She'd become a spoiled brat. Her mother would roll over in her grave if she could see Kiernan's behavior.

Half the time, Kiernan didn't even mean to be so cruel. It was as if some sarcastic beast took over her vocal cords, cutting a swath of destruction. And while most people seemed to anticipate her caustic remarks, that just made it more of a challenge to break them apart, to make them uncertain and afraid of her next action. *Disgusting. I don't like myself.* It was no wonder she had few people close to her. And as for her fans, they either didn't know or didn't care about her shenanigans.

Maybe her questions had to do with a series of fan letters she'd received over the last few months. They were provocative, making her rethink the way she lived, and she found she enjoyed it. Though once the show ended, she wouldn't receive any more letters since all of them were addressed to the theater. The writer discussed how her perspective of a calla lily could be much different than another person's perspective. Another letter spoke of music, how it connected people through the emotions it evoked. All the letters circled around the subject of how one experienced life, but Kiernan feared she had stopped caring long ago. It was much easier to coast along.

These letters were causing Kiernan to question how to become a better person, and she had no idea what that meant. She knew what qualities she didn't like, but she had trouble even capturing the essence of meaningful, sustainable, positive ways of being. Over the years she'd become used to getting what she wanted, when she wanted.

*Is it even possible to change?* Kiernan knew that, ready or not, she would have to. Her play was coming to an end. Although they hadn't discussed it, she was sure Rudi had heard how the show was folding at the end of the week. The producers hadn't even bothered to notify Kiernan until last week.

The producers already had a new show in the works, but they hadn't offered her a role. She had packed the theaters for years, yet they had the audacity to leave her behind. Shying away from the possible reasons why, Kiernan took comfort in how she would shove their noses in her future success. She didn't need them. She'd made it on her own in this business, and if she had to act confident, charming, and ruthless, so be it.

*This late night slide into self-doubt is a waste.* It was too hard to change, never mind chase after a silly dream. Regardless of how much those letters fascinated her, they were a bunch of words with no power over her unless she allowed it. Everyone had an opinion, but she had the choice of ignoring them.

# Chapter Three

PRINCE UBEL CHECKED HIS recordings once more before logging his final report on the meteor. All tests indicated humans would react to the materials comprising the mass, their DNA rewriting itself. Once the process began, it was hoped the subjects would transform into superior beings who could be captured and bred with select Katakitites to transfer their new powers. Although Ubel abhorred the thought of touching a human, he was willing to sacrifice for his royal lineage.

This wasn't the first time his family had exploited other worlds to better its own, but in the past they only preyed on less advanced civilizations closer to their own world. They knew not to abuse any nearby space-faring worlds since they might seek retribution. Earth was in the beginning stages of exploring space and, like the other planets they had mined for raw biological materials, was technologically primitive. None of its inhabitants would recognize the meteor was engineered to enter their atmosphere in a particular area to affect humans in a specific way. Even if they were more advanced than his commanders believed, humans would not be able to stop the transmutation process once it began. Or the herding process thereafter.

This mission was Ubel's chance to prove himself once and for all. His father had been killed in the last uprising, and his older brother, captured. Although his mother would become the ruler of his people after removing the rebels, Ubel knew the day would come when he would become king. Women were weak—they never lasted as rulers. Even though he loved his mother, he knew she was not meant to lead. By providing an heir with DNA programmed to create exceptional abilities, Ubel would be hailed a vanguard for his people's civilization. They would overthrow the insurgents who dared to repudiate his family's rightful authority and rule with a firm hand, crushing any other usurpers.

Noticing the time, Ubel decided to make his way to the command wing. Before leaving the protection of the science wing, he stood before the atmospheric container, grimacing at the pressure he felt against his chest. This planet's atmosphere was comprised of more sulphates, and he found it harder to breathe when he was outside of the constructed habitats. Counting to sextorix, he hit the release button and walked outside, crossing the mammoth quad in the center of the complex. His breathing became harder, his muscles screaming in protest. He would be glad when he could return to his home planet, if only to breathe easier. He glanced at the orange sky and frowned. He could feel the electrical charge in the air and knew what that meant. He picked up his pace, taking shallow breaths while making his way to the correct building. As the first few fat raindrops fell, Ubel flashed his credentials at the automated scanner and entered.

Ubel walked through the atmospheric container into the oxygen-rich welcoming room before pausing. He listened to the rain hit the window panes while his breathing regulated. Relieved to feel the pressure dissipate, he strutted down a long corridor to the meeting place.

"I am here to meet with Supreme Commander Flerg." A guard in a dark uniform led him to the inner office, where his commander leaned over a map of Earth's solar system. Ubel waited, head bowed and hands clasped behind him.

Several cakrae later, Commander Flerg looked up and beckoned him closer. He pulled out a map from underneath the one he'd been studying. It was of the Andromeda Galaxy where they were currently stationed. "Ubel, I have good news. Our scientists are confident they can set up a portal here." He pointed at a neighboring moon. "From there you will be able to travel near the site we have chosen for the meteorite. You are to leave tomorrow at katrinet two. What is your best estimate for the time it will take for the transmutations to take full effect?"

"All experiments indicate six karinan cycles." Ubel winced, knowing his commander would be disappointed.

"That's ahead of the original timeline, but it won't give us much time to train them. They're no good to us if we cannot harness their powers to regain control of the government. Breeding may take little time, but their gestation periods are several karinan cycles longer, and other species we have used for similar purposes were powerless while impregnated."

"The advantages outweigh any dangers," Ubel replied. "Once we harness their powers, we will no longer have to use technology. We will have the advantage of surprise against our enemies, and we will reclaim our rightful place."

Commander Flerg nodded. "Take a team of eight. Retrieve the meteorite once it has landed, determine who is affected, and monitor them. I expect regular reports."

"I shall do as you command." When Commander Flerg turned away, Ubel took it as a dismissal. He hurried to his quarters to ready for his mission. Excitement coursed through him. This would change his life.

***

### TUESDAY, JUNE 6, 2017 7:42 P.M.

*What a crappy day.* Patricia pushed her front door shut with her foot. She usually delighted in taking a moment outside her home to gaze at the clapboard shutters and flower boxes emphasizing the brick brownstone she purchased three months ago. She had splurged on the flowers, planting yellow monkey-faced pansies and pale blue forget-me-nots, hot pink dianthus and royal purple hyacinths. The overflowing boxes popped with color, and her heart fluttered every time she saw them. But today, she felt deflated. Not bothering to turn on the lights in the atrium, she trudged upstairs while carrying her luggage. It wasn't heavy, but to Patricia it felt like a thousand pounds—as heavy as her spirit.

The day started out so well before promptly going downhill. First Rudi cancelled their lunch date with profuse apologies, but little explanation. She didn't even know when she would see Rudi again, if ever. Then, she had nearly missed her flight, only to sit on the runway for two hours while the airline waited for the wind to die down. Once she left the subway, or as the locals called it the T, she walked the short journey to her home on the hill in the rain.

After retrieving a towel, Patricia stripped down to her panties and donned a short silk robe before moving to the window, regarding the rain. Her mind wandered to a recent weekend trip to New York. The infamous northeast weather had asserted itself, and as she watched the rain hit the hotel window, a crane swung a load of steel across 48th Street. The wind caused the bundle to sway, yet underneath it people scuttled along. The crane operator delivered his burden to the desired destination without mishap. Perhaps the passersby had reason not to worry. Perhaps they knew they weren't in danger...or they just had no idea what was happening. Perhaps their perceptions of reality didn't allow them to see enough.

*It's like eyes connecting across a room. So many different ways to interpret the connection.* Patricia flopped on her couch. She half-heartedly sorted through her mail, her mind running a mile a minute.

*I don't even have her contact information. Maybe I should have taken her to bed yesterday.* Patricia snorted. Of course, she wouldn't have done that. She wasn't a one-night stand type of gal. If she really wanted to contact Rudi, she supposed she could leave a message at the theater where she currently starred in her latest Broadway smash, *Modesty Will Get You Nowhere*. It had been running for several months and showed no signs of stopping any time soon. Not only was she a great stage actor, she had successfully crossed over to television and film. According to Rudi, though, her first love was the stage.

Checking her cell phone, delight stole through her. She had a message from Rudi. Listening to Rudi's voice, Patricia felt the familiar fluttering in her stomach. "Patricia, I'm truly sorry I was unable to meet you for lunch. I entirely forgot I agreed to help at a charity event. Please, please do let me know when you'll be back in New York. I should like to see you again. Call me."

Smiling as she wrote down Rudi's phone number, Patricia moved to her refrigerator to see what she could scrounge up for supper. *A whole lot of nothing.* Sighing, she placed a delivery order at the local Chinese restaurant. It didn't take long for the food to arrive, and she changed into silk pajamas before consuming the food as if it were her last meal.

Once full, Patricia relaxed in her favorite overstuffed chair with a cup of tea and her journal. Her life was changing. She liked writing in her journal before going to bed, allowing the day's events to flow through her fingers and onto the page. Over time she'd found it to be a great way to sort through her reactions, often surprised by what she wrote. She had plenty to relay regarding the last few days.

For years she dreamed of writing books. Patricia focused on reaching her goals of writing each chapter, revising words until she finished the story. After finishing the book, a new set of goals supplanted those, propelling her to write. Finding a publisher, working with an editor, waiting for each month's book sales reports, arranging book readings and book signings, and traveling and promoting—she tried to live in the present even while she planned future books. The process was exhilarating, frightening, illuminating, and perfect.

*Star Light, Star Bright (Make My Wish Come True Tonight)* was her love letter to Rudi, wrapped up in fantasy. It astounded her that somehow it had worked like a love potion, drawing her heart's desire into her life. Most would never recognize the lead protagonist as the actress simply because Patricia had changed the character's sex, adhering to socio-normative conventions in order to tap in to a broader readership base. It was the coward's way out, but she felt that once her reputation was established, she could take more risks by featuring same-sex relationships. Although those closest to her recognized some of the scenarios she included in the book, only Marcia knew Rudi was the lead character, and Patricia planned to keep that her little secret.

Her cell phone's ringtone intruded upon the quietness. "Hello?"

"Sweetie. How was the book signing?"

"Hi, Mom. It was great. People actually showed up." Butterflies flitted in her belly as Rudi's sexy smile flashed across her mind.

"Of course they did. You're a wonderful writer. I'm glad other people are noticing."

"Thanks. I got to see Marcia, too. It was good to catch up with her."

"Oh, she's so sweet. You should invite that girl up here so we can all visit."

Patricia nodded, even though her mom couldn't see her. "I'll mention it to her. How's everything? Dad?"

"You need to talk to him. He'll listen to you."

Hearing the change in her mother's voice from lighthearted to stressed, Patricia winced. She didn't want to argue, but she and her mom had disparate viewpoints regarding her father. "Mom, he has a right to decide what he wants to do."

"He also has to think of his family."

"I know. But, Mom, if he's constantly weak and in pain, what's the point?"

"The point is that he may go into remission. He may add more time to his life, more time that he can spend with his family, with me."

The break in her mother's voice tugged at Patricia. This was hard for her. It was hard for everyone in the family to deal with her father's illness. "I told you what he said when I spoke to him last week. I don't think he's going to change his mind. I think we need to concentrate on spending time with him while we can and enjoy those opportunities."

A soft sob reached Patricia's ears, and she found herself holding back her own tears. "I'm sorry, Mom." She didn't know what to say. Badgering her father to go through more rounds of chemo seemed ridiculous when the latest prognosis painted such a bleak picture. Lots of pain for minimal gain. Taking a deep breath, Patricia said, "I'm really tired. I'll talk to you soon. Okay?"

"Yes. I love you."

"Love you, too. Bye."

Patricia thought about her father, now in his late sixties. He looked like Grampy did before he died twenty years ago. With the same crinkly, washed-out blue eyes, balding thin red hair, and a smile that lit up the room, Don "Red" Steitz was succumbing to cancer. Much heated debate surrounded the best course of treatment for him—every family member had an opinion. The questions of quality versus quantity of life as well as the uncertainty of success effectively immobilized her father's ability to move forward, wherever that may lead. Patricia sat down with her father just last week to discuss what he wished to do, regardless of anyone else's feelings or desires. His answer surprised her.

*"I want to live for as long as I am able but without this constant pain. The trick is to take medication that can dull the pain but keep me lucid enough to enjoy the time I have left with the ones I love. That's why I don't want to go through chemotherapy. I would be sick, and it would only buy me a few more months. It's not worth it, and it's certainly not how I want all of you to remember me."* He patted Patricia's hand as she processed his answer.

*"You're giving up,"* she accused, her eyes to the floor.

*"No, honey. I'm just accepting life as it is instead of indulging in fantasies of how life should be. The reality is that I don't have*

*enough time or physical strength to combat this disease. I'm dying. So, I intend to make the most of the time I have left." He corrected her so gently it brought tears to her eyes. As Patricia reached up for her daddy's comforting hug, she allowed those tears to pour forth, accepting that he had the right to choose how to live the rest of his life.*

Shaking away such thoughts, Patricia glanced down at the journal next to her knee and turned her focus on her suppositions for the upcoming course. She was looking forward to discovering more about the class, the professor, and herself. She held high hopes, wanting to be pushed into self-reflection and maybe self-enlightenment. She certainly tried to better herself, but she needed some guidance on where to focus her energies. With all the changes occurring in her—her father's illness, her success with her book, her new home, and now this crazy thing with Rudi—she knew it was past time to consider what she wanted and how to get it. That would take some serious work on herself, on facing her fears and insecurities. Her days spent leaning on her daddy for advice and reassurance were coming to an end. *It would help if I had a life syllabus*. Smiling, Patricia wrote down a few more thoughts before closing her journal. She moved around the house, closing it up and making her way upstairs to the bedroom to unpack her suitcase and get ready for bed. She wanted to fall asleep at a reasonable time so she would be ready for tomorrow's class.

***

Arriving at the college campus early the next day, Patricia settled herself at the Beach, a grassy area behind the Marsh Plaza and the College of Arts and Sciences building. Some of the students played with Frisbees, others sunbathed, but most were talking in small groups. Tuning in to a group near her, she heard them discussing Professor Corelli.

"She's a great professor. She doesn't just review the classics. She helps us to understand humanity. Like, she's able to connect us to the protagonists, and she tries to get us really involved in conversations instead of just lecturing to us. How many professors do that?" a male college student said. The redhead wore a red Boston University T-shirt with the school's bulldog mascot and ripped jeans. Patricia leaned closer, wanting to hear more about why the professor was so respected.

"Yeah. I had her for a class on feminism through literature. I thought she'd be a man-hater or something, and I was ready to heckle the hell out of her," a woman said. "But she's not like that."

Grinning, Patricia got to her feet and made her way into the building. She was withholding judgment until she saw the professor in action, but she had a good feeling about the class. Entering the lecture hall, Patricia could feel the current of excitement sizzling through the air. The place was packed. Patricia sat toward the back of the auditorium and observed her classmates for several minutes before movement at the front of the room captured Patricia's attention. A petite brunette with curly, shoulder-length hair entered. She wore a lilac blouse, an unbuttoned ivory sweater, and light gray slacks with dark gray pumps. A long silver necklace rested below her collarbones. The woman exuded a confidence that made her appear much larger. Patricia felt the room's energy intensify as the other students noticed the woman, waiting for them to acknowledge her.

Professor Corelli began to welcome the class, expressing her pleasure at seeing so many happy faces, when a slamming door interrupted her and two people raced into the room.

"Get away from me, you freak," a teenager in a T-shirt and jeans screamed as a man followed her, demanding that she stop. "It's mine. Get lost." Staring at the professor, who sported a bemused look on her face, the teenager said, "Help me. This pervert won't leave me alone." Then the young lady ran up the lecture hall stairs, skirting through a row as people pulled their feet back to let her pass, and ran out the back exit.

"She stole that book," the exasperated man said and raced after her, leaving the room. Silence reigned.

Staring at the class, the professor asked, "Did you see that?" Several people chuckled. "Everyone, write down what you just saw. Don't discuss it. Just write down as many details as you can. No names on your papers, please. Do it now."

Patricia grinned. *How interesting*. She began to relate in her notebook what she saw. A few minutes later Professor Corelli asked for the papers to be passed down. Whispering to a young man who collected some of the papers and handed them to her—*that must be her assistant*—the professor scanned them before giving half to him and keeping the rest for herself.

"Some girl busted in chased by a guy. She was trying to get away from him. She ran through us and out the back. He followed," the professor read. "Okay. That's a start." Taking a sheet her assistant passed to her, she read, "At 10:04 a.m. a thin, brown-haired teenager, around fifteen, wearing baggy jeans and a red T-shirt with a dove imprint on the front, ran into the room via the front left door."

"Good description," Professor Corelli said, nodding. "Do you hear the difference?" she asked the class. "What makes it different?" Taking answers from the class, she smiled. After discussing those answers, reading several more sheets, and fielding more comments, Professor Corelli got to the point. "We all were in this room when those two people arrived. Yet, we saw different scenarios, didn't we? Some saw how they dressed more vividly than others—their visual impressions. Some heard their voices more distinctly—the emotions reflected. Some observed how they arrived and left—their locomotion. Others felt the energetic shift—the urgency. We were all here, but we all experienced their presence in different ways based upon our experiences, our knowledge, and our ways of sifting through the sensory stimuli. Have you ever wondered why a car accident is hardly ever clear-cut? Even with eyewitnesses, no one can ever accurately relate all the details. And many of the details are refuted by other witnesses. Why is that?"

Time passed quickly as they discussed perceptions and possible reasons why each person perceived reality differently. Patricia loved the lesson. She'd never thought about perception in quite this way. The professor turned on a projector, as her assistant shut off the lights. Slides of people with various facial expressions lit up the darkened amphitheater. Professor Corelli asked for volunteers from the audience to identify the emotions reflected by each expression.

"How do you know?" she asked each participant before opening it up to the class to add to the opinion. Most were in agreement with the offered answers for each picture, although a few debates erupted for the more intangible, complex emotions reflected.

Next, she projected an abstract painting and asked them to identify shapes found in it. After receiving some rather inventive answers, the professor suggested their upbringings, education, and imagination contributed to what they saw, causing the answers to be as diverse as the students in the room. As a last example of perception, Professor Corelli played several audio recordings of people conversing in different languages, asking after each one what feelings were emoted. Most of the time it was easy to interpret the emotions by the tone of voice.

"Nowadays, it's easy to misinterpret a message, particularly when not seeing the speaker, such as through a telephone conversation or when not hearing the person's voice, such as through an email or text." She paced the length of the room. "We use so many societal cues to interpret what we hear, what we see, and how we process that information. This is one of the areas we'll examine. Now, let's take a look at the syllabus."

Excitement coursed through Patricia, as the professor and her assistant passed out the document reflecting the course topics. The next class would focus more on point of view, commonality of experience, and being present. Quickly reviewing the rest of the subject matter listed, Patricia's interest increased. Noting her writing assignment—to discuss how people with different upbringings, viewpoints, and thoughts are able to connect with each other—she clapped along with the rest of her classmates before gathering her belongings and leaving. Many students remained to chat about the class. *So much to think about*, Patricia mused. She knew Marcia would love it. *Well, I'll just have to be sure to tell her all about it.*

She appreciated how the professor neatly set up a complex lesson in an effective display of sensory stimuli and wondered how different people's memories would have been affected by the staged interruption if they'd known what to expect ahead of time. Personally, she would have taken notes as the events unfolded. Due to the quickness, however, she doubted she could have added much to what she wrote in class. Plus, how could she have fully experienced the event if she were worried about writing every moment down? Patricia shook her head. She once held a job as a movie reviewer. Taking notes while watching a movie hindered her from experiencing the overall effect, as she ended up concentrating on recording each element instead of the whole. Often, she watched the movie a second time to feel it. This class gave her hope that she could find some way to observe and experience life simultaneously—find some way to be more present.

***

## MONDAY, JUNE 12, 2017 8:57 P.M.

Marcia had arrived at Sunny Horizon Resort two days ago, ready to have a good attitude while participating in team-building exercises with her colleagues. The property was idyllic, with the lodges grouped according to a visitor's goal, whether it was a conference, retreat, or spa treatments. The lodgings surrounded five large buildings, each one dedicated to a different function. The main building where Marcia registered had a common area with several chairs and tables sprinkled against the back wall and around an immense fireplace. Floor to ceiling windows showcased grassy areas defined by walking paths. Further away, a small lake sparkled in the morning sun, canoes and kayaks beached near a boat dock. To the west, Marcia saw a large walkway leading to a water fountain, and to the east, hedges in the shape of a labyrinth were enveloped by beautiful flower arrangements—a kaleidoscope of yellows, greens, oranges, and pinks. She chose to splurge on the lodging so she didn't have to share it with anyone. Her room was a tiny cabin attached to a private bathroom. *Perfect.*

The next two days weren't nearly as horrible as she feared. Through several exercises geared toward trust and collaboration among the law firm's employees, Marcia became more familiar with people she'd seen for years but never gotten to know beyond what small talk revealed. After the group activities ended, Marcia had plenty of time to explore the surrounding area. She even made some connections with colleagues from other departments.

Tonight, though, she had decided to indulge herself by getting a deep tissue massage after dinner. It felt fantastic. After the treatment, Marcia had decided to walk around the lake. Tomorrow was the last day of the company-mandated retreat, and Marcia admitted that she'd miss this picturesque locale.

It was a balmy evening with a full moon, and she could hear the sounds of frogs and crickets merging with a cacophony of voices floating toward her from the garden. No doubt some were walking the labyrinth while others sat on benches beneath the oak trees. The voices faded as she circled the far edge of the lake, the sound of the water's lazy current soothing Marcia's mind. It was exactly what she needed. Although she made sure to seem calm and confident, the months leading up to the case she was to litigate next week was taxing. Not only was the product liability case complex, but also she was facing her former law firm. She knew this was her chance to release old grievances and move on, but she feared her emotions might get the better of her. She perched on a rock, tilting her head toward the brook. Perspiration gathered on her arms, and Marcia grimaced, knowing mosquitoes would soon find her. The smell of burning sycamore tickled her nose—Marcia guessed a small bonfire was the cause—but a pleasant flower fragrance captured her attention. Looking around she spotted several clumps of forget-me-nots, their beautiful blue petals and bright yellow centers beckoning her to take a closer look. Bending down, she gazed at the flowers.

Marcia finally leaned back. She allowed her mind to wander, the sounds coalescing into pleasant background noise. The voices were too far away for her to distinguish any words, but the feelings behind them were clear, engaged, and happy. The ambiance of the resort soothed her tattered soul. It was rare for her to find solace since her husband died, but here it seemed so easy.

Rising, Marcia followed a nearby trail ascending a grassy knoll before zigzagging up a steeper incline, leading her farther away from the resort. Having followed this trail before, she knew the view would be worth the effort. Once she breached the crest of the steep hill, she leaned over, hands on knees, taking deep breaths. She felt so out of shape.

Noticing part of the sky brightening from navy blue to indigo, Marcia squinted as two streams of smoke cut through the sky at a downward angle. The sky became brighter and brighter. A massive boom sounded, and a concussive force traveled in waves toward the ground. The light—now a fiery yellow—became blinding and moved directly toward her. Horrified, Marcia ducked, and a moment later she felt her body lifted in the air, debris raining down around her. She hit the ground hard. Pain blinded her.

Marcia had no idea how long she was unconscious. It could have been a few seconds or several minutes. Her head throbbed, and a loud ringing filled her ears. Her head felt worse than the time she'd gotten drunk in college and spent the night hugging the toilet. She'd never allowed herself to drink like that again. She tasted bile, and she tightened her jaw as she focused on getting her body under control.

After breathing through her nose for several minutes, the ringing receded. A quietness replaced it. An unnatural silence. A chill ran through her. No wildlife stirred, no far-away voices carried on the breeze, no rustling leaves or gurgling water. Marcia could hear nothing.

Reaching for her head, Marcia felt wetness coat her fingers. She opened her eyes, squinting. Her eyes were sensitive to the moonlight. Sound eventually returned, and Marcia was glad that any hearing loss was temporary. She sat up, groaning at the spike of pain shooting through her head. She must have hit the ground hard. Her ass certainly was sore. Looking around she saw that she was about fifty yards away from the top of the trail.

"Jeez," she whispered. "What the hell was that?"

The area around her was flattened, and several rocks about the size of her fist were smoking. *Well those couldn't have done that.* Rising, Marcia wandered around the area. As she got closer to a steaming meteorite, she inhaled some of the fumes. It was like breathing in a hot spring. She'd never seen a meteorite up close. It was massive. At least the size of a compact car. As black as a crow and as smooth as steel.

Stooping, Marcia gathered some leaves. She knew this was a stupid idea, but that didn't stop her from extending her hand and allowing the leaves to touch the space rock. When nothing happened, Marcia stepped forward enough to hold her hand close to the meteorite. She didn't feel any heat. Worrying her lower lip between her teeth, Marcia tried to talk herself out of it. *Don't be stupid. It's probably hot enough to give you third degree burns.*

The problem was that she was always so in control. She never allowed herself to color outside the lines. She did what was expected. She bottled her desires, big and small. But when would she ever get the opportunity to touch a meteorite again? And with no one around…

She placed her hand on the side of the meteorite. Nothing happened. It was warm, but certainly not hot. She studied the material, and to her it looked like any other black rock. It could have been mistaken for onyx.

Hearing people approach, Marcia bent to gather a few of the smaller rocks that had the same consistency. She stuffed the rocks in her pockets, seeing two people in dark clothing approach her. They didn't look like anyone from the resort. They seemed too serious. Not exactly hostile, but certainly not friendly.

"Are you all right, Ma'am?" asked one of them. He was slim and tall, certainly over six feet.

"I think so. I hit my head when I fell," Marcia said. She watched the other agent turn and wave. Soon two more people joined them, both carrying medical supplies.

"Let's have them check you for injuries," the same man said. "I'm Agent Thacker. This is Agent Blackstone. The meteorite and space debris that came through the area has been monitored for months. When they entered the lower atmosphere, most of it burned up, but their speed broke the sound barrier and caused this area to be flattened. We had hoped the meteorite would burn up entirely once it entered our atmosphere."

Marcia could see the destruction of the surrounding area more clearly now. "Was anyone hurt? Did the resort get hit?"

Agent Blackstone, a woman with dark eyes and a trim build who looked to be in her mid-thirties, chuckled. "Oh, no. The point of entry was far enough away not to cause any property damage. So, let's get you patched up."

"Right. Okay." Marcia could only guess that these people wanted to search the area for any other rocks that had fallen from the sky. It didn't take long for her to be cleared, and she hurried back down the trail.

Once she descended a bit, she hid behind a tree. Peeking around it, she gasped. People were everywhere, and most were wearing some type of white hazmat suit complete with oxygen masks—close to the type she'd seen in movies about viral contamination or zombie apocalypses. She could now see that they used instruments on the meteorite.

"They must be trying to figure out what it's made of," Marcia said, shaking her head. Groaning at the slight throbbing, she decided it was time to get back to her cabin and take something to ease the pain. *At least I have some unique paperweights.*

Once she was in her room, Marcia took out the stones to really study them. They were light, about half the length of her palm, and smooth. One of them was sliced in half, and she could see threads of color running through it. "Not just black," she murmured. Purple, white, and silver wove through the ebony. The light from the lamp hit each strand as she turned the stone slowly, making each color glow. The other rocks were whole and smooth, yet when the light hit them just right, she saw specks of color— gold, green, and white.

Glancing out the window, Marcia saw the moon high up, reminding her that it was late. Her head felt better, at least. *Maybe tomorrow I won't feel like I have a hangover.* Deciding to turn in, Marcia walked over to her carryon to store the stones, but once there, she hesitated. She squeezed them in her fist, not sure why she was balking at releasing them. With a sigh, she crossed over to the bed and placed them under her pillow. After climbing into bed, her hand reached for the rocks. Feeling their smoothness against her palm, a sense of calmness flowed through her, and she drifted off into a restful sleep.

# Chapter Four

PATRICIA GOT OFF THE plane and hurried toward the exit. Marcia was picking her up, and in a matter of hours, she would see Rudi again. It had been two weeks since they shared dinner and some promising kisses. During that time she'd reflected on their dinner, attempting to understand herself—her desires, hopes, and fears. After some soul-searching, Patricia decided that she wanted Rudi. She wanted to dispel the fantasy and live the reality. They were attracted to each other, and Patricia was undeniably in love with the actress—well, she was in love with the woman she imagined her to be. Now, she wanted to find out who Rudi really was behind the fame and public persona.

Seeing Marcia, she rushed over to the sleek, champagne-colored Lexus and hopped in the passenger seat. She bit her lip. "I can't believe I'm here."

Her friend raised an eyebrow. "I can't believe it took you this long to get your ass back here. God, if Rudi wanted to spend time with me, I'd have dropped everything. She's worth dropping everything." Marcia wiggled her eyebrows, as Patricia groaned.

"You know I'm taking that course this summer. I can't just fly back here whenever she wants." Patricia would, though, if she could. "As it is, I can only stay for a few days."

"Then, you'll just have to make the most of it." Marcia winked. "Are you sure you don't want to stay with us? We have plenty of room."

"No, no. I'd rather stay at the hotel. That way I can get some writing done, too."

"Oh, come on," Marcia scoffed. "Who are you trying to kid? You won't have time to write a single word."

Patricia felt heat travel up her neck and across her cheeks, and she looked away. She hoped she would be kept busy by Rudi, but she didn't want to get her hopes up. She shrugged. "I don't even know how much time we'll get to spend together. How's work? Aren't you going to trial soon on that Delaney case?"

"Yes." Marcia heaved a sigh, but Patricia knew her friend better than that. "It's been a bear. The defendants have been inundating us with depositions, requests for productions of documents, interrogatories—you name it, and they've demanded it. Their only saving grace will be if they decide to settle, and it will have to be for a damn good amount."

Marcia's eyes gleamed as she chatted about the product liability case. It had been in the newspapers for months. Speculation of how this case would put the defendants out of business had caused their stocks to drop. Right now they were trying to implement damage control to no avail. Patricia admired Marcia's ability to use her skills to help the less fortunate, particularly after turning her back on a much more lucrative law career.

Marcia once told her the only reason she went to B.U. and later law school was because she was in love with a B.U. alumni who had wanted to attend law school. Marcia claimed she'd wanted to understand him. Now, many years later, she used her training to give back to her community. *Someday I'm going to have to pull the rest of that unrequited love story out of Marcia.*

After Patricia checked in to her hotel room, they made their way to a restaurant for a bite to eat. Once they placed their orders, Marcia asked, "So, how's the class coming?"

One of the things she appreciated about Marcia was how she took an interest in her life. She always asked about her latest writing endeavor or what was happening in her world. More importantly, though, Marcia sincerely cared to know the answer.

"The class is wonderful." Shaking her head in wonder, Patricia added, "I wish you were taking this course with me. I bet you'd love it."

"I know I would. I'll have to take the course through you. Make me smarter, dear Patricia."

"I doubt that's possible," Patricia joked, "but I'll try my best. The professor has made me question everything. That's a good thing. At our last class she talked about music, how it interacts with our emotions. I never thought of it that way before. She then linked music to language. Our tone of voice, the words we use, the emphasis we place on syllables all contribute toward how we connect with others. She makes me think, Marcia. I've never encountered such a fascinating person."

"Sounds like you're developing hero worship," Marcia teased.

Patricia punched her on the arm while confirming it with a smile. "It's more than how words are delivered. How we receive words, the way we interpret the message, those are just as complex. I mean, I could stay up nights just thinking about this stuff. I do." She bit into her turkey wrap, realizing she was famished.

"And yet here we are, communicating." Marcia grinned before taking a sip of her lemonade.

"Yes, but we can still misinterpret each other, right?"

"Right, although since we know each other so well, it's less likely."

"And then there's the added complexity of the senses. They can be easily manipulated. Scented candles can trigger the olfactory senses, creating sensual stimuli. Suddenly, you can imagine tasting the crispness of cinnamon apple slices, touching the velvety texture of rose petals, or hearing the crashing ocean waves against the rocks. Our beliefs, our thoughts, and our experiences remind us that we smell only a candle. However, without such knowledge and discernment, our senses may interpret reality differently." Patricia popped a few French fries in her mouth before nudging the plate toward the center of the table and gesturing for Marcia to have some.

Marcia tilted her head, a faraway look in her eyes. "That's interesting. I recently read that singers use different types of microphones to enhance their voices." She sighed and picked up a few fries, moaning as she chewed them.

"Isn't that cheating?"

Marcia chuckled. "The microphones or the French fries?" She shrugged. "I felt a bit cheated when I read it. If performers use special microphones to manipulate how they sound, how can we trust our senses?"

"Or even the reverse. What if the voice is manipulated when it's recorded and sounds different when the singer performs live? But you know from all those singing competitions on TV that the talent must exist in order to be enhanced. Modern technology merely enhances present talent in the best possible way. It's a positive development, like athletes using the latest advances to aid them in their competitions."

"I wonder, though," Marcia said, wiping her mouth with her napkin before placing it beside her plate, "why do we need such enhancements? As a society, how did we become so demanding that these performers must manipulate their talents? Are they manipulating society's perceptions of what they can do?"

Patricia smiled. "See. It's as if you're taking the class with me." They sat in amiable silence, and Patricia's mind wandered to her plans to meet Rudi for a late dinner after she finished her show. When Patricia spoke to her on the phone the day before, Rudi seemed thrilled with the prospect of seeing her. *I really want to see Rudi, too.*

"Oh, I see that moony face. You're thinking about tonight."

Nodding, Patricia could feel her face heating up. "How can I not?" She grinned at Marcia's chuckle. "Now. No more stalling. You promised to tell me all about that conference you went on last weekend when you saw me in person. So spill."

Marcia leaned back in her chair. "It wasn't much different than any other retreat created to make colleagues trust each other."

Patricia raised an eyebrow and smirked. "Yeah, right. Give me the dirt. A bunch of type A's stuck together, learning how to trust one another?"

Marcia chewed on her lip. "Well, we did have some fun activities. Like the human knot. We had to take the hands of two different people, neither next to us, and then once that was done, untangle ourselves without breaking our grips. It was a bit like playing Twister."

"That sounds fun, although perhaps a bit awkward if you have to deal with sweaty hands or certain body parts in your face." Patricia could only imagine the odd positions. Marcia was one of the most fun people she knew, but in her professional life, her friend hated looking silly. "What else?"

"You know what? We can talk about that later. Suffice it to say, we had some fun, and I got to know people from other divisions."

Patricia watched Marcia take a sip of her drink. It was unusual for her to skimp on details. She was holding out. "Okay, what haven't you told me?"

Blue eyes stared at her. Patricia tilted her head and waited. After a pregnant pause, Marcia sighed. "Well, something really weird happened the last night I was there. There was a meteor shower."

"I didn't see anything about it in the newspapers."

"Nor did I, and I was an eyewitness. If you ask me, it's all hush, hush. Whenever the government gets involved—"

Patricia waved both her hands. "Wait. Wait. Back up. The government? What the hell?"

Marcia wiggled in her seat and leaned forward, eyes bright. "I know. So, I went for a late hike after dinner. It was gorgeous out there, and with the full moon, easy to see. I crested the top of a hill and could see everything around me for miles. The lake, the wooded areas, the resort, and the gardens. A bright light caught my eye, which wasn't too hard since it lit up the entire sky. This huge fireball came right at me."

"You're kidding."

"I swear upon my husband's grave."

Patricia grimaced. She knew Marcia was still dealing with John's death. Two years wasn't a long time to process such a loss, and she had her daughter to comfort, too.

Marcia continued in a soft voice. "Anyway, it was coming right at me and so like any rational person, I ducked." She sipped from her cup, her eyes twinkling.

After a few moments, Patricia gave in. "And?"

"And I swung around just in time to watch this huge meteorite skim over the trees before plowing into a bunch of pines. The entire area was totally flattened. I fell on my ass. Got a nice bump on my head, but no concussion. It sounded like those whistler fireworks, the really loud ones. Lots of small rocks rained down, so I pocketed a few. I figure that when I have the time, I'll have one checked out to see what they're made of."

"Wow," Patricia said, leaning back in her chair. "Did you get to see the meteorite? Was there a fire? Who else saw it?"

Marcia leaned forward again. "This is where it gets really interesting, and you have to keep this to yourself. I was the first one to the site. It was huge, like the size of a car, and it was smoking, just like you'd expect to see in a sci-fi movie. There wasn't much of a fire, probably since it had rained the day before. It was giving off steam that smelled kind of like a hot spring. I held up some leaves against it to see whether they'd burn. Since they didn't, I touched it. It was cool."

"Wait." Patricia rubbed the bridge of her nose. "You touched the meteorite?" At Marcia's chagrinned expression and slow nod,

Patricia rolled her eyes. "You do realize that you could have seriously burned yourself?"

"That's why I used the leaves first. I—" Marcia protested, stopping when Patricia raised a hand for silence.

"God, Marcia! Really?"

Marcia's eyes softened. "I'm fine. It was like touching tinfoil after taking it from the oven. It had cooled down."

Patricia bit her tongue to stop herself from yelling at her friend. Marcia wasn't a reckless person, and it was perplexing to hear how she'd taken such a stupid risk. "What happened next?"

"I heard something and jumped back just as the government lackeys got there. I gave a short statement of what I saw, had my head checked out, and returned to my room."

"That's it?"

Marcia shrugged. "Pretty anticlimactic, huh? It seems few people even know about it. A local station reported it, but I don't think many saw the broadcast. I tried to look it up online, but I found nothing. And the meteorite was gone by the next morning."

Patricia shook her head. "It's amazing how you always get caught up in these incredible events. You didn't feel sick or anything afterward, did you?"

"Not at all. I feel great."

"Just making sure. And here I was expecting to hear you hooked up with someone," she joked.

"Now that would have made the evening news," Marcia said, chuckling.

After eating lunch, they made plans to meet again before she left for Boston. While hugging, Marcia said, "Don't do anything I wouldn't do. Be safe."

Affection rushed through her. "That pretty much leaves me with carte blanche, doesn't it?" Stepping away from a playful swat, she waved at her friend as she made her way to her car. Noticing the time, Patricia returned to her room to write a bit and get ready for the evening ahead.

After working on an outline for her next book about a young pediatrician who falls in love with her patient's widowed father, Patricia turned her mind toward what to wear. Deciding on a form-fitting, mossy-green colored dress to emphasize her green eyes and copper hair, Patricia took her time preparing for her date. By the time Rudi rang up to let her know she was waiting in the hotel lobby, Patricia felt ready. She looked in the mirror once more while applying some lip gloss and winked. She felt sexy. Joining Rudi in the hotel lobby, Patricia accepted a kiss on her cheek.

"You look breathtaking," Rudi murmured.

"You don't look so bad yourself," Patricia said, allowing herself the luxury of raking her eyes over Rudi's body. She wore a maroon, silk, button-down shirt and black pants that hugged her curves. Patricia squeezed her hands into fists to prevent herself from reaching out.

"Ready to go?"

"More than ready." Patricia grinned.

They walked a couple of blocks before entering an unassuming French restaurant. One would never know how luxurious the interior was from outside with its crumbling, weather-stained facade. Eighteen-foot coffered ceilings towered over arches, balustrades, and delicately carved pilasters, reflecting a neo-classical look complemented by sleek, elegant designs. Etched glass light boxes shimmered throughout the room. Wrought-iron wall sconces branched out, a pleasing contrast to the handmade porcelain tiles decorating the walls. Grays, browns, and tans were accented with reds and blues. Even the leather and velvet textures evoked an undeniably romantic ambiance.

"Is that by Manolo Valdes?" Patricia asked. She indicated to one of several pieces hanging in the main room.

"Yes." Rudi's eyebrows hiked up her forehead. "The artist created the paintings especially for the owner, whom I happen to know. I take it you're familiar with his work."

"I am. I was admiring some of his paintings the last time I visited MoMA, and, of course, I've admired his outdoor sculptures throughout Manhattan." Before she could say more, Patricia noticed Rudi's attention shift toward a man heading their way.

"Do you like wine?" Rudi asked.

"Yes," Patricia answered while nodding. Wine sounded perfect to her. She wasn't one to drink hard liquor or mixed drinks. Give her a glass of wine, though, and she was a happy girl.

"Do you have a preference for red or white?"

"No, not really."

"Will you trust me to order for you?" Rudi asked softly.

"Of course. Thank you."

Patricia barely held back a gasp as a pleased smile crossed Rudi's face. Once the sommelier reached their table, Rudi conferred with him in low tones. Soon after, their server arrived.

"We'll have the tasting menu." Indicating Patricia, Rudi continued, "She'll have the crab salad, scallops, halibut, beef, and the chocolate coulant. I'll have the sardines, scallops, the bass, the lamb, and the chocolate coulant. All with the wine pairings."

Patricia's mouth opened in surprise, not expecting such a decadent meal. Seeing Rudi tilt her head at her in question, Patricia gave her a dazed smile. "That sounds wonderful."

Throughout dinner, Patricia made approving noises as she bit into the various courses. At first she was mortified, and she tried to stifle her responses, but when, after a particularly loud moan escaped once she tasted the flaky, seared halibut, she looked up to see Rudi's expression of mild arousal, Patricia decided not to hold back. Their conversation flowed easily throughout dinner, focusing on more intimate conversation than when they were last together.

By the time their plates were cleared to make way for dessert, Patricia wondered whether Rudi was going to cross the polite distance between them in their rounded booth and kiss her. For someone who'd just eaten such a lovely dinner, Rudi looked positively starving. Her eyes were so dark Patricia had a hard time looking away. Even though Rudi maintained her distance, Patricia recognized the promise of much less distance between them once they were no longer in public. She looked away to regain her equilibrium. *Remain cool. Do not climb over the table and into her lap.* She could feel beads of perspiration forming at her hairline. She reminded herself to not fan herself with her napkin, but it was difficult to appear unaffected. The smirk on Rudi's face told her she wasn't succeeding. While attempting to regulate her breathing, Patricia nearly missed Rudi's next comment.

"You wrote your book about me, didn't you?"

*How do I answer that?* She finally decided on the truth. "Yes. I got the idea after I received the thank you note. I let my imagination run wild." Looking away, she glanced around the decorated restaurant, recognizing several other well-known personas seated at the surrounding tables.

"An actress I've worked with in the past, Kiernan Connelly, told me about the book. She said the lead character bore a striking resemblance to me, except for being male. Well, of course i had to read it for myself. When I read about the roses the man received during a standing ovation and the note he sent to his adoring, beautiful fan," here she moved her eyes over Patricia's face, "I had no doubt that I must see you again."

Patricia thought about her book. She had channeled her infatuation for Rudi, her knowledge of her characteristics, and her love for the theater into that fluff novel. She supposed that was why it sold so well—it had more substance than the normal light reading, and it tapped into the public's love for celebrities.

"I hope you're not upset that the lead character fell in love with a man." She gave Rudi a sheepish grin.

Patricia watched as the faint pout on Rudi's face, emphasizing full lips she wished to kiss again, melted into a small smile. "No, I understand. My sexuality is a bit of an open secret. You removed one large stumbling block for creating a successful book by keeping to the traditional coupling. Your book became a hit because of that choice. Who knows whether that would have proved true if you hadn't made the switch."

Patricia hummed her agreement as she sipped of her wine. Dessert came, and they ate in silence. The small cake was delicious. Patricia made quick work of it, loving how the chocolate middle oozed onto the plate. Once finished, Patricia leaned back and studied her date. She appreciated how Rudi didn't interrupt her scrutiny. *She's probably so used to it that it doesn't bother her.*

"You love it, don't you? The adoring fans, the publicity, the money, the opportunities." Patricia hesitated. "Don't you ever miss your privacy? You have to be 'on' all the time, right? You can't do whatever you want, wherever you want, without having to consider how your fans will view your actions."

"I love the attention. Have since I was a little kid. Losing my privacy so I can do what I love is a small price to pay. I don't know what I'd do if I were unable to act anymore. It's the love of my life, and the reason I live." Rudi leaned forward and covered Patricia's hand. "I'm so glad you're here. All the fame and glory in the world becomes meaningless if I can't share it with someone."

Patricia noticed how Rudi swallowed and looked away, her leg bouncing and fingers tapping. She realized with surprise Rudi was nervous. *Guess she doesn't share her feelings too often.*

Rudi became motionless, her eyes unfocused, before she blinked a few times and leaned forward. "I have tomorrow all planned for us. I'm bringing you to some of my favorite places."

For the next hour, Rudi described where they would explore. Patricia allowed the change in subject, thankful Rudi wanted to spend time with her. She dared not think beyond tomorrow, afraid she'd find this miraculous weekend coming to an end.

After dinner they took their wine glasses onto the side balcony to enjoy the summer breeze. Rudi stood next to Patricia, their hands clasped together. As Rudi grazed her thumb across Patricia's knuckles, surprise and pleasure skittered through her.

"I have to be honest. I've never met anyone like you. You are refreshing. I feel good when I'm around you," Rudi confessed, her voice soft.

Rudi skated her other hand over Patricia's arm from wrist to shoulder, her eyes following her fingers' path and continuing to rest on Patricia's face. Her smoldering look inflamed Patricia. Rudi leaned in as if in slow motion. Patricia met her halfway for a scorching kiss. With a sigh and a prayer of thanks, Patricia released her desires from their constraints, allowing her passion to rule.

Patricia pressed her lips firmly against Rudi's while pulling her neck down and melted into Rudi's body. Groans of pleasure came from both of them. She kept her eyes tightly shut, focusing on the multitude of sensations bombarding her. The softness of Rudi's lips combined with the taste of her mouth—passion mixed with port and chocolate—were an aphrodisiac.

Restless fingers itched to wander, but Patricia had the presence of mind not to give in to these urges, instead gliding her hands through Rudi's dark, spiky hair. Breaking away, Patricia was thankful for Rudi's close hold. She leaned her ear against Rudi's chest, listening to her hammering heart.

"I need you," Rudi rasped.

"Come back with me." Although a simple response, she tried to express much more through her eyes: desire, need, adoration.

Rudi beamed, and Patricia shivered at the look on her soon-to-be lover's face.

"Let's get out of here, shall we?" Rudi's voice was seductive. Patricia shuddered with awareness. She nodded. Taking a few steadying breaths, she retrieved her wrap and purse while Rudi paid the bill, and they moved into the night air without any more conversation.

It was a lovely summer evening for the short walk back to Patricia's hotel. She felt a buzz of excitement. She promised herself that she wouldn't squander another moment to insecurity or fear. Patricia's only desire was to reveal all of herself to Rudi in the hope it would be enough to make her happy. She wanted Rudi to know her in every way. *First things first.* She had her fantasy woman coming back to her hotel room, and she intended to love her. She grinned. *Maybe all those fantasies I've had over the years will become reality tonight.* And she had a great imagination.

Eyeing Rudi, she sucked in her breath as she saw the lustful look on Rudi's face. Tendrils of heat wrapped themselves around her heart, abdomen, and groin, even while her legs shook and her breath hitched.

"Almost there," Rudi said, an unspoken promise caressing Patricia's ears.

Turning the corner, they moved toward the hotel. Once at the door to her suite, Patricia inserted the passkey and invited Rudi in. After illuminating the room, Patricia poured two glasses of wine. Returning to Rudi, who had moved toward the window to see the gorgeous view of Manhattan's skyline, she passed one of the glasses over.

Patricia began a toast. "To taking a chance, being in the moment, and living life fully."

"Yes." After taking a sip of the beverage, Rudi placed the crystal on the coffee table. "I can't wait much longer."

Patricia understood and managed to place her own glass down just before Rudi swept Patricia into her arms. Lips parted, the length of their bodies touched, and their tongues sought out each other. Without a second thought, Patricia broke the fiery kiss and led Rudi to the bed.

At the foot of the bed, Rudi turned to Patricia. Bringing both of Patricia's hands to her lips, Rudi kissed each fingertip with touching devotion. Patricia felt as if, with each kiss, her sense of being was grounding itself. For the first time in her life, she felt complete. Safe.

When she felt Rudi's lips touch the pulse points on her wrists, Patricia gave herself over. The actress's eyes, stained with passion, darkened to a swirling mass of gunmetal gray. As their lips met and her body responded to Rudi's touch, the rest of the world fell away. Moaning, Patricia felt strong arms enfold her.

They settled down onto the bed. Patricia lifted her hand to touch Rudi's strong jaw, gliding her fingers up her cheekbone before guiding Rudi toward her for another kiss. What started out as a gentle exploration spiraled into a passionate exchange, and clothes slipped off. As they came together, promises of spending more time together and getting to know each other better were exchanged and throughout the night, they laughed and shared, touched and explored, until they both fell asleep.

The next day the couple roamed Manhattan. Rudi spoiled Patricia to no end. They walked through Central Park, hand in hand, enjoying the summer weather. With her personal assistant's help, Rudi had organized a picnic on a grassy hill overlooking the lake, complete with appetizers, sandwiches, drinks, and dessert. Later they went to Tiffany's, where she bought Patricia a stunning tennis bracelet. Patricia was even able to coerce Rudi into granting her request to visit St. Patrick's Cathedral. She humored Patricia by walking beside her, taking pictures and answering questions while Patricia marveled at the architecture, sculptures, and stained glass.

Eventually, Rudi dropped Patricia off so she could get ready to perform that night. Promising she would attend Rudi's play and accompany her to an informal cast party afterward, Patricia kissed her lover farewell.

Several hours later, Patricia enjoyed Rudi's show. *The last time I sat in this theater, I handed Rudi a dozen coral roses during the standing ovation. Now, I'm sitting here as her guest, still as infatuated by her smile.* After another fabulous performance, Patricia idly watched the crowd disburse.

Kissing her in greeting moments later, Rudi asked, "Wasn't that a great crowd? I was feeding off of their energy. As soon as they laughed at the first joke, I knew this would be a magnificent night."

She guided Patricia behind the stage curtain to a crowded area set up with drinks and assorted snacks. Patricia gasped, as she noticed the crowd was filled with not just the cast but also other assorted guests connected to the theater. Producers, directors, actors, actresses, casting agents, friends, family, singers, and whoever else could manage an invitation were milling around the stage. As if all the "it" people who lived in or around Manhattan had found their way to the soiree.

Rudi was the perfect host, introducing Patricia to whomever she saw. To Patricia's chagrin, Rudi told each person how Patricia authored a book about her and beamed when Patricia demurely received praise while redirecting attention toward the actress.

"Kiernan, come here," Rudi called out to an actress crossing the stage from the drink table. A lovely lady with high cheekbones, long ebony hair, and cobalt eyes came toward them without breaking stride. *She's striking,* Patricia thought as the woman neared. Stepping in front of the pair, she looked at Rudi, a slight smile gracing her classical features.

"I'd like you to meet Patricia Steitz. She's the author of that book you pointed out to me as being about me. Patricia, this is Kiernan Connelly." Smiling, Kiernan bowed her head while maintaining eye contact with Patricia, who felt her heart begin to accelerate. Kiernan was sophisticated and talented. Patricia saw her on Broadway once, and Kiernan's performance mesmerized her. She was able to express emotion through her eyes, her facial expressions, and the way she held her body. Her performance left Patricia breathless, and her mind kept returning to particular parts of the play for weeks after that show.

Hoping she wouldn't make a fool out of herself, Patricia said, "It's a pleasure to meet you. I love your work."

# Chapter Five

"IT IS A PLEASURE to meet you. Is your book really about Rudi?" Kiernan asked.

After a slight hesitation, Patricia said, "Well, it's a composite. I took some real experiences and let my imagination run wild."

"You certainly did," Kiernan answered, amused. Sipping from her cup, she observed the younger lady's Irish features and petite figure, wondering how she wangled an invitation to the party. With her bright emerald eyes, red mane of hair, and generous smattering of freckles across her face, she exuded vivacity. She was autumn in Vermont.

Kiernan couldn't help thinking Rudi was the one who invited her. "How did you two meet?" She waved vaguely between Rudi and Patricia.

Rudi smoothly interjected herself into the conversation. "She was in town recently for a book signing, and I took it upon myself to invite her to dinner. It seems the least I can do is to show her the behind-the-scenes world of stage acting, wouldn't you agree?" Rudi smiled while sweeping her arm out in an all-encompassing arc toward the room where conversations abounded.

Kiernan quirked a brow and turned back to Patricia. "Are you working on a sequel?"

The young writer paused, no doubt wondering at the strange undercurrent between them. It wasn't that Kiernan wanted to make the writer uncomfortable, but she was an unknown factor in Rudi's life, and Kiernan felt threatened.

Patricia cocked her head, eyes flittering to Rudi before finally answering, "I'm taking a summer course in preparation of a new book. I don't anticipate it to be a sequel, though, so no."

Kiernan asked, "Oh? What course are you taking?"

"It's called Enlightenment 101: Musings of a Madwoman. The course is about spiritual growth and self-actualization in today's world. Quite interesting, really. Over the last few classes, the professor's been focusing on perspective and communication. For example, she discusses how it's possible to empathize with others and their experiences. She explained that people tap into two basic emotions—fear and love. We instinctively understand these feelings even when we haven't lived through a specific set of circumstances. I've learned quite a bit. Certainly enough to make me question my perspective."

Glancing over at Rudi, Kiernan was disappointed to notice she looked bored. A moment later, Patricia turned to Rudi. "Rudi, I'm going to take a look at the food. Do you want anything?"

Noticing how Rudi continued to look around the room while sporting a small grin, Kiernan elbowed her. Rudi looked at Kiernan's arm, her face, and at Kiernan's head jerk toward Patricia before she realized she'd missed something.

"Patricia offered to get you something from the food table," Kiernan explained.

"Oh." Rudi's eyes widened, her mouth opening for a moment before she turned toward Patricia and gave her an apologetic smile. "Thank you, but no. Go ahead. I'll talk to Kiernan for a bit."

Breathing out her disappointment and watching the writer leave, Kiernan asked, "Where were you this time?"

"Huh?" Rudi snapped out of it again, shaking her head like a confused dog. "Oh. I was thinking about tonight's show. It was great. The energy was electric."

Kiernan nodded, her lips twitching. Rudi never changed. "You know, what Patricia was saying about her class applies to us. You might want to listen to what she's learning. Maybe you'll even learn something."

Waving her hand, Rudi replied, "That's her thing. I'd rather use my instincts to connect with my audience. I don't need to be told how or why it works. I just need it to work." She smirked.

"I've received some intriguing letters that seem to touch upon what Patricia said. I wonder if there's a connection."

"Hmm, yes. Would you like to have dinner tomorrow night?" Rudi turned back to Kiernan, finally looking as if she were present.

Lips curving, Kiernan glanced in Patricia's direction and raised her eyebrows. "Won't you be busy?"

Rudi glanced Patricia's way. "Her? Oh, no. I was just her tour guide, so to speak. You know I love spending time with you, and we haven't been able to lately because of our schedules. We could go to your favorite restaurant for a late dinner after the play, say eleven?"

"Not this week. I need to get some sleep. Make it Monday at eight." Leaning forward, Kiernan pecked Rudi's cheek. "Until then, darling." Walking toward Patricia, she paused to deposit her empty glass on the table. "It was a pleasure to meet you. I hope your class is enlightening." She smiled at her unoriginal pun and turned to leave.

"It was a pleasure to meet you, too," Patricia replied, her words running together as Kiernan turned away.

Kiernan veered off to retrieve her purse. She stood to the side and watched Patricia rejoin Rudi, who linked their arms together and led her toward the exit. The vibes they gave off indicated more than polite interest. Kiernan followed them out the door, staring in the direction they walked long after she lost sight of them. She had the strongest feeling they were together. She and Rudi never claimed to be exclusive, but the thought still hurt her. It seemed like everyone was turning her in for a younger version. *Why aren't I enough?*

The next day Kiernan opened an envelope covered with now-familiar script. She had two letters forwarded to her through her agent, along with the warning that all other received mail would be refused by the theater. She knew no other person who received letters like these—thought provoking, honest, and demanding—and she skimmed over the latest letter once more. Since talking to Patricia so briefly, she couldn't stop wondering whether the letter writer was the professor she mentioned. It seemed like too much of a coincidence, yet her gut told her it was true. As true as the fact that Rudi and Patricia were intimately involved.

*I have long wondered why we must experience suffering and how such experiences make us stronger, wiser, and interesting. I must admit that I struggle with struggle. Heartbreak, setbacks, upheavals, disappointments—most humans must come to terms with these types of events. These trials and tribulations may cause a person to barricade the heart and mind from further anguish.*

Considering the words, Kiernan thought about the struggles she endured to become a successful actress. She still struggled. Take for instance her present circumstances. She had no role and no idea why. She had acted steadily since graduating high school. However, she was getting older, and the parts she was offered were slowing to a crawl. No one thought she could continue to headline shows. With a sigh, she continued to read.

*Yet, there are times when I feel I cannot seize a piece of peace, when no matter what I do, life provides no rest for the weary. It's an uphill battle where I try to pull myself up the precipice, hand over hand, grasping at the small indentations in life that may crumble at any given moment. Others struggle just as painstakingly as I am—my spiritual brethren. At those times, I focus on each moment—it's all that exists—each foot plodding forward, body swaying, hands clutching onward and upward.*

Kiernan thought back to when she first began her search for acting jobs twenty-five years ago. Breaking into the business was an arduous task. She often told young actors that if they weren't absolutely dedicated to acting, it would be better to choose a different profession. Kiernan went to countless auditions while working as a waitress at one of the restaurants near Times Square known for its clientele of Broadway producers, directors, and actors. It took her two years to get an off-Broadway part. Much longer to get to Broadway itself. She never looked back.

*Toward the top I see people who not only reached their goals but have returned down the mountain to cheer me on as I keep going, using inner reserves I did not know existed. And so life becomes that much sweeter, profound, and meaningful, as I overcome whatever life throws at me. My experiences provide me with an inherent understanding of other people and their struggles, bringing me closer to them. We connect. I can't help wondering, though, wouldn't it be more pleasant if all could connect through positive experiences?*

The unanticipated joke caused Kiernan to laugh. *This writer has a dry sense of humor.* Indeed, it would be more pleasurable not to have to struggle so much. On the other hand, she was right that the moment felt sweeter when success was borne through struggle. It was also true she didn't take many chances these days. *But that's being smart, isn't it?* Her life had an easy quality to it.

*So, there is hope. As we experience these struggles, we have the opportunity to release patterns that no longer coincide with our desires. We create new ways of being—new beliefs, actions, thoughts. And we learn from each experience, regardless of the outcome. We invite change into our lives.*

*Sometimes I do not embrace change. Whether the change occurs through an external or internal force, it all stems from my reality and my choice. I have given permission for the change to occur. Otherwise, I would not attract that change. We waste great opportunities, mostly due to not being present, or we pull back due to fear. We look ahead and behind, not appreciating the moment at hand.*

Kiernan leaned back in her overstuffed chair. *Interesting. She's saying we create everything that occurs in our lives, good and bad. I created not having a new acting job, this casual relationship with Rudi, and this reality where I'm not able to carry a show because I feel I am too old.* These were hard truths. Kiernan didn't know whether she was ready to accept them.

She tried to remember the last time she was totally present and in the moment. It surprised her that she couldn't remember a specific event. It wasn't that she was unhappy. It was more apt that she had become comfortable. She lived life on automatic pilot, and life had passed her by without comment. *Where exactly have I been focusing my attention?* For all she knew, she might have blown several chances to procure a new acting role just by not being aware.

It made her wonder whether she was squandering her life, fighting against changes instead of accepting them. Maybe it really was time to change, to use her senses by being present each moment.

*With change come opportunities to connect with others. To make a difference in others' lives. How we leave our mark and how we affect others are our choices. We all play a role not only in our own lives but in others' lives.*

Chuckling, Kiernan noticed the gentle ribbing she was receiving from the letter writer. Every actor wished to make a mark. In fact, the success of an actor's career turned on whether her performances were compelling enough to attract admirers. That was why some celebrities fell into the trap of allowing their every movement to be captured by the media. Any publicity to them served as a way to remain in the public's eye. Kiernan tried to not feed the media. She was a private person, only allowing so many interviews and photo shoots, and only when they were preplanned. Firm in her decision to keep her private life separate from the public, Kiernan cloaked herself with an aura of mystery.

*In the end we do make a difference by existing, but we are mere blips at most. Yet, to ourselves and to others we have touched, our existence has meaning. It makes a difference. In the end, it's my willingness to live life and climb mountains that creates my reality.*

Kiernan reread the paragraph once more before placing the letter on a small table. She felt ill-equipped to contemplate all these ideas. How could she find the time to figure out why events occurred in certain ways? She was as guilty as many others of taking life for granted, looking ahead instead of focusing on the present. If pressed, she might even admit that when acting she wasn't always entirely focused. Not that she needed to be. She portrayed each Broadway role hundreds of times with the same words, the same inflections, the same movements, day in and day out. She didn't need to be entirely present to act out the play. Or so she thought. Now she wasn't so sure.

She wanted to respond to the letters, but the truth was she had so many questions about the writer. She had no idea who this person was, really. For all she knew, the letter writer could be paparazzi or a rabid fan waiting for Kiernan to write back, only to post all her answers on the web or sell them to the highest bidder. She was asking Kiernan to bare her soul, her innermost thoughts, and Kiernan had no idea what those even were. She couldn't afford to trust this person. It made her too vulnerable.

Besides, she had so many conflicting thoughts that she felt she didn't have the time necessary to devote to an honest response. *And this writer*—she glanced to the bottom of the letter where it was signed—*Thea Corelli, deserves a heartfelt response. Perhaps once I get my career in order.*

With determination, she contacted her agent and told him that she was ready for another job even if she was not the top-billed star, even if she had to audition for a part. After a stunned pause he assured her he'd be in touch soon. Kiernan grinned. She had rejected several roles in the past because she would have had to share or relinquish top-billing. As for auditioning, she hadn't entertained the notion in the past. She had a feeling that, with her changed attitude, much better parts would crop up. Her reasons for acted had changed over the years, and she wanted to reassert her past motivations. She loved the craft, loved tapping into the stories, the characters, the connections with others. Change, although scary, was overdue for her. She needed to clean house, as it were, and climb the mountain. Focusing on her craft was a step in the right direction.

***

### MONDAY, JUNE 26, 2017 8:57 P.M.

On Monday night, Kiernan played with the napkin in her lap while waiting for Rudi to answer her question. The meal was the same as all the others, meaningless chitchat and excellent wine. Still, she deserved a truthful answer.

"I don't understand what your fascination is for that girl," Rudi huffed. "I was just being polite. I doubt I'll ever see her again." Kiernan watched Rudi take a deep breath and slow her breathing as she refocused on her. "You know I adore you. This jealousy is unnecessary." Her eyes pleaded with Kiernan to believe her. The problem was, she didn't believe Rudi, and she didn't trust her. She had never caught Rudi cheating in the past, but she watched them interact. Having studied human nature and emulated it for most of her life, she knew what she saw—the lingering looks, the sparks of energy whizzing between them.

*Rudi must think I'm a fool.* And maybe she was, for she wanted desperately to believe her. They were two peas in a pod. Both loved acting. Both were successful in theater, television, and film. Both methodically translated their mastery of the craft into believable characters. Both loved the same restaurants, people, and relaxation activities. They fit together well.

Words floated through Kiernan's mind, unbidden. *How does one find truth without fear?* She asked this question once in an interview, and Thea had tried to provide her with an answer in one of her letters—by totally accepting what is, without judgment. The situation she needed to accept was she and Rudi were comfortable but not necessarily right for one another. They were drifting apart. Maybe it was because they were at different points in their lives. She faced an uncertain future while Rudi's career flourished. Kiernan needed to take a good, hard look at where she was and how she had arrived at this point in her life. Only then could she live life fully. Only then could she move forward.

<*"If I act offended and keep denying it, maybe she'll believe me."*>

Kiernan looked at Rudi, cocking her head to one side. *Surely she didn't say that out loud.* Rudi gazed at her with wide eyes and a beseeching look, giving no indication she had spoken. *What the hell? Am I hearing things?*

<*"Just hold the pose. She'll believe me. She always does."*>

"Did you say something?" Kiernan asked, studying Rudi's face.

"No. Kiernan, are you all right?"

Kiernan waved her hand. "Yes. It's the surrounding noise. I thought I heard you say something about believing you."

"No," Rudi repeated, her response slow and eyes filled with confusion. <*"Well, at least her focus is off Patricia. Maybe she really knows nothing."*>

*I'm hearing Rudi's thoughts.* Kiernan didn't know what to do. *How am I able to listen to Rudi's thoughts?* "You're right, of course. I guess I am a bit jealous."

Kiernan could see Rudi's uncertainly. Schooling her features to a bland expression, Kiernan took a sip of her wine while she thought about what to do. It was scary to think of ending her relationship with Rudi. Even if she had cheated on her, she knew the woman. Kiernan was comfortable with her. They maintained their individuality but spent time together comparing stories, supporting each other, and frequenting celebrity functions together. If they broke up, she would be alone. Kiernan wasn't sure she was ready for that. Ready or not, though, she understood Rudi might have already made that decision, even if she didn't seem ready to reveal it to anyone, not even to herself.

With a sigh, Kiernan decided to let it go for now. "I'm sorry, darling." Leaning forward, she placed her hand on top of Rudi's where it rested on the table. She gave her a sad smile. "Just promise me that if you decide to move on, I'll find out from you and not some tabloid."

Rudi blinked and drank from her wine glass. "There's a charity ball to raise money for AIDS research next week. Would you like to go?"

"Sure." Kiernan agreed, her mind still focused on the words she could have sworn Rudi said moments ago. As the conversation continued, she marshaled her wayward thoughts and concentrated on Rudi, knowing their time together was winding down.

"Rudi, are you happy?"

Stopping mid-sentence, Rudi looked askance. Not even taking any time to think about the question, she answered, "Yes, of course. Aren't you?"

Kiernan frowned. "I don't know. I thought I was, but now I'm not so sure. I feel like I've been sleepwalking. And now that I've awakened, I want more from life and from myself."

Rudi tittered. "Oh, Kiernan, don't worry, honey. You'll have a new acting job before you know it. Take this time to relax, maybe travel. You'll feel better in no time. You'll see." Patting her hand, Rudi resumed where she'd left off, telling Kiernan who would be at the charity ball and what she planned to wear.

Kiernan felt a bit lost. Rudi's behavior grated on her more and more. Maybe it was her fault. Maybe she had never shown any interest to get to know her on a more intimate level. But she was trying now, and Rudi rejected any opportunity Kiernan presented for her to open up.

It seemed that Thea's powerful letters were unleashing an entirely new reality, and Kiernan felt poorly equipped to deal with it. *Well, as Thea says, we attract everything. Nothing is a mistake.* Kiernan pulled her thoughts back to concentrate on the present. On Rudi talking about the latest gossip.

Once they exited the restaurant, Rudi said, "So, nightcap?"

*It amazes me how obtuse she can be.* "No, dear. Not tonight." Kiernan delivered a kiss to Rudi's cheek. "We'll talk soon." With a nod to the valet, a cab was hailed down and, ignoring Rudi's look of consternation, she left.

Back in her apartment, Kiernan looked around as if she were a stranger viewing it. The entranceway flowed into the living room, which showcased floor to ceiling windows with a view of the Hudson River and the city skyline. The building, built before World War I, boasted hand-painted moldings, tiger oak flooring, and sculpted light fixtures. To her right, a buffet lined the wall with her family's silver tea set placed upon it. Above it hung pictures of family and friends. Rich oriental rugs with reds, dark blues, brown, and white hexagonal patterns adorned the living room and dining room floors. An overstuffed white couch and matching white and blue patterned chair surrounded an oak coffee table. The dining room table, a mix of cherry and oak wood with matching leatherback chairs, cast an elegant air to the apartment. An original oil landscape painting from a dear friend hung on the wall. The swirling yellows, reds, and blues accentuated the furniture colors.

Her home looked warm and inviting. Empty. A perfect reflection of who she'd become. Truth be told, she hardly ever entertained here. It might be time to change that.

Rudi suggested she get away, but Kiernan already did that. Two weeks ago she traveled to a spa to relax and unwind. Sunny Horizon Resort was world-renown for its top-notch services. Kiernan spent two days being pampered, and if it weren't for a strange meteorite experience, it would have blended into her memories as merely another spa retreat.

"At least I have a souvenir," Kiernan murmured, moving to her mantle where three small rocks rested. Picking up one, she admired the speckles of gold, green, and white all over the smooth, ebony rock. She'd have to get it checked out at some point to find out what it was made of. Maybe she could even have one shaped into an amulet. She was certain the unique rock would make a great statement piece. She liked holding them and felt calmer when she had one in her hand. Wearing one would probably quiet all the roiling thoughts that kept jettisoning her peace of mind.

# Chapter Six

SITTING IN HER APARTMENT Patricia threw down her pen, crumbling up the piece of paper half-filled with scribbles and tossing the useless writing into the basket beside her desk. She got up from her chair and stretched. *I need to clean anyway.* Stopping halfway across the room, she slowly swung around and returned to her desk, plopping down with a sigh.

Labeling what she was doing—trying to find something else to occupy her thoughts so she wouldn't have to focus on this paper—Patricia shook her head. The paper was due the next day, and she was procrastinating. Honestly, she didn't know what to write. How was she supposed to know what personas she utilized on a regular basis? Professor Corelli explained in class that a persona was a façade, a mask donned. Each persona directed that person on how to follow acceptable societal norms.

But Patricia's personas had changed radically over the last couple of months. Take Rudi. She never would have flung herself into such a passionate, soul-consuming whirlwind romance before she wrote the book. It was as if she were another person around the actress. An infatuated fan, gaga-eyed, flushed, and tongue-tied, Patricia found it hard to concentrate on anything except her body's instinctual responses. It wouldn't surprise her if Rudi thought she was a total idiot. She could hardly put together a coherent sentence when they were together.

As a child, Patricia used the "fly on the wall" persona—quiet and aware. Once an adolescent, she began to assert herself more with mixed results. Her friends, family, and peers helped her to develop personas for school, social events, family interactions, church, and dating through positive and negative responses. Patricia never really thought about it, though. She just knew that she acted differently, according to the situation and the people present.

As an adult, she became gregarious, outspoken, and fun-loving. There were times when she would revert back to old behavioral patterns while in the company of family, former classmates, or other people from her younger years. Even now, she would sometimes fall back on the lessons she learned while growing up when she found herself outside her comfort zone.

Over the last few years, her personas again shifted. Writing changed her outlook on life and started her on the road toward self-discovery. The book, in some ways, became her confessional, her way of releasing childish fantasies. Surprisingly, now those dreams were manifesting. She got the famous actress, but Rudi wasn't quite what she expected. It was unsettling—this meshing of fantasy with reality—and she developed new personas accordingly.

Refocusing on the assignment, Patricia began to brainstorm the types of personas she used. When in class or with the professor, she was inquisitive and open. Her dialect reflected a student trying to master the classroom lingo, often grappling for the best terminology. She was also wary about what she didn't know, but she felt passionate about the subject matter, which often spurred her to speak. One moment she was silent in her seat, the next she was practically out of it, hand raised so she could voice her opinion. *Professor Corelli must think I have a split personality*.

Nowadays with her friends and family, Patricia tended to be confident and quick to laugh. She was used to asserting herself into conversations, having found it necessary with two sisters and one brother. The friends she attracted also loved to debate issues from every angle for the academia inherent in such exercises, if not for the love of the subject matter itself.

The phone rang, breaking her from her thoughts. Patricia jumped up to reach for the cell, a smile in her voice as she answered.

"Hey, Patricia. When are you coming back to New York?" asked Marcia teasingly.

"I was just thinking about that. I was going to call you today. I'm just trying to finish this damn paper."

Marcia sighed. "Ah, the agony of writer's block. Should I let you go?"

"No, no. Maybe the break will help. As it turns out, I'm free this weekend." Patricia smirked as her heart rate spiked.

"Great. I'll pick you up from the airport, and we'll grab dinner. How's your dad?"

"We booked the trip to Italy," Patricia answered, sadness leeching through her system.

"Oh. I'm so sorry, Patricia. Is there anything I can do?"

"No. You've been great through all of this. I can't thank you enough. We'll talk once I'm there. It's a bit too hard right now." Patricia played with her pen, swallowing back her sorrow. She had no intention of crying again, although she knew Marcia would comfort her as best she could were Patricia to lose control of her emotions.

The family was planning a trip to Italy at the end of the summer. She was looking forward to the trip, but she also felt distraught, knowing they were going to create their last loving memories with her father before he died. This trip would be bittersweet at best.

Marcia sensed her hesitation and changed topics. "Hey, how's everything going with Rudi?"

"Great. Awesome." Patricia felt giddy every time she thought of her blooming relationship with Rudi.

"Wow. That good, huh?"

"That good," Patricia replied, taking a seat on her couch. "I've never met anyone like her. She is so sexy. Sensual. A great storyteller."

"Not to mention easy on the eyes."

Patricia nodded, but it bothered her how everything came back to Rudi's sexiness. There had to be more to the actress.

"What?" Marcia's voice was filled with concern.

"I don't want to sound judgmental, but all she does is talk about acting. I mean, I tried to lure her into conversation several times about different subjects, but she doesn't seem interested. And she doesn't really talk about her interests, family, friends— nothing except her roles. I feel like I don't really know her." Patricia sighed. "I've been infatuated with her for years. Here's my chance to know the woman behind the persona, and I feel like I'm failing miserably at drawing her out."

"These things take time. She's used to hiding, protecting herself from her fans. When are you going to see her again?"

"I'm not sure," Patricia murmured. "Probably this weekend."

"You're going to see her again, aren't you?"

"Yes. How can I not? She's irresistible. A great lover." Patricia's face reddened as she realized how much she'd revealed, and she was glad this conversation wasn't taking place in person. Marcia laughed, and Patricia whispered, "I need to see her again. If I give her enough time, I'm sure she'll trust me enough to let me in."

"Well, it sounds like you've already let her in several times."

Patricia sighed.

"Seriously, though, I'm sure it will work out. And, this is so exciting!"

Laughing, Patricia had to agree. This thing with Rudi was incredible. She'd be a fool to let it go without a fight.

"See you this weekend."

"Okay. I'll send you the flight details soon. Love you." Patricia hung up the phone, deep in thought. Marcia was a wonderful friend. She had drafted the will, health care proxy, power of attorney, and all the other necessary legal documents for her father without charge. But that wasn't what made her a great friend—she was ready to talk at any time, full of supportive, encouraging words. She understood what Patricia did and didn't say. Moreover, she always seemed to know when to push Patricia to discuss her feelings and when to break through the sadness with jokes.

Patricia grew up in a middle-income, albeit fractured family. Her father doted on her, often taking her out separately from her siblings for walks, ice cream, and movies. Once she entered adulthood, they drifted apart. Although they still shared a strong connection, she missed that relationship. Even harder for her to accept was how his body was failing him. She remembered an energetic man. Now he looked like a shadow. She walked back to her desk and sank onto the chair. It was time to get the paper done.

***

The next morning, Patricia wondered where Professor Corelli was. She was usually punctual, yet here she sat five minutes past the start time with no one to lead them. The room hummed with energy. She couldn't think of a class in this course where she'd been disappointed. On the contrary, her admiration for the professor grew with each hour. She felt privileged to spend time with Professor Corelli, debating points brought out that day.

Hearing the door open, Patricia's eyes widened. In waddled the professor wearing a costume which consisted of an oversized, purple pajama suit, a green beret with two vines of grapes and leaves attached, and a sign on her chest that read: "Don't tell Welch's that I'm here!" She was a runaway Concord grape.

After a moment of complete silence, the room exploded into laughter, whistles, and clapping. Patricia joined in. Their illustrious professor stood in front of her class, hands clasped around her girth, a pleasant smile gracing her lips. As the class quieted down, the professor's gaze cased the room, catching the eyes of several students.

"Today we are going to talk about façades, masks, personas, and society's effect on each," Professor Corelli announced. "We get labeled, often inaccurately, according to a variety of factors. Have you ever thought about your behavior while with another person? More particularly, how your behavior changes according to whose company you keep? Why?"

"Maybe because it's expected?" a blonde young woman said.

"By whom?" Professor Corelli asked.

"By society. Or by whoever is there," the blonde answered.

"Yes. From an early age, we learn to interact in certain ways—when to speak, when to be silent, when to act, when to remain still. We are shaped by our parents, friends, teachers, and siblings. Through this process we develop our personas. As we grow older, we become more adept at interpreting reactions and anticipating the best mask to don."

Patricia shook her head, amazed at how Professor Corelli made it sound so simple.

"Have you ever attended a function where everyone is proper? Then in comes a stranger, flamboyant, flitting from group to group. Have you seen the reactions of others? Some are amused, others envious, and a few are downright angry—angry this person seemed to ignore the tacit decorum which everyone else has been following. This newcomer did not don the right mask!"

Chuckling with the rest of the class, Patricia enjoyed Professor Corelli's way of laying out so plainly how people might feel. Patricia knew exactly what she was talking about.

"As an extension of these façades, a person may naturally slip into different dialects. While talking to a loved one, one may speak casually, yet while speaking to a colleague that person may adopt more formal speech. They complete the persona the person wishes to portray. So I ask you to consider this—can a person ever just be himself or herself in any and every given situation, making no changes to his or her persona whatsoever, regardless of the circumstances? Is it possible to know what that is like?"

As the class continued, Patricia's mind wandered to Rudi. Was Rudi ever herself? Did she slip into a character she once portrayed, or did she shed those roles when not being paid to act? She saw shades of different roles during their time together, but how could she really know?

She listened as the professor drew them into a discussion about society's rules and how a person's behavior may be measured against them, and she felt her perception shift. Now the last paper assignment made sense. Society influenced people's actions, the pressure of those with whom they interacted cuing them on how to act. How a person reacted with a family member as compared to a friend in the same situation could be different. As the class ended, Patricia saw the professor's gaze sweeping the lecture hall, stopping as it locked on her. With a raised eyebrow and a slight grin, Professor Corelli waited for Patricia to gather her belongings and bound down the steps to join her.

"That was wonderful," Patricia said as she reached the front of the classroom.

"I'm glad," Professor Corelli answered, unzipping her fleece suit and unpacking herself. Patricia watched in amazement as her mentor produced air-fill packets, one after another, from her costume, placing them on top of the table. She could now see her professor's flushed cheeks. *The costume must've been warm.* Underneath, the professor wore only shorts and a T-shirt, and Patricia noted her professor was quite pretty. Toned arms, flat stomach, defined legs. With a sigh, Professor Corelli divested herself of the remainder of the costume and slipped some flip-flops on her feet.

"Whew, that's much better," she said with a wide grin. "Let's get something to drink. I'm parched." As the professor led them to the GSU, Patricia relished their upcoming conversation.

"Professor Corelli," Patricia began. "Weren't you afraid that you'd make a fool out of yourself by showing up in that costume?"

"Do you think I made a fool of myself?" the professor asked in an amused voice.

"Not at all." Patricia flashed quick smile. "I don't think I could ever get up the nerve to do something like that, though."

"Yet you've given book readings across the country to strangers for months. Weren't you afraid of not reading the right words, not connecting with your audiences?"

"Sure I was nervous, but I believed in what I was saying." Patricia nodded.

"And, did my showing up to class in that outfit lessen the impact of the lesson I gave? Lessen your respect for me?"

"No," Patricia stuttered. She gathered her scattered thoughts. "If anything, your appearance reinforced the lesson. It also brought forth the idea that our perceptions can be manipulated by our senses. We need to be careful when making judgments. Truthfully, I thought your appearance drove home your lesson more than mere words could have."

The bright smile Patricia received for her words blindsided her into speechlessness. *What is going on with me? First I have a manic fan-worship complex for Rudi, and now it seems I'm creating hero-worship for my professor.* Shaking her head, Patricia looked up in time to see a frown linger on her professor's lips.

Silence reigned as they sipped their beverages, both lost in thought. Eventually, conversation began again, and they fell into the comfortable ebb and flow of their well-practiced philosophical conversations.

"I've read your book. Was that based on a real person?"

Though stunned, Patricia answered, "Yes. As a matter of fact, she came to one of my book readings while I was in New York last month. I was totally unprepared for the reality of meeting her. I created her into this larger-than-life persona, and now I'm trying to reconcile that with who she really is."

"She's an actress?" Professor Corelli leaned forward.

"Yes, a well-known one."

"Are you...keeping in touch with her?" Professor Corelli asked.

Patricia tensed, but in the next moment she relaxed into the feeling of trust she held for her professor. "Yes. I guess you could say that we have embarked on a relationship, but I'm having trouble releasing the dream woman I created in my mind."

Patricia laughed self-consciously as her fingers twisted a napkin into a useless wad.

"I understand." Her professor gave her a soft smile. "Expectations can kill any relationship, but if you keep working at learning who she really is behind her public persona, you may find that it's enough."

Happy they were speaking on a more personal level, Patricia thanked her. She felt a real need to connect with her professor on a more intimate level. She didn't understand the emotions roiling under the surface, but she knew that she welcomed spending time with Professor Corelli.

She thought back to her last visit to New York City. She had attended another after-play party at the theater. Once they had returned to Patricia's hotel, she and Rudi spent the night discussing the future in broad terms, careful not to say it would include the two of them together, as a couple. Instead, they had tiptoed around the elephant in the room. They had made love, getting to know each other more throughout the night. The morning light found them spooned together, Patricia stroking Rudi's toned forearm and wondering how often she exercised. Their conversation flowed back into her mind.

*"These last few weeks have been wonderful. I don't want it to end."*

*Rudi squeezed Patricia's midsection. "Who said anything about ending it? I love spending time with you. I'm glad that you're able to come down to New York so often."*

*Patricia turned around within the circle of Rudi's arms. "You are?"*

*"Of course. I adore you. I adore how you make me feel. It looks like I'll be working the show for the foreseeable future, but we're able to spend most of the weekdays together, and let's not forget the marvelous late nights."*

*Kissing her, Patricia agreed.*

Her thoughts returned to the present when Professor Corelli rose, indicating that she had to go. She touched Patricia's forearm. "I'll see you next class." and with that she was gone. Patricia remained in her seat for several minutes, processing the change of energy between them. With a smile, Patricia left campus with unhurried strides. It was a beautiful summer day.

Hopping on the inbound T, Patricia took the green line to Government Center, where she disembarked and walked down the steps to Faneuil Hall. Strolling through the indoor food court, Patricia decided on a cheesesteak for lunch before climbing the stairs to find a seat on the upper level. Patricia made a game out of determining which of the tourists were couples. Glimpsing one couple who ate without talking, she concluded they had been together for several years, complacent with silence. Rudi became uncomfortable with their silences, often taking pains to fill them with stories.

She wanted more in their relationship, but she'd have to talk to Rudi about it. She wanted to be closer with her, to know about her childhood, how she became the woman she was now. She knew all the normal biographical facts about her—Patricia had memorized them long before she wrote the book. But she didn't know Rudi's outlook on life, her thoughts on spirituality, politics, metaphysics, and energy. She didn't know what Rudi strived to accomplish, other than maintaining a successful acting career. She didn't know what drove her into acting and how that career satisfied her. She didn't know what she did when she wasn't on stage or at an event. This weekend, Patricia decided, she would attempt to find out.

# Chapter Seven

## *TUESDAY, JULY 25, 2017 7:35 A.M.*

AS THE MORNING LIGHT sifted through the thin curtain material to caress Kiernan, she opened her eyes to a new day an indolent smile crawling across her face. She felt different— grounded. Over the last several weeks she'd made life-altering decisions in just about every part of her life. She had taken inventory to better understand what made her happy and what did not. Kiernan began to take the necessary steps to make happiness a fixture in her life. Now she wondered why she had taken so long. *Fear, probably.* She had realized that she was afraid to let herself be vulnerable.

Yet she had auditioned for a new role and found herself excited to explore it. The last time she auditioned for a part was well over ten years ago. Such a hurdle nearly took her out of the game before it even began. Her nerves had gotten to her, telling her she was too old, too much of a prima donna, too out of touch with honest emotions, too stuck in her ways. But she was willing to reevaluate, change, and grow. With that in mind, she put aside such negative thoughts and nailed the audition.

It was an ensemble piece, and she was content with it. Another milestone. She felt the changes in herself and in her lifestyle, and it was all she could do not to embrace the fear that shadowed each moment. Fear of the unknown. Fear of failure. Fear of being alone at the end of the day and not liking who she was when there was nothing around to distract her from looking in the mirror.

Thea had asked her some interesting questions in the last letter she received, now over a month ago. She seemed to enjoy exploring the ideas of personas and empathy. And her comments made Kiernan reevaluate how she approached her craft.

*As an actress, you are a master at slipping into a given role. You make the character your reality, at least while playing the role. Tell me, though, how are you able to separate yourself from the mask that you wear while acting? I was contemplating how we need not have personal experience in order to empathize with another's circumstances. It is enough to know about the situation producing joy, heartbreak, laughter, or sorrow. How are you able to act out a scene where you have no personal experience from which to draw? What do you take away from your roles? Do you allow your fans' expectations to impact your behavior? At public events, do you ever become one of your characters? Or, after playing a role for a long period of time, does the role become a part of you?*

*So many interesting questions.* Stretching, she rolled to her side to gaze at Rudi. As usual, they had a wonderful time the night before. It used to be the perfect relationship, but Kiernan was ready to release her security blanket. Broaching the subject last night, it became clear Rudi didn't want to change their dynamics and could persuade her to drop the subject. Kiernan smiled ruefully. She supposed this romp in the sack could be labeled the last hurrah, a bittersweet, temporary union with a person who had fit in her life for a while. She was grateful for the time they'd spent together, but it was time to say goodbye.

Slipping from the bed, Kiernan wrapped herself in her cranberry-colored silk robe and padded out of the room. She peered out a window overlooking the Hudson Bay, a calm silver sheet in the morning shade, recognizing the irony with allowing Rudi to join her at her home. Truthfully, she was afraid of what her future held for her. Rudi functioned as a constant in her life. With all the changes occurring to her, what would her touchstone be? What would calm her fears?

Kiernan kept telling herself that she was creating a wonderful, fulfilling life. She believed in herself—in what she was creating. She believed in the words Thea wrote, the words that changed her so much.

Several times, Kiernan flirted with the idea of contacting Thea. She knew, however, that she wouldn't take such a step. She'd been burnt too many times before by fixated fans to want to take the chance. When she gave an inch, they took a mile—expecting everything and resenting any boundaries. It was flattering at first. Yet, she quickly learned that if she were not careful, she would have no private life. Through some embarrassing mishaps, including some overzealous fans sitting down at her table while she was sharing dinner with her director, Kiernan learned she needed to layer her identity so people couldn't easily track her down. Acting was a job, after all, and at some point she needed time to be just Kiernan. Lately, the problem she faced was her uncertainty about who she was. The letters helped her explore that question. Perhaps, if she received any more letters once she was back on Broadway, she would contemplate answering.

Kiernan wanted to reactivate her love of the craft. What better way than to teach acting? What fascinated her was how easily everything fell into place once she made that discovery about herself. Two days later she was approached by her former acting coach to teach a class on how to tap into the senses, reflect emotions, manipulate the audience into empathizing with the characters, and make not just the confused heroine understood but also the hateful villain. Such objectives were quite challenging, and she relished the opportunity. She felt more alive than ever. Just preparing for the class was changing her perspective. She was exploring feelings long locked behind her protective walls, and she intended to use such self-reflection to help others connect with their audiences. Turning toward Rudi when she heard her step into the room, Kiernan stared at her.

"You're serious, aren't you?" Rudi walked toward her. "Is this about Patricia? She means nothing to me. I'll stop seeing her. We've been together for a long time. Doesn't that warrant another chance?" Rudi grasped Kiernan's hand. "Please, Kiernan. You know how much I care for you."

<*"How did she figure it out? I thought she believed me when I denied I was with Patricia. Jesus! It's just a fling. I can't lose Kiernan. I can't."*>

Something in Kiernan balked at the blatant lies Rudi was spewing. It confounded her that she could hear Rudi's thoughts. She didn't know how to react—whether to confront Rudi or not. Hearing people's thoughts was a very new development. At first, she thought she was going crazy, but after she asked some careful questions, overheard thoughts were validated. The hardest part was not reacting to the caustic thoughts, often about her. They were ego-crushing, and she had spent many years inflating it. When she first began hearing people's thoughts, it was overwhelming. She couldn't control what she heard, and it was hard to identify whose thoughts she was hearing. She didn't know how to turn them off, and she learned more than she ever wanted to know about those around her. No one realized that she could hear their internal monologues, and she felt she had invaded their privacy.

Thankfully, she found she was able to block unwanted thoughts by visualizing erecting an impenetrable wall. It was the only way she could achieve quiet moments. Although this gift proved useful when she needed to know what someone was thinking, she found herself more comfortable not listening.

"Do I?" Kiernan gave her a mocking smile. "When's the last time you asked me about my hopes, my dreams, my fears? We have chemistry, I'll admit. For a long time, that was enough. Not anymore. Rudi, it's time to let me go. You don't need me. You have Patricia and if that fails, you'll find another person to listen to your stories and stroke your ego. I need someone who will stimulate my mind, not just my body. I need more in a relationship. It's time for us to get out of this rut and move on. It doesn't mean that we can't spend time together in the future, but it does mean that we won't spend it in this way." Kiernan waved her hand between them before letting it drop to her side and looking away. Kiernan could feel the fear Rudi felt, radiating off her in waves. She felt bad but not bad enough.

"Is there anything I can say to change your mind?" Rudi asked, pouting.

"I'm sorry. You'll see this is for the best."

"I should leave." Rudi slouched out of the room, returning within minutes dressed. "When will I see you again?"

"In a few weeks *The President's Other Mistress* will be offering a public reading. There will be a party afterward. Perhaps you and Patricia would like to come?" Kiernan raised an eyebrow.

"Wouldn't it bother you if Patricia came?"

"No," Kiernan replied. "Actually, I like her. You'd do well to let her in. She has a lot to offer."

Rudi hugged her tight before leaving without another word.

"Goodbye," Kiernan whispered to the empty room.

Tears began to fall, cleansing her soul as one part of her life came to an end. Grieving for the loss of this relationship, even while knowing it was the right course of action, Kiernan allowed herself to feel the waves of confusion, hurt, sadness, and emptiness washing over her. Hugging herself, she broke down completely, sobbing. Alone and afraid.

Kiernan stumbled to the couch and clasped a pillow, tears continuing to fall. She thought of the changes in her work, in herself, in her relationships. *Am I doing the right thing or being a fool?* She feared she would become too lonely and run back to Rudi, run back to the hollow, unfulfilling relationship, if only because it was better than not having anyone to hold her.

Finally, her tears began to abate, and calmness blanketed her. In the loud silence, she heard her rapid breathing, intermittent sniffles, and a pattering against the windowpanes. *Rain?*

Kiernan loved the rain. It served as a reminder of nature's complexity and power. Off the east coast, clouds would roll in over the ocean, enveloping the area with a thick and all-encompassing fog. Lightning would brighten the sky as energy played among the clouds, sometimes escaping to strike the ground. Rain was always a comforting sound. Kiernan loved the smell before the clouds released. It mingled well with the sea air.

Moving back to the window with the pillow in her arms, Kiernan watched, mesmerized, as the rain pounded the city. Sheets hit the bay in a diagonal pattern, creating a ripple effect across the water. The trees far below swayed, losing many leaves. In spite of the storm, traffic flowed at a steady pace, seemingly unaffected. She would take their example to heart. Wiping away the last vestiges of her grief, she shifted her mind toward making her heart sing. The new play and teaching job were good starts. She intended to begin today with creating the reality she wanted and deserved. Smiling at the soothing rain, Kiernan said a silent thank you for the reminder and began the day in earnest.

\*\*\*

## SATURDAY, JULY 29, 2017 6:26 A.M.

*Today will be better than yesterday. That's what I've always told myself. I told myself yesterday, and I'll probably feed myself that line tomorrow.* Marcia didn't have to open her eyes to start her mantra. She started each day with those words because, up until today, she always disliked waking in the morning. She always felt like death warmed over, like she was suffering the effects of a hangover even though she hadn't enjoyed the transient pleasure of getting drunk. Yet, today she awoke feeling more refreshed than ever. Stretching, she didn't feel any of the usual pops and cracks. She flexed the arches of her feet and felt no danger of cramping. Her ribs, back, neck all felt fine, a big deal since she'd broken a rib some years earlier and often felt a dull ache, particularly when it was overcast like this morning. As for her back and neck—she'd abused her body for several years, all in the name of sports. Although not one to readily admit it, she was a bit competitive. A bit driven. Today she felt different, though.

Lying in her cozy bed, tucked under a white down comforter and amber-colored faux-fur blanket, she felt hard-pressed to get moving. However, work didn't stop for a Manhattan attorney, even on a weekend during the summer, not even when said attorney was pretty damn content to remain in bed.

Getting up, she donned her eyeglasses, flicked on the bathroom light, and screamed. *My hair.* It was white, pure white, as white as newly fallen snow. Salt, John's undershirts, cotton balls, polar bears, icebergs, paper before she printed legal briefs on it—white. Luckily her daughter Sammy had slept over her best friend's house the night before. Marcia was going to need some time to figure out what happened so she could explain it to her. Of course, she needed to find a way to explain to herself. Staring at her reflection, she lifted a hand to her hair and marveled at the change. But the color was brighter than white—purer, colorless, unblemished. That was when she noticed her skin.

She had perfect skin. Soft, supple—no wrinkles, no crow's feet, no laugh lines, no color imperfections—flawless. And besides the white hair on her head, eyebrows, and eyelashes, she seemed to have no other body hair. Pulling out her drawstring pants and panties, she confirmed that little fact. *Good Lord. What the hell is going on?* She undressed. *Okay. Baby's skin, no stretch marks, no cellulite, no imperfections, no body hair except for the head, eyebrows, and lashes, no aches, and violet eyes.*

*Violet eyes!* Staring into the mirror, she blanched as glowing violet eyes stared back. Leaning closer toward the mirror, she studied her new eye color. She felt herself falling into those eyes—her eyes—and zooming through tunnels at high speed. Soon she came back to herself, feeling shaky and dizzy. Her eyes were unfocused, but they remained that same unearthly color.

How would everyone react to these changes? *I can't let anyone see me. How do I explain this?* She leaned against the sink, nauseous. Taking some deep breaths, she decided she needed some time. *First thing's first.* Leaving the bathroom, she walked over to the phone and dialed the office. Hearing the weekend switchboard operator, she asked for her assistant. With a quick glance to the computer laptop, she confirmed that Brenda should have just gotten into the office.

"Brenda? Hi. It's Marcia. I'm going to work remotely today. Is there anything I need to know?"

After a pregnant pause, Brenda answered, "No. I'll be finishing up the research you asked for today—"

"Right—on the Delaney case. You can email me the research. Call me if anything comes up. Thanks." Hanging up, Marcia removed her glasses and squeezed the bridge of her nose, trying to think. *Did I do something different last night?* She thought for a moment. *No. Last night I worked late at home, took a shower, and fell into my empty bed. Am I still sleeping?* Shaking her head, she knew she needed a plan, one that would keep her colleagues from seeing her like this. Or Sammy. Or anyone else. Plus having a plan helped her calm down...if only a little.

Logging online, she decided to check out contact lens websites. *I can't go to work with purple eyes. One look at them, and everyone will freak out. Like I have. Or worse.* Which led Marcia to another discovery. She could see perfectly. Although she was wearing neither contacts nor glasses, she saw no blurriness, no fuzzy, indistinct shapes. *Cool.* Except now she'd have to wear contacts to hide her eye color.

Reviewing the websites, she realized she might have a problem—okay, another problem. There was a wide range of blue contacts. How was she going to match a pair to her eye color? She doubted there was much of a demand for washed-out blue eyes. Would anyone notice the difference if the shade was a bit off? *Not many people stare into my eyes, not since John.*

John, her husband, died two years ago while they slept. Heart attack. He was thirty-six years old. She didn't really know how much she loved him until he was gone. She fell into that sorry group of people who took their significant others for granted, dwelling on the negatives surrounding everyday life instead of the positives. She missed him. She missed his steady presence, his gentle humor, and his loving demeanor. They were married for eleven years. Now it was just her and Sammy.

Stella blue, ocean blue, baby blue, topaz, blue angel, powder blue: so many types of blue contacts, but no pictures were available on the websites for review. Some were tinted, others solid. Filling out the online form, Marcia ordered baby blue and powder blue to be delivered later in the day. Same-day delivery was one of the best perks of living in New York City.

Next on her list: dealing with the bright white hair. Pulling it back into a ponytail, Marcia donned a baseball cap and sunglasses, dressed, and left the house. She was a woman on a mission. For a hair-coloring kit. An hour later she found herself in the bathroom covering her hair with blonde coloring goo and plastic, hoping it would take care of the problem. She also applied some to her eyebrows, figuring blonde hair and white eyebrows might look odd. She looked at her reflection. Everything would be fine soon enough. As she waited the prescribed twenty minutes before washing out the coloring solution, she puttered about the house.

She loved her home. Built in 1910, the living room, with its window-paned French doors, opened onto Juliette balconies overlooking a quiet neighborhood on the Upper East Side of Manhattan. On the opposite side of the room stood floor-to-ceiling bookshelves. She was a booklover through and through and often spent hours curled up on her maroon leather chair before a roaring fire, reading.

Walking through the connecting formal dining room to reach the kitchen, Marcia idly viewed the cross-beamed ceiling, red oak hardwood flooring, and hand-painted moldings. She preferred to live in a house that oozed character and comfort. Opening the curtains and one of the balcony doors overlooking a private atrium, she breathed in fresh air tinged with the scent of roses, before continuing to her destination. Retrieving orange juice from her state-of-the-art refrigerator, she marveled at how retro her kitchen seemed with its antique façades. Looks could be deceiving.

Returning to the bathroom, Marcia stripped and showered. Quite a bit of hair-coloring solution washed out by her feet. Shrugging, she finished her shower, grabbed a peach towel to dry off, and strolled into her walk-in closet to find sweatpants and a T-shirt to wear.

She wasn't quite sure what to do about hiding her eye color from Sammy. Could she arrange for Sammy to stay at her friend's house for one more night? Otherwise, she had three options: wear sunglasses in the house, tell Sammy that the violet eye color was actually contact lenses, or hide in her room, claiming a headache. Of course, she could tell the truth, but it didn't seem to be a good idea. Or maybe she was just a coward.

She would need to be prepared to face her daughter's questions, though. Delaying the inevitable wouldn't remove the necessity of explaining the eye color since Sammy would notice even if the colored contacts worked. After all, some of the violet would bleed over the sides. If she claimed to be wearing purple contacts, Sammy would realize pretty quickly she wasn't. Sammy had a fascination with contacts, often watching Marcia put them in or take them out while asking how she could touch her eyes like that and didn't it hurt having something plastic in her eyes and why couldn't she wear contacts, too. *So, I'm stuck.*

Blowing out her breath as she sat down on the edge of her bed, Marcia decided she'd just have to tell the truth. *Yes, honey, I know it looks strange, but I woke up this way.* She blew her breath out again, while shaking her head. *This will be fun.*

Taking the towel off, Marcia worked her hands through the mass of hair as she walked to her vanity. She shook her head, confounded. It was still white. All of it. Not one bit of hair dye had taken hold. Not even on her eyebrows. Her hair remained thick, luxurious, and white. Throwing her hands up, Marcia tried to figure out how she would explain her new look to her daughter. She sank on the bed, noticing how her hands trembled. Squeezing her eyes shut, she rubbed her temples. *This can't be happening.* She placed a hand on her chest, concentrating on her breathing. She had no idea how to deal with this. *And what do I do about work?* She had a trial starting on Monday, a high profile one. She couldn't just waltz into court like this. The opposing counsel would think she was trying to disrupt the court by directing undue attention toward these changes instead of to the legal arguments. *One thing at a time. Think.*

*Should I call my hair stylist? Maybe I've applied the hair coloring dye incorrectly. How will I explain it to her, though?*

Marcia had a sinking feeling that just as the hair-coloring kit was unsuccessful, so would a trip to the hair salon. *Should I buy a wig?* It would have to be customized. That would take too much time, and she had already wasted her entire morning on her new looks. Not only did she look the same, but she had no idea why her body changed while she slept. Her stomach lurched, and Marcia jumped up, running to the bathroom. She leaned over the sink, taking deep breaths before splashing her face with cold water.

This was all so much easier when she was younger. She could roll with the punches, then. Adapt. Change. Accept. But, she hadn't been so good with those concepts over the last few years. Even when Patricia talked to her about such ideas, Marcia shied away, delivering jokes to cover her insecurities. *I should call her. She can help me make sense of this. I need help. I need a calm head.*

She dialed Patricia's number and began pacing, listening to it ring. "Hello?"

"Patricia, it's me." Marcia paused, unsure how to begin this conversation.

"What's wrong?"

Hearing the concern, Marcia grasped the phone tightly, trying to get the words out. "I...I don't know if I can explain. I'm afraid you won't believe me unless you see me. Patricia, something's happened to me, and I'm freaking out." Sighing, Marcia sat down. "I woke up a totally different person, and I don't know how it happened."

"Start from the beginning."

"I know you weren't planning on coming here for a couple of weeks, but is there any way you can come here today? I know I'm asking a lot, but I really think everything will become clearer once you see me." She ran her hand over the bedcover, focusing on the feel of the plush faux-fur.

"Yes, yes. I'll come on the air shuttle today. Can you pick me up?"

Marcia winced. "You know that normally I would, but these aren't normal times. Can you take a cab here? I promise you'll understand once you see me."

"Sure. Are you all right? You're scaring me a bit," Patricia said.

"Not really, but it's not necessarily bad. I truly don't mean to sound vague, but it's better to wait until you're here."

"Okay. You know, modern technology makes it easy to see each other."

"No," Marcia replied, her voice firm. "This is an in-person reveal. I need my best friend with me, in person. I need a hug, and I need you to hold my hand and tell me everything's going to be okay."

"Right. I'll call you back to let you know my flight time. I can stay there, can't I?" Patricia questioned, uncertainty coloring her voice.

"Of course. I'll see you later. And, Patricia, I truly appreciate this. I do."

"I know," Patricia answered. "I'll talk to you in a bit. Hang in there."

After the call ended Marcia sat on her bed, staring around her room. It looked the same as the day before. Her watch and jewelry sat on her dresser, yesterday's clothes waited to be added to the drycleaner's pile, some shoes peeked out from underneath the bed. None revealed clues as to how or why her body had transformed. *Maybe I've finally cracked up. Maybe I look the same, but I'm seeing something else. Maybe I've been working too hard.*

A scream tore through the room. Marcia jumped. Sammy stood in the bedroom doorway. Marcia shot off the bed toward Sammy to placate her, but Sammy backed up, bumping into her friend, Rosie.

"What's happened to you?" Sammy shouted, wide-eyed. She covered her mouth with her hand, her eyes jumping from Marcia's eyes to her hair. "What did you do?"

Marcia didn't know what to say, and she reached toward Sammy in a useless gesture. "Honey, it's still me."

Sammy shook her head. "This is horrible. You have white hair and purple eyes! What am I going to do when everyone hears?"

"Sam, it's not that bad," Rosie piped up, putting a hand on Sammy's arm. Rosie was one of Sammy's closest friends. They looked like bookends. Both of them had long, wavy black hair and cornflower blue eyes. The only difference seemed to be Rosie's height—she was a few inches taller. "It's kinda cool. Who has purple eyes? My mom wouldn't do that. And that hair is so white. And she's a lawyer, so it looks good on her."

Marcia let out a breath, grateful to Rosie. *Always did like that girl.* Sammy seemed to be calming down a bit, simply staring at her.

"Why didn't you tell me you were going to do this?" Sammy asked.

"I'm sorry it scared you. Really." She figured telling her that she had reacted similarly, that she had no hand in her new looks, might cause more problems. Better to tell her later. Walking to the doorway, Marcia hugged Sammy. "It's still me. I just look a little different. Okay?" Pulling away to see Sammy's face, she watched her daughter nod. "Patricia's coming for a visit this afternoon. Go do what you were going to do while I get some work done. Life goes on, even with different colored eyes and hair."

Marcia grinned and waved them away. Shaking her head, she turned her mind back to the case she was supposed to be prepping, determined to use some of the time to prepare for trial. That, at least, hadn't changed. She looked forward to showing her stuff in the courtroom. As for the rest, well, she hoped Patricia could help her find a way to reverse the changes so that, come Monday, people would pay attention to her legal arguments instead of her new look.

# Chapter Eight

## SATURDAY, JULY 29, 2017 1:38 P.M.

AS SOON AS THE cab pulled up to Marcia's townhouse, Patricia handed cash to the driver. "Thanks." She pulled her carryon behind her as she exited the car and stood in front of the building. Bracing herself for whatever problem she was about to face, Patricia climbed the handful of steps to Marcia's front door and rang the doorbell.

The door opened. Patricia gawked. She heard her suitcase fall on its side, but she couldn't tear her eyes away from Marcia. If she didn't know any better, she'd think this was an elaborate joke. The wild look in her friend's eyes and trembling hands confirmed how real these changes were. *She looks like a goddamn superhero. All she needs is a leather suit.* She cocked her head. *And maybe a cape.*

Patricia finally found her voice. "I can see why you needed me here. Somehow I don't think telling me over the phone would have done this justice. I can't wait to hear the details." She picked up her carryon and swept past Marcia in to the atrium, tossing back over her shoulder, "Where's Sammy?"

"She's in her room with Rosie. Let's get you settled, and then we'll talk," Marcia replied, as she led Patricia toward the guest bedroom. "Do you want to freshen up?"

"Yes. Why don't you make us some coffee, and I'll be out in a few minutes." Patricia placed her luggage on the bed. Before Marcia could leave, Patricia stepped forward and captured her in a tight hug. She could feel Marcia grip her, conveying just how upset she was. She was great at covering up her emotions, but Patricia knew how to read her. And it was clear that Marcia was freaking out, as she should. Even if she weren't trembling in her arms, Patricia could feel how Marcia held herself, and the coiled tension and jerky movements were dead giveaways. Add on how she was like a furnace, and Patricia had no doubt that her pulse was racing. She let Marcia go and turned toward her bag, knowing Marcia would want a moment to regain control of her emotions before they discussed anything.

"Will do," she said. "Patricia."

Glancing toward the door in surprise, she raised an eyebrow.

"Thank you for coming." Marcia gave her a shaky smile.

Patricia could hear the emotion in Marcia's voice and wanted to pull her in for another hug. Instead, she nodded. "Of course."

After Marcia left the room, Patricia sank down on the bed, trying not to freak out. It wouldn't help the situation. She knew that. But Marcia had white hair and purple eyes. She looked like a witch or a sorceress. Or a mage. Marcia the Mage. That had a nice ring to it. Patricia smirked. *Well*. She slapped her hands against her thighs and rose. *We just need to figure out what happened and whether it's permanent. No problem.*

By the time Patricia entered the kitchen, it seemed Marcia had found her equilibrium. Marcia smiled, setting the steaming coffee cups on the table. Patricia noticed the laptop set up beside a stack of papers. She sat down, ready to listen.

"Part of the reason why I asked you to hop on a plane to see me, besides needing your support," Marcia covered Patricia's hand, squeezing it before letting go, "is to make sure you can see the changes in my physical appearance with your own eyes."

"I do. Boy, do I. Yup. Physical changes noted. Those eyes— wow! Penetrating and distinctive with the white hair."

Marcia's lips twisted into a wry smile. "Thanks. I tried to dye my hair blonde, but the dye didn't stick. I've ordered colored contact lenses. We'll see whether that at least work to hide the eye color."

"Okay. What else? What's the paperwork all about?"

Marcia rifled through the papers. "I've searched all morning for some viable explanation. All the research suggests that hair cannot turn white overnight. Some reasons the body may decrease or stop the production of melanin include stress, autoimmune disease, gene mutation, or playing in toxic radiation or chemicals."

Patricia snorted. "I think you'd be dead in that case."

Marcia shrugged. "Otherwise, all these processes are gradual. There is a disease where one loses all the colored hair while gray hair remains, but I didn't have any blonde hair on my pillow this morning, and my hair isn't gray."

"Yes, it certainly isn't. How about albinism? Doesn't that affect eye and hair color? Can a person become an albino as an adult?" Patricia leaned forward and grasped the warm coffee cup.

Marcia nodded, tapping a pen against a pad of paper. Her mug of coffee was untouched, and Patricia wondered how many cups her friend had already drunk.

"I researched that, too. Some people with albinism have white hair and violet eyes. However, melanin production is at the root of it. Also, it occurs at birth, and it always impairs vision. My vision became perfect when I metamorphosed."

"Really? This just keeps getting more mysterious," Patricia responded. *How does someone wake up with changed hair and eyes? Will this hurt her? Are there other changes she hasn't noticed?*

Marcia kept tapping her pen. "I know. With everything I've read, it seems clear that I have no pigmentation in my hair and no production of melanin. The politically correct term for my hair color change is 'pigment challenged strands.' Kind of like how I'm not an aggressive attorney. I'm a zealous advocate."

Patricia laughed. She loved how Marcia tended to fall back on humor when she was stressed.

"Hair stylists recommend to people with gray hair to use violet-based shampoo so their hair won't develop a yellow tinge. The violet-colored shampoos make the yellow appear white. So a connection between my hair color and my eye color does exist. I just haven't a clue how."

"Maybe we're looking at this the wrong way. White is void of hues, while violet is at the visible spectrum of light. One is absent of color, while the other isn't." Patricia picked up a page that caught her eye while Marcia refilled Patricia's cup. "This is interesting. White symbolizes peace, unity, royalty, and death. Purple is usually associated with royalty, too."

"Yes, but violet and purple are different," Marcia huffed.

"But people use them interchangeably," Patricia said. "Violet can appear blue when light density increases. There seems to be a connection between your old eye color and your new one. Here it states that violet can signify royalty, death, inner wisdom, and unity. So, white and violet overlap to some extent with the symbolism for royalty, unity, and death."

"I have no idea what that means." Marcia pushed back against her seat and rubbed her eyes. "And, we haven't even touched the perfect skin conundrum. The research says I'm producing large amounts of collagen causing my skin to look great and my body to feel younger and stronger. If I could bottle that change and sell it, I'd be a rich woman."

"No kidding."

"Perhaps I'm the new queen of peace. I'll have to start taking yoga classes and acting like a saint."

Patricia chuckled and shook her head. "Yeah, I can just see you now." She leaned back against her chair and pressed together the thumb and pointer fingers of each hand so they formed little circles, holding each hand at chest level while closing her eyes. "Ah-ummmm," she chanted, then cracked one eye open. "Am I doing this right?"

Marcia wadded up a piece of paper and threw it at her head. Patricia ducked. *Whoa, Marcia's getting upset.* She leaned forward and laid a hand on Marcia's forearm. "Marcia, it will be okay. You're not in pain. It's just how you look and your eyesight. Right?"

"So far. I just don't understand. Because really, what the hell is the purpose to these changes? Why me? Why now? And how did this happen? I'm an attorney. I live a pretty ordinary life."

"Aren't you forgetting something?" Patricia asked, raising an eyebrow.

"What?"

"That little meteorite encounter?" Patricia was surprised to see Marcia's shocked expression.

"How could I not think of that?" Marcia said, squeezing the bridge of her nose.

"Give yourself a break." Patricia squeezed Marcia's arm before letting go. "You said you brought some pieces home. Can I see them?"

Marcia rose and led Patricia to her bedroom. On her fireplace mantle sat several small rocks. Patricia approached them, noticing that they looked pretty normal. Nonetheless, she was afraid to touch them. Marcia picked two up and held them out for inspection. One was cracked open, displaying several veins of white, purple, and silver.

"Beautiful," Patricia murmured, cocking her head and gazing at them. The other rock was smooth and black with specks of color.

"Do you want to hold them?"

"I think I'll pass for now. Just in case. Has Sammy seen them?"

"No. You know how she gets. I didn't want her to get upset. She doesn't usually come in here. Maybe I'll put them some place safer, though." Marcia crossed over to her closet. "I'll be just a moment."

"Have you thought about getting checked out by your doctor?" Patricia asked once they sat down at the kitchen table again.

"No way." Marcia shook her head, her eyes widening. "I don't want to be a guinea pig." She waved her hand. "It's not like I'm in pain. I look different, but I feel great."

"Yeah, but if this was from the meteorite, it could be a chemical reaction, and don't doctors treat people for physical reactions?"

"I doubt any doctor will be familiar with the composition of meteorites or their effect on people. I'd be better off talking to a scientist."

"Then do that." Patricia crossed her arms.

Marcia pursed her lips. "I don't have time for this. I have a trial that starts on Monday. I have responsibilities. And Sammy. I don't have time to go through a battery of tests which will probably tell me nothing."

"Marcia, we're talking about your life."

"Exactly. My life." She glared.

Patricia huffed. "Being inconvenienced isn't a good enough reason. When something life-changing occurs, you have to deal with it."

"Like your dad's imminent death you refuse to talk about?"

Rearing back, Patricia looked away, blinking several times to clear away sudden tears. She took a few deep breaths. She knew Marcia was upset, but she hadn't expected to be on the end of a verbal attack. She leaned an elbow on the table, resting her chin on her hand while she continued to breathe through her nose. Tapping her finger against her cheek, Patricia chewed on her lower lip while telling herself to calm down.

"I'm sorry."

Finally looking over at Marcia, Patricia saw her contrite expression and sighed. "Do you really think that?"

Marcia shrugged. "You never want to talk about it. I worry that by avoiding it, you're distancing yourself from what's going to happen. I know you can't prepare for his death, but talking about it can help. Talking to you has helped me deal with John's death. I know I'm not an expert on grieving, but I'm here for you."

Nodding, Patricia asked in a soft voice, "Why did you ask me here?"

"You make me feel safe, and you tell me the truth, even when I don't want to hear it." Marcia covered Patricia's hand, a bittersweet smile on her face. "I'm realizing how unfair this is to you, though. I'm sorry I dragged you away from your weekend. I'm sure if you called Rudi, she'd be delighted to spend time with you."

Patricia warmed at Marcia's words. Even after so many years of friendship, it was rare for Marcia to open up this way. Rolling her eyes, Patricia said, "Don't be silly. Even if we can't figure out anything, spending time with you is enough. Plus, I haven't seen Sammy in a while. I can kidnap her tomorrow so you can prep for trial, too."

"What would I do without you?"

"Oh, you'd be fine. Not that you'll ever have to find out. So, if this is the effect of the meteorite, maybe we should try to do some research online of similar experiences? Let me get my laptop, and I'll meet you in..."

"The den," Marcia finished for her. "It's more comfortable."

"Okay."

The doorbell rang, and Marcia said, "That's probably my contacts. Be right back."

Patricia grabbed her laptop, wandered down to the den, and saw Marcia standing in front of a small mirror, a contact on her finger and an expression of fierce concentration on her face. She watched Marcia try to insert it, only to have the contact fall onto the cherry wood bar buffet. "Frick-frack!"

Chuckling, Patricia moved over to her friend. "Don't tell me you've forgotten how to put those puppies in. Haven't you been wearing contacts since before you met me?"

"Yes. They keep sliding off. It's like my eyes are coated with something that repulses them."

"Well then, that's that. You can't hide. Let's see what information we can find online." Patricia crossed the room to get comfortable in one of the overstuffed chairs and booted up her laptop. She glanced up, watching as Marcia tried a few more times to insert the contacts. Failing, Marcia sighed and left to get her laptop before joining her.

"What was the name of the place where it happened?" Patricia asked, opening up her search engine.

"Sunny Horizon Resort. I'll send you the link." Marcia sank into another overstuffed chair, balancing her laptop on her knees.

"Thanks." They sat in a companionable silence as they searched for any news related to the meteorite. "It's strange. I don't see anything. Did you see anyone else there besides the government employees?"

"No." Marcia scratched her chin. "I think most people were at a bonfire or in the resort. The meteorite hit a few miles away. I'm sure people heard it, but anyone who wasn't nearby wouldn't have seen anything."

"Curiouser and curiouser."

"Thank you, Alice," Marcia groused. They grinned.

"Was there a crater? That'd be hard to miss."

"You'd think so, but no. Now that I'm thinking about it, why wasn't there an impact zone?" Marcia sat back, rubbing her eyes. "Nothing makes sense."

Patricia shrugged. "Maybe sci-fi movies have it wrong." After a frustrating hour of not finding anything about the meteorite online, they decided to take a break.

"I do think you should contact Rudi. No need for your entire weekend to be a waste of time," Marcia said.

"This isn't a waste of time. I may not be any help with figuring out how the meteorite changed you, but I can be here to support you while you and Sammy adjust. Besides, I don't know whether this thing with Rudi is going to work out."

Marcia gasped. "What?"

"I think I might break it off." Patricia kept her gaze on her computer screen. "We don't seem to be on the same path."

"Why? I don't understand," Marcia replied, exasperated. "Do you have to go into every relationship as if you were planning to marry the person?"

Unaccustomed to Marcia speaking to her in this way, Patricia's hackles rose. "Look. Even starting this relationship with her was totally unlike me, but I took the leap. Rudi isn't looking for a real relationship. She doesn't open up or share her thoughts. I doubt it even matters to her whether she's with me or someone else."

"That's exactly what I mean. Why not stay with her and see where it goes?" Marcia tilted her head. "Some people take a long time to trust another person. Be patient with her, and stop trying to change her."

"She'll never be the woman I created in my mind. It's unfair to her to continue this relationship. I'll be constantly disappointed and might even treat her poorly."

"Then drop the expectations. They're based on your overactive imagination, anyway. You have the flesh and blood, real woman in your life. How can you throw that opportunity away?"

Patricia ticked off the reasons on one hand. "She isn't on a spiritual journey. She doesn't care about releasing negative patterns or bettering herself. All she cares about are her adoring fans and her career. The bottom line is that I can do better," Patricia huffed, hurt by Marcia's disapproval. "I thought you'd understand. I need to be more than just a warm body in her bed. I want to be her confidante, her friend, her partner, and her lover. But, she won't even discuss it. She basically told me to take her or leave her as she is. What else can I do but leave her?"

After a few moments of silence, Marcia said, "Not everyone is on a spiritual path. Many are just muddling through life, trying to survive, to get through each day. And that doesn't mean they are destitute or hopeless...just not in touch with themselves. Why are you faulting her for being human, for just enjoying what she has created, without wanting more? And need I remind you that, not so long ago, you were one of her admiring fans?"

Patricia scowled. "I'm not judging her. But I want to confront our fears and insecurities and release them. I want to embrace happiness and being in the moment. I can't do that if my partner isn't...I don't know. Maybe I am judging her, at least to the extent that I have decided we're not on the same path."

Marcia looked down at her hands and sighed. "Who am I to give you advice? My marriage was a sham, and I did exactly what you did but worse. I indulged in fantasies for years." Marcia got up and walked toward the credenza where several family pictures were displayed. She straightened the frames. "For years I fantasized about what it would be like if Peter Dullard ever gave me the time of day. I had it all worked out in my head. Years later I bumped into him. It was as if a day hadn't passed but worse. I was given a second chance, and I threw it away." Marcia turned to her, a trembling hand going through her white locks. "It was horrible. He told me how he'd made a mistake and took me in his arms. He pulled me close and said, 'Don't you think I've wanted to do this?' and he kissed me like he had dreamed of it for years. As I had. I was shocked. Angry. Confused. Scared. So fucking aroused I thought I'd explode. I didn't know how to react."

"Marcia..."

"No." Marcia turned and held trembling hands out in front of her. "Just let me get this out." She sniffed, blinking quickly.

Wanting to hear about a part of Marcia's life she knew nothing about, Patricia nodded.

"I was so angry. It was too late. He'd had his chance and rejected me. How dare he do this? But I wanted it so badly. I slowed down his kisses and took control." She looked over at Patricia and smirked. "You know how much I like to be in control."

Patricia barked out a laugh, watching Marcia as she placed her hand over her heart. When she spoke again, it was in such a soft voice that Patricia needed to lean forward to hear.

"That control didn't last long. Our kisses became more passionate. I acted in a way that wasn't like me." Her chuckle was filled with sadness. "I'd only felt that out of control once before, and we won't be discussing that encounter today. In many ways that was even worse, and I'm still dealing with it."

Raising her eyebrows in surprise, Patricia said, "Got it." She was nearly as desperate to hear that story as this one. Marcia hated surprises, hated the unknown, hated not being in control.

"I was so hungry for him. It was crazy, but I knew it would go no further." Marcia smiled. "He felt me pulling away and tried to pull me closer. It was torture, and I let him hold me for a bit longer before I backed up. This all-encompassing feeling of despair came over me." She shrugged. "You know, timing can be a real bitch."

"Yes, it can be."

Marcia shook her head. "I shouted at him. He knew of my feelings for years, and we no longer had any chance of exploring them, never mind any type of relationship. As he launched into a rationalization, I said that I loved him. Those words hung between us while I searched his eyes and saw proof he harbored the same emotions."

Patricia gasped, feeling her heart twinge. How had she not heard about this before?

"He asked what I wanted to do, but what was I supposed to say? I kissed him again. The world stopped for me in that moment and I felt alive. When the kiss came to an end, I answered his question. I said, 'We do nothing.' So, I drove away from my dream." Marcia blew out a deep breath. "I married for stability. I wanted a child, and I figured I couldn't have him. I had already given birth to Samantha by the time that happened. I didn't feel I had any option but to walk away. I stuck to the vows I made to my husband, but at what cost? In many ways, I chose the easier path. I settled because I feared an uncertain future if I took the leap. I feared failure. I feared how others would view me. There's one thing I learned from that...not to live in a fantasy world, because when it clashes with reality, the fallout can be brutal. Sometimes, I regretted marrying John because I didn't feel I could ever entirely give myself to him. And now he's gone, and I've realized too late what a good man he was. I don't want you to regret not giving Rudi the time she might need to measure up to what might be the ideal mate for you. I don't want you to regret your actions the way I have."

"Marcia, I didn't know," Patricia whispered, crossing the room to hug her friend. Sighing, she led Marcia to the couch and sat. "I just don't know how to get through to her. Maybe she's afraid I won't accept who she really is. Or maybe she doesn't know who she really is. Whatever it is, I want to connect with her in a deeper way, and she won't or isn't able to let me. I need some sign that it will be worth it."

"Don't give up." Marcia clasped her hand. "Maybe she needs your help. Just try to enjoy your time with her. Maybe she'll do something that will reassure you. You know how we see things when we least expect to and take them as signs? Stop looking, and you'll see signs everywhere."

"Perhaps. As for my helping her, every person must experience self-actualization alone. She may look to others to see how they found their way, but she's a different person with different perspectives, experiences, reactions, and knowledge. Her journey may even become similar to others' journeys, but it won't be the same. Much like how experiences with those we fantasized about were similar, but different."

Marcia smirked. "Yeah, in this reality you've been getting some with your fantasy. I, on the other hand, must still resort to my overactive imagination." They laughed quietly.

"At some point, if we are to forge ahead with this relationship, she has to remove the barriers."

"I don't disagree. But don't concentrate so much on the future that you forego enjoying your time with her now."

Nodding, Patricia acquiesced. "Hey, has anyone ever told you that you're a great lawyer?"

"That's why I get paid the big bucks."

Smiling fully at Marcia, Patricia rose from the couch to prepare something to eat. "I still believe that there are no mistakes, that events happen as they're meant to unfold. Professor Corelli talked to us about how every moment is perfectly orchestrated, and I agree."

"But it doesn't help knowing that little nugget sometimes, though, now does it?" Marcia commented, delivering a crooked smile.

***

### SATURDAY, JULY 29, 2017 6:45 P.M.

Marcia stretched her arms above her head, taking a break from her trial preparations. Her mind dwelled on the dream she had last night, starring a familiar person. It was her dream lover, a constant companion since college. When she first began to have these dreams, they consisted of two strands intertwined like energetic DNA. Wrapped around each other, they emitted a glow from within. Marcia couldn't determine the beginning or end, but she did know they could never be separated. She felt a thirst she'd never experienced, a yearning. Each time she woke up after dreaming about her dream lover, she reached out, only to find herself alone.

Over time, her dreams turned toward her desire to learn more about this dream lover. She would have settled for seeing a face. All she knew was what the person felt like, the feeling of rightness and comfort, excitement and love. In some of these dreams, Marcia sought to understand this person's deepest, most closely guarded secrets. They took the form of old, dusty tomes hanging on thick cords from the ceiling of her dream lover's family home.

Marcia would cast her eyes about the room, musty and stale, before attempting to read from the pages. Each time she would feel a hand on her arm, turning her toward an indistinct form. She sensed a somberness as the person took her hand. Staring at Marcia, her silent companion would release her hand and turn away. The message was clear. This person was not ready to divulge any secrets to her.

In later dreams Marcia's enigmatic lover reached out, and she accepted the offer of timeless love, unbridled passion, and boundless desire. She could feel them coalesce into her dreams like the most colorful threads weaved through the most magnificent cloth. She belonged with this being. She dreamt of awakening to find this perfect person watching her. She came alive as the heated gaze glided over her. She felt the promise of a life not yet shared, and she despaired. Every time, she was unable to distinguish the countenance of her mystical observer. She saw bright energy, fuzzy facial features, and an indistinct form.

It didn't matter. Marcia had been so sure she'd recognize this person when they met. She woke up for years wanting to return to those dreams, and she was prepared to make her dreams a reality. She knew this person was getting closer. She knew they'd be together one day.

Sitting in her home office to work while Patricia prepared dinner, Marcia allowed her mind to wander once more. The dreams stopped right before she met John. She had assumed he was her dream lover, so when the dreams began again, she ignored them. She pushed away the hunger, the emptiness and need which left her bereft after each nocturnal visit. Although the subconscious was a merciless creature, Marcia refused to listen. She was determined to move on with her life with John by her side.

Marcia never saw the face of her mystery lover in her dreams. She sometimes wondered whether her mystery lover was Peter, the one who got away. She wondered whether he was calling out to her. She had no obstructions other than of her own making now. She could contact him. If he wasn't interested, she could get on with her life, knowing she'd tried. After losing John, it seemed silly for her not to take the chance.

Last night she enjoyed a wonderful, magical dream. A dream where she was transformed. She spread her wings wide and took a spin around the universe. She remembered how powerful and infinite she felt, how she soared to immense heights with only a focused thought and self-given permission. When she woke, it was with the thought that she couldn't be beaten down in this world unless she allowed it. And in that moment between dream and reality, she unfurled her spirit and rode the waves of energy through that realm and beyond. It was a glorious feeling. A sated, complete, free moment. *And then I awakened to a brand new world.*

Two days later Marcia pretended not to hear the murmurs her arrival in the courtroom provoked. Giving into her gallows humor, she chose to wear a sharp slate-gray suit and purple blouse to emphasize the changes in her appearance. She decided that if she couldn't hide them, she would show them off.

She moved to the plaintiff's table with her client, striving to calm herself as she unpacked her attaché case. Feeling a presence at her side, she looked over at Lexie Yamin, one of the senior partners of Finklestein, Krauss & Yamin, P.C., with a raised eyebrow.

"Interesting hair style, Marcia. Finally decide to stop coloring your hair?" opposing counsel said with a smirk.

"At least I'm not trying to look younger than my years, Lexie," Marcia replied in a bored voice as she sat back in her chair, folding her hands on her lap and eying the formidable litigator. *She looks as gorgeous as ever.*

Lexie chuckled. "Take your best shots now. With age comes experience, and I intend to use that to my benefit." Leaning in closer, she whispered, "Sure you don't want to drop the case before you embarrass yourself?"

Marcia laughed. "If you want to offer a reasonable settlement, we'll consider it."

Marcia watched Lexie sashay to her table. Marcia spared no more thought to her poorly contrived plan to rattle her. Instead, she marshaled her thoughts toward the opening arguments. She had reviewed the file so many times that she could recite the facts in her sleep. That freed her up to focus more on strategy and presentation. In the courtroom, Marcia liked being able to focus solely on each moment, shifting her strategy in reaction to what was revealed throughout the trial. To that end, her assistant took notes of each proceeding so that she could review them and use them during the next court appearance.

By the end of the week, Marcia had decimated the defense with a strong opening statement and two reputable witnesses. After the novelty of her looks wore off, people became entranced by the facts she presented. Her goal was to wow everyone with her confidence, charisma, and passion.

That wasn't to say that Lexie had been doing a poor job. On the contrary, she was as impressive as ever. If she hadn't prepared so thoroughly, Marcia had no doubt Lexie would have ripped her apart like a frothing pit bull.

Striding toward the courtroom doors at the end of the day, Marcia's steps faltered as her eyes latched onto an unexpected sight—Peter Dullard. *Am I hallucinating?* He looked as if he hadn't aged a day since their illicit kiss nine years ago. His shaggy blond hair, light gray eyes, and strong jaw sent a thrill through Marcia. She worried that if, after her emotional talk with Patricia about him, she'd lapsed into a fantasy where he played a starring role. He was her Moby Dick, and such a dream seemed safe and harmless. But, no, he wasn't a figment of her imagination. Taking a deep breath and slamming her court persona into place, Marcia stopped in front of him.

"Hi." He greeted Marcia with a quirk of his lips. "I was hoping we could share a meal before you return home. If you're pressed for time, perhaps coffee instead?"

Flustered, Marcia agreed to the meal, knowing Sammy wasn't due back from the softball clinic for a couple of hours. *A girl needs to eat, after all.* Once settled in the restaurant, Marcia found herself being scrutinized.

"How are you?"

"I'm fine," she answered, slightly confused. *Did he come all the way from Boston to ask me that? Hasn't he heard of the phone? The internet? Snail-mail?*

"I have a confession to make. Out of curiosity I watched you litigate a case a couple of years ago."

Marcia sucked in a breath, stunned. "A couple of years ago?"

Peter lowered his eyes. "Yes. Since then, I've watched you a number of times."

"When do you work?" Marcia blurted out.

Peter grinned. "Summers off. Remember?"

"Right." *Still teaching, then.* "Why didn't you approach me?"

"Lots of reasons. I thought you wouldn't want to see me. It's been a long time. And, I didn't really know how to approach you." Laughing, he admitted, "So I left it to fate."

"And remaining in the gallery," Marcia noted. Noticing his frown she pressed on. "Why now?"

She found it hard to believe he'd traveled to New York over the last couple of years just because he had some time to kill. Her mind turned to the last time she saw him and that exhilarating, terrifying, mind-blowing kiss. *For the love of baby ducks. Could the timing be any worse? I'm in the middle of complex litigation. At least we're both single.* She had so much work to do. She had to work late into each night, preparing for the next day's witness examinations. Even though it was Friday, she'd still work once Sammy went to bed. The weekend meant more time to prepare for a trial, which would continue for several weeks.

She was tired of playing it safe, tired of always planning and thinking and weighing the pros and cons before acting on her feelings. Right now she felt a great need to feel those lips on hers, to breathe in his breath, and feel his body mold against hers. To see whether she'd romanticized their last encounter or if the embers were still hot enough to fan into a blaze of passion. She blinked, confused by where her mind went.

*Turtle doves. It's been nine years. What the hell? I feel like a schoolgirl fantasizing over kissing the quarterback.*

"I don't know, really. I didn't exactly plan to see you today. I meant to slip out. But you were different today. Don't get me wrong. You've always controlled the courtroom. But today you were irrepressible. Undeniable. Magnetic." Peter shook his head. "At first I thought it was the change in your appearance, but the way you were today seemed more powerful. I couldn't take my eyes off you. I hope I haven't offended you."

"Offended me? Never." Marcia couldn't help but chuckle. "I've been thinking about you lately."

She didn't know whether it had to do with all her physical changes, Lexie's presence, or her recent dreams of a lover, but lately she'd been thinking about her past regrets, times she hadn't entirely processed because they'd hurt too much.

Peter leaned back. "I'm sorry for your loss. I realize I'm about two years too late with my condolences, but they are sincere. I feared that if I came to you, it might seem like I was trying to take advantage of the situation."

Marcia shook her head, surprised he would assume that she'd hold his motives suspect.

Reaching over, he squeezed her hand. "The truth is I might have taken advantage, if given the chance. Even though you refused me so many years ago, I couldn't let you go. It was in that moment I realized what I'd thrown away."

"Poor timing. What happened that day, I dreamt about it for years. Yet, by the time you stepped up, I couldn't accept your love. It was too late." Nor was she willing to give up the life she'd created. She was doing well at her firm, John was her best friend, and Sammy was such a sweet girl. Her life was settled. Comfortable. She wasn't willing to take the risk then. *Am I ready now?*

"I know. When I heard your husband died, my first instinct was to hop in the car. I forced myself not to rush to you. So instead, when I felt myself missing you too much to stay away, I attended your trials. And I hoped that when the time was right, you'd see me. It was hard not to say anything, though, because I realized there was nothing stopping us from being together but inaction."

Marcia raised an eyebrow. *Does he really think it will be that easy? It's been nine years. I don't even know him anymore.*

Peter shrugged. "Those few moments together, you made me feel alive. I can't stay away any longer, not if there's a chance to be with you."

Marcia narrowed her eyes. This was out of character. He was saying everything she wanted to hear, but it was as if his lips were moving out of sync with his words. *Still.* She turned her hand over so she could hold his hand. "This is a strange time in my life. I'd like to spend some time with you, but I don't know that it's a good idea. I try not to live in the past. I can't help but think I would be going backward by indulging in these emotions."

"Please let me see you again," Peter whispered.

"I don't know. These feelings are from a long time ago. I buried them, and I thought I was over you. Now I'm not so sure," Marcia replied just as quiet.

"Then let's see what we have. Let's not hold on to any more regrets, any more what-if's. Please, Marcia."

As indecision gnawed at her, Marcia stared at him. She'd always been attracted to him—loved him. The years had augmented his attractiveness. Yet, there was something off. The longer she stared, the more certain she became that something was different. Too different. She could see a muddy pink color surrounding him, and she wondered what that might mean.

Why after all this time did he decide to pursue her? She searched his gray eyes for some clue, but they seemed shuttered. It made her wonder why she was even considering his request. Was it the allure of finally giving in to an attraction denied for so long? Was it the idea of finding out once and for all whether they could cultivate a relationship?

"I can't promise anything," she warned, "but let's get together again and see what happens."

Peter nodded. "Thank you. I won't take this opportunity for granted."

"I have to get home soon to my daughter." Marcia paused, tasting the significance of the next few words. "Do you want to come with me?" She held her breath, afraid he'd say no, afraid he'd say yes.

Peter leaned forward, his breath ghosting across her lips. "There's nothing I'd rather do than come with you."

Marcia's breath left her as she heard, saw, and felt the innuendo. She lifted her gaze to his eyes, seeking confirmation that he was, indeed, propositioning her. *Yup. Okay then.* She licked her lips, unable to help herself. He made her feel so damn sexy, so desirable. Even though she knew she should act more circumspect, particularly in light of her recent transformation, it was hard for her to keep her guard up. She wanted to accept what he was offering—the gift of completing unfinished business.

They walked home in companionable silence. After unlocking the door, Marcia stood aside and ushered her guest inside. This man was an enigma, a puzzle she wanted to piece together. Whereas before he was the forbidden fruit, no such barriers separated them now except that which they created through fear.

And Marcia was a bit afraid. So many changes in her life. She didn't understand what happened to her, what was still happening. The physical changes were hard for her to accept. Knowing Sammy would be home in moments, knowing all the trial preparation ahead of her, Marcia couldn't help thinking that this was yet another instance of poor timing. Although she didn't want Sammy to find them in a compromising position, Marcia needed to kiss him. She needed to know whether she had romanticized her reaction to the one time she'd given in to her desires and allowed herself to indulge in a kiss. *Just one kiss.*

Peter sported a soft smile as he roamed the townhouse, his steady tread reflecting an attitude of belonging. She felt the shift of energy in her home—a new sensation since John's death. She wasn't sure whether she liked it. She shook her head, fighting to not get ahead of herself. *We hardly know each other. My knowledge is based on observations I made many years ago. This man before me, he's a stranger. I need to be cautious.*

As Peter continued to familiarize himself with her home, Marcia walked into the kitchen to find a bottle of wine. She needed a distraction. A moment to catch her breath. She realized quite quickly that she wouldn't have the time, however, when she felt him enter the room. She didn't need to look. His gaze on her back felt like a bold caress. Closing her eyes, she took a deep breath, immersing herself in the feeling of him.

Sensing malice, her forehead furrowed. Her eyes flew open, and she turned around, seeing a mustard-colored haze surrounding him. He moved toward her, a look of determination on his face. Her body tensed just before his hand landed on her shoulder. Seeing his smile, she forced herself to relax. She wound her arms around Peter's neck and tilted her head. Their breath mingled.

When their lips met, Marcia's reality shifted. She saw armies and spaceships and explosions and death. Marcia tried to pull away, but Peter pulled her closer and entered her mouth with his tongue. Marcia squeezed her eyes closed to block out the world while she focused on the images appearing in her mind. She could smell the destruction of worlds, taste the hatred of those vanquished, see the innocent cut down, hear the vows for revenge, and feel the evilness crawl up her spine.

*Holy crackers! What's happening? Who is this? What does he want? Am I going crazy, or is he really from outer space?* Marcia consciously relaxed her face, slowing down Peter's fervor, knowing this wasn't really the man she'd desired for so long. This person was an imposter. Someone who could harm her, could harm Sammy.

Marcia continued to kiss him while lightly scratching the base of his head, eliciting a groan. She saw the flash of a humanoid head and somehow knew it was the true face of the person kissing her. His skin was blue, like a robin's egg. Oval-shaped eyes, as black as the meteorite she found, rested high on a long face, framed by two large ears, one on each side but closer to the forehead. Although she didn't see a nose, she noticed a gaping mouth full of serrated teeth, comparable to a shark's terrifying maw. Horrified, Marcia's first inclination was to pull away, and it took all of her resolve to continue the kiss. She knew she needed to press the pause button while making it seem like she was reluctant to stop. She leaned back against the counter, staring into his slate-colored eyes while taking long, soothing breaths. She smiled, and he pulled her in for a quick hug.

"Wine?" she asked, moving around the counter with the pretext of picking out a bottle. She needed a barrier right now.

"Sounds great."

Marcia set about the task while attempting to figure how to get him out of the house without raising any suspicions. She didn't want him there when Sammy arrived. "My daughter will be home soon, and for now I'd rather she not meet you. So, one drink only, mister. Salut." Marcia touched her glass to his and took a sip.

"Those aren't contacts, are they?" Peter asked.

"No. They aren't," she replied.

"Your eyes were blue before, weren't they?"

"Yes." Marcia knew that trying to lie would only place her in danger. Whoever this person was, he was dangerous.

"And your hair was blonde, wasn't it?" His eyes ran over Marcia's face.

Marcia nodded.

"How—" he began, only to be interrupted by Sammy's exuberant entrance.

"Mom! How was court?" Sammy asked, as she bounced into the room and headed straight for the refrigerator.

"Good." Marcia answered, turning her head for a peck on the cheek. "How was practice?"

Sammy took a sip of water. "It was really good. They had me try second base. I really like it, and I hit a triple off Lori." A wide grin graced her face. Lori was her archrival on the field, and one of her closest friends. Marcia chuckled. Noticing Sammy's curious glance at Peter, she cursed silently before introducing them.

"Peter was just leaving," Marcia said, placing her hand on his forearm and tugging. "Don't eat any junk. I'll be making dinner soon."

"Oh, I'm not in any hurry," Peter said.

"Don't you have a lot of work to do tonight?" Sammy asked while looking from Peter and Marcia.

Marcia raised her eyebrows. Her daughter was so intuitive. "I do," she confirmed with a sigh.

"I'm going to wash up. Be right back."

At Marcia's loud clearing of the throat, she stopped her exit. "It was nice to meet you." She turned to Marcia and rolled her eyes. "Okay?"

Marcia could tell that her impetuous child wasn't asking about her behavior. If Marcia gave any sign, Sammy would call for help.

"Yes," Marcia said, nodding. Once Sammy left, Marcia turned back to Peter's impersonator. "Peter, why me, why now?"

"I could list all the reasons I find myself attracted to you, how beautiful you are, how keen your mind is, how funny and humble and persistent you are, but it all comes down to what my instincts tell me. I may not know your life history, but I know you. I fought these feelings for a long time." Peter took Marcia's hands in his. "I still needed to try."

Marcia stared at him, dumbfounded. If only this were really Peter. These were the words she had longed for, and it sickened her to realize that somehow this person knew. Still, she couldn't let on that she was aware of the duplicity. Instead, she reached for him and gave him a kiss. He tasted of coffee and mint, exotic and sweet, dark and light. She hated that she loved it. Her fingers mapped his strong jaw line, the definition of his chiseled cheekbones, the curve of his ear lobes, and the texture of his silky, blond locks. She massaged behind his ears, ripples of pleasure trembling through his taut frame. She knew it was false, not really the Peter she knew and once loved, but she kissed him anyway, allowing herself to fall under the illusion. After this encounter, she knew she'd have to find a way to keep him away. Whatever he was after must have to do with her metamorphosis. The timing was too coincidental. She'd have to take steps to protect herself and Sammy from his plans.

"I'm sorry, Peter," Marcia said, pulling away. "I'm not ready for this. I don't even know you, not really." She placed a placating hand on his chest.

Peter looked a bit angry, but he didn't try to change her mind. "I'll be in touch," Peter said when they stood before the front door.

Closing the door, Marcia leaned against it and let out a sigh. Eyes shut, a sob tried to work its way out, but Marcia refused to express it. That wasn't Peter. He hadn't come back into her life to tell her how much he loved her. People didn't do that. Not in real life.

*Whatever he's after, he's not getting it.* Marcia locked the door before collapsing on the sofa. She had no idea what to do. Patricia would be in town tomorrow. *I'll tell her. She can help me.* Placing a hand over her eyes, Marcia shuddered. The visions she saw scared her. *What does all this mean? What does he want?* Hearing Sammy open her bedroom door, Marcia straightened up and pasted a smile on her face. *No matter what, I won't let anything happen to Sammy. Or to my family. And if it comes to it, Earth.* Seeing her daughter, she felt the tension in her shoulders ease. She might not understand why the meteorite affected her, but somehow she'd use every advantage she had to protect what she loved. She'd find a way to keep them all safe.

# Chapter Nine

## *KARINAN CYCLE 2 KATRINET 3*

"WHAT IS YOUR PROGRESS, Ubel?" Supreme Commander Flerg asked.

"I have acquired the guest manifest and interviewed or ruled out nearly all subjects who may have come into contact with the meteorite." Ubel slouched on a wooden chair, holding the communicator near his mouth. His eyes traced the names on the list on the table before him, as he thought about how best to finish interviewing the rest.

"Good. How many more do you have?"

"Twelve. I was prepared to question Marcia Struthers, but it became unnecessary when I saw how her physical features transformed. I used the actinometer to determine she was exposed to the meteorite gases, which may have caused the physical changes. I have yet to determine whether it has affected her mind."

"Your next steps?"

Grimacing, Ubel got up and began pacing in the small room where he slept—a facility called a motel. It was dark and dirty. Worse, he found he could not sleep on their beds in his natural form, as they were too small and soft. "I have assumed the identity of someone she knew years ago and struck up a new acquaintance. I gained admittance to her home, and although I did not see any proof, I am certain she houses some fragments of the meteorite there. I scanned the area with the vibrometer, and it indicated the rocks are in what appears to be her bedchamber. My hope is to continue in the guise of this persona long enough to retrieve them and determine what further effects they may have on her."

"And what of the other subjects?"

Ubel stood in the middle of the room, tapping his fingers on his thigh. "We will find them and determine whether they have also been exposed to the meteorite."

"You realize your timeline is diminishing? You must finish your assignment before the portal collapses."

"I will, Commander." Ubel stared out the dirty window, watching a man and woman kiss. It reminded him of his earlier interaction with Marcia. He shuddered, swallowing back the bile filling his mouth.

"What of securing the meteorite?"

"We have studied the location where it is secured. I will take five members of the team to infiltrate the hangar and retrieve it at the beginning of the next lunar cycle."

"Good. Continue on. I expect progress within three karinan cycles."

"I shall do as you command."

"Star One, out."

Ubel pressed the necessary button sequence to secure a recording of his conversation with his commander, cross-referencing it with relevant keywords: meteorite, test subjects, and timeline. Looking at himself in the mirror, Ubel scowled. He loathed this human form. When he entered the courtroom earlier in the week, he was able to use the telepathy reader to isolate two people Marcia desired for at least a decacycle: the opposing attorney and Peter Dullard. Although the body-changing process was painful, he was committed.

If they were able to determine how the meteorite affected test subject Marcia Struthers and how it activated the transmutation process, they might be able to enact the same changes on his people. The Katakitites would easily gain dominion over those who, based on their false precept of justice, exiled them from their homeworld. In the past, they had borne offspring with the valuable mutations through similar use of lesser species, but within a generation, such powers disappeared from the Katakitites. He would find a way this time. His years of studying biogenetics would make all the difference.

He sneered. People cried justice when they were too weak to enforce their own laws. Those who cast out his people had only succeeded due to an alliance they formed with neighboring rebels. *We will destroy them all and take back our land. It is only a matter of time.*

# Chapter Ten

"I'M SURPRISED YOU AREN'T at Rudi's matinee show," Marcia commented, placing two glasses of lemonade on the kitchen table and sitting down.

"Oh, I've watched her show several times, and I'll see her later tonight when we go to Kiernan's party," Patricia said. "Besides, I wanted to spend time with you. Hear about the trial."

Wincing, Marcia thought about how best to tell her friend about an imposter posing as Peter appearing yesterday. It was hard for her to believe, and she had no clue whether Patricia would think she was crazy. A warm hand squeezed her arm, redirecting her attention.

"What's wrong?"

"Remember I told you about the man who got away?" Once Patricia nodded, Marcia continued. "He showed up at court yesterday."

"What? Why didn't you call me? What happened?"

"We went for coffee, and he said all the right things. I had to get back to Sammy, so I invited him home. We kissed. I saw a bunch of visions that scared the shit out of me and let me know he wasn't really Peter." Marcia's voice got faster with each word. "I think I saw his aura a couple of times. I got rid of him without tipping my hand, and I've been avoiding his attempts to contact me ever since. I don't mind telling you I don't know what to do."

"Wait. He wasn't himself? Do you mean he's changed? People do that, Marcia. It's been years since you last saw him. Maybe you need to give yourself some time to get to know him again."

"No. You misunderstand. He wasn't the same man. The person who showed up in the courtroom gallery may have looked like Peter, but it wasn't him."

Patricia raised an eyebrow, a thoughtful expression on her face. "And you said you had visions when you two kissed. What visions?"

Marcia stared at her fingers as she twisted them together. "I know it sounds crazy, but when we kissed, I saw all these visions of death and destruction. I felt this sense of evilness sliding down my spine. And spaceships. I saw lots of spaceships." Looking up after a loaded silence, Marcia couldn't help but crack a smile at the incredulous look on Patricia's face.

"I'm sorry. What?" Patricia muttered.

"You heard me. Whoever that was masquerading as Peter isn't from here. As in from Earth. And the only reason I can imagine why some being from space would approach me is due to the meteorite and the effects it's had on me."

Patricia leaned back. "My brain stalled at the word spaceships. How are you not losing it?"

"I've had all night to think about it," Marcia replied. "All night to revisit what that imposter really looks like. To revisit the destruction I saw and the hate I felt. At first I thought he was evil, and that his intentions were malevolent. Now I'm not so sure. I mean, if it was his people who were killed, they might be the victims. He might not be the bad guy."

"Do you think you're in danger?"

"Do you think I'm in danger?"

"Well, why else would he hide? Why pretend to be someone else?"

"Right." Marcia exhaled. "You're right. Although I don't think the average person would be open to being visited by an alien with an agenda to wage war. I don't know what to do. I can't help thinking that since he's hiding his true identity, no one knows but us. I don't trust anyone else. I mean, maybe other aliens might be masquerading as humans. I can't go kissing everyone to find out."

Patricia bit her lip. "You can't find out without kissing a person?"

"Not that I'm aware." Marcia shrugged. "His hand touching mine wasn't enough, and I can't read minds. I did see his aura, but that's a new development. I don't really know how to interpret the colors I see. At any rate, I refuse to run away. Certainly not while I'm in the middle of this trial. That would raise all sorts of red flags, and I already gained people's attention when I strolled in with my new looks. He doesn't know I'm aware that he's a pod person. That's an advantage I don't want to surrender."

"Okay. Let's figure this out." Patricia held a finger up, as if preparing a list of topics. "First, we need to deal with the whole alien thing. Do you think you should contact anyone? You said you spoke to some government people after the meteorite hit. Did you get a name?"

"Yes. Agent Thacker and Agent Blackstone. I didn't get a card or number, though. I'd have to do some digging, and I don't know that it's a good idea. They'll want to do tests. Who's to say that'll be any better than what an alien has planned?"

"That's a bit of a leap, isn't it? I think you've been watching too many government conspiracy theory movies. Besides, you could just call them. Get a burner phone or find a payphone or something."

Marcia guffawed. "Now who's watching too many government conspiracy theory movies?"

"Okay. Let's leave that for a moment. What if he shows up in the courtroom again? And what the hell, Marcia?" Patricia reached over and slapped her arm. "Have I taught you nothing about safety? How could you bring him home?"

"Ow," Marcia muttered, rubbing the area. "He seemed okay when we went to get coffee, and I can ignore him if he shows up in court. I doubt he'll interrupt the trial to get my attention."

"Well, yeah, but if he's from another planet, I can't help thinking he won't give up easily. And what's this about an aura? Can you see mine?"

"Yes. You have a blue color. And lavender. I have no idea what the colors mean. Yet another thing to look up." Marcia shook her head. "I'm sliding down a slippery slope. My perceptions are changing. I constantly question what my senses are telling me. When I look at someone, I see colors encasing the body, shimmering off like mist emitted from a frozen lake on a sunny day. I see energy waves joining and separating constantly. I can map where my energy weaves into the surrounding network of energy. And then I blink and see none of that."

"Fascinating. Theoretically, you could connect with the energy waves by touching them, and through that, you could touch someone across the room. We're gonna have to experiment!" Patricia squirmed with excitement in her seat, a wide smile on her face.

"Yes, yes, I'm your personal guinea pig. Better you than the pod person impersonating Peter."

"No kidding, but before we get to testing your powers, we need to come up with a plan of action to at least keep him from getting you alone again."

Marcia shook her head. "I really can't think of anything. I mean, I know I can't ignore this, but it seems like all these things are coming up at the same time, and I feel paralyzed." She placed a hand over her eyes. "Usually I'm maxed out focusing on litigating a case, but now I'm dealing with my feelings for Peter and the meteorite and these physical changes and new abilities and my feelings for Lexie—"

Patricia rubbed Marcia's arm. "It's okay. Let's talk about what else is happening. Sometimes leaving a problem alone for a while helps." Patricia clasped her hands together and raised an eyebrow. "I didn't realize the one and only Alexandria Yamin was litigating the case against you." She smirked. "She's a hottie. Did you ever work with her while you were part of her firm?"

Marcia took a deep breath. "Lexie's the reason I left."

"Really? I don't think I've heard this story. Do tell."

"It's funny," Marcia said, sidestepping Patricia's request. "I knew the case was against her firm, but I didn't expect to see her. Yet, I've seen more of her during the last two weeks than I'd seen her the previous fourteen years. I can't help but take pleasure while pummeling her in the courtroom. I feel vindicated. Validated. Powerful. Finally I'm affecting her. I may not have impressed her while I was a lowly associate at her firm, but I have garnered her attention during this case. She can't ignore me now. I can tell she's looking at me differently, perhaps seeing who I really am. Seeing that I am just as good as her."

"So…you want her to notice you. How? Professionally? Personally?"

Marcia sighed. *Am I ready to tell Patricia about this?* With all the changes occurring in her life, Marcia needed to confide in Patricia, if only to clear her mind and receive some advice on what to do. She allowed herself to think about what she had long ago dubbed "That Night." Just remembering it brought a mix of pain and longing. She stared off as the memories flooded her mind.

*"I want you to pick up an order of lobster for a party I'm hosting tonight. It's in the Upper East Side at a place called Joe's Lobster Shack. Bring them to my house. You do know where I live, don't you?" Flicking her glance up toward Marcia for confirmation, Lexie waited a beat before returning her gaze to the brief in front of her.*

*Dismissed. "Right. I'll go." Marcia backed out the door and made a mad dash for her purse and attaché case, muttering. She'd been hired as a junior associate nine months ago, and this was the* first time Attorney Yamin had seen fit to address her directly since she'd called Marcia in to her office months ago to rip apart her work on one of her files. Attorney Yamin was known to be fastidious, and anyone who worked on her files was expected to not miss anything. Marcia didn't care that this was a menial task. She was dying to see the senior partner's home, a beautiful brownstone at Chelsea's London Terrace.

Attorney Yamin was the youngest senior partner, earning her spot among the good old boys' network of stalwart, boring attorneys. Intelligent, quick-witted, sharp, and ruthless—these words were often bandied around to describe her. People hired her because she was a pit bull, attacking the other side with a ferocious offense, instilling fear, and often eliciting fair settlements, lest she rip apart the opposing party in the courtroom.

She was also reputed to chew up and spit out lowly law associates with glee. However, Marcia was determined to make a positive impression. If that meant picking up lobsters, her dry-cleaning, or anything else to appease her, so be it. And the fact that Attorney Yamin was a gorgeous, single woman didn't matter at all.

In Marcia's mind, she called the senior partner Lexie, which rhymed with sexy. Sexy Lexie. Auburn hair, flashing eyes that changed colors with her mercurial moods like a storm-tossed sea, a body that exuded sex—Lexie was magnetic, compelling, and dangerous. It wasn't smart, it wasn't safe, but there it was. Such emotions guided her to Finklestein, Krauss & Yamin, P.C. Marcia looked forward to each instance of crossing paths with her, feeling she had accomplished so much when she received a fleeting quirk of the lips or a nod of the head in passing. Shaking her head to refocus her thoughts, Marcia left the office building, intent to complete her lobster mission.

Marcia was no slouch. She graduated top of her law class. Several firms sought to woo her onto their team, but she knew where she wanted to go—where she belonged. So, although she played it cool when Lexie's law firm contacted her for an interview, she was ecstatic. Then the reality of working in a highly-renown law firm hit her full-force. What a reality check. At the end of the first day, she felt like a balled-up piece of paper. Since then, she worked long hours doing whatever anyone asked without complaint. It wasn't long before she became the go-to gal for the tough assignments, particularly for researching case law.

Striding to the subway, Marcia hopped on the uptown train. Once there, Marcia realized Lexie neglected to pay for two hundred forty-seven dollars' worth of lobster. At a bit past six in the evening Marcia stomped her way toward Lexie's home in high heels, searching for Lexie's residence. Reaching the correct walkway, Marcia was surprised to see Lexie throw open the front door and rush forward.

"What took you so long? They'll be here in an hour." She quickly hustled Marcia in the elevator, not offering to take the bags from her. Once they reached her floor, Lexie walked through the door. "You'll have to assist me. This way." Lexie pointed toward what Marcia presumed was the kitchen. A large pot of water sat boiling on the stove.

You're welcome, Marcia didn't say, although she really wanted to. Instead, she walked through Lexie's home with her burden.

"Set the lobsters down there." Lexie pointed to the butcher's block in the middle of a huge kitchen. The entire room boasted complex brickwork and detailed brass etchings. The hardwood flooring complemented the earthy tones, as did the throw rugs interspersed throughout the room. "My personal assistant was sick, so I have no one to help me except you."

Marcia didn't know how to feel about this development. However, when she agreed to the errand, she did so hoping to impress Lexie or at least to gain her attention. Staying to assist seemed to be in her best interest. Maybe Lexie would remember her in the future.

Lexie's eyes slowly traveled over Marcia's powder-blue power suit, crème silk blouse, and matching high heels. "Although you look a bit worse for wear, you're still presentable."

Hopes of impressing Lexie shriveled up like grapes in the sun. She would wager that Lexie knew her reputation among the associates. She probably didn't care, though, as long as she got the best work possible from her subordinates. The legal field was cutthroat—Marcia learned that early on. It was rumored that a pretty face and a beautiful mind enticed Lexie, although she was discreet with her dalliances. Supposedly, her ex-husband, also an attorney, had left her for one of his clients years ago. It was whispered that Lexie's heart had been broken—that was assuming quite a bit. Like she had a heart.

Assigned the chore of setting the table, Marcia completed the task. Sexy Lexie. Sexy Lexie. Sexy Lexie. Catching a glimpse of herself in the hall mirror, Marcia groaned. Her face was flushed, and hair mussed. She quickly patted down the flyaway strands, reminding herself that even though Lexie disregarded the non-fraternization rules, it didn't mean she could afford to do so. Or that she wanted to. Of course, she didn't. So what if she found Lexie attractive. It was an aesthetic appreciation for the Celtic beauty. It was not—there was no way it could be—sexual attraction. She shook her head. No way.

Marcia returned to Lexie's side. "Do you need me for anything else?"

Lexie gave her a noncommittal look. "You don't plan on deserting me, do you? Surely you must realize I still need you?"

Answering a question with a question—how typical. She squirmed, feeling guilty for wanting to leave and knowing Lexie had guessed her intentions. "No, of course not." Seeing Lexie quirk her lips in amusement at Marcia's quick acquiescence, anger coursed through her body. She didn't like being manipulated.

"Good. They should be here soon. Why don't you open this bottle of wine while I freshen up a bit? It doesn't look like you need to clean up, but you can once I return, if you'd like." Lexie swept away.

With a sigh, Marcia committed herself to remaining for a while. The evening went by quickly, and at long last, all the guests left. Marcia deposited the dirty dishes in the dishwasher and looked up to find Lexie leaning against the kitchen doorjamb, waiting to be noticed. Marcia allowed her eyes to slide over Lexie's body. She'd changed for dinner into a forest-green sheath, bringing out the vibrancy of her hair and seemingly her fiery personality, too. Marcia liked it. A lot.

When their eyes reconnected, she felt as if a bolt of electricity hit her. Lexie smirked, raising two wines glasses and an opened bottle of wine she held. "You're off the clock and free to leave, but I was hoping you'd like to join me for a drink on the rooftop patio. It's a magnificent night."

*Marcia took the invitation for what it was. She was being propositioned. Excitement ran through her at the realization that Lexie wanted her. Walking through the door, Marcia stopped short, her eyes widening in wonder as she turned her head to take in the view. To the right, a flower garden spewed forth a myriad of vibrant reds, purples, yellows, and oranges. To the left, a waterfall fountain burbled while lit from within. Straight ahead were two mosaic tables with comfortable chairs arranged around them. But it was the city view that took Marcia's breath away. Below them stretched Manhattan, sparkling like party streamers.*

*Lexie poured the wine and crossed over to one of the tables to deposit the bottle. Turning to Marcia, she passed one of the crystal goblets to her. "Here. You earned this." At Marcia's quizzical look, she explained. "I know I didn't give you a choice with helping me tonight. So thank you, Marcia. You are, indeed, the go-to gal. Have a seat." Lexie graced Marcia with an inviting smile, as she sat down by way of example.*

*Once Marcia acquiesced, a surprisingly comfortable silence enveloped them. Marcia relaxed into the sounds of the city and the caress of the evening air, but she could feel Lexie studying her. It made her nervous and excited. Not able to mistake the heated look Lexie directed her way, Marcia blushed—hard. She read the hunger reflected plainly in Lexie's turbulent blue eyes, so dark Marcia believed she could fall into them and never hit bottom. It unleashed a ball of heat in her belly. Goosebumps rose on her arms, and Marcia admitted to herself that the attraction was mutual.*

*"Your feet must be sore by now," Lexie observed, her voice a soft burr, while running an elegant hand down the nearer leg. Marcia gasped, her leg on fire, as Lexie lifted it by the calf and slipped the shoe off, scratching the arch. Magical fingers wrapped themselves around her foot—an erotic vision—massaging the tired appendage. Overwhelmed, Marcia groaned her pleasure. Never in her wildest dreams could she have imagined the exquisite feeling.*

*After rubbing Marcia's foot until it felt like butter, Lexie lowered Marcia's leg onto her lap and reached for the other foot to repeat the special treatment. Marcia closed her eyes, trying to control her erratic breathing. When those talented hands began to massage her calf, then her thigh, her eyes flew open to gaze into eyes* glazed with desire. Lexie's hands stalled over the run on Marcia's left upper thigh.

"What happened here?" she questioned.

"The lobsters," Marcia answered, finding it hard to concentrate. She wasn't sure what to think. Was Lexie seducing her, or was she overreacting?

"Mean lobsters," Lexie murmured. She leaned forward and kissed the scratch.

Marcia hummed her agreement.

"Well, you won't be wearing these again, now will you?" Lexie mused.

Before Marcia could understand, both of Lexie's hands glided up her thighs and inward. An excited pulse of arousal shot through her a moment before Lexie's thumbs came to rest on either side of her panties. Marcia' eyes bulged.

Lexie leaned forward, fingers rubbing lightly over her clitoris. "Let's see if there are holes anywhere else, shall we?"

Her legs fell to either side of Lexie's hips, and Lexie drew circles through the drenched panties, a predatory smirk in place. Moments later, Lexie ripped the fabric open and her hot mouth covered her center. Marcia moaned, drowning in glorious sensation.

She's taking me, and I'm not going to do a damn thing to stop her. How could she? Her body, bombarded with so many strong responses, begged for Lexie's touch.

As Lexie's fingers played with the edge of Marcia's panties, her stomach muscles clenched in anticipation. Lexie's other hand found the catch on Marcia's skirt, drawing it down without pausing the feather-light circular motions she made through the paper-thin barrier. Reaching up, Lexie pulled off the skirt, hosiery, and panties in one fell swoop, baring Marcia from the waist down. She next unbuttoned Marcia's silk shirt and unfastened her bra, leaving them hanging on her trembling body, now glistening with perspiration and need.

Pulling Marcia forward by the legs so she was flush against her abdomen, Lexie touched Marcia's breasts with capable hands, twisting and pulling. Marcia closed her eyes in ecstasy. Suddenly, she felt both hands supporting her backside and then breasts brushing her abdomen. Lips latched on to one of Marcia's tightened nipples. Marcia's stomach muscles fluttered. Alternating with lips and tongue, Lexie made a show of laving each peak delicately with the same circular motion she used while moving her fingers lightly over Marcia's clitoris. Marcia was in heaven.

Marcia held her breath, her stomach muscles jumping as she watched Lexie kiss a path down it, arriving at the touchstone of her womanhood. She tried not to hyperventilate when Lexie bent toward her legs and, replacing fingers with tongue, licked her with relish. Marcia's body hummed, and she knew it wouldn't take long to lose control. When Lexie added her fingers to the mix, Marcia couldn't help moaning. With permission granted, Lexie thrust her fingers into her opening, sucking hard in counterthrust. Marcia screamed, as Lexie slowed her movements to draw out the exquisite feelings she evoked.

Marcia stared into wild, hooded eyes while attempting to regain her breath. Lexie removed her fingers and licked them. Recognizing Lexie's need for release, Marcia stroked Lexie's thigh before lifting the edge of her dress and rubbing against her. Moisture seeped through Lexie's silk panties. Lexie groaned, her motions erratic, signaling that she was close. She removed her fingers, surprising Lexie by dropping to her knees and stripping her of clothes. Marcia burrowed her fingers within Lexie, causing her to cry out. She lifted one toned leg over her shoulder and began to lick. As Lexie's body began to shudder, all Marcia heard was Lexie's keening, breathless sounds ended with a sustained shriek of satisfaction when she climaxed. She held the woman, never stopping her agreeable assault until Lexie began to sag, totally spent.

Carefully lowering Lexie's leg, Marcia rose and turned away to give her time to recover. Retrieving her drink, Marcia tasted the mixture of wine and sex. She smirked. Picking up her clothes, she hazarded a glance behind her. Lexie, leaning with one hip against the table, stared across the city, seemingly lost in thought as she sipped her wine.

To Marcia, it seemed as if the air had changed. Lexie's face held a shuttered, faraway look. It was as if they were miles apart. She winced. Although she despaired that Lexie wouldn't want her as a lover, she didn't regret one moment of this incredible night. Redressing, Marcia cast her mind around, seeking some way to leave without appearing as awkward as she felt. If the rumors *were true and Lexie had indulged in this behavior before, she will expect Marcia to be sophisticated enough to leave without asking questions about a possible future together. Besides, Marcia knew. Right now, they had no future. This was it. It was possible that Lexie might not ever acknowledge just how great they were together, how extraordinary they could be if she allowed for more than one romantic tryst.*

*"Well, it's getting late. I'd better get going." She headed toward the door. She knew better than to try for a goodnight kiss. Hell, Lexie hadn't kissed her at all, the one regret for this night.*

*At the door, Marcia stopped and looked over her shoulder. Lexie hadn't turned her head to acknowledge Marcia's exit. "What you did, how you touched me, was perfect. I wouldn't want to change a moment." She left without a backward glance.*

Blinking away the memories, Marcia cleared her throat. She stalled, drumming her fingers on the table. "I never even told John about this."

Patricia's hand covered hers, and Marcia looked into a soft gaze. "It's okay. You can tell me anything."

"I know," Marcia muttered, embarrassed. She felt like her skin was being peeled away, revealing her in a way that made her want to hide under her thickest blanket. She rubbed the back of her neck. "If I'm being honest, Lexie's the reason I joined the firm. She was everything I aspired to be professionally. It was a confusing time. I admired her, and she took advantage of that. I worked to capture her attention, to be given the privilege of working on her cases." Marcia looked at Patricia through her eyelashes. "I got her attention." After a moment, Patricia's eyes widened, and Marcia nodded. "We shared one night together. It was mind-blowing. I had never experienced anything like it. And I never have since."

Eyebrows crawling up her forehead, Patricia breathed out. "Whoa. That must have been some night. Why didn't you tell me? I mean, that can't be normal. She was your boss, after all."

Marcia frowned. "I didn't work for her directly. I was in a different division, and she chose to stay away from me after that night. It didn't affect my partner track, if that's what you're thinking. I waited six months, and then I couldn't stand it anymore. I couldn't continue seeing her every day, knowing we would never share that type of intimacy again. So, I resigned. She was too close and too far away. It hurt so much that I ran away. Self-preservation at its best."

Patricia covered Marcia's hand with her own. "I'm sorry."

"She broke my heart, and John was there to pick up the pieces." Marcia drank her wine, eyes faraway. "I don't think I ever fully recovered."

"But weren't you in love with Peter? And weren't you with John back then?"

"I'm beginning to understand that I was in love with the idea of Peter and no, John and I got together after I changed firms." Marcia looked at Patricia. "Lexie is the one who got me my present job. She sought me out on my last day. Asked me to allow her to help. Said she was sorry. Even then, though, I was afraid to ask her why. Why she hadn't given me a chance. After I left the firm, I decided to date John. He was gentle and kind. Safe. John was like a favorite sweater you wear on a cloudy day. Accepting his love was easy. He was an open book. Uncomplicated. Exactly what I needed."

"I can see why you found that attractive. You know, you're a single, attractive, intelligent woman. You could pursue whoever you want now. Like Lexie." Patricia waggled her eyes.

Chuckling, Marcia admitted, "Well, she did ask me to dinner."

Patricia leaned forward, a look of outrage on her face. "And you're just telling me now?"

Marcia held her hands up in a placating gesture. "Need I remind you of the other topics we've covered today?"

"Sure, sure, aliens, breathtaking sex, heartbreak...I guess I can excuse it this time. So, what happened?"

"I asked for a rain check until after the trial ends. I'd like to avoid any ethical difficulties. Or emotional ones, for that matter." She shrugged, pretending she wasn't scared to death about spending time with Lexie.

"Do you want to go to dinner with her?"

Marcia paused, considering what it would mean to be in Lexie's alluring presence again without any distractions. "I can't deny that I'm curious. I'm also still wildly attracted to her. We have two more weeks of trial, and I can't stop thinking about her. I guess when all is said and done, I want to hear what she has to say, but I'm terrified she might reject me again."

"Be brave, Marcia. I don't think she'd ask you out if she didn't intend to make amends."

"Brave. That seems to be a theme lately. Any suggestions on how to deal with the pod person?" Marcia arched an eyebrow.

"Not yet. For now, just make sure you aren't alone. Ever. If he shows up at your door, don't open it. If he tries to get to you with others around, use them as a shield. So far the only changes the meteorite has caused is in your appearance, right?"

"Well, no. I've noticed some other changes, but we'll have to discuss them later since I can hear Sammy at the door." Marcia looked toward the doorway, and sure enough, Sammy walked in with a smile. "Hi, sweetie."

"Hi, Mom. Hi, Patricia," Sammy said, leaning in to deliver a kiss on Marcia's cheek. "What's for supper?"

"That is a good question," Marcia said. She looked over at Patricia. "Ideas?"

Patricia clapped her hands together and smiled. "I know just the thing."

# Chapter Eleven

As PATRICIA AND RUDI entered the gathering, Patricia looked around. They were in a private backroom of a restaurant frequented by Broadway performers. Several round tables were littered with bottles of wine and half-filled glasses, like abandoned books left in favor of hunting for better stories. People sat, their voices mingling to create a wall of conversations, all interesting, all stimulating, all beckoning Patricia to listen closely.

She saw a strip of square tables with red paper tablecloths against the far wall. Various trays of food sat on top, their enticing aromas attracting Patricia's attention, but she ignored her growling stomach. Well-known celebrities interacted with each other as if this were the last party they'd ever attend—loud, vivacious, and engaging. She knew Rudi would soon join their ranks, trotting out her best stories and hamming it up for laughs. It wasn't that Rudi was two-dimensional—she actively chose to not be introspective.

It surprised her when Rudi suggested they attend this party, specifically mentioning how Kiernan Connelly had invited her. Patricia still remembered their previous interaction and found the older actress interesting. However, she felt the undercurrent thrumming between Rudi and Kiernan. They had a history together. Patricia was certain. Conflicting emotions filled her—excitement, trepidation, curiosity, and fear—all linked to the distinguished Italian actress. The heated conversation she and Rudi shared before leaving for the party made her feel a bit off-kilter, but she was determined to push those feelings aside. She would have to attend to the ramifications of that exchange later, once she was alone and had some time to think.

After obtaining drinks, they joined a group of actors Rudi knew that were talking about their upcoming projects. With the conversation swirling, Patricia watched Rudi as if they'd just met. In some ways, they had. She still knew so little about her, and that was the impetus for their disagreement. It seemed Rudi was content, but of course she was. Patricia did all the traveling, rearranging her life and often placing her own needs on hold by sidelining her doubts and insecurities to make sure their time together was full of lightness, intimacy, and joy. However, this situation was no longer light, intimate, or joyful. She needed more from Rudi.

Unfortunately, as she had found out an hour ago, Rudi was unwilling to give more to this relationship. If it could be called a relationship. It was more like a scheduled booty-call. She had been so convinced that as they spent more time together, Rudi would open up to her. Her jealousy spiked. Patricia wondered if Rudi had revealed herself in such a way to Kiernan.

"Oh, good. You made it. I'm so glad you came." Kiernan smiled at Patricia, leaning over to receive a peck on the cheek from Rudi before returning her attention to Patricia.

Patricia warmed as she realized Kiernan wasn't merely being polite. Perhaps under a different set of circumstances, they could have become friends. *Who am I kidding? We're from different worlds. Right now we're in parallel orbits, but soon we'll be pulled back into our own gravitational wells.*

"How are you?" Kiernan continued. "Are you still taking that summer course?"

"Yes, but only for a couple of weeks more. It's been an incredible process. I'll miss it," Patricia replied.

"What are you covering right now?"

"Expectations. I never thought of it in quite the fashion she has laid it out, but then, if there's one thing I've learned from Professor Corelli, it's to expect the unexpected." Patricia chuckled, picturing her professor's face in her mind.

Kiernan, seeming a bit preoccupied, asked, "What will you do once the class ends?"

Patricia paused a moment before answering. She could feel a well of sorrow rise up, and she swallowed. "I'm going to Italy with my family. My father is dying, and we all wanted to spend some meaningful time together."

"I'm sorry you're experiencing something so painful." Kiernan grasped Patricia's forearm.

"Thank you." Kiernan's obvious distress surprised her. *It's not as if they were friends. In fact, if what she suspected was true, Kiernan should hate her.* She had nothing to lose by asking Kiernan a question that had burned in her mind since Rudi had showed up at her book signing. She glanced at Rudi, noticing she was well into telling a story, and asked, "Were you and Rudi together, at some point?"

Kiernan pursed her lips and nodded. "When did you and Rudi begin?" After Patricia told her, Kiernan said quietly, "Perhaps, you'll be able to reach a part of her I could not. We were comfortable but not good for each other. She needs someone to breathe new life into her. Someone who will challenge her, push her out of her comfort zone. You may be the one to do it." Kiernan squeezed Patricia's arm, a bittersweet smile flittering across her visage.

Patricia mulled over the actress's words. Eventually, the room's noises seeped back into her consciousness, and Patricia realized Kiernan had left her side. Her eyes sought out Rudi, who was laughing with several others, seemingly free of all the emotional turmoil Patricia currently felt. It was clear Rudi was content with her life and didn't feel any inclination to stretch her spiritual muscles.

It wasn't enough. She needed to be with someone who was also taking the journey toward self-discovery. Like Kiernan, she couldn't reach Rudi, either. It was possible the actress didn't understand what that entailed, and her pride would bar anyone from guiding her.

It was tough to surrender a dream she had spent so many years creating. Patricia had devoted much energy to who she thought Rudi was. The reality could never measure up, of course, and she grieved. Try as she might, she couldn't help comparing her fantasies to the reality, and her expectations could not be realized. It was time to release them or Rudi.

Patricia remembered with faint disgust the scenarios she had envisioned, many revolving around her somehow saving Rudi's life and having Rudi fall in love with her. In one, she sat in the audience watching Rudi perform. A man shouted, "Prepare to die!" and pointed a gun toward the stage. Patricia lunged toward the man, blocking the bullet with her shoulder as several others tackled him. Once she woke up in the hospital room, Rudi told her she owed her life to Patricia and proceeded to spend all her time with her while she recuperated. Soon, they were in love, and they lived happily ever after.

Patricia smirked, realizing how damaging these fantasies were and vowing to end them. If this relationship was to work, she needed to be totally present. Rudi saw nothing wrong with being placed on a pedestal, but Patricia did. One way or the other, it was time to move forward.

Waking up the next morning, Patricia chided herself for being weak. She had intended to force a conversation with Rudi once they left the party. Instead, she found Rudi was too tipsy to discuss anything of importance. All she was good for was a spirited round of sex before she felt asleep. When Rudi woke in the morning, she dressed quickly, full of apologies and charm. Patricia had to hand it to her—she was an expert at deflecting questions. Patricia gave up any more attempts to force a conversation and ate breakfast with her before they said their goodbyes. Not wanting to dwell on where their relationship was headed, Patricia chose to focus on the other reason she was in New York City. She was committed to helping Marcia in any way she could.

***

## SUNDAY, AUGUST 13, 2017 8:46 A.M.

Marcia sighed, sitting up in bed and rubbing her eyes. The dreams had returned, making Marcia thirsty. The craving for her mysterious lover had intensified so much that she found herself shaking with hunger once she awoke. She wanted this dream person in her life. She knew Peter was not the one. Seeing Lexie over the course of the trial had shaken her, and she no longer knew what to think.

Looking in the mirror after her shower, Marcia struck a pose, flexing her biceps. Widening her stance, she pulled her abdomen muscles in and bent a bit at the knees. "Wow." She was impressed with the changes in her body. *All muscle, baby.* Not that she had changed her exercise regimen at all. Yet, as the days passed, her body was morphing into a lean specimen of fine living. She'd never been overweight, but neither was she overly toned. Before all the changes began, she could suck in her gut enough to see a vague outline of a six-pack and the telltale signs of ribs, but certainly nothing like this. She was a career woman, working long hours and exercising little. Now it didn't seem to matter.

Donning some jeans and a T-shirt, Marcia left her room in search of coffee. Smelling the enticing brew, she fixed a cup, satisfied with her first taste of caffeine. The hum of the house followed her as she made her way to her favorite chair in the living room. After pulling a soft blanket over her, she curled up. She felt good, really good.

Not even being dubbed the "Indigo Woman" in the media could get her down. She was getting better at rolling with the punches. Before the meteorite changed her life, Marcia was sleepwalking through life. Now she was excited about what would happen next. She constantly felt energy surges as if endorphins were pumping through her. She felt vibrant and powerful.

Staring aimlessly around the room, Marcia wondered when Patricia would be gracing her with her presence. She dreamed the night before of waking Patricia, of frightening her. Unintentionally, of course. It was a very odd dream. She had appeared in Patricia's hotel room quite suddenly, feeling a bit disoriented. In the dream she was looking down at Patricia and Rudi as they slept, and Patricia must have sensed her presence. When she opened her eyes and looked up, Marcia realized that she was several feet above her friend, hovering. Patricia gasped, Marcia gasped, and Marcia felt the room spinning. Then, she found herself in her own bed.

Once Patricia arrived, she strode past Marcia into the living room and plopped down on the couch. "You scared the shit out of me last night. Why didn't you tell me you could do that?" Patricia began as soon as Marcia handed her a mug of hot coffee and sat in a nearby chair.

*So, not a dream.* "I'm so sorry. I didn't know. I swear," Marcia sputtered. "One moment I was lying in bed thinking about all we had discussed, and the next moment I was hovering over you."

"Hovering," Patricia scoffed. "That wouldn't have been so bad, but it was just your head. You were decapitated, staring at me, all fuzzy, with eyes glowing. You're damn lucky I didn't scream. I don't think Rudi would have liked that."

"Oh, really? I bet she'd love to hear you screaming while in bed together," Marcia said, laughing at her friend's look of outrage. Teasing her about her love life never got old. "Seriously, though, I promise to not pop in on you like that in the future. At least, I'll try. In fact, I think we should experiment with it a bit both while you're here and then once you're back in Boston. I promise to give you proper notice." Marcia laughed at her friend's dubious look. It seemed like Patricia had gotten over her fright fairly quickly, and Marcia was impressed.

"Fine. Whatever you need. Just try not to pop in on anyone else."

"Yeah, about that," Marcia said, rubbing the back of her neck.

"Oh, no. What did you do?"

"I have a confession to make," Marcia muttered.

Patricia cocked an eyebrow. Marcia looked toward the cold fireplace, studiously avoiding Patricia's stare. "I may have, um, dropped in on other people last night."

"Who?" Patricia asked.

"Rudi, for one." At Patricia's intake of breath Marcia glanced up, seeing a look of shock crawl across Patricia's face. "I know. I know. I couldn't help it. I'm surprised she didn't say anything to you."

"What did you see? Did she see you? Was anyone with her?"

Images of the night before paraded across Marcia's mind's eye, as clear as when the events occurred. "She was in her dressing room, talking to a blond-haired lady about the show. Evidently, someone in the front row had fallen asleep, and she was outraged." Marcia hesitated to relate the next part.

"What happened next?"

"She was looking in the mirror, removing her makeup. Our eyes connected. She got this horrible look on her face, like she was seeing a ghost. It scared me so much that I blinked and was back in bed."

"Ah."

"I hope I didn't scare her too much," Marcia mumbled, looking away.

Patricia sighed. "We'll find out tonight. She invited us to Kiernan's cast party."

"You mean you," Marcia said.

"No. I attended Rudi's after-play party last night, and I told her I wanted to spend time with you tonight. She suggested you join us. It might be just the thing for you. Get out for a few hours, relax, get a new perspective. Don't worry. She'll talk herself into believing she saw nothing, that it was all her overactive imagination." As Patricia squeezed Marcia's arm, she began to feel better.

"Well, okay. It sounds fun. I could use something to get my mind off of everything. In the meantime, maybe you can help me do some research on this newest ability, like how to not make unplanned visits."

"I'll try."

"Finding a way to clear my mind before going to bed so I don't end up in any more awkward situations might be a good start." Picking up a pillow wedged between her body and the chair, she hugged it. "Patricia, I truly appreciate all you've done for me. I knew I could turn to you to help me make sense of it all."

Patricia made a sound in the back of her throat. "I don't know about that. I have no clue how to help you and the list of incredible things you can do keeps getting longer."

"It doesn't matter. You're here for me, and that means more than I can ever say. Thank you." Marcia reached out and hugged her, secure in the knowledge she was fully accepted even in this new form, even after scaring the bejeebers out of Patricia. "Since you're here, Sammy will be dragging herself in soon for breakfast..."

"Ah, I get it. It's my superior cooking skills...that's why you keep me around."

"You caught me," Marcia said, rising and leading the way to the kitchen. She watched Patricia take over the kitchen, trying to recall more of what happened the night before. A wave of information swept through her, making Marcia dizzy. She blinked several times, mouth dropping open as she realized another ability was added to her steadily-growing list. Jumping up from her chair, she paced.

"What's the matter?" Patricia asked.

"I remember everything," Marcia replied, eyes flitting as memories flowed through her mind.

"And?" Patricia prompted, a puzzled look on her face.

"No. I remember everything. Since the time I was born, perhaps a bit before then. I remember every moment, experience, action, thought, conversation—everything. It's like a switch was flipped, and now I can recall all the events of my life." Marcia swung around, standing in the middle of the room, unsure of what to do with this new development.

"Let's test this," Patricia suggested, a gleam evident in her green eyes. "What was the first case you litigated?"

"Strauss versus Global, L.L.C. on January 24, 1998. The trial lasted three days before the defendant asked to settle. Try something harder."

"Okay. Maybe something more subtle." Rubbing her chin, Patricia took a few moments to formulate a harder question. "Tell me what happened the second time I met you from beginning to end."

Leaning back against the counter, Marcia scoffed. "Oh, come on. Is that all you can come up with?" At Patricia's raised eyebrow, Marcia began. "We met on March 24, 1991, at the undergraduate housing office to get our lottery number for lodging. We pulled a great number and were able to secure one of the best rooms in one of the smallest dorms. While we were waiting for our turn to choose, we ate Sugar Daddy lollipops that were given to everyone." She looked at Patricia and shook her head. "I haven't thought about this in years."

"No stalling," Patricia teased, pointing at Marcia with her spatula.

"I'm not. Once we were called, I continued to chew on the lollipop. When I tried to rip off part of the caramel, I accidentally flung a chunk of it onto the shoulder of the administrator. She was wearing a white silk blouse." Marcia chuckled.

Patricia joined in. "All true. What were we wearing?"

"I had on brown corduroy pants and a chocolate brown cable-knit sweater with a white turtleneck sweater beneath it. And black boots. I wore a long black wool overcoat with white wool gloves and a matching scarf." Marcia paused to watch Patricia's reaction. She looked suitably impressed. "You wore blue jeans, a red button-down flannel shirt, and sneakers. Your coat was the rattiest thing I'd ever seen, not to mention outdated."

"Hey, I lived in that Levi's jean jacket. I had a lot of good times while wearing it."

"And I'm sure many others when you took it off," Marcia rejoined with a suggestive quirk to her lips.

Patricia tsk'ed. "You are incorrigible. Okay. Continue with what happened when the Sugar Daddy hit the administrator's shoulder."

"I was mortified. She didn't notice, so I said nothing. Instead, every time I looked at the piece that got away, I began to giggle. Then, you'd join in." Marcia shook her head. "She must have thought we were the most immature kids. When we got outside the room, we laughed so hard we fell to the floor. After that, we ate in the cafeteria and separated to attend our classes."

Patricia nodded, wiping away tears of mirth. "Right on. What else can I ask you? Who was the last person you kissed besides pseudo-Peter?"

"Oh, no," Marcia answered while wagging her finger at Patricia. "I would remember that even if I didn't have this new ability. It's not like I kiss that many people. The last person would have been John, of course—"

"That's not true," Patricia interjected. "I'm sure you've kissed other people, just not in a romantic way. Discounting family and me, who did you last kiss, say, on the day of John's funeral?"

"Gladys," Marcia answered.

"Gladys?" Patricia echoed, seemingly confused.

"She was one of John's co-workers."

Patricia cracked some eggs into a bowl and whisked them with milk and cheese. Once she poured it into a frying pan, she picked up the thread of their conversation. "Let's take stock of all the changes. Your appearance has changed. No hair on the rest of your body if you discount the top of your head, eyebrows, and eyelashes. Let me tell you, my friend, at our age many women would love that!"

Marcia gave her a lopsided smile. "I know, and many would love to be able to think of a person or a place and be there, presto change-o, but I didn't exactly ask for this, and I can't control it. The scariest part, by far, is I don't know what else I can do."

"Besides see auras, astral project, and now remember everything."

"Exactly. It's not like I have an owner's manual—" Marcia stopped as a new thought crossed her mind. "Do I have a manual?"

"Do you?" Patricia asked, leaning forward.

Marcia tilted her head, trying to make sense of what she was visualizing. She saw snapshots of her life, each moment blending into the next. She closed her eyes and concentrated on slowing down the flow. Once she was successful, she took a deep breath and wondered how she could recall a particular event. An answer popped into her thoughts, and Marcia rocked back on her heels.

After a few moments of silence, she replied, "Kind of. It's like a whole host of memories, or files, are stored in my brain. When I think of something in particular, a bunch of instructions come to mind. Like for the memories. I need to be prompted by one of my senses to trigger a memory. Or I can think of a particular person or event. Even a particular date in time. I just need to focus on what I want to remember." She looked over at Patricia. "Can you believe this? I have a how-to manual stored in my brain!" She laughed shakily, drawing a hand through her hair. "Wow."

"You'll have to explore these directions. Maybe it will tell you how to control your powers better. And who knows what else you can do. It's like a Choose Your Own Adventure series." Patricia grinned.

"What's like an adventure?" asked Sammy as she entered the kitchen.

Shooting Patricia a warning look, Marcia answered, "My new looks now that I've been photographed."

"You were?" Sammy asked, pulling the paper over in front of her. "Where?"

"*Page Six*," Marcia answered, handing over the *New York Post*. She watched her daughter skim the paper while Patricia placed the cooked eggs and some juice on the table.

"Thanks, Patricia," Sammy said without looking up. "They're calling you the Sage Mage."

"It's better than the Indigo Woman. Must be because I'm winning my case."

"You are? That's incredible." Patricia faltered when she saw Marcia's expression. "I just mean Lexie's one of the best litigators around. Not that you aren't." She looked over at Sammy, who rolled her eyes. "Are you going to throw me a life jacket here?"

"Don't get me involved," Sammy said, shoveling the rest of the eggs in her mouth as if she were afraid they would be taken away.

"I'm a great attorney. Perhaps you should come see me in action."

"Oh, I already know. I've watched you on that court TV station. Come on, Marcia. You know I didn't mean it that way," Patricia whined.

She was so pathetic Marcia couldn't keep up any pretense of being hurt. She chuckled. "Yes. I know."

"Phew," Patricia said, pantomiming wiping her forehead. "I got worried for a moment." They all smiled.

"What did you want to do today, honey?"

"Can I go to Rosie's? Her mom has offered to take us to the movies."

"That sounds okay. I'll call over there after breakfast." As she went to retrieve her cell phone, Marcia couldn't help but feel relieved. She didn't want Sammy around while she and Patricia tried to make sense of her new abilities. With her luck, she'd end up appearing in front of Sammy and scaring her senseless. *No need to scar the girl any more than I have already.* Once she had this new parlor trick under control, she would demonstrate it to her daughter.

***

### SUNDAY, AUGUST 13, 2017 10:28 P.M.

Marcia followed Patricia into the restaurant, curiously looking around. The last time she ate at this restaurant was the day she was sworn in as a New York attorney. Her family splurged for the occasion, making the reservation months in advance. Opulent with deep reds and gold splashed throughout the room, large mirrors, and mahogany tables, Marcia swore she could breathe in the wealth and elegance such an atmosphere exuded. They made their way to the function room at the back, and Marcia was bombarded by myriad sounds, smells, and sights. She heard Rudi greet Patricia, but Marcia was unable to get a clear view since she was blocked by people chatting. Patricia half-turned to introduce Marcia, motioning that she step forward.

*The moment of truth*, Marcia thought.

"Hello. It's a pleasure to meet you. Patricia's mentioned you often," Rudi began, as she extended her hand in greeting. She froze as their eyes met, and Marcia's stomach sank. Opening and closing her mouth like a gaping fish, Rudi's eyes bugged out. "You're that woman from the mirror," Rudi exclaimed, pointing at Marcia.

Patricia laughed, grasping Rudi's forearm. "You're so funny, Rudi. Seeing people in mirrors now, are we?"

"No. I saw her last night," Rudi insisted. "She had the same glowing, purple eyes." Rudi raised her hands, pantomiming circles with her fingers and holding them in front of her eyes.

"Oh, come on, Rudi. Really?" A rich voice interjected. Marcia looked over, recognizing Kiernan Connelly, who shook her head in amusement. "You knew you'd be seeing them tonight. Maybe you were letting your mind wander. And really, glowing purple eyes? Obviously, she's wearing contacts. They look marvelous, by the way." She pinned Marcia with a brief but intense glance.

Agreeing, Patricia steered the conversation away by asking Kiernan about her upcoming show. "When does it premiere?"

"Not for another six weeks or so. We'll have some workshops open to the public as we get closer. We have a great cast," Kiernan answered.

As their words washed over her, Marcia took the opportunity to observe Kiernan. Marcia didn't mind admitting to herself that the actress, with her high cheekbones, deep blue eyes, and shapely figure, was captivating. Realizing how flagrant she was being while checking Kiernan out, Marcia shifted her eyes back to Kiernan's visage, recognizing an amused look flitting across her face. *Bagged.* Flustered, Marcia excused herself and strode to the restroom.

She stood in front of the mirror, splashing water on her face in an attempt to dissipate the redness from her cheeks, no doubt created by her absolute mortification over what occurred. Shame enveloped her. Ogling Kiernan was unacceptable. *What is wrong with me? I don't do that. Where are my manners?* After drying her cheeks with a paper towel, Marcia reached into her purse to retrieve her lipstick but stopped when she felt a hand on her shoulder. Looking up, Marcia's eyes latched on to Kiernan, amazed at the compassion she saw. Frozen, she watched a warm smile light up her face and felt her fingers tighten. Compelled to face her, Marcia turned. Her eyes widened in surprise when Kiernan closed the distance between them to deliver a hug.

"Marcia," she whispered. "Don't worry. You're doing fine." Kiernan released her and stepped back.

Confused, Marcia asked, "Do you know me?"

Smiling, she replied, "I do." As she opened her mouth to say more, the restroom door opened. Kiernan's smile was apologetic. Marcia could do nothing but watch her leave. For a moment, Marcia wondered if she imagined the entire event. Steadying herself, Marcia took several deep breaths to slow down her thudding heart. *What just happened? Why did she hug me? What did she mean? Will I see her again?* That last thought made her pause. Exiting the restroom, she scanned the area, already knowing that Kiernan was no longer at the party. She also knew she'd be seeing Kiernan again, although she had no idea why. It was a gut feeling. *And when I do, I'll get my answers.*

***

## WEDNESDAY, AUGUST 16, 2017 11:21 A.M.

Hearing a knock on her door, Kiernan crossed her living room and looked through the peephole. A tall man in dark clothes stood waiting. "May I help you?" She said through the door, wondering how he gained access into the building.

"Ma'am, my name is Special Agent Thacker. I'm an agent at the FBI." He flashed a badge with his name and credentials. "If you have a few minutes, I'd like to discuss a recent event you might have witnessed."

Kiernan cocked her head, listening for his thoughts. She'd become better at focusing on the constant stream of words surrounding her. <*"The vibrometer indicates some meteorite rock is here, but the door is blocking the actinometer readings. All I need is to get inside."*> It was hard to understand what the man was thinking, but Kiernan got a distinct feeling of danger. Before she could respond, she felt a tickling at the back of her mind. Gasping when the feeling became more invasive, she visualized a wall to block it. It felt like tar oozing into her mind, though, and she tried not to panic. She created a bright, golden force field and pushed the blackness back. Trembling, she heard, <*"Why isn't the telepathy reader working?"*>

"I'm sorry, but I value my privacy. You'll have to make an appointment with me through my management company." She continued watching him through the peephole.

A thunderous expression darkened his features. "All right. I just need the contact information."

"You're a special agent. I'm confident you can track it down. Good day." Kiernan held her breath, listening. She was certain he wasn't a real government agent, and she wouldn't meet with him unless she was surrounded by other people.

"Very well. I'll be in touch."

<*"I'll send Remik to interview her,"*> she heard as he moved away from the door.

With a sigh of relief, she moved over to the sofa, surprised to feel her body trembling. She leaned back and closed her eyes. She didn't feel as if someone were trying to get inside her mind anymore, but she'd never felt anything like that before. It was scary. *He mentioned the meteorite.* She wondered whether Patricia's friend received a similar visit. *I have a feeling Marcia and I will be crossing paths again.* For now, she wanted to forget the meteorite and the ramifications of finding some of the space rock.

Spying the large padded envelope on her coffee table with familiar writing on the front, she opened it. Kiernan received it at the theater yesterday. Inside were several letters dated weeks earlier. She had hoped she would receive more now that she was acting again. She read through all the letters, marveling at how they seemed to mirror events in her life. Over the last few months, Kiernan had traveled this road of self-actualization, and these letters served as her how-to guide. At some higher energetic level, Thea had connected with her as surely as if she were talking her through the process of realizing life every minute.

Kiernan smirked. *Next I'll be having conversations with her in my mind.* Amused, Kiernan released the thought. She might be able to hear people's thoughts nowadays, but as far as she could tell, no one could hear hers. Kiernan was learning how to block extraneous thoughts as if she were using the controls of a radio. She could tune in to a person's thoughts but turning up the volume with her mind, or reduce others' thoughts to background noise by turning the voices down. She was even able to turn it off. What she still needed to learn was how far away she could be from a person and still hear his or her thoughts.

Being an actor helped her while she became used to hearing others' thoughts. Most times, she was able to hide her reactions. *Not that I did such a good job with Patricia's friend.* Still, it was illuminating to hear Marcia's thoughts about her. What made her follow to hug the woman was the unique feel of her mind. It felt like the first rays of sun hitting her face after a rainstorm. More than that, though, on some level she recognized a kindred spirit. Although it was clear Marcia was unable to converse with her through telepathy, she had some unusual talents of her own. Kiernan tapped her lips with a finger. They had some type of connection, thanks to the meteorite.

Noticing the time, she placed the letters on her desk and rose to prepare for that day's rehearsal. Their last public reading was well received, and today they planned to implement some changes based on the feedback they received. Kiernan was looking forward to finding out what she needed to do.

*How did I attract Thea into my life? Do I want to meet her?* Such questions flew through her mind and sparked her imagination. *Would I even recognize Thea if she showed up at one of my performances? Would our eyes meet and a gong sound in the recesses of my mind announcing who she is? What would we talk about?* She was afraid to meet Thea. She had the distinct feeling she would have to be absolutely truthful, holding nothing back, removing all walls and masks, and giving herself over to the bond they shared.

And there was a bond. It vibrated between them. Yet, meeting Thea would be to acknowledge that connection within this reality instead of allowing it to merely exist at some spiritual level. That scared her. Maybe she was romanticizing their connection. At this point, though, Kiernan understood it would be up to her to reach out, if she dared.

*Do I dare?*

# Chapter Twelve

"WELL, HERE WE ARE. Our last class. And I must confess, I have become rather attached to you all." Professor Corelli's eyes swept the room, pausing on different faces with a smile or a nod. "We undertook a marvelous journey to discover ourselves and each other. Think about all that we've discussed. Think about where you were in your life when we began traveling this road and where you are now." Patricia held her breath when Professor Corelli's eyes found hers and held them. The professor continued in an even tone. "I want you to know how much I have enjoyed our interactions, even when we disagreed on certain issues." She quirked an eyebrow and smiled before breaking their connection, looking at the class at large. "My goal was to guide you on your path toward self-enlightenment. I think I reached that goal. For that, I humbly thank you." She dipped her head, and the class stood and clapped, Patricia included. The professor straightened, abashed, and blinked several times. Once the class quieted down, she provided information on their final project deadline and the grade posting date.

"Many have asked whether I'll be teaching any more courses like this one. In fact, our illustrious school has consented to allow me to play some more." She gave them a wide smile. "I'll be teaching Enlightenment 201: Conversations with a Madwoman next semester, and I'd love to see you again. This course will delve deeper into our perceptions, beliefs, and foundations of what creates and sustains us. We'll discuss religion and politics, right and wrong, interactions and individuality. I hope you will continue your journey with me. Whatever you decide, though, I wish you a life full of happiness. Just remember, you create your reality—so make it a great one."

Patricia packed her belongings in her bag and followed the students flowing out of the rows. Several approached Professor Corelli, no doubt for more information on the new course. Patricia felt the warm buzz of excitement wash through her as she thought about taking it. She stood on the fringe of the enthusiastic students. Finally, the crowd trickled out.

The professor smiled. "Are you hungry?" Patricia nodded and waited for the professor to gather her teaching materials before they fell into step. "I'm famished. Let's grab some grub."

Patricia laughed at the slang. "Lead the way, professor."

"Call me Thea."

Patricia was surprised to hear this, but she agreed.

Once they were settled in their usual spot, Thea looked at her. "So, how are you?"

"I feel like I've been running a marathon. So many things have been happening. I just want to catch my breath." Patricia paused, thinking about what she wanted to share. She trusted Thea, and it might prove helpful to get a different perspective on Rudi. "You know how I'm in a relationship with an actress? I guess you could say that we've hit a rough patch, or rather I have. I've tried to release my expectations, but it's so hard. I can't seem to get behind her masks. I want to accept her fully for who she is, but at the same time, I know she could be so much more. I see this potential within her if she only tried."

Patricia's sighed and shock rippled through her when Thea covered Patricia's hand with her own.

Thea's eyes shined with compassion. "Patricia, have you ever thought about what exactly you want in a mate?" Raising her other hand in front of her, Thea warded off any response. "Now, I know you wrote about the perfect man in your book and the book was about your lady, but realistically, have you thought this through?"

Patricia took her time before responding. "No. I suppose not. I've been processing the lessons you've taught in class, particularly the last few classes about loving unconditionally, being present, and releasing expectations. It's hard to put these concepts into action."

"Does she make you happy? Do you miss her? You don't have to answer these questions right now, but think about it." Thea leaned back in her chair, allowing her hand to slip away from Patricia's and sipping her coffee, a look of curiosity on her face.

Patricia blurted out, "It's Rudi Singlewood. I've been seeing Rudi." She laughed nervously, then looked at Thea's frozen expression and began laughing earnestly. Thea joined in.

"I thought she was with Kiernan."

"Kiernan Connelly. Yes, I didn't know that for a while. I guess I didn't want to know. But Kiernan pretty much confirmed it the last time we spoke. Oh, and I have to tell you she asked about your classes." At Thea's surprised look, Patricia elaborated. "The first time I met her, it was right after your class started. I told her about it, and she was interested. Since then, whenever I see her, she asks about the subject matter. She seems to really be interested in the topics you've introduced."

"I greatly admire Kiernan. I've seen some of her interviews over the years." They grew quiet, each picking at their food. Patricia could see that Thea had something on her mind, and she waited. She watched Thea cross her arms, her forehead scrunched up as she deliberated on what she wanted to say. "I know this is highly irregular, but I've come to depend on our weekly deconstruction of the lessons. Do you think..." Uncrossing her arms, she leaned forward, struggling to vocalize her feelings.

Patricia also leaned forward, and this time it was she who covered Thea's hand. "Yes."

Thea's face lit up. "Really? Wait, you mean?"

"I mean I would love to keep in touch." Patricia tried to spell it out for both of them. "I've felt a growing closeness with you throughout this course, and I've come to depend on our interactions, too. I look forward to them. And, I am disinclined to let that end just because the class is ending."

Grinning, Thea turned her hand over to squeeze Patricia's before letting go. "That's great. I was afraid I was feeling something you weren't. I have to admit, it took me by surprise. However, you're an amazing individual, and I firmly believe that when you connect with someone, you should try to nurture it. Can we make plans to meet next week?"

At those words, Patricia's face fell. "Actually, I'm taking a trip to Italy with my family next week. My father is dying, and we wanted some time together. He has reconciled himself with death, and I think he wants to help us come to terms with it."

"Oh, Patricia," Thea said, reaching out once more to squeeze her hand. "I'm sorry. I know how hard it is to accept the death of a loved one. Nothing can prepare you for the loss."

"Actually, your class about grief helped me quite a bit. Dying is natural. Grieving is a part of that process. I can't say I'm ready for his death, but I feel better equipped to accept it. I could call you once I return?" Patricia offered. She knew it was silly, but she was nervous making the suggestion. Patricia didn't often make new friends. She was a private person and tended to keep a tight grip on her emotions. Patricia's instincts told her she could trust Thea, though.

"Of course, let me give you my contact information." They exchanged numbers and email addresses.

"Tell me about your new class," Patricia said.

"Well, I'm still structuring it, but I'm really excited. I'm going to start with politics. It interests me how people choose a party. From there, I'll extend the conversation to encompass religion. I truly believe that as long as we can get to the crux of these topics without judging anyone, if we make the classroom a safe place to explore these ideas, we can really grow and connect."

"That sounds fascinating. I don't think I've ever heard of anyone teaching such provocative topics in that way." Patricia bit into her turkey breast and provolone cheese sandwich, chewing as she contemplated Thea's new class. She would make sure she could take it.

Smiling, Thea replied, "You know, I've visited Italy a few times. As a matter of fact, on my first visit, I got lost in Florence. I was one of the teacher chaperones for a high school trip. We had taken part in a walking tour early one morning. After the tour, we split up to explore, planning to meet again a few hours later to hop on a bus to visit Pisa. I hadn't been paying attention. Every street leading out from the Duomo, like the spokes of a wheel, seemed the same. In a panic, I circled the cathedral again and again, looking for some clue as to which road would return me to my hotel. As I walked, I searched for those who belonged to my traveling group—any of the twenty-four individuals. But I saw no one, and I continued to walk in circles. Have you even been alone in a strange land, not knowing how to speak the language?"

Patricia shook her head, grinning, and Thea chuckled. "That was me. I knew very few words—costa, ciao, cappuccino. I didn't even have a map. After a few hours, I sat down, admitting defeat." Thea took a sip of her drink and glanced at Patricia. "This is the embarrassing part. I realized that I had my hotel card in my pocket. I had taken it that morning. I walked to the nearest hotel for directions. A few minutes later, I left with a map sporting a black line that reflected the route back to my hotel. Fifteen minutes later, safe once more, my feelings of anxiety, panic, confusion, and loneliness faded away. And as soon as I changed my shoes, I was back out the hotel door to explore Florence. And this is what I learned, years later. If I had known I was going to get lost, I would have paid better attention to where I was going. It's acceptable to alter course, to deviate, as long as I'm aware of what I'm doing. That's why it's so important to be present every minute." Thea raised a finger to make her point. "If lost, it helps to take deep breaths, think of the experience as an adventure, and check your pockets."

Patricia laughed, affection rushing through her as Thea joined in. Rising much later from the table, they faced each other, knowing they had turned a corner within their relationship. Patricia was thrilled about their deepening connection. They were more than professor and student or mere acquaintances. What they were building was exciting. She could see the beginnings of a strong friendship. Thea pulled Patricia in for a hug.

Whispering in her ear, Thea said, "Enjoy yourself in Italy. Be present and try not to dwell on the future. Let it unfold as it must." Pulling back, she looked Patricia in the eyes. "I'll be here when you return."

Tears filled Patricia's eyes, and she felt ridiculous. *How did I come to care for her so much? Why does the thought of not talking to her for a few weeks make me so sad?* She had a hard time composing herself, and she turned away, swiping at tears. "I'll send you a postcard," Patricia uttered, catching Thea's nod through the corner of her eye before making a beeline for the exit.

*I can't believe that was the last class.* The class had helped her sort out so many aspects of her life. The entire course, fraught with philosophical questions, deep-rooted beliefs, and cutting-edge scientific interpretations stimulated Patricia in ways she hadn't anticipated.

Walking up the pathway to her brownstone forty minutes later with a spring in her step, Patricia wondered what to do next. She loved how Thea learned from every experience. *That woman*, she thought in amazement, *has changed my life.*

She contemplated whether to begin packing for her upcoming trip. It would bring her one step closer to vacationing with her family. One step closer to not creating any more happy memories with her dad. *I shouldn't think of it that way*, she chastised herself. She looked up as she reached the stairs to her home and stopped short. Leaning against the brick façade at the top of the staircase, ankles crossed, was Rudi with a bouquet of roses in her hand. She grinned at Patricia's stunned expression.

Standing up straight, Rudi swooped in for a breathtaking kiss once Patricia reached the top step. "Surprised?"

Surprised didn't begin to describe what Patricia felt. After she had finally decided that Rudi was a self-absorbed narcissist, here she'd gone out of her way to be thoughtful, spontaneous, and lovable. A juxtaposition of conflicting thoughts collided, causing a mild headache to develop. Trying to clear her mind, Patricia unlocked the door and walked through without saying a word, holding the heavy wooden door for Rudi. She offered coffee to her guest, placing her class materials on her desk. Strong arms wrapped around her from behind once she stood in the kitchen. Leaning back, Patricia indulged in the embrace, closing her eyes.

She deserved a partner who was her equal in every way—willing to be open, to work on releasing negative behavior, and to grow as they integrated their lives. Up until this moment, Patricia was convinced Rudi didn't have the desire or ability to become such a partner. Now, a spark of hope fluttered to life. Maybe she was willing to try after all.

"I knew you were leaving for Italy next week and couldn't bear the thought of being away from you for so long. Is this okay?" Rudi said as she nuzzled Patricia's neck.

"Yes, of course," Patricia breathed. "This is a wonderful surprise." Turning, Patricia grasped her forearms. "I can show you some of my favorite places. How long can you stay?"

Rudi's smile and sparkling eyes sent a shiver down Patricia's spine. "I would be disappointed if you didn't. I can only stay for a couple of days before I must get back to the show. As it is, I can only hope the understudy bombs tonight and tomorrow so that my role will be waiting for me upon my return." Although said lightheartedly, Patricia could hear the insecurity Rudi harbored that she might be replaced.

Trying not to get too excited, Patricia wondered whether Rudi was ready to allow another person into her life. Rudi wasn't stupid. Maybe she had begun to question whether her life was perfect. Maybe she could see the writing on the wall that Patricia was close to breaking off their relationship, and she decided to do whatever she could to change Patricia's mind. Whatever Rudi's motivations for the visit, the first step to saving whatever they had was to spend time in Patricia's world, and she saw Rudi's appearance as a good sign.

As Patricia showed Rudi around her home, she felt like she was seeing it for the first time. After the success of her first book, she splurged on a three-story brownstone on Beacon Hill. She was close to the Boston Commons, the Theater District and Back Bay, as well as Government Center, Faneuil Hall, and the North End. Her house—with its hardwood floors, brick walls, intricate inlaid moldings, and bay windows—was a throwback to the 1800s. It oozed warmth from the large fireplace stacked with logs, to the wool afghans topping the sofas and chairs. The large kitchen had cast-iron pans strung above the stove. A kitchen door led to a private stone courtyard with potted flowers, a birdbath, and a built-in barbecue pit. Upstairs, she showed her the two bedrooms and den before leading Rudi up one more flight of stairs to the rooftop terrace. She was proud of her home. When it came on the market, Patricia jumped at the chance to buy it for a song since it needed extensive renovations. Her siblings and parents had helped her update the rooms a little at a time.

After getting Rudi situated, they left the house to explore Boston. They walked the Boston Commons, stopping to watch some children partake in the Swan Boat rides. Traveling through the Theater District, they decided to buy tickets for the *Nunsense* show. Their next stop was at an outdoor café where they drank cappuccinos and discussed Italy. Rudi told her what she knew about Venice since Patricia and her family intended to travel there next week. Her family had rented a villa near San Marco Square.

Rudi put her cup down and stared at her. "Tell me about your family."

Surprised Rudi wanted to hear anything about her life beyond small talk, Patricia jumped at the opportunity. "I have an older brother and two younger sisters. We're a typical Irish Catholic family. We look out for each other. You know, the whole blood is thicker than water concept. Family always comes first."

"That must be nice. Knowing you can always rely on them. Are you a practicing Catholic?"

"Not so much, much to my parents' eternal disappointment." Patricia laughed. "I'm more of a holiday Catholic, though my parents call me a lapsed Catholic." She grinned, sipping her cappuccino slowly. "How about you?"

"Oh, no. Not religious in the least." Rudi sipped her drink and looked around them at the people walking by with feigned interest. After a stilted silence, Rudi asked, "How did they take your sexuality? I thought Catholics were dead set against it. You know, going to hell and all that."

Patricia nodded. "It was hard for them, but they've come around, probably due to how close we are. Love won out. That said, we don't really talk about it, and I doubt we will unless I start bringing someone around." She was surprised when no one mentioned her relationship with Rudi. Pictures surfaced every so often on *Page Six*. Then again, her family didn't normally follow celebrity gossip, so she doubted they'd know anything unless she told them or they saw it on television. "What about your family? Do you have any siblings? Are you close with your parents?"

"I have a younger sister, and she's the perfect daughter for my parents. I haven't spoken to her in years. Tell me more about your family." Rudi didn't make eye contact while she revealed these details, so Patricia picked up the conversation ball after an awkward silence.

"Both my parents worked hard to put food on the table and to protect me and my siblings from the ugliness of the world. They made sure we knew that no matter what, we could turn to them whenever we needed help or someone to listen. I'm really lucky to have them."

"It sounds like it." Rudi finished her drink and smiled. "Ready to roam some more?"

Patricia accepted Rudi's extended hand, and they explored Faneuil Hall, enjoying the unique stores and the kitschy items. Patricia felt something shift within her as they wandered around the tourist attractions. She gave herself leave to fully enjoy this experience without attempting to think about what would happen next. They would deal with the future later. Right now she was determined to not think about anything other than each moment she was sharing with Rudi. After all, it might be the only time Rudi visited.

As they sat in the North End eating a scrumptious Italian meal a few hours later, Rudi admitted to what had compelled her to hop on a plane to see Patricia. "I feel like we've been drifting apart." Engulfing Patricia's petite hand into her larger ones, she continued with an earnest expression. "I may not be the perfect woman, but I'd like to try to be what you need. I've heard what you've been saying about my needing to open up to you. There isn't much to tell, and I don't even like thinking about my upbringing. Nevertheless, you make me want to work on who I am, and I'm just asking for more time. I'm giving you everything I can. With your guidance and understanding, I can learn to be what you want."

Patricia stared at their intertwined hands, resenting Rudi's decision to bring this up in a public place. *She knows I don't want to argue in public. Why couldn't she wait until we were home?* Struggling not to give in to her anger or pettiness, Patricia tried to navigate through Rudi's words to the real message. Although she was encouraged by Rudi's willingness to change, it concerned her she was only changing in order to appease her. Rudi was a woman who liked being admired and having her ego stroked. It wouldn't surprise her to find out that Rudi didn't mean a word and was merely spouting out what she thought Patricia wanted to hear in order to keep her from walking away.

"How are you going to change?" Patricia asked in a soft voice while searching those gray eyes she loved so much.

"I'm not sure." Rudi looked uncertain. "I'll admit that I'm a confirmed bachelorette. Changing my attitude, my way of living, to let you in may take some time."

"So, what attitudes do you plan to change?" Patricia was genuinely curious.

Rudi gave her a charming smile. "Well, what would you suggest?"

Patricia let out a breath with a grimace, the truth slapping her in the face like an unexpected ocean wave. *She isn't serious. If she were, she would have thought this through.*

"It doesn't matter what I think or what I want," Patricia replied, her tone harsh. "You need to figure out your own road. If I tell you what to do, you'll be doing it to appease me, not to become a better person." Patricia removed her hand from Rudi's grasp and wrapped it around her wine glass.

"Why can't it be both? I don't know what to do, and I need your help." When Patricia remained silent, Rudi's eyebrows lowered, becoming a flat line. She sat back in her chair, crossing her arms across her chest. "Look, you don't know what my life is like, what I deal with every day. I have to be careful."

"Yes, and isn't it sad that after dating you for months, I don't know you any more than your legion of fans." Patricia clenched her teeth, waving her hands in front of her. "If you want a successful relationship, you have to be willing to trust. But you just can't make that leap of faith, can you? Well, you've got what you want. You're safe. You're surrounded by fawning fans. God forbid you let anyone closer." In a less heated voice, Patricia continued. "Until you truly see who you are and realize what you want in your life beyond a successful career, you'll be alone, even in a crowded room. It's time to face your fears. You have the potential to live a wonderful, rewarding life. But, as long as you keep those walls up, that potential will remain unrealized. Half the time we're together you seem preoccupied with how others are viewing you, what you'll do next, whether you're playing the part correctly. You need to focus more on the moment. Perhaps at some future time we can reconnect, but for now I think it best that we let go."

Even though Patricia had known they were headed toward this decision, it still hurt to say it aloud. She'd wanted to be wrong and had felt a glimmer of hope flare when she found Rudi on her doorstep. That spark was extinguished by the reality that Rudi wasn't willing to become vulnerable.

Rudi laughed, but then a look of consternation crossed her face. She captured Patricia's hand once more. "Darling, I've always coasted along while hiding behind my masks, but you've made me rethink everything. You make me want to be a better woman. If you'll be patient with me, if you'll help me, I know I can be a person worthy of your love."

Patricia grimaced again. She recognized the pretty words, dredged up from a movie Rudi starred in several years before called *The Lady Behind the Mask*. She leaned forward. "I'm not Henry, and I'm not going to take you into my arms, declaring my undying love and willingness to help. This isn't a movie. You have to be willing to do the work yourself in a relationship."

"You're being unreasonable. Why recreate the wheel? I can't give you what I don't have. This is what I am." Rudi opened her arms. "No one else has ever complained. Did it ever occur to you that you ask for too much? I'm a girl who wants to have fun."

Patricia sighed. "Yes, and how fun, how fulfilling is it when your partner doesn't know who you are? It's exciting in the beginning, but after a while, the lack of intimacy is tiresome."

Rudi stared at her in dismay, at a loss for words. She sat back. "If I try to change, to allow you to know the true me, will you give me a chance?"

"Not right now. I don't want you to do this just to placate me. You might begin to resent me, believing that I'm always judging you." Patricia took a quick drink, soothing her dry throat. This was a hard conversation, but it had to happen. Rudi had to see the truth.

"Aren't you?" Rudi arched an eyebrow.

Patricia shook her head. "No. I'm honoring myself. I don't ever want to resent you. Similarly, I don't want you to resent me by trying to change in order to keep me. Change because you want to, not because someone is asking you to do so."

Rudi mulled over her words. After a few minutes, Rudi's face cleared, and the tension released from her frame. "You know, maybe I should have listened to you more when you talked about those classes you were taking."

Humming agreement, Patricia relaxed, confident in her decision. If they were meant to be together, they'd find each other again. If not, she was glad for the experience.

The rest of Rudi's visit was surprisingly lighthearted. Only one uncomfortable moment occurred on the night of their talk. Rudi wasn't thrilled by the idea of sleeping in the guest bedroom. Patricia rejected her advances, stating it would muddy the waters too much and finally throwing a pillow at her while threatening to not take her to the best Chinese restaurant if she didn't stop pouting. After a tense few moments, Rudi accepted defeat. She seemed to push aside her wounded pride and concentrate on enjoying their time together. True to her word, Patricia did introduce her to a fabulous restaurant in Chinatown the next day.

When it came time to say farewell, Rudi extracted a promise that Patricia would contact her every so often when she was visiting New York. "After all, you can never have too many friends, can you?"

Patricia had to agree that friends were a valuable commodity. She enjoyed spending time with Rudi, and with the sexual component taken out of their relationship, she had high hopes they could become good friends.

# Chapter Thirteen

PUTTERING AROUND HER HOUSE in her bathrobe, Kiernan tried to release the memories that kept popping to the forefront. Today was the twenty-fifth anniversary of when she left home to be an actress. It was also the anniversary of the last time she spoke to her father. They had a terrible fight over a taboo subject—acting. It went along with the other taboo subject—her mother. Memories invaded her mind, as they always did when thinking of her childhood home.

*Returning from kindergarten class, full of stories to share, Kiernan could not understand why the house was so quiet. Skipping through each room, calling, "Momma," Kiernan looked all around the two-floor French villa before checking the surrounding yard. Inhaling the ocean air as she rounded the corner, Kiernan, only six years old, saw her mom sleeping under a tree. Feeling tired, Kiernan curled next to her, snuggling under the limp arm, and relaxed into a deep sleep. When she awoke several hours later from restless dreams, she was in her own bed. Disoriented, Kiernan sat up and listened for her mother's voice. She overheard her father and several strangers speaking in hushed voices instead. Rubbing her eyes, Kiernan joined them. They quickly switched topics, giving her their full attention and care.*

At the time, Kiernan didn't understand that her mother had died. Shaking her head, she showered and dressed, wondering what to do for the day. Of course, she knew what she wanted to do. The idea had taken hold of her mind for several weeks now, but she cautiously approached it even now. She was exhilarated and terrified. *I'm afraid he'll reject me. What if he won't see me?*

She worried her lower lip between her teeth. Her eyes caught sight of Thea's letters, and she made her decision. She would take control of her reality today. Reaching for the phone to make the proper arrangements, Kiernan was determined to make it work.

Three hours later Kiernan found herself flying across country toward her childhood home in California. Her mother had been a successful film actress. They moved to a beautiful estate in Santa Barbara where Kiernan spent countless hours exploring and dreaming. She used to visit her mother on the filming set, fascinated as she ran through her lines, stood on her marks, and became different people at the sound of "Action!" Her mother always encouraged Kiernan to express herself. Kiernan frowned. She never did find out how her mother died. Her father refused to tell her as did anyone close to the family. It was as if her mother never existed.

After Kiernan left home to live in New York, she promised herself not to pursue the truth. Every conversation devolved into arguments whenever she broached the subject with her father, and it hurt too much. The fights drew a wedge between them. As if that weren't enough, her father refused to allow her to act. She participated in the school theater without his knowledge, but it felt like a dirty secret. Her resentment grew to a boiling point once she graduated from high school, knowing she could no longer shield her activities, and she left home to make her own way as an actress without her father's consent. After all these years, he still remained in her childhood home, a home she missed every single day.

Kiernan hoped she could somehow get through to her father. So much had occurred in her life that she wished to share. She had allowed too much time to pass. And what excuse did she have? He tried to contact her over the years, but she stubbornly refused to respond. *I hope it's not too late.* Kiernan was prepared to do everything she could to make amends. If that meant groveling and apologizing, she'd do it. She just wanted Papa back.

When he opened the door, they stared at each other in shock. Kiernan was astounded at how old her father looked. She berated herself for such foolish thoughts. It had been twenty-five years, after all. Her childhood memories of a tall, muscular man with a full head of black hair, a strong jaw line, and bright blue eyes no longer matched the man in front of her. His thin body was stooped, hair gray and receding. Wrinkles crossed his forehead as if someone had raked sand, and his eyes were dulled by years of heartbreak.

Kiernan heard fractured thoughts. <*"My daughter...so beautiful...just like her mother...she's here."*> She took a deep breath at the pain and sorrow reverberating through each one. She stepped into the doorway and embraced him. Stunned, it took her father a few seconds to return the hug. He made up for the delay with a fierce embrace, holding her as if he never wanted to release her. Tears rushed to Kiernan's eyes.

"My only child, my only child," her father whispered.

Kiernan finally pulled back. "I'm sorry, Papa. Please forgive me."

Her father shushed her, clucking his tongue as he led her into the house. "No, no. It is I who must ask your forgiveness. How could I stand in your way? You are as great an actress as your momma, even better. You look so much like her." Taking a handkerchief from his pocket, he wiped his eyes and blew his nose, as he led her into the drawing room. "I have watched your progress. I should have come to you, made you listen to me. I have no excuse." His eyes sidled away in shame.

Kiernan took his wrinkled, sculptor hands in hers. "Let's agree to forgive each other and move on. We've wasted so much time. I want you to be a part of my life. Please, Papa."

Nodding, he smiled, if not a bit awkwardly, making Kiernan wonder when he had last expressed pleasure in such a simple way. *Well, I'll make sure he smiles more often.* Today would be the beginning of a new chapter, for both of them.

Several hours later found them in front of the fireplace, sipping sherry and viewing old family photographs. They talked about their lives and how they changed since she had struck out on her own. Kiernan saw for herself how similar her appearance was to her mother. Before today, she had only the memories of a six-year-old. She began to understand why her father was unable to cope with her mother's loss, particularly as Kiernan reminded him of it through her looks, vivaciousness, and artistic bent.

She learned that her father never sculpted after her mother's death, and sadness rushed through her at the discovery. Sculpting was her father's passion. Some of her fondest memories included watching him sculpt, creating beauty from a lump of clay, as if he were reaching in and pulling out a well-concealed treasure. Looking around, her eyes found the small bust of her mother. It shocked her when she realized it was like staring into a mirror.

"For the first time in so long, my fingers itch to sculpt again. I want to capture your beauty. You remind me so much of your momma." His eyes brimmed with tears again, and Kiernan nodded.

"I'd love that, Papa."

They sat by the fire in a silence full of memories and regrets, hope and forgiveness. Kiernan could hear her father's thoughts. It was always easiest with people she knew, perhaps because she didn't feel as disoriented while trying to make sense of that person's thoughts. Moreover, since she wasn't actively trying to block unwanted thoughts, they were clearer. She was tempted to say something, but she didn't want to invade his privacy any more than she was. Her hand toyed with the amulet she wore. She knew she was being selfish, listening to him as he processed their reunion, but Kiernan wanted to be closer to him. Listening to his thoughts helped her understand how destructive her absence was.

They shared a simple dinner her father insisted he prepare before returning to the living room, and Kiernan asked the question she knew her father dreaded. "How did Momma die?" Her words were so soft they hardly competed with the crackling of the fire, but Kiernan could tell by the tightening of her father's eyes and jaw that he heard.

Taking some steadying breaths, he replied, "She overdosed on some sleeping pills."

Kiernan failed to hold back her gasp. Nowhere had she read about her mother's death as being a suicide or accidental drug overdose. Her insides twisted, and she bowed her head, unable to watch her father fall apart while telling her. The pain rearranged his face into a patchwork of misery. She pressed her lips together, unwilling to interrupt now that he was finally telling her the truth.

"She experienced many insecurities. When she was passed over for a part she desperately wanted, she stole herself away from our family. For years I blamed myself. I thought that if I had loved her more, showed her how important she was to me and to you, she would not have ended her life."

"No, Papa, no." Kiernan took her frail father into her arms, holding him tightly, telling him through her embrace she didn't blame him. Kiernan grieved anew the senseless and premature ending of her mother. Sighing, Kiernan kissed his temple before pulling back. "It wasn't your fault. I'm so sorry."

Exhausted, Kiernan suggested they turn in for the night. They said their goodnights, hugging each other again. Both smiling now, "I love you" echoed off the walls.

Entering her childhood room, Kiernan wandered around after she changed into sleepwear. She had missed being here. A white desk was pushed under the window in the room. She could see the ocean, and she remembered spending countless hours staring at the deep blue water while dreaming of becoming an actress. *Well, here I am. I struggled all those years to become a star. Was it worth all the sacrifices? All the loneliness? Am I happy?*

Sighing, Kiernan opened the window to allow the ocean breeze in. Taking some deep breaths, Kiernan grinned. She might not have all the answers about how to sort through these feelings of uncertainty, but she knew coming here was a good first step. If there was one thing she learned over the last couple of months, it was that she needed to put the work in if she wanted to lead a more rewarding life. She had worked hard for her career, and she needed to work just as hard for lasting relationships. With that in mind, Kiernan climbed in her bed. *No more shortcuts. Time to take stock in my relationships and figure out what I want.*

The next morning Kiernan walked through the estate, reacquainting herself. Stepping out through the living room's French doors onto a side courtyard, she gazed at the ocean, listening to the roar of the waves. She missed this. Although she had fought hard to push aside her need for reconciliation, Kiernan was glad she took the chance instead of listening to her deep-seated fears.

She had a startling thought last night. Rudi reminded her quite a bit of her father. They both had refused to let her in. Well, she had broken through her father's barriers...or more likely, he had finally realized he could take them down. While Rudi was obviously not ready to trust anyone with her heart, Kiernan realized that she was. Taking steps to rectify her actions with her father was the first step. Next, she would concentrate on widening her circle, trusting others. *Had Patricia been able to break through Rudi's walls?* Kiernan feared not. Rudi didn't let anyone get close.

Too soon she had to leave. Surprisingly, Papa offered to fly back with her, admitting he would like to see her play. They were readying for the opening night, and although she warned him it was still a work in progress, it didn't matter. Wanting to strengthen their fragile bond, Kiernan agreed. Her home was certainly large enough to accommodate a guest, and she wanted to spend more time with him.

That night he sat in the front row, beaming as he applauded. Seeing him so proud, bursting with love, filled Kiernan with a feeling of warmth she hadn't experienced since she was a child. She was determined to hold that close to her heart. She introduced Papa to the cast after the run through, and she was grateful when they made him feel welcome. Seemingly overwhelmed, his composure slipped in front of the group. Before Kiernan could do anything to comfort her father, her cast mates gently teased him.

"No need to cry. She isn't that great an actress," Jack said while handing him a tissue.

"Hey," Kiernan yelped, embarrassed by the ribbing but thankful her father grinned. She wanted to point out that the only reason he was funny was due to the playwright, but she was grateful his cajoling made Papa smile. Jack played the president in *The President's Other Mistress*, and he served as their de facto ringleader. He was warm and genuine and, although she would never admit it aloud, funnier than he had any right to be.

"No, no. You've got it wrong," said Felicia, who played the mistress in the play. "Obviously, he's crying because he's overwhelmed by the rest of our brilliant performances."

"Obviously," several actors repeated before everyone chuckled. Much laughter permeated the room, everyone competing for the best reason as to why Papa had shed tears. Kiernan shook her head and joined in the fun.

\*\*\*

## KARINAN CYCLE 4 KATRINET 4

Darkness blanketed the compound, and Ubel peered at his luxfactorum, daring to set it to the lowest level so he could see. Crouching with his group, he whispered, "Remik is with me. Dugrin and Katri will enter here." Ubel pointed on his map before moving his finger to another area. "Tagi will enter here with Teug. Any questions?" Once he was sure they were ready, Ubel said, "Our primary mission is to retrieve the rock by attaching the captislacus to it. Whoever reaches it first will secure the six discs on it. Then, retreat and notify the other two teams. If you are discovered, you must not be caught." He stared at each team member, making sure they understood what went unsaid—no one could be taken alive. All team members squeezed their eyes shut before reopening them, indicating their readiness.

All were disguised as humans who worked at the military instillation. Ubel had obtained current employment records and based their identities on those who worked this shift, assuming their identities after incapacitating them. He would have preferred to kill them, but his instructions were to accomplish his objective while preventing undue attention. The transformation results were unattractive. At least they were able to transform into forms of those who were the most powerful within this society—males with light skin and chiseled facial features. He knew their best chance lay in acting as if they worked in the facility, and the history of this planet proved these human specimens to be superior. Even if they weren't in charge, they would be respected.

"On my mark," he said, observing a side door where two humans stood. He held his vibrometer, checking one more time that the meteorite was inside the far building. He took out the telepathy reader, scrolling through for any indication of who else might be inside. He couldn't find any specific thoughts. Maybe the night shift was composed of a skeleton crew.

"Go, go," he ordered, watching his team disburse. Donning his uniform hat, Ubel stood and glanced at Remik before stepping forward.

About halfway across the courtyard, a guard said in a loud voice, "What're you doing here, Stewart? You're scheduled for tomorrow night."

Ubel furrowed his brows and scratched the back of his neck, as they continued to move closer. He stopped about three clarks away. "I switched with Woods."

"Who? Do you mean Ward?"

"Yes. Ward." Ubel stood motionless, his mind racing. Two guards were in front of the door which housed the meteorite. If they were caught due to a small error with the person's name, all would be lost. His future depended on the success of this mission.

His fingers twitched, the compulsion to kill the guard becoming stronger with each breath.

"Don't tell me you switched schedules, too," he said to Remik.

"I shall do as you command."

Ubel bit back a groan. Human language was quite different from their own, particularly in this part of the planet. Remik speaking in a literal fashion was bound to get them discovered. "We do not want to be tardy." He walked toward the door, Remik behind him.

"Wait."

Ubel sighed, not turning. He could see inside the cavernous hangar through a small window in the door. Two guards stood at attention, and he was sure more were at the other end of the storage facility. Ubel turned. "Yes?" He was unhappy to note both guards holding primitive weapons aimed at them.

"We have to check with the squad leader before you can enter," the blue-eyed guard said.

Ubel nodded, standing at ease with his hands clasped behind him. He had a weapon hidden in his waistband, but he waited for the perfect moment. One guard held his weapon pointed toward the ground, while the other spoke into a black electronic clipped to his chest. When he saw his focus shift, Ubel lunged forward, knife in hand. With a flick of the wrist, the man expired. Ubel turned away so he wouldn't have to see the blood. Remik disposed of the other human with efficient speed. Ubel opened the door, and they entered without delay. Once they crossed the wide open floor, they turned to the right, where another door impeded their way. The two guards he had noticed before still stood at attention.

Ubel lunged forward as soon as he saw them leveling their weapons. Dispatching these two took longer. They were better trained. Remik received a glancing blow to his shoulder, and his ugly simulacrum undulated before reverting back to his true Katakititesta form. Ubel shuddered at the mess of bone, flesh, and blood before him. Remik tried to rise. He stumbled, placing a hand over the wound to staunch the blood flow. Rapid footfalls alerted Ubel to the next wave of humans, and he made the decision to stash Remik behind a large motorized vehicle before entering the next room.

"Stay here," he whispered.

He heard heavy footfalls, and five humans turned the corner at a sprint, weapons ready. Ahead of Ubel, Dugrin and Katri were engaged in combat. He hurried into the room, skirting the area where they were fighting, and he noticed a large window revealing a smaller room. That's where he needed to go. He searched for a way in and saw a white, digitized pad to the side. Before he could get closer, he heard a shout, and the five men ran toward him.

He had to retrieve the rock. It was that simple. He ran toward the closest human, throwing his blade at his throat. The sickening gurgle of death caused his stomach to lurch, and he swallowed several times before retrieving the fallen man's weapon. He turned toward the next human and pulled the trigger, but nothing happened. He twisted his hand to better view the mechanism, pulling back the hammer before aiming it and pressing the trigger again. This time it issued a projectile, and Ubel blinked at the remains of the human less than a clark away. It was grotesque.

A projectile whizzed close to Ubel's head, and he ducked, scrambling behind an upright records manager cabinet. He cocked the human weapon and leaned forward to see what was happening. Dugrin and Katri were down, and Tagi and Teug were waging hand-to-hand combat. Three humans stood in front of the digital pad, weapons ready. He aimed at the window and fired several rounds, but the bullets bounced off. His breath caught in his chest. He needed that meteorite.

Flinching when he heard Tagi cry out in pain, Ubel saw him and Teug on their knees, hands laced behind their heads, weapons raised against them. Ubel raised his weapon.

"Drop it," a female voice said behind him, and something poked him in the back. He scowled. Females could not be effective warriors. Before he could react, Remik dove into the room, stabbing one of the humans in the neck. Remik uttered a soft groan, then pitched forward, a wide hole in his chest. Dead. Jerking back, Ubel head-butted the woman behind him and rolled away, pulling an ignis canister from his belt and throwing it into the middle of the room. Arms around his head and body wedged under a metal table, Ubel felt more than saw the explosion. He popped up from his hiding place and glowered. Everyone was dead, including his entire strike team.

Yet the window obstructing him from the meteorite was still whole. Ubel ran to it, studying the digital pad beside it as he retrieved a digitizer to unscramble the code. Hearing noise, he looked back and saw another squad running toward him.

"Faex!" he cursed. He ran to each Katakitite, removing their information modules and name badges. Without pause, Ubel exited the room and ran toward their escape route. Dugrin and Katri had completed their duties, taking out the guards in that quadrant. Ubel pushed aside his heartache at losing his team and started the quick-jump portal. It would deliver him to his temporary abode.

Flerg would not be pleased with this setback. All he could do was make sure he was able to finish the rest of his assignment. Although not retrieving the meteorite would delay them for several cycles, they could still salvage the mission by finding the affected humans and retrieving them—and Ubel was determined to do so or die in the attempt.

\*\*\*

### THURSDAY, SEPTEMBER 14, 2017 11:24 A.M.

Patricia sat with Thea on a blanket, discussing her trip to Italy. "We participated in all the tourist activities, like taking the guided tours of San Marco's Square and the Basilica. It's incomparable to the United States. Our country is so young. When I walked around Italy, it was as if history was coming alive. We had a great tour guide who told us stories as if he'd experienced them firsthand.

"And the nights—they were the best. We picked different restaurants for dinner and then meandered down to the Piazza San Marco for coffee and chocolate. We'd listen to an orchestra play and reminisce about family events." Sadness stole over Patricia's features. "Dad made sure to spend time with each of us separately. With me, he told me how proud he was of the person I'd become." Patricia couldn't stop her voice from shaking with emotion. She could feel Thea's eyes on her as she bowed her head and sought to regain control of her feelings. "How did you do it? How did you deal with your mother's death?"

Thea shook her head. "Not well, I'm afraid. I struggled. I was angry with her for leaving me. I was upset we had ignored our problems because we didn't want to fight. I threw things around, I yelled, I sobbed, and eventually I got to a place where I could forgive. I forgave her, and more importantly, I forgave myself."

Patricia sniffed. "Yeah. That's how I feel. Angry and sad and powerless, and I'm afraid how I'll feel once he dies."

"Dealing with death doesn't happen overnight. For me, well, I fell into some old patterns, but I worked hard at picking myself up when I fell down those black holes, and I released those feelings again. And again. And again. Give yourself time, Patricia. Allow your emotions to surface, and process them as well as you can."

They sat on a blanket on a grassy knoll as Patricia mulled over their conversation. It comforted her to hear no one dealt with grief perfectly and her feelings were natural. She absorbed the sight of colorful dinghies, lobster buoys, and sailboats moored throughout the harbor flowing outward toward the horizon. To their left stood a functional, alabaster lighthouse. Marblehead Neck boasted a beautiful coastline with green grass, supple sand, and screaming seagulls. The waves struck the rocks, creating their own rhythm. The structures in Old Town crowded each other, allowing only a few feet to exist between neighboring homes. The coastal town oozed a distinctive charm full of hidden gems waiting to be found.

Patricia switched to an easier topic. "I think Peanut is a hilarious misnomer for this gentle giant." She grinned, stroking the back of Thea's dog, a black Great Dane, while the dog chewed a bone.

"She's a sweetie," Thea said, her eyes tracking a sailboat tacking across the water. "Have you ever been on a sailboat?"

"No. I always wanted to, but I never had the chance."

"I took a sailing class years ago, and now I rent one a few times every summer with friends. They offer classes here, but you may want to take one in Boston. I bet you'd enjoy it."

"Yeah. I'll have to check it out."

They sat in silence, enjoying the weather, the companionship, the feeling of not having any time constraints. Patricia's voice pulled Thea's attention back to her. "How did your meeting go with Jerry?"

Thea's brown eyes gleamed. "He took me on. I just signed the book contract, and we've started the editing process. Well, you know more about it than I do. I'm supposed to get the edited version back in a couple of months, and we'll take it from there. He believes they can get the book on the shelves by the end of the year."

Patricia's smile widened. "That's fantastic. Don't get disheartened when you get the edited version back. Much of it will probably have to do with formatting, not content. What type of format are you using?"

Thea blushed, looking away. Patricia became curious by her reaction, watching as she took a deep breath to calm herself before answering the innocuous question. "It's in a letter format. It was a good way to corral my thoughts into an orderly format."

"Did you send them to anyone?" Patricia asked, intrigued.

"Well, yes, but I never received a response. I doubt they were ever read," Thea answered. Her eyes flitted across the horizon, obviously discomforted.

"Who?"

"I'd rather not say. The person is rather well known. It's not that I don't trust you. I offered a platform of utter discretion and safety to that person. Even though the person didn't write back, I would be remiss if I broke my word."

Seeing Thea's sincerity conveyed through her eyes, Patricia dropped the subject.

"How are things with Rudi?" Thea asked.

"I broke up with her." Patricia pulled at blades of grass, her face shielded by her hair.

"I'm sorry to hear it didn't work out. Are you okay?"

"Yeah. It was hard, but it was the right thing to do." Patricia sighed.

"Why was it the right thing to do?"

Patricia shrugged. "It turned out she didn't want to share herself with me, or with anyone from what I've heard."

Thea frowned. "That's too bad. Does she have a reputation for keeping her distance from anything more meaningful than a casual relationship?"

"Kiernan hinted that she broke up with Rudi for similar reasons."

"That must have been an interesting conversation," Thea murmured. "Are you friends with her?"

"I think there's potential, particularly since Rudi and I decided to maintain a friendship."

"I remember when we discussed your expectations for Rudi. It can be hard to let those go. Like with the letters I wrote, I really wanted a response even though it was unreasonable. It took me a while to change my perspective. So, there's always room to grow."

"Well, that's certainly true in my case," Patricia joked, smiling at Thea when she looked up from the grass she'd been absentmindedly plucking.

The afternoon flew by as they explored the various antique shops until it was time for Patricia to leave. Although sad the day had ended, Patricia was confident that they'd share many more days just like this one.

*** 

## FRIDAY, SEPTEMBER 29, 2017 10:14 P.M.

As Kiernan sipped water backstage, waiting for her cue for her final bow of the night, an usher appeared at her elbow.

"Ms. Connelly, this is for you." The timid usher extended his hand.

She took the proffered flower and envelope with a smile and thanked him. Reacting to her name, Kiernan strode to her mark and took her turn to thank the patrons of that night's show. Tonight she felt as if she were on fire. Energy seemed to sizzle through her veins. Swinging her eyes across the theater, she took in the enthusiastic response. Feeling loved, she clapped her hands in delight, only to be reminded of the items in them. Glancing at the envelope, she saw the familiar writing and froze. She was holding a red calla lily, reminiscent of the first letter she received from the good professor, and what must be another letter.

*She's here!* Looking more carefully at the crowd, she felt a zap of anticipation and fear. Not knowing what Thea looked like, Kiernan stepped back to rejoin the rest of the cast, taking her final bow with them. Holding hands, they backed up as the curtain descended. Her last view was of a petite brunette with flashing eyes and a knowing smile. <"*I see you*,"> she heard clearly.

Ripping open the envelope as she paced to the privacy of her dressing room, Kiernan's eyes swept the page. The silence in her dressing room reverberated through her. *Will it be an invitation?* It looked like a goodbye letter. Kiernan began to panic as she read about the dangers of people worshipping celebrities.

*The problem with elevating people onto hero-worshipping pedestals is that they are viewed as the ultimate examples of how to succeed. When a boy living in a low-income, inner-city environment looks to his favorite basketball star as his hero, he follows the athlete's behavior as a step-by-step how-to-get-out-of-the-ghetto rulebook. If that athlete has a tendency to be hotheaded and explosive, so the boy will follow suit. Looking to others' successes, coveting them, is a recipe for disaster. After all, what do we have in the end? Castles built on clouds.*

*Does she really believe this?* Kiernan believed many people in the limelight exemplified strong work ethics and unflagging drives to succeed. *If people didn't fantasize, if they didn't build castles in the clouds, just imagine how many dreams wouldn't come to fruition.* It did bother Kiernan how admirers would draw connections between their lives and hers by relying on superficial, and often fabricated, facts about her. They believed they knew her, but they didn't.

*Realistically, these heroes do not know their admirers and cannot help them. They are living their lives as best they can— making and avoiding mistakes, all the while overexposed and dangerously vulnerable to influencing others. These people wield the power to affect their admirers. These are the people who are "loved," even though they are strangers to their admirers.*

Kiernan couldn't please everyone without losing herself. She was watched constantly, like an amoeba under a microscope. It was impossible for her to remember what she had said in every interview, yet each comment was tracked and compared. She wasn't left to grow, expand, or change her mind without having to defend herself. Yet, the reality remained that her fans kept her working, and she was thankful for the life she had.

*I thought I was smarter than these admirers, but it turns out I was worse than all of them. I placed you on a pedestal and tried to climb up next to you. I asked for your time, your thoughts, your friendship, but I don't deserve them. I'm sorry, Kiernan. I've seen the changes you've made, and I know you deserve all the adulation you attract.*

Kiernan released the breath she held while reading the last words of the letter and sank into a chair. She read it two more times, just to absorb it entirely. More than ever, Kiernan wanted to reach out to this woman. She wanted to remove the masks, lower the walls, and reveal herself. Kiernan felt grateful to Thea. In a way, Thea had become her hero. Kiernan laughed at the irony.

Kiernan wondered how she affected her fans. The responsibility of being a good role model was tough to bear at times. She cringed at how she had indulged in temper tantrums over the years in order to get what she wanted. *But, I've changed.* And she had. She found herself at a period in her life where she was surrounded by people she could trust. It seemed the more she allowed others to see who she truly was, the lovelier her life became. It made her feel more courageous, more willing to take chances. *Starting now.*

Kiernan rushed through her dressing room door to the front of the stage, only to see the crowd had left. Knowing it was hopeless, she peeked into the lobby, but no one was waiting. Of course, Thea wouldn't be there—she wasn't a fan. *Thea had extended her hand in friendship as would a peer, not a subordinate.* Not wanting to open the backstage door where many fans awaited her exit, Kiernan returned to her dressing room, knowing she had just let someone precious slip away without the least bit of resistance. She must be absolutely mad, waiting so long to connect with Thea. *Too long. And now it's too late.*

# Chapter Fourteen

*SATURDAY, SEPTEMBER 30, 2017 7:32 A.M.*

MARCIA WOKE UP DRENCHED in sweat. *These damn dreams!* She wouldn't be able to get back to sleep. Closing her eyes and pressing against the corners with her thumbs, she attempted to vanquish her wayward thoughts. She knew it would be foolish to ignore the possibility of happiness, even in light of her past romantic failures.

The touches, those were Lexie's hands. Marcia would never forget how the woman had felt. But that didn't mean she was her dream lover. Couldn't mean. It was more likely her subconscious had pieced together her sexual experiences, creating a composite of what she desired. Someone who yearned for her, loved her, satisfied her, and accepted her.

She wished these feverish creations were linked to someone reaching out to her. She wanted these imaginary unions to mean as much to her mysterious dream lover as they did to her. As exhilarating and terrifying as it was to consider Lexie as her dream lover, it was also dangerous. She refused to be susceptible to her charms tomorrow night when they met for dinner. Somehow, she was going to have to resist Lexie long enough to find out what she wanted. Marcia wasn't sure whether she wanted to solve the mystery of who her dream lover was. She didn't know if she was brave enough.

Four hours later, Marcia and Sammy walked down the main marble hallway of their local museum. Marcia glanced at Sammy before studying the museum map. It was close to lunchtime, and she knew Sammy would start fidgeting. Sammy had so much energy. Marcia wished she could bottle it up and drink it when lethargy overtook her, particularly in the late afternoon hours. Whenever she voiced such thoughts, Sammy laughed.

"Mom, look at this," Sammy said, as she grabbed her arm. Marcia turned to study the robust statue, appreciating its smooth planes and detailed lines. She glanced at the title, *La Frileause, Bronze* by Jean-Antoine Houdon, 1787. "Isn't she beautiful?" Marcia nodded.

Sammy had pointed out her favorite pieces all morning, and Marcia couldn't help but be pleasantly surprised by how broad her tastes ran. Earlier, Sammy had admired *Three Men Walking II* by Alberto Giacometti for the angular, elongated figures, the precision of their placement, and the resulting shadows they cast. She had also stared at Max Weber's *Athletic Contest* for several minutes, tilting her head this way and that, as she tried to make sense of the chaotic brilliance of the painting.

Marcia was more partial to Georgia O'Keeffe's *Black Iris* with its clear lines and sensuality and Gustave Courbet's *The Desperate Man,* which reflected what she felt, a personal crisis. Her favorite piece, though, was the statue *Sappho* by Comte Prosper d'Épinay. Her expression of fierceness, of being ravished or having just ravished another, that aimless gaze of introspection as she clutched at her breast, struck a chord within Marcia's soul. Lexie's face flashed before her eyes, and she sucked in a breath.

"Ready for lunch?" Marcia asked, directing herself to snap out of it.

"Yes! Can we go to Two Boots for pizza?" Sammy pleaded.

Pizza was their go-to meal, and Manhattan housed some of the best pizzerias in the nation. The meal was cheap, easy, and comforting. It was a great idea, so she nodded, grinning at Sammy's jubilant victory fist thrust. They walked east on 82nd several blocks before turning north on Second.

"Do you still want to go to the Guggenheim or are your feet sore? We can always go there next week," Marcia suggested.

"No. I'm fine. Let's go today."

Marcia looked over at her to make sure Sammy wasn't fibbing. She seemed sincere. She was walking with ease, bouncing down the street. "If you're sure. The exhibit is by Cai Guo-Qiang. It's called *I Want to Believe.* He uses gunpowder and explosives to create his art. It was here several years ago, and he came back with more pieces added." Marcia read a preview on the exhibit that was in the Sunday Arts section of the paper. "He's attempting to connect his art with ideas like transformation and instability. He works a lot with energy—positive and negative energy, energy waves, and energy transformation." She glanced over to see a puzzled expression on Sammy's face.

They entered the pizzeria and ordered before Marcia began to explain. "It's like Q from *Star Trek.* You know how they talk about time and space, how to manipulate it. He's trying to show that even with negative energy, represented with blowing things up, he can create positive energy, like the results which we'll see at the museum. He's trying to transform the chaos into something we can appreciate. Trying to make something good out of the bad."

"Like you dealing with the way you look now? It's no big deal now that I'm used to it. Or like how you work at home a lot more since Dad's death, except when you're on trial?" Sammy asked.

Marcia felt like Sammy punched her in the gut. They hadn't really talked too much about John's death. Marcia hadn't felt ready, and Sammy hadn't seemed inclined. Instead, for the first year Sammy often came into Marcia's room at night and slept cuddled into her side. Sometimes she cried, but she never talked about her feelings. Not once.

"I suppose. I want to spend as much time with you as I can, sweetheart."

Sammy shrugged. "I know. It's just that Daddy used to spend time with me after school, and you would come home for dinner or sometimes after that. But now you're always home for supper, and most of the time you're home before I get there. It's different. Good, though. I've liked it."

Marcia squeezed Sammy's arm. "Me, too. You know, we were doing the best we could with our schedules. I knew he was around for you when I wasn't. Once he died, I did make a point of getting home earlier. I'll continue to do that. So, yes, I can see what you mean about making something good out of the bad." She bit into her slice of veggie pizza, closing her eyes for a moment as the flavors hit her. She used to eat pepperoni or sausage, but with the changes in her body, she found herself craving vegetables more and meat less.

Sammy matured so much in the past year. She was about to begin seventh grade at a new school. Her athletic prowess paved the way since she met older students while playing on regional teams. Yet, entering a new school with so many older personalities could be intimidating, and Marcia worried for her. "I hope you know you can talk to me about Daddy or anything else on your mind. You don't have to deal with your emotions all by yourself."

"I know. Do you miss him?" Sammy's voice was so soft Marcia had to lean in to hear her.

Marcia searched Sammy's eyes, concerned. *Does she really think I don't?*

"I mean, you never cry, and you never talk about him." Sammy began to tear up.

Marcia felt her heart breaking. "Oh, honey. I do miss him. Terribly. More than I thought possible. If I think too much about it, I become sad. And I don't want to make you sad by seeing me like that. So I've pushed those thoughts away. Lately, though, I've been allowing myself to feel the loss and grieve." She squeezed Sammy's hand. "I'll always love your dad. He was a great man, a wonderful husband and father, and my best friend." Marcia paused to gauge how Sammy was receiving her words. She seemed a bit calmer. "You know, I was thinking that I'd like to make a memory box."

"What's a memory box?" Sammy asked, sniffing.

"It's a box we decorate. Inside it we place items that remind us of him. It can be pictures, clothing, books, letters, really anything we connect to him. And we'll place it somewhere special where either of us can open it whenever we want to. Do you want to help me?"

"Yeah. We can put the Civil War collection he loved in it and his Yankees cap. I have some pictures, too."

Tenderness stole over Marcia as she listened to Sammy list all the items she wanted to include. "We'll have to use a big box," Marcia said with a chuckle.

"Do you think you'll ever get married again?"

Blinking several times, Marcia tried to make sense of her question. Sammy stared at her, a serious expression on her face, while she twisted her fingers together and waited for a response. This was rather unusual for her. Although rather emotional, she was usually pretty upbeat.

"I don't know, honey. It's not something I've thought about." Marcia tilted her head. "How would you feel about that?"

"I'd want to meet him, get to know him. I mean, I know Dad would want you to be happy, and you're still kinda young. But, not to Peter, right? I mean, you're not going to marry him, are you?" She made a face.

A laugh bubbled up, and Marcia smirked. "Glad to know you don't think I'm too old." She reached across as if she was going to tickle her, and Sammy giggled. *She is such a sweet child.* "No, I'm not going to marry Peter. I know you don't like him. Is it him in particular?" At her silence, Marcia offered a small smile. "It's all right, honey. I won't get mad."

"I don't like him. There's something about him. He seems sleazy. I don't trust him."

"You know that I met Peter in college, years before I ever met Dad, right?" Marcia held Sammy's gaze with her eyes. Sammy nodded. Even though Marcia was beginning to question whether she had really been in love with him or merely infatuated, for all those years she had dedicated toward him, she had believed herself to be in love. "Well," she sighed, "I thought I was in love with him."

Sammy bit her lip. "You weren't?"

"I spent a long time believing I was in love, but he wasn't interested, and then I came back to New York and started practicing law. I met John. We started out as friends, you know. He was always so easy to be around." Marcia sighed. "I miss him."

"Me, too," Sammy whispered. She could see Sammy's eyes starting to tear up, and she squeezed Sammy's hand again. It would be easy to turn this into a conversation about John. Certainly it would be easier than explaining her feelings about Peter. But since Sammy mustered the nerve to ask what it was about Peter that had attracted her, Marcia felt she had to answer. Without bringing up the whole pseudo-Peter, pod person development into the conversation.

"Peter was the one who got away. No matter what I did, it never seemed to be good enough. I wasn't good enough."

"You're good enough," Sammy exclaimed. "He's stupid!"

Marcia smiled at her ferocity. "Thank you, honey. I know I'm good enough. How would you feel if I decided to date someone else?"

Marcia needed to know. She was going to meet Lexie for dinner that night while Sammy was sleeping over Rosie's house. She had no idea what would happen, but she had her hopes. *Why would she want to spend time with me unless she is finally ready to continue what we had started so long ago? Or, if she wanted to be friends, wouldn't she have suggested we meet for lunch instead of dinner?*

Not that Marcia was sure whether she wanted any type of relationship with Lexie. *She must know we will not be indulging in casual sex again. I have no interest in sleeping around.* Actually, she hadn't intended to have sex on "That Night," either, and her hopes of anything more had died. She was afraid to indulge in hope now.

"While you're dating Peter?"

"No, honey. I don't believe in dating more than one person at a time. Not that there's anything wrong with it, but I'd rather concentrate on one person." She watched Sammy chew the rest of her pizza slice for a few moments before looking up.

"I don't know. I'd have to meet him, I guess." Sammy looked away and made circles on the table. "Are you dumping Peter?"

*Yes, because he is an alien interested in my meteorite-driven changes.* Marcia sighed, knowing it was better to have Sammy think that she was dumping him rather than scare her with the truth of how some alien had assumed Peter's appearance to get close to her. "I wouldn't characterize it that way. The truth is he's not the same person I remember. He's changed." She released Sammy's hand and motioned toward herself. "And I've changed. I'm not the same person I was then. So, I'm not attracted to the same things that I used to be. Do you understand?"

"Yeah. You used to think he was cool, but now that you've been with Dad and you're a famous lawyer, he's boring and stupid."

"Samantha!" Marcia huffed. "That's not true. We both moved on with our lives, and we can't go back in time." Marcia imagined that would be true if the real Peter Dullard had shown up to see her.

Sammy blue eyes gazed at Marcia, as she tilted her head. "So you like someone else?"

This part of the conversation scared Marcia. She'd talked about same-sex relationships with Sammy before, but her reaction had the potential to hurt. Marcia gazed around the pizzeria, bracing herself. "You know the case I litigated for the last few months?"

Sammy nodded. She had taken to clipping the newspaper articles and placing them in an album that contained clippings from past cases. She began collecting them years ago.

Taking a deep breath, Marcia said, "I want to date the opposing counsel, Lexie." Marcia waited for what felt was a thousand years but was actually only a few seconds before Sammy reacted.

Wide-eyed, Sammy half-whispered, "You love a girl?"

Marcia firmed her lips to keep a nervous laugh from escaping. "You don't date girls. And she's the enemy!"

Now Marcia did chuckle. "She isn't the enemy. Just opposing counsel. I actually used to work with her at an old job of mine, and we left on bad terms. And you're right. I don't normally date women. Not that there is anything wrong with dating one. There isn't. As far as dating females go, I'm only interested in her."

"You really like her?"

"Yes, and I think you'll like her, too." Marcia got up and stretched, hands on her lower back. "This entire conversation may be overkill, of course. She may want to clear the air for the way we had left things all those years ago, and that's it. I may be creating all these crazy, romantic scenarios in my head while she just wants to be friends. Actually, she may not even want that."

"I bet she likes you. You'll stare at her with those eyes, and she'll go all gaga."

Marcia watched Sammy position her hands under her chin and flutter her eyes. Waves of yellow vibrated around Sammy, and Marcia grinned as she swooped down to tickle her, eliciting a series of lighthearted squeals.

"That's enough out of you. Let's get going so we have plenty of time at the museum."

"Okay, Mom." Sammy jumped up and threw out her empty plate before delivering a tight hug. "I love you."

Marcia hugged Sammy and replied, "I love you, too, sweetheart." *She took that much better than I anticipated. Perhaps I can begin to tell her about the other changes I've experienced.*

A half hour later Marcia watched Sammy study the exhibit pieces while wondering whether she was making a mistake by agreeing to have dinner with Lexie. It was the look on her face when she asked her that haunted Marcia. For one moment the smooth veneer cracked, and she saw something. It stirred her, touched her so strongly it scared her. And now her life was once again changing due to that insufferable, superior, arrogant woman. That beautiful, intelligent, unforgettable woman. Forcing air through her nose in frustration, she wondered how to deal with these emotions. They hounded her. She thought she'd excised those demons years ago, and then the trial came along.

*What a fool I've been. All I did was bury my feelings. Just like with Peter. Just like with John's death.* She was unwilling to ignore them any longer. Although tempted to call Patricia to relate her conversation with Sammy, she didn't want to tell her about the pending dinner. *Maybe tomorrow, once I know what Lexie wants, if anything.*

Once they returned home, Sammy went to her room to choose some belongings to use for the memory box. Marcia retired to her own room and approached John's old bureau. Opening it, she breathed in the faint aroma of vanilla, amber, and sandlewood from his cologne. She covered her mouth with shaking fingers. Lifting out a cable-knit sweater, she rubbed her face slowly against it, remembering the many times he wore it, particularly to ward off the morning chill. *I'll keep this one.* Laying it on the bed, she sorted through his belongings, often stopping as memories assailed her.

Sammy was right that her grieving process wasn't healthy. She had stuffed her grief deep down, swallowed her pain, and backed away from the many platitudes delivered by well-meaning individuals. When she cried, the grief would burst through her chest without warning, often triggered by something innocuous. Two years gone and still Marcia hadn't removed his clothes from the closet or bureau, hadn't thrown out his toothbrush or razor, hadn't stopped the service for his cell phone. Marcia hadn't done anything except avoid the truth. He was gone. Her conversation with Sammy made her realize that she needed to do better. She needed to move on.

***

### SATURDAY, SEPTEMBER 30, 2017 7:17 P.M.

"I've dreamt about you for years. I promised myself that if you agreed to have dinner with me I would be startlingly honest. How am I doing so far?" Lexie smirked in a self-deprecating way.

Marcia looked up, searching glittering eyes for any sign of deceit. "Astoundingly well." She winced at the sound of her voice. A bit breathless, a bit high. *Shut the front door. I need to get a grip here.*

"It's difficult to be open. I've spent most of my life attempting to protect myself. But with you," Lexie smiled slightly, "I handled things between us poorly. I've regretted it."

Marcia found it rather hard to believe Lexie regretted anything in her life. "Why didn't you contact me, then?"

"You were leaving to get away from me, and I felt I had nothing to offer you. Not then. You had stunned me, and I wasn't emotionally equipped to deal with those feelings."

"You are now?"

"I have no idea, but I'm willing to risk everything for an opportunity to find out."

Marcia's eyebrows rose. She didn't believe her and felt anger roll through her. "What are you playing at?" she asked in a low, shaking voice. *Is this some type of game for her?* She felt out of control, and she clenched her hands to focus on the bite of her nails.

"I assure you I'm not playing with you. Have I ever lied to you?"

"Well, no." Marcia struggled to keep a firm hold on her righteous indignation.

"I find it hard to believe you hadn't heard the rumors about me. As discreet as I was back then, I was aware of what people were saying. I made no promises to you," Lexie said, her face serious.

"I know that. I knew that. I was...it felt...I thought." Marcia sighed. "I was naïve and foolish. I had hoped after that night..." She shook her head. "Stupid."

Lexie covered one of her fists with her hand and leaned forward to catch Marcia's eyes. "Not stupid. Not even far-fetched. You weren't alone, Marcia. I felt the connection, too."

Marcia leaned back to break their connection, placing her hands on her lap while she stared at Lexie, confused. Frustrated. She saw ribbons of white and green blanketing Lexie's body, braided through with strings of bright red and pink. While strutting around the courtroom, Lexie often had emitted a dark red color. This morning when she looked in the mirror, Marcia saw her body radiate gold with flashes of purple, green, and pink. *I really need to do some research on auras.* It would give her another way to interpret people's feelings. She didn't know what to believe.

"Then why didn't you do something?" Marcia hissed, leaning forward and wrapping her hands around her wine glass. She looked around the restaurant, its modern, sleek lines and light colors creating an elegant ambiance. They were seated in front of a large window, and she glanced outside, saddened the days were getting shorter and the temperature cooler. Saddened the trial was over, and along with it any opportunities to admire Lexie without having to work through her feelings. She took a large sip of the expensive red wine Lexie ordered for them and waited for Lexie's answer. She knew they needed to have this conversation. She also knew that placing Lexie on the defensive by throwing accusations at her, no matter how warranted, might defeat the purpose of the dinner. So far Lexie was much more forthcoming than she anticipated. A hand covering hers startled Marcia out of her thoughts.

"You have every right to be upset with me. I should have done something. Even on your last day, I had the opportunity, but chose to remain silent. I thought you were better off without me."

"That was my choice to make, not yours. You should have given me a chance. You were a coward." Marcia withdrew her hand and took a large sip of her red wine. She wondered whether the bitter aftertaste sitting on her tongue was from the wine or her feelings.

"No more than you. Or did you think hiding in your little cubbyhole, head down and shoulders rounded like a beaten puppy was attractive?" Lexie threw back.

Mortified, Marcia ducked as if Lexie had just swung at her head. The perceived condemnation felt like fists pounding against her. She hated it, hated that Lexie still had that hold over her, that she affected her so much. She felt her composure slipping, tears burning her eyes. She bent over to grab her purse. *I can't take any more of this. It's too much.*

A hand grasped her bicep. Marcia saw Lexie kneeling before her. She looked panicked and radiated grayish-blue. "Marcia, please don't leave. I am realizing that my inaction gave you the idea that I despised you, or that I didn't like you. That is untrue and unacceptable. Nearly as unacceptable as being the cause of your tears."

Frozen with shock, Marcia's bag thumped on the ground. She tried to make sense of what was happening, but the hurt and the anger made it hard to think. *And why? For something that happened fourteen years ago? Get a grip!* Marcia wanted to spend time with Lexie, and yet here she was about to run away. Again. *Who's the coward?*

Lexie's grip tightened. "I'm sorry, Marcia. So many times I wanted to reach out to you, but it was better to stay away. You were rising quickly within your firm, you were married, had a child. I wanted you to be happy. It seemed you were."

Marcia stared at her. *She kept tabs on me?* "It didn't occur to you that we might be able to talk it out and become friends?" Unbelievable. Marcia shook her head. She needed another drink. "I won't leave. Get up." *It's like she's begging me.* Marcia couldn't help but wonder how such a proud, strong woman could act this way. *Maybe she's a pod person, too.* That thought shook her. She looked around for their server, nodding when she caught his eye. He hurried over. "I'll have another," Marcia said, indicating her glass. Lexie also ordered another drink.

"I could never be just your friend." Lexie swallowed much of her drink while Marcia remained silent. "I heard about your husband's death, and I am sorry. With the trial over, I won't be able to see you anymore unless you allow it." Lexie grasped Marcia's hand again. "Seeing you at functions a few times a year is simply not enough. I want you in my life."

"Why? What do you want?" Marcia could see she had taken her by surprise, but what did Lexie expect? *Surely she doesn't think I'm just going to fall into her arms after a few pretty words.*

"Your well-being is important to me. I know I have no right to insert myself back into your life, but I have never stopped caring. What do I want?" Lexie shrugged. "Whatever you're willing to give me."

Marcia looked at her, skepticism no doubt reflected on her face. She studied Lexie, trying to discern the real reason she barged into Marcia's life and turned it upside down once more. With all these changes, Marcia really didn't know whether she could deal with this. And yet, hadn't she wanted Lexie to admit she had been wrong? Didn't she want to spend time with her? Hadn't she told Sammy as much?

For the last two months Marcia watched this woman take control of the courtroom. She used her charisma and presence to persuade the judge, jury, even the media to trust her. Each day she found another reason to admire Lexie. It was clear that over the years, she had refined her techniques. No longer all raw power, she exuded a controlled intensity that compelled Marcia to watch her. And due to their history, Marcia was leery. This was dangerous. Lexie was dangerous. She was unsure whether she was ready to face her feelings. Much like her process of grieving for John's death, Marcia had stuffed those feelings for Lexie far down in her psyche.

And then there were the countless dreams she'd had over the years. Her mysterious dream lover who felt like Lexie. She couldn't see the face, couldn't hear the voice, but she felt the energy, the essence of the person, and she recognized it—recognized Lexie.

"What did you think would happen?" Marcia sneered, disgusted with herself.

Once more Marcia's self-control began to slip, and this made her angrier. Over the years she became so good at controlling her emotions. Yet, an hour alone with Lexie, and she was reduced to an out-of-control ball of angst. Lexie had a way of piercing through her defenses, and Marcia wasn't confident she could withstand being hurt by her again.

"I won't betray your feelings again." Lexie gazed at Marcia. "There's something between us. I know it, and you know it. I may have acted the fool, but I know you aren't one. Let me in."

"And what am I supposed to do when you decide you're done with me? How am I supposed to—" Marcia stopped herself with a choked off curse and took a deep breath. Several deep breaths. "I have my daughter to consider. There are so many changes right now, even within me. You may get more than you bargained for by spending time with me. It may be more prudent for you to stay away."

"I've been curious about that. Will you tell me what's happened?"

"Not tonight, but if I do, it will be hard to believe."

"I'll consider myself warned," Lexie said drily. "I'm done with being prudent, though. I can understand if you want to take this slowly, but my mind is made up. If you feel anything, anything at all for me, then spend some time with me. I'm not above begging, not when it comes to you."

Conflicted, feelings of anger and undeniable hunger made Marcia hesitate. She wanted to break her, to make her understand that nothing was simple. She wanted to reject her and leave with her head held high. It took years for her to stop looking for Lexie at the courthouse, on the street, even at her own firm. For years she suffered through whiffs of her unique scent tickling her senses at the most inopportune times. Years of harboring feelings of loss while hiding her sadness.

Over the last two years in particular, she shelved the yearning by dealing with the more immediate concerns, which came with John's death, caring for Sammy, and hiding in her work. Now, though, Lexie was pleading with her to let her in. What excuse did she have to refuse other than fear? And anger. *How dare she waltz back into my life and ask this of me!*

She had a sneaking suspicion her only chance at happiness lay in securing Lexie's presence within her life. Her heart wouldn't allow her to enter any type of closeness with blinders on, though. If Lexie walked away from her again, she didn't know whether she could survive another rejection. *Is Lexie worth all this effort? All this risk?* Marcia recognized in Lexie her hope, her sincerity, her desire.

Rising, Marcia whispered, "I'm sorry. I don't think I would survive another heartbreak." As she turned away, she felt pain sear through her being. Caught by surprise, Marcia stopped mid-stride, clutching her chest. She took several deep breaths, but the pain intensified. She felt it radiating through her chest, arms, and legs. Tears leaked out, creating trails of fire down her face. She stumbled back to the table, grabbing the edge to steady herself.

She turned to stare at Lexie, who had tears in her eyes. *Tears! This woman is crying because of me.* Lexie's face contorted, her agony plain. She did nothing to stem the flow of tears, and her body shuddered with soundless sobs.

She never could have imagined that Lexie's feelings were so strong. It made Marcia question her decision to walk away. Her reasoning stemmed from her fear of being hurt. She had convinced herself that she felt so much more than Lexie. Now she knew that wasn't true. Marcia acknowledged that truly cutting Lexie out of her thoughts and out of her life was no longer an option. It was simply too painful. For both of them.

Kneeling before her and wiping away the tears, Marcia said, "I feel you. This pain, that's you, isn't it?" Marcia saw the pain and confusion painted in waves of gray, green, and red wrapping around the area of Lexie's heart. The anguish was so incapacitating Marcia could hardly see straight. She held Lexie, who squeezed her tight.

"Please, please, Marcia. I'll do anything. Don't walk away," Lexie whispered.

Swallowing back her tears, Marcia wrestled with the chaotic emotions still echoing through her, feelings that, although not hers, certainly resonated. She had felt these feelings, the gaping hole, before.

"All right. We'll try it. But, Lexie, for both of our sakes, let's go slow. I wasn't kidding. You really hurt me. In some ways, I don't think I've ever recovered." Marcia swallowed, her nerves tense. "How about lunch next week?"

Lexie's laugh caught Marcia off-guard as Lexie pulled her into another hug, her body shaking. Marcia wondered whether it was from laughter or tears. Maybe both.

"Lunch sounds marvelous," Lexie whispered. They remained that way for long minutes, each taking solace in the closeness as their breathing slowed down and tears dried.

After returning to her seat, Marcia took another sip of her wine. Lexie really had upset her equilibrium. She sighed. Even after all this time, Marcia wanted to prove she was worthy. *I haven't quite convinced myself, unfortunately*. Why did Lexie want this chance? Was she consumed with the idea of the one who got away? *What if she realizes after we spend time together her romanticized version of me doesn't live up to reality? John did most of the work when we were married. I might not even know how to be happy. Not really.*

Once more Lexie's warm hand covered Marcia's, squeezing it to gain her attention. "Stop worrying. We'll figure things out."

Releasing a shuddering breath, Marcia turned her hand over, tangling their fingers. Marcia nodded. She saw relief shining through Lexie's eyes. And so much more. Promises Marcia needed but wasn't ready to hear. *Great. I'm a love-sick idiot. My doom is sealed.*

They spent the next hour catching up on the important parts of their lives, although Marcia didn't divulge any information about the meteorite or the resulting effects that experience caused. Although she didn't feel in danger, she was still wary. She supposed if Lexie was an imposter, she would try to kiss her, just like pseudo-Peter did. If that happened, Marcia was confident she would receive similar visions to reveal her true identity. Marcia's heartbeat quickened at the thought of kissing Lexie.

"I have missed you."

The whispered words thrummed through Marcia. She could do nothing but nod. Rubbing the back of Lexie's hand with her thumb, she allowed hope to well within her. She couldn't remember the last time she felt so content holding someone's hand.

"Do you believe in fate?"

Marcia tilted her head. "Not until today." It was Lexie's turn to nod. After several more minutes spent in companionable silence, Marcia sighed. She was exhausted. She squeezed Lexie's hand before letting go. "Next Wednesday work for you?"

"Yes. I'll call you to make arrangements," Lexie replied, as she signaled the server for the check. "Let me pay," she said when Marcia started to pull a credit card from her wallet.

"Thank you." Marcia smiled, appreciating the gesture. "I'll pay next time." She could see Lexie's reluctance to agree, which made Marcia smile wider. Once out of the restaurant, she turned and surprised Lexie by pulling her in for a tight hug. "Thank you, Lexie." She kissed Lexie's cheek, pulling back to gauge her reaction.

"I should be the one thanking you," Lexie said, sounding breathless.

"Don't worry." Marcia winked. "You'll have other opportunities."

"For the record, I intend to woo you, Marcia Struthers, the way you deserve. I won't let you walk away this time."

"I look forward to it," Marcia said, a frisson of excitement rushing through her. She delivered one more smile and walked away, knowing Lexie watched her go. It felt good.

# Chapter Fifteen

WHEN PATRICIA AND MARCIA first began experimenting with her ability to transport, Marcia was exhilarated and terrified. It didn't help that she couldn't seem to control when she would astral plane. *Or is it astral project?* She couldn't find much research on it. Usually she appeared as a fuzzy head with flaming eyes.

Late at night when Marcia was exhausted, she wasn't always able to control her wandering thoughts. After scaring Patricia and Rudi, Marcia attempted to focus her thoughts more before falling asleep so she wouldn't make any other unintended visits. Often she was successful and would visit Patricia, watching her sleep for a moment before walking through her home. Once Marcia returned home, she made sure to write down her observations. Patricia began leaving certain items, such as the first page of her newest chapter or a piece of mail, out for Marcia to notice. The next day they would compare notes. As Marcia's visits became more frequent, she became better with remembering what she saw.

The trips were illuminating. She visited Kiernan, Peter (the real one), Lexie, and family members. It was a relief each time she found the person she visited was sleeping. She felt like an intruder. Most visits occurred in the wee hours of the morning. Of course, the last thing she wanted to do was scare anyone.

Marcia and Patricia set up a schedule for when Marcia would attempt to visit. On those nights, Marcia would focus on her friend's face while lying down in bed, and eventually she was able to pop into Patricia's home. During the first few attempts, Marcia's body remained insubstantial, and she was unable to move. Instead, she hovered above Patricia, able to see but not able to communicate. As she visited Patricia more often, she found she was able to control her body better, finally able to stand in front of Patricia. Using her internal user manual, Marcia learned how to pull her body with her by shifting her focus from finding Patricia to materializing in front of her. Last week, Patricia stayed awake, and she relayed how she could still see through Marcia, like one would a ghost, but her body seemed more substantial. Lately, Marcia had experimented with remaining awake while astral projecting. She found that it was much like meditating, using her imagination and senses to execute her wishes.

The first time she left her body, Marcia had remained in her bedroom and saw herself in bed. It had surprised her so much that she was pulled back to her body with a jolt. Since then she accomplished that feat several times and became more comfortable with seeing herself on the bed.

Tonight Marcia was determined to appear in solid form at Patricia's home. She wanted to be able to engage all her senses. She wanted to hear Patricia's voice and touch the desk. She wanted to be present to the same extent as she was while sitting on her own bed. It was all a state of mind. By tapping in to the surrounding energy and following the strand that connected her to Patricia, she would be able to teleport. No hesitation, no doubt. *Just focus on Patricia—what she feels like, and how her energy resonates.*

Lying back, Marcia took some deep breaths and visualized her friend's face. She didn't allow her mind to wander, and after a few minutes she felt an unsettling pulling sensation, like tiny pinpricks racing over her body. She remained still, afraid that if she moved, she would break the meditation and have to start over. Her body trembled enough that the mattress shifted beneath her, but Marcia kept her focus on Patricia. Her body felt lighter, and a moment later, Marcia stood in front of her friend. Marcia concentrated on feeling each part of her body solidifying. This time felt different than her past attempts. She could hear the radio playing in the background. Feel the hardwood floor beneath her feet. She turned her head toward the fireplace, smelling the firewood as it burned. She was as fully formed and lucid as if she had walked through Patricia's door.

Marcia sat on the couch next to Patricia and stared at her. She reached out and touched Patricia's arm, laughing when her friend flinched.

"You did it!" Patricia shouted, pulling Marcia into a hug. "This is incredible, Marcia. Do you think your body is still on your bed? Or are you all here? Are you split in half? We're going to have to pull someone else into this to see what happens to you at the other end."

"I'm not sure who I could have checking on me. I haven't told Sammy about this ability because she is dealing with my new appearance and now..." Marcia hesitated, contemplating Patricia's suggestion.

"Well, you could have Lexie watch you or," she said in a teasing voice, "your dream lover."

Marcia stared at Patricia, wondering whether she should reveal what she had so recently realized. Patricia's eyes widened. "You know who it is, don't you? You have to tell me!"

Waggling her eyebrows, Marcia drawled, "I have to? Really?"

"Come on. If you know who your dream lover is, that means I do, too. Right?"

"I didn't realize who it was until a short while ago. I don't think I wanted to know." Marcia pressed her lips together, shrugging. "It's Lexie. After the trial ended I agreed to dinner with her. We cleared the air. And..." Marcia stopped. She felt Patricia shifting on the couch.

"And? Come on, Marcia. You can't stop there." Patricia huffed.

"After many tears, we agreed to spend some time together." Marcia smiled. "We've shared lunch several times, and I'm planning on inviting her to meet Sammy soon."

"Oh my God! That's amazing. You give hope to all the hopeless romantics out there."

"Like you?" Marcia laughed. "I doubt it. I'm happy. Terrified but happy. I've never gotten over her. It astounds me that she feels the same. I'm afraid to trust her, but I simply can't walk away from this chance." Marcia shook her head. "I'm so attracted to her that I have to fill my mind with other thoughts before I go to bed. I don't know what I'd do if I popped into her bedroom one night."

Patricia snickered.

"Well." Marcia slapped her lap with her hands and stood up. "I need to get back. I wonder how this will work." A wave of exhaustion hit her. She blinked several times and grabbed the sofa arm.

"Are you okay?"

"Tired. Maybe I should lie down instead of trying to stand while I do this." Marcia stretched out on the sofa and looked at Patricia. "Thank you for everything. I don't know what I'd do without you. But more than that, you're one of the only people I trust." Marcia had trouble keeping her eyes open. Her last thoughts were of Sammy and home.

"Marcia. Marcia, wake up."

Groggy, Marcia found it difficult to concentrate on the voice calling her away from her dreams. She felt lethargic. Heavy. She struggled to open her eyes and stared in confusion at Patricia. "What happened?"

"You fell asleep. I thought you'd want to try to get back home while Sammy's still asleep. It's six o'clock."

Marcia pulled herself into a sitting position while wiping her eyes. "Thanks. I was so wiped out last night." She stretched, feeling energy surge through her body. She felt good. "Okay. Let me try this." Marcia lay back down and concentrated on Sammy. Sammy. Sammy. Sammy.

Feeling her body pulling her forward, Marcia remained focused on her daughter. Her body vibrated. A rushing noise filled her ears. Opening her eyes, she saw Sammy in bed, blankets tangled around her feet. Spreading out her awareness, Marcia felt her body tingle. She imagined a wave of energy flowing from head to toe, filling every molecule. She imagined air filling her lungs and abdomen. When she heard Sammy's steady breathing, Marcia turned her head and smiled. *I made it.* Returning to her bedroom, Marcia reached out and felt the bedspread. Her eye widened, surprised her hand didn't sink through the material. She climbed in bed, cell phone in hand.

"I'm here," Marcia said as soon as Patricia connected to the call.

"I saw you disappear. It was really interesting—" Patricia began.

"Can I get the details later? I'm really tired again. I just want to sleep for an hour before I have to get up with Sammy."

"Oh, yeah. Of course. Call me tonight."

"Thanks. I will. Have a good day. Bye." Marcia smiled just before sleep reclaimed her.

*** 

**MONDAY, OCTOBER 9, 2017 10:57 A.M.**

Kiernan sat in the auditorium, watching Thea teach. Mesmerized, she listened to one of the many lessons Thea wrote about in the letters to her during the summer. Her mellifluous voice soothed Kiernan's nerves. She was glad she took the chance of coming to the lecture.

"I love mulling over the feeling of a word like a fine wine. Rolling it around in my mouth and mind to feel it vibrate with its essence. When we invoke a word, the significance attached to it depends upon its delivery. Intention is paramount. I can crush or embrace with them. We use words in such a cavalier fashion. Yet, it is one of our best tools for connecting with others. How can I have such power? Why do I allow others to possess such power?"

Kiernan listened to people contribute to the lesson, and she saw firsthand why Patricia loved taking the class so much. Why Kiernan found herself attending the guest speaker series on a Friday morning. Columbia University held them each year, and professors from across the country visited for a week to teach their specialties. Submitting Thea's name for consideration was easy enough since Kiernan was slated to teach some acting classes at the university next semester.

After the class ended, Thea took time to answer questions without making anyone wait too long. Kiernan was surprised to see Patricia waiting patiently for Thea to finish, although in retrospect, she shouldn't have been.

*Maybe I shouldn't intrude.* Just as quickly as Kiernan thought the words, she dismissed them. Instead, she remained in her seat, watching and listening. It took her a moment to realize she could listen to their conversation even though they were at the front of the room. *When did this start?*

"I didn't realize you were in town," Thea said to Patricia. "Are you going to see Rudi?"

"I'm going to the after-play party tomorrow night. Why don't we do some touristy things together tomorrow? You can come to the party, too, and I'll introduce you. My friend, Marcia, will be coming. I'd like you to meet her."

"That sounds great. If you're free tonight, let me know." Thea smiled.

"I'm going to spend tonight with Marcia, but have fun." She leaned in and reached down to squeeze Thea's hand for a moment before letting go. "See you tomorrow."

Kiernan's heart jumped when her gaze connected with Thea's mesmerizing eyes a moment later.

<*"Oh, my God, she's here. What do I do?"*>

Kiernan's lips lifted when she heard Thea's thoughts, feeling much more confident. She rose from her seat and made her way to the front. Kiernan could hear Thea's thoughts racing, disjointed words that revealed her excitement and fear. That simply wouldn't do.

Once in front of Thea, Kiernan pulled the woman into a tight hug and whispered, "This is long overdue." She felt Thea's body melt into hers and stifled a moan. They felt wonderful together.

<*"Holy shit! She's hugging me. Don't think about her curves. Hug her back before she lets go."*>

The running commentary Kiernan heard amused her. She felt Thea's arms wrap around her waist, and Kiernan tightened her hold. She was so tempted to turn her head and kiss Thea's neck, but she refused to take such liberties without explicit consent.

Pulling back just enough to catch Thea's eyes, Kiernan grinned. "Would you like to have dinner with me tonight?"

Thea's forceful yes made Kiernan blink in surprise. Only hearing a stream of propositions helped her to realize Thea hadn't uttered a word. Kiernan raised an eyebrow, prompting Thea to answer out loud. Although certainly illuminating to listen in on Thea's internal monologue of how she wanted Kiernan as her main course, Thea would be mortified if she knew Kiernan could hear all her prurient thoughts.

They arranged to meet at the restaurant located in Thea's hotel that night. Kiernan gave in to the urge to kiss Thea on the cheek before they parted ways. The burst of desire-driven thoughts she heard as she pulled away promised her a new beginning, if she chose to embrace it.

\*\*\*

Kiernan made her way into the busy Japanese restaurant, weaving through the tables and dodging countless shopping bags half-tucked under them to reach the back. "Darling," Kiernan greeted Rudi, leaning in to kiss her cheek before sitting down. She watched people strolling past, most wearing sweaters or light jackets to combat the autumnal breeze and wondered whether Thea was among them.

"You look ravishing today. Is that for me?" Rudi asked with a smirk.

Chuckling, Kiernan answered, "No. I went to a lecture before coming here, but I'm glad you approve."

"Oh? That's surprising," Rudi commented after their server took their orders.

"Thea Corelli was the guest speaker. Remember Patricia took a summer course? It's her instructor."

"Small world. Why did you go? It's not like you took the class."

Kiernan unrolled her napkin and placed it on her lap before glancing up into curious eyes. "She was my letter writer."

"She wrote you letters?"

"Yes, a series of letters about the subjects she taught in class. I told you about them. The letters interested me enough that I wanted to meet her."

"Oh. Well, good."

Rudi looked perplexed, but Kiernan let it pass. They hadn't shared a meal together in quite some time, and she wanted to enjoy it. "How's the play going?"

"Wonderful. I'm killing it. It's extended to May at the least. Oh, Kiernan."

"What?" Kiernan asked, surprised by the change in tone of Rudi's voice. She sounded contrite.

"I forgot your play folded yesterday. I remember the last time that happened. Don't worry." Rudi leaned forward and patted Kiernan's hand. "You'll find something else."

"I'm not worried at all. It's perfect timing. I want to spend more time with my father, and beginning in January I'll be teaching some acting classes."

"You don't have to hide your feelings. If it were me, I'd be crushed."

"You never change, do you?" Kiernan shook her head, equal parts amused and saddened.

"Wha...I've changed. And I've missed you." Rudi grabbed Kiernan's hand. "Give me another chance. I've grown."

The server came with their food, and Kiernan took the opportunity to take her hand back. She studied her plate, gathering her thoughts. Although she didn't want to hurt Rudi, she also didn't want Rudi to keep trying to be more than friends with her. "Rudi, we aren't going to have sex anymore. Our foundation was made of loose sand, and it kept shifting and spreading until it scattered too far."

"Why can't we start again? We get each other."

"No, darling, we don't. Not really. Our friendship is easy and comfortable, and I want to keep it intact. Trying again will surely rip apart what we have now."

"You sound like Patricia," Rudi replied.

"Perhaps if more than one person has given you the same message, you should listen to it." Kiernan smiled affectionately. "I'm glad to talk to you about Patricia or whoever else might be important to you. I'd also love to hear about your background and family, whenever you're ready."

Rudi's gray eyes were dark, her forehead furrowed. "I'll think about it. Truthfully, what we had was fun and easy. Patricia, she was different—vivacious and passionate. I thought she was asking for too much, but maybe at some point I'll be able to give her more. As it is, I'm friend-zoned by you and her."

Kiernan smirked. "You'll work it out when you're ready, and I'll always be your friend."

"All right then, what's the deal with this instructor? Will you be seeing her again?" Rudi's eyes danced.

"Yes, I'm meeting her for dinner tonight."

"Really?" Rudi said, adding a suggestive inflection to her voice.

Kiernan shook her head. "Just because you took your author to bed doesn't mean I'll do the same with my letter writer."

"Why not? She wrote to you for months. Doesn't that tell you something?"

"It tells me she has a fascinating mind. I expect nothing, but I hope for everything."

Rudi sat back in her chair, staring at Kiernan with a contemplative expression. "Everything? I thought you'd never met her before."

"I haven't, but I know her to some extent through her writing. I have a feeling she wants to share things with me, and I want to tell her about my life, too."

"This sounds serious."

"Yes, and presumptuous." Kiernan rubbed her hands together. "I'm actually a bit nervous."

"Just be yourself. She'll love you."

"I'll know soon enough. I believe you'll get to meet her tomorrow night. I overheard Patricia making plans with her for the after-play party."

"Huh. Well, if she's intriguing enough for Patricia and you, I'd like to meet her." Kiernan shot her a warning look, and Rudi raised her hands in surrender. "Don't worry. I'll be on my best behavior. I would never do anything to jeopardize a budding romance for one of my dearest friends." <*"Besides, I have my hands full trying to persuade Patricia to take me back."*>

"Tell me about your latest interactions with your adoring fans," Kiernan said.

"That I can do," Rudi said, grinning as she launched into a tale regarding a mother and two daughters who bickered about which person would get to stand on either side of Rudi during a group picture.

Sitting back to enjoy the story, Kiernan allowed herself to forget about the possibilities tonight's dinner presented. Sometimes slipping into a ripped pair of jeans was easier than wrestling into a stiff new pair.

\*\*\*

### MONDAY, OCTOBER 9, 2017 6:58 P.M.

Kiernan was nervous, and it was absolutely ridiculous. She felt like she did on her first audition. She took a deep breath and wrung out her hands, stretching her neck to release some of the tension. She was meeting Thea in twenty minutes at her hotel restaurant. It wasn't as if she had any reason to feel like this. They were merely meeting for dinner, taking the opportunity to talk to each other.

It was the fear of acting like herself and somehow falling short of Thea's expectations that made Kiernan so uncertain. She was afraid she wasn't good enough and would be rejected. That this would be their first and only meeting. She wanted to prove she was worthy of those letters. The future was murky and frightening and exciting. She needed to talk herself down, remind herself that she was meeting a person interested in getting to know her. She was worthy. She was interesting. She was ready.

Kiernan applied some lipstick and gathered her purse and coat. She made her way to the hotel in record time, ducking into the restroom to check her hair and makeup. *You look sexy and personable and elegant.* She stared into her eyes through the mirror, giving herself a pep talk and willing herself to believe. She saw flashes of gold light up her eyes and glanced at the chandelier above her head. *Odd.* She adjusted her meteorite medallion and studied her visage. Her dark blue eyes stared back, matching her dark blue dress. *No gold. Okay.*

With a nod, Kiernan left the bathroom. She sashayed toward the elevators, stepping up to the area as Thea exited into the lobby. Her heart skipped a beat when their eyes connected. She wanted nothing more than to stare into them and pick out all the colors peeking out. She watched the slow smile that inched its way over Thea's beautiful face, lighting it up from within, and felt her own smile broaden as they walked toward each other. She sank into the hug a moment later, wrapping her arms around Thea's waist.

"I could get used to this," Kiernan whispered.

"Me, too." Thea held on another moment before pulling back. "I'm glad you're here."

"Shall we?" Kiernan swung a hand out in the direction of the restaurant, keeping her other hand around Thea's waist. They stepped forward together, and soon they were seated.

After ordering their meals, Thea sat back. "It really is great to see you. How are you?"

"I'm in a much better place than when I first began receiving your letters." Kiernan leaned forward and covered Thea's hand. "You may not believe this, but you changed my life. Those letters guided me, helped me to make sense of my life and what I wanted to do. You've affected me in every way. I changed my relationships, career, perspective. You did that. I want to thank you for reaching out to me. I have no idea why you did it, and maybe you'll tell me why today, but I will always be grateful."

Kiernan gazed at Thea's stunned expression and smirked. She supposed Thea didn't expect her to be so forthcoming, and why would she? Up until today, Kiernan had never indicated any interest in speaking to her. Thea turned her hand over so that their palms met, and her fingers lightly stroked the inside of Kiernan's wrist.

"Kiernan," she said in a low voice. "I did nothing more than share my thoughts. You made the changes, and I know how hard that can be. Are you happier?"

"Oh, yes. I love what I'm doing. Next semester I'll be teaching some acting courses, something I've wanted to do for years but never felt confident enough to try."

"That's wonderful. I'm so happy for you."

"More than that, I was able to make some changes in my personal life. I was feeling pretty stuck, but I realized that only I could make my life better, attract better people into it. So, I broke up with my paramour and reached out to my father."

Their salads arrived, and they ate in companionable silence. Kiernan allowed herself to listen to Thea's steady stream of thoughts. <*"Is it weird that I'm so proud of her? She's working so hard on herself, and it shows. Her eyes seem different. Is it the lighting? They seem golden. She's dazzling."*>

"I've heard a bit about your former paramour. I should tell you upfront that I'm friends with Patricia," Thea said once she finished her salad and the main course was served. <*"God, I hope she doesn't become upset. This is going so well. She's holding my hand again. When did that happen? Oh, my God, she's holding my hand!"*>

Kiernan circled a thumb across Thea's hand to gain her attention. "I know. I've known for a while. I like Patricia, and through the limited number of conversations we shared, I was able to piece together your connection with her. I've told Rudi to bring her around to the theater parties. I think Patricia is good for Rudi."

"And are you okay with the change in your relationship with Rudi?" Thea asked, withdrawing her hand and reaching for her glass of white wine. "Do you think you and Rudi…"

Kiernan studied her, listening to the words Thea wasn't saying out loud. <*"Will you reconcile? My feelings are ridiculous. You're a star, and I'm just a professor. God, I'm such a fool."*>

"No. Rudi and I are friends now. We were together for a long time, but it wasn't what I wanted in a significant other. I want more."

Thea took a sip of her wine. "I understand. Compatibility between a couple and feeling comfortable around each other are important in a relationship, but so are an interest in your partner and growth in the relationship."

"You sound like you're speaking from experience," Kiernan said, an eyebrow raised.

"Yes. Several months ago my relationship ended with a wonderful woman. We were traveling different paths, and neither of us wanted to hold the other back." Thea leaned forward. "It showed me I wasn't in love with her anymore. We're two old friends now."

"Well, you deserve to be with someone who will grow with you. You're astonishing."

Thea flushed, and she shook her head. "Hardly. I have clay feet, I assure you. I'm searching, growing, stretching. I'm as insecure and afraid as the next person. I just try not to let that stop me from walking through the door to the next adventure."

"That sounds promising," Kiernan said, her voice taking on a rich, seductive register. Her lips quirked, as she noticed how Thea's eyes dilated. Kiernan waved for the server to bring the bill. When Thea began to search through her purse, Kiernan leaned forward. "Please let me pay since I invited you to dinner."

"Thank you," Thea said. <"*Will I ever see you again? Do you want to spend more time with me?*">

Kiernan asked, "How long are you in town?"

Thea grinned. "Another two days. Patricia and I are going to do a bunch of touristy things tomorrow. I don't suppose you'd like to join us?"

"I wouldn't want to impose."

"I think her friend may be joining us, and I'd like to spend more time with you. She also mentioned attending Rudi's after-play party tomorrow night."

Thea gasped when Kiernan leaned forward and took her chin between thumb and forefinger. Their eyes locked. "I want to spend more time with you, as much as you'll allow, in any capacity you desire."

"I want that, too," Thea answered, swallowing when Kiernan rubbed Thea's bottom lip with her thumb.

Kiernan watched with satisfaction as Thea blinked several times, fighting not to close her eyes. Kiernan's eyes were glued to parted ruby-red lips, and it took all her willpower to raise her gaze to sparkling eyes instead of leaning forward.

"Good. We can work out what that means as we spend more time together. I'm looking forward to getting to know you."

<*"Damn, do I want to know you. Every inch. Preferably with my lips. Is now too soon?"*>

Warmth shot through Kiernan as Thea's thoughts rolled over her, and she shivered. They rose from the table, and Kiernan placed a hand on the small of Thea's back as they walked into the lobby.

"I'm so glad you came by the lecture," Thea said.

"Me, too. I missed you at the show you attended and feared I had thrown away any chance I might have to get to know you. I wasn't willing to let another opportunity pass by."

They stood by the elevator banks, smiling at each other like teenagers.

<*"Should I ask her to come up? Is it too much too soon? Will I be able to control myself once we're alone?"*>

Kiernan leaned forward and whispered, "Ask me." She delivered a kiss behind Thea's earlobe before pulling back.

After a pregnant pause, Thea asked, "How about a nightcap?"

Kiernan took her hand and kissed her knuckles reverently before intertwining their fingers. "Lead the way."

# Chapter Sixteen

APPRECIATING THE BEAUTY OF the marble Ionic columns lining the entrance hall, Marcia glided across the mosaic floors toward the bar. Although she wasn't a drinker, a glass of wine after a long day at the office sounded like a fine idea. Every year she attended this shindig, hosted by the New York City Bar Association, to schmooze all the movers and shakers and play nice with those attorneys she normally stared down in the courtroom. At least the venue was beautiful. The food was tasty, too, although she probably wouldn't eat much of what was offered. Her stomach was tied up in knots. She hoped to see Lexie tonight.

She dressed carefully for the evening, wearing a shimmering black satin Valentino sheath with a one shoulder bodice-cut, plunging neckline, and pronounced slit up the right thigh. Sleeveless and slinky with virtually no back to speak of, she would normally never wear something so sexy, but with the changes in her body, she felt much more confident. And she wanted to catch Lexie's attention. Since their dinner, she had acted like the perfect suitor, and Marcia wanted to break through her control. She grinned at the thought of seeing some of Lexie's passionate nature shine through those blue-gray eyes. Not that she would complain over the way Lexie treated her.

Just two days ago Marcia arrived at her office to find a large bouquet of dark red calla lilies coupled with white roses—elegant and gorgeous, like the sender. The card simply said, "Miss you." Marcia tried to call her, but she had been unavailable. As far as she knew, Lexie was returning from her business trip late this afternoon and would be attending this event. For the past couple of weeks, Marcia hadn't had an opportunity to speak with her, but Lexie had warned her of the constant meetings. *She must be back in the city by now, though.*

It was possible she wouldn't come. Yet, Marcia was aching to see the woman. Now that they'd spent time together through several shared meals, Marcia was ready for more. The past two weeks without Lexie had tested her restraint. She came close to popping into Lexie's hotel room in Atlanta. How would she have explained that, though? She knew she needed to tell her about these abilities, soon—certainly before their relationship became more intimate. As it was, they had only held hands and shared hugs.

Wine in hand, Marcia looked around for familiar faces. She saw several of her colleagues standing in a loose circle and smiled when Brad waved her over. A tall, slender man with kind hazel eyes and a full head of white hair, he always acted as her mentor, taking her under his wing and shielding her from much of the office politicking while she climbed the corporate ladder. Even though she was a partner of the firm, he still protected her. She joined the group, murmuring her greetings. The obligatory small talk served as a welcome distraction.

Feeling the energy change, Marcia straightened. *Lexie is here.* Marcia searched for her. As their eyes met, Marcia felt something settle within her belly. Yes, Lexie was worth the effort, worth the wait, worth exposing herself. She looked ethereal tonight. Everyone noticed her entrance. The surrounding conversations faded away as she approached. Marcia lost her breath, blazing eyes burning her soul. They seemed to glow, and Marcia could only stand motionless, as she watched Lexie weave through the crowd.

*How does she do that? Everyone gets out of her way,* Marcia wondered. *Everything about her turns me on.* Heat suffused Marcia's body. She sipped the air and held her hands tightly together. Once Lexie reached her, Marcia held her breath, not quite knowing what would happen next.

"Marcia," Lexie murmured.

She peered into Lexie's eyes, searching. So many emotions—when had she ever seen so much feeling stirring within those turbulent eyes? Lexie leaned toward her, tilting her head. Marcia froze, believing for one breathless instant they were going to share their first kiss. Well, she was partly correct. In the next moment, Lexie gently touched her lips to her cheek as Marcia stood paralyzed before pulling back to study her face. Her smile reached her eyes. Marcia couldn't help but respond in kind.

All surrounding motion ceased, and the world became Lexie, only Lexie, always Lexie. She studied those complex eyes as they darkened and beamed forth such a strong band of energy Marcia was jolted by its surge. She felt as if they were traveling through a tunnel, colors merging and separating at a dizzying speed. She couldn't feel her body, yet she knew Lexie was next to her, experiencing this incredible journey. And in the next moment, Marcia was back in her body, gazing into glowing, silver eyes before they faded to well-known steel-blue. Before she could begin to make sense out of what happened, the world sped up again, intruding upon the most spectacular, life-changing moment Marcia ever experienced.

It was hard to believe how unaffected Lexie appeared. Her amusement at Marcia's befuddlement did a great job of shaking her from the Lexie-induced haze she'd fallen into, and she looked around the group, noticing their curious gazes. Marcia was going to have to try harder to shake Lexie's calm demeanor. Once again, she effortlessly had gained the upper hand through a simple kiss on the cheek. *I must have imagined the rest.*

Brad greeted Lexie. "Come to pay your respects to one of the few attorneys able to beat you in the courtroom, Lexie?"

Marcia listened to the round of chuckles and smiled in relief. She could just kiss that man. Now, she just needed to act like a person with an available mind, a mind that worked to the extent of stringing words together to form intelligent sentences used to impress others with witty conversation. Nope. She had nothing. No repartee.

"Of course. Marcia is one of the best litigators in the country and certainly a worthy adversary," Lexie answered smoothly.

Marcia saw the gleam of mischief in Brad's eyes. "Makes you wish you had never let her go, huh, Lexie?" He turned to the rest of the group. "Marcia began her law career as an associate at Lexie's firm." Several of Marcia's coworkers looked at her and Lexie more appraisingly, as if seeing a new association.

"Worst mistake I ever made, letting her leave," Lexie admitted.

Surprised by her honesty, Marcia turned to Lexie, who captured Marcia's gaze and then swept her eyes over her form before returning to her widened eyes. Marcia was sure everyone witnessed it. The passion Marcia recognized encapsulated within dark gray eyes latched on to her pounding heart. If they were alone, she would pull Lexie forward and feast until her desires were sated.

Slowly, Lexie extended her hand. "Dance with me?"

*Intriguing.* Lexie was making a public statement tonight—she was serious about being with her. It was time for Marcia to make the commitment, too. Marcia looked at the glass in her hand and smiled when Brad took it. She linked her fingers with Lexie's, and they walked to the dance floor.

"You look exquisite," Marcia whispered once they faced each other. Lexie wore a midnight blue evening gown with velvet trim. The cut emphasized her small waist before flaring outward in a loose swirl. Her shoulder-length, auburn hair was perfectly styled, just waiting for Marcia's hands to be buried in it. Lexie smiled again as she took her right hand in her left and pulled her closer. This Lexie, the private one few were allowed to know, attracted Marcia to such an extent that she ached with the need to get closer.

They moved across the floor in time with the music. Flashbacks of their bodies moving together so long ago made Marcia gasp. She was relieved to note Lexie didn't seem immune to their closeness either.

Lexie gazed into her eyes. "You have never looked more beautiful." She pulled Marcia closer, placing her hand on the small of her back, causing her to suck in her breath. Lexie took the opportunity to explore Marcia's back, and each stroke of her fingers against her skin heightened Marcia's arousal.

*God, how am I supposed to behave around her? I thought I was supposed to throw her off kilter, not the other way around.* Drawing in a deep breath, Marcia leaned in, moving her hand from Lexie's shoulder to the nape of her neck. *Two can play at this game.* She stroked along her hairline, as she moved her lips closer to Lexie's ear.

"I was hoping to see you tonight." She smiled, feeling Lexie's body shiver. Pulling back, Marcia gazed into flashing eyes. "I dressed for you."

They didn't speak any more as they danced, their eyes locked. She had never experienced dancing like this. One song blended into the next, as they continued to move against each other. She felt Lexie's hand wander up and down her spine before resting on her tailbone. *Definitely a statement.* Marcia ran her fingers through thick curls before removing her other hand from Lexie's grasp and trailing it up her arm. Marcia smiled when she saw how her touch made Lexie shiver again. She brushed the back of her fingers along Lexie's neck before joining her hands together at her nape.

Marcia wished they were alone. She wished they were in her bedroom or in Lexie's bedroom or in a private vestibule—anywhere but surrounded by people. She wanted to give in to these feelings and connect with Lexie in a more fundamental way. Feeling energy flow through her, Marcia popped her eyes open, afraid she had begun teleporting. But no, she was thinking of Lexie, and she was in her arms. Once the song ended, the music stopped. They pulled apart and shared a smile. Lexie took her hand and kissed the palm, thoroughly charming Marcia. One of the coordinators of the event announced the waitstaff would be visiting the tables to take dinner orders. Marcia looked at her dance companion. She knew she had to sit with her firm, as she was sure Lexie did with hers. She wanted to spend more time with her, though.

"I'll find you after dinner," Lexie reassured her. Marcia nodded and squeezed her hand before walking away. She could feel herself being watched and added a little more sway to her hips. Once seated, everyone stared at her. "What?" She looked from person to person, seeking an answer.

Brad, bless his heart, answered. "I didn't realize you and Lexie were so close. You make a handsome couple."

Marcia felt her face flush. "Thank you."

She refused to explain herself. She lifted her chin, jutting it out in an unspoken challenge to anyone who would dare criticize her choice. She could practically feel her body crackling with energy. As she stared at her colleagues, their eyes slid away. Marcia took a deep breath. *Calm down. No one knows of your past with Lexie, and you were married up until two years ago. You've never even dated since John died. Let them get used to the idea.*

Turning back to Brad, Marcia asked about his wife. She hadn't attended tonight, opting to remain at home with their children. Marcia felt the rest of the table sigh and hid a grin. Soon, others began separate conversations, and the cloud of discomfort dissipated. As time passed, Marcia found herself looking around, noticing energy strands—blue, red, green, gold. Wherever she looked, she saw strands crisscrossing the room, and all of them led to a person. One strand seemed thicker, stronger, brighter, it's green color seeming to pulse as if it were breathing. She followed it with her eyes, astounded to find Lexie at the end. She didn't know why she was so surprised. Lexie looked up as if she heard her thoughts, and Marcia saw the strand brighten, like a yellow-brick road to Emerald City.

*Why exactly are we taking our time with this relationship? We know how good we are together, we know how much we have in common, and we both feel the connection. Oh, yeah, that whole not-getting-my-heart-broken-again issue.* Marcia allowed herself to be guided into another conversation, pushing aside her salacious thoughts for now. Just as the topic became exhausted—*how much is there to say about movies when we all work so many hours*—two warm hands on her bare shoulders made her shudder. She cocked her head upward, knowing she would see Lexie.

Smiling, Lexie asked, "Are you planning on staying much longer?"

"No," Marcia answered, wondering what she was getting at.

"I'll drive you home," she offered.

*Oh. Oh!* Marcia jumped up, appreciating how Lexie reacted quickly enough to pull her chair back so she wouldn't hit the table. "I just need to get my coat."

"I'll get it for you while you say goodbye to everyone."

Marcia handed the coatroom check slip to her with a smile before turning back to the table. It took several minutes to wind up last-minute conversations and bid everyone a good night. Brad had the audacity to wink at her. She chuckled. Heading toward the front entrance, she saw Lexie chatting with a couple, Marcia's coat draped over her arm. As Marcia reached her, Lexie stepped forward to place the coat over her shoulders, lifting her hair gently from beneath the collar. Marcia shivered, relishing the feel of Lexie's hand sliding down her back before she wrapped an arm around her waist.

"Marcia, I want you to meet Jessie and her husband, Mike. Jessie joined my firm about ten years ago," Lexie said. "She's one of my closest friends."

Marcia extended her hand to shake theirs. "It's a pleasure to meet you both." She knew they were sizing her up, but she didn't mind. She suspected Patricia would behave similarly when she met Lexie. While they sized her up, she did the same, appreciating their style. Jessie wore a red floral wraparound dress while her husband wore a dark blue suit with a crisp white Oxford shirt. Classy. "Are you heading out, too?"

"Yes, we just wanted to meet you first," Jessie replied, her dark eyes piercing into Marcia's soul. Marcia's eyebrows rose, surprised by her honesty. *I like her.* Tucking a strand of her dark-brown hair behind her ear, Jessie said, "I'm sure we'll meet again soon. Have a good night." She leaned forward to kiss Lexie's cheek. "I'll talk to you later."

She felt Lexie's breath caress her ear. "Ready?"

Marcia nodded. Lexie led her to a silver convertible Mercedes-Benz and unlocked the passenger door, holding it open while Marcia slid in before rounding the car and getting in. Marcia felt energy buzzing so strongly through her body that it seemed to vibrate. She needed to calm down.

"Where do you live?" Marcia gave her directions and sat quietly, happy to be in Lexie's presence. After the first turn, Lexie took her hand and held it on her lap.

"I can't believe you found a parking spot," Marcia said a few minutes later. She usually had to circle the block to find one this late at night. "Do you want to come up for a nightcap?"

"I'd hate to wake your daughter," Lexie said, "and I'd like her first impression of me to be favorable. I'll walk you to your door, though."

*Can she be any more gallant?* Marcia really wanted her to come in, but she was probably right. She wanted Sammy to like Lexie, and Sammy was known to be grumpy when awakened from her beauty sleep.

Marcia floated up the stairs while her mind whirled. The entire night was a revelation. Lexie captivated her on so many levels she had a hard time refraining from expressing her elation in some immature but totally satisfying fashion. A picture of herself donning an iPod and dancing around to some type of fist-pumping music Sammy favored flashed through her mind.

Marcia slid the key in the door lock and walked across the threshold into the low-lit hall. She turned around. "Thank you for walking me to my door. It wasn't necessary, though." Marcia shifted from foot to foot. She knew what she wanted to do.

Lexie closed the door and approached. "Sure it was. How else could I do this?" She left Marcia with no time to prepare, as she leaned in for a kiss.

The connection was mind shattering. All thoughts vacated Marcia's mind, sensation taking control. Lexie's lips barely grazed hers, and yet she was immobilized by the shock of desire sizzling through her.

*I've felt these lips before.* Flashes of dreams she'd had over the years crossed her mind, blending into a montage of desire and too-brief kisses. The kiss was so slow, so gentle. Marcia could not speed it up, could not apply more pressure, could not even pull Lexie closer. All action was held captive by the sweetness of the moment.

The kiss served as a conduit, connecting them in ways more intimate than Marcia could ever have anticipated. She could taste Lexie's affection, desire, conviction. In turn, Marcia communicated her absolute commitment toward allowing Lexie behind her walls. She got lost in the kiss, reveling in the taste and texture of reverent lips and just the slightest brushing of a tongue.

Lexie drew back, and Marcia mourned the separation, taking a few moments before opening her eyes. She allowed her gaze to drink in Lexie's parted lips, dark eyes, and heaving chest. But Lexie was leaving. Marcia wrapped her arms around her body to prevent herself from pulling Lexie forward again.

"Patricia's coming into town this weekend. Are you free Tuesday night? She mentioned going to an after-play party. I'd like you to meet her," she offered instead.

Lexie grinned. "That sounds fun."

Marcia chewed on her lip, debating whether to chance extending another invitation. Lexie's eyes were so warm and inviting, though, she decided to take the chance. "Will you come over for dinner a week from Sunday? I'd like you to meet Sammy."

"I'd love to."

With a short kiss that stretched her restraint, Marcia stepped away. After the door closed, she slumped against it while attempting to regain her equilibrium. *What she does to me!* In a daze, Marcia managed to change into her black silk negligee. All she could think about was the look in Lexie's eyes, the feel of her hands, their bodies moving together so provocatively as they danced, and those kisses—glorious, passionate. Sunday couldn't come soon enough. She was relieved she saw no visions during their first kiss, which would indicate an impostor in Lexie's form. That would have been heartbreaking.

Climbing under the covers after looking in on Sammy to make sure she was sleeping, Marcia felt her body relax. She pictured Lexie as she looked just an hour ago—her swollen, smeared lips, her passion-glazed eyes, her trembling body. She longed to cause that loss of control again. Feeling lethargic, Marcia smiled. Whatever else may be occurring in her life, they hadn't affected this budding relationship. Their shared trial had been docketed long before she woke up to these physical changes, and she was confident Lexie would have tried to reconnect with her regardless.

*God, how I wish I was still in Lexie's arms.* Hearing a dull buzzing in her ears and feeling her body vibrate, Marcia's eyes popped open. She realized too late what was happening. Her body began to materialize, and Marcia looked around, afraid to confirm what she suspected. Lexie stared at her, still in her evening wear, her mouth dropped open in shock. Marcia wished she were invisible with all her heart. *Just let me disappear, so she can chalk this up to an overtired imagination.*

Lexie gasped.

Looking down at herself, Marcia realized her body was surrounded by a fine mist. Before she could transport out, Lexie rushed forward. Marcia didn't have enough time to move out of the way, and her breath got knocked out of her as she toppled back, Lexie on top of her. All those fantasies of Lexie—they were different from this reality.

Marcia froze under her, not sure what to do. She stared into unworldly, flashing silver eyes, the same glow she witnessed at the bar function, and felt the heaviness of her body as it materialized. Lexie grabbed her head between both hands and captured her lips. Desperate, hard—these kisses were more passionate than she could ever have imagined. Their tongues dueled for dominance. Marcia took control, exploring her mouth, seeking out every secret. Lexie shifted, like a lioness ready to strike. Marcia cupped her ass and squeezed in synch with each tongue stroke, gratified to feel Lexie moving against her.

For all her sophistication, control, and grace, right now in Marcia's arms, Lexie was the epitome of wanton abandon. She felt Lexie's groan in her core, and it made her crave more.

Disappointment coursed through her when Lexie broke away, stilling her body's rhythm and staring into Marcia's eyes.

"Don't even think about disappearing now," she commanded.

"I won't. You can see me?"

"Yes. If I get up, do you promise to stay?"

"I promise." *Does she think I'm crazy enough to want to leave after those kisses?*

Lexie pulled back and rested on her knees. Marcia sat up, not able to rise while Lexie remained on her lap, and wrapped her arms around Lexie's waist, waiting for her to make the next move.

Lexie traced Marcia's face with gentle fingers. "How is this possible?"

Marcia swallowed and stared at the floor, attempting to calm down. "About that. Why aren't you upset about how I just appeared in your bedroom? How can you sit here so calmly?" *And how could you stop us when it felt so good?*

"Should I be concerned?" Lexie quirked an eyebrow.

"Answering a question with a question?" Marcia griped. Lexie just smirked. "No, you shouldn't be. I'd never hurt you."

"I feel that. I've based my life on listening to my instincts, and that has served me well. When I'm with you, I feel safe. Familiar. If it were someone else, I would probably be angry at the invasion of privacy. But not with you."

"That seems a bit odd."

"Perhaps, but there's something about you. I can always tell when you're in a room. I recognize you on some other level. I feel you. In court, I always knew when you arrived at the courthouse, as if you tripped some type of silent alarm system hotwired to my heart." Lexie's brows drew downward, and Marcia knew she was weighing whether to say more. "I've dreamt of you for years. I've become familiar with how you feel in my mind, and that's how you feel whenever you're near me. So, I'm not upset. I'm not afraid of you."

Marcia pulled Lexie in for a quick hug, and they both rose from the floor. Marcia grasped her extended hand and held on to it, as they walked into the living room. Marcia looked around. Although the rugs and some of the décor had changed, she still recognized the main furniture pieces. They sat down on a leather couch, and Lexie stared at Marcia's sleepwear while her thumb stroked the inside of her palm. She felt her body respond. Marcia growled and leaned toward her, the urge to pin her against the couch overwhelming. A hand on her chest stopped her.

"Marcia," she gasped, all amusement leaving her face. "We need to talk—"

She didn't wait for her to say anything else. Instead, Marcia leaned closer and kissed her pulse point. She could taste Lexie's heartbeats, strong and rapid, fluttering beneath her lips. Marcia moved to her collarbone, licking the indentation she coveted all evening. Lexie's guttural moan resounded through the room. Through a haze of desire she felt Lexie's hand pushing her away and groaned.

"Darling, we have to stop. I want you, but you'll have to leave soon, and I don't want to rush this. I want to be able to hold you all night. We deserve that."

Lexie's fingers ran through Marcia's hair as she rested her head against her chest. She sighed and chuckled. "Yes, of course, we do. I'm sorry. I shouldn't have pushed." Marcia shook her head. "You're irresistible."

Lexie cupped her cheek. "So are you."

Taking a deep breath, Marcia let it out. She could do this. She could control herself. Although she was certain Sammy wouldn't wake up until morning, she didn't want to rush making love with Lexie. And really, the woman deserved to know everything before they became any closer.

"I want you to know that I've never lied to you, and I never will. What I'm going to tell you will sound ridiculous, but I swear everything is absolutely true."

Lexie placed her hand over Marcia's trembling one. "I believe you. I saw you appear in my room out of nowhere, turn invisible, and reappear. I know you have abilities, some extraordinary abilities." Lexie gestured toward her face. "And I know those aren't contacts or a dye job. So, tell me what happened. I promise to keep an open mind."

Marcia told her about her transformation and powers, every last detail save for the meteorite.

Lexie sat quietly, listening to her story. Finally she asked, "You have an idea of what caused this, don't you?"

"Yes. I went to a retreat a few months ago, and I touched..." Marcia realized how farfetched this sounded and stalled. She really didn't want to lose Lexie, but sounding like a nutcase might spur her to back away from what they'd been building.

Lexie gave her a warm smile. "You touched a meteorite."

So lost in her fears, it took Marcia a moment for the words to sink in. Her eyes widened. "How can you know that?" For a moment Marcia feared Lexie was an imposter. That thought was quickly discarded, though. She would have known when they kissed.

"I was at the Sunny Horizon Resort the day the meteorite hit. In fact, wait here." Lexie rose from the couch and walked into her bedroom. She returned a moment later, sat next to Marcia, and extended her hands. In them were four small stones—pieces of the meteorite. Black fragments had different colors threaded through them—silver, purple, and white in three of them, and gold, green, and white in the fourth.

"Have these affected you?" Marcia asked, studying the stones.

Lexie nodded. "My senses are sharper. I can listen to a whispered conversation in the front row of a theater from the back exit door and see the smallest motion from blocks away. When you gazed at me from across the room tonight, it felt as if you were touching me. And evidently I can find you even when you're invisible."

Marcia chuckled. "Your eyes glowed silver. As if your eyes weren't mesmerizing enough."

"So, your ability to travel places through thought—that must come in handy."

"Well, that's a work in progress." Marcia told Lexie everything—the astral traveling, the practicing, the challenges, and her recent full-materialization success. She even told her about the user's manual. "The invisibility is entirely new. I don't know of any other abilities, but I'm willing to bet there's more." Marcia sat back. "And that's it."

They sat together quietly, staring off into space. Before tonight, Marcia worried Lexie would find all these changes too daunting to want to explore a more intimate relationship with her. Finding out Lexie had her own powers reassured Marcia that Lexie wouldn't be scared away. That meteorite was a blessing. It bonded them in a different way. Still, she needed to be sure.

Marcia steeled herself and looked over. "What do you think?"

Lexie tilted her head, taking a few moments before answering. "I think these changes are incredible. Do you realize just how awe-inspiring these gifts are? If you can figure out how to use these abilities, you can use them in countless ways. And if a scientist could study your physical changes, the research could push us forward with restoring youth and muscle vitality. Botox would go out of business, as would exercise equipment. How can you be so blasé about it?"

Jumping off the couch, Marcia ran a hand through her hair. "I'm not, but this is my life we're talking about. I don't want to be some guinea pig to be poked and prodded. What if the wrong people found out and tried to persuade me to use these abilities in nefarious ways?" Marcia added with a softer voice, "I can't tell the world. I need to find out what I can do before I make any decisions." She sat back down next to Lexie. "Besides, you seem to have some abilities yourself. Have you tried to control them at all? How have they affected the way you live your life?"

Lexie turned more toward Marcia so that their knees touched. "I seem to be able to control them naturally when I concentrate on a particular sense and what I want to have happen." She reached out to cover Marcia's knee. "I understand your point, but your abilities are much more impressive and potentially much more helpful to humankind."

"Please, Lexie. I'm trusting you. Please don't tell anyone." Marcia could feel herself getting upset. She was in love with this woman. She didn't know how she'd recover if Lexie betrayed her.

"Shh, darling. I won't tell anyone. I promise. And I'll help you in any way I can," Lexie said. "Thank you for telling me. I know you didn't have to. I'll prove that your trust is well-placed. With your metamorphosis and with your heart." She rose from her seat and moved across the room, stalling at the window.

"Lexie, has anyone approached you about the meteorite?"

"Some FBI agent." She turned around, one hand playing with her necklace. "The interview was at work, and it was quick. I told him I didn't see it, which was true, and I hadn't noticed anything suspicious. He doesn't know I took home any souvenirs or about my senses being affected. He felt...off. He emitted this feeling of darkness, like ash, and I didn't trust him."

Marcia warred with whether to reveal what happened with the person impersonating Peter. The last thing she wanted to do was scare Lexie, and she hadn't seen him in weeks. He stopped trying to corner her, and she didn't have another trial for at least another month. Still it concerned her that someone was contacting everyone who'd been at the resort on the night the meteorite appeared.

"Have you talked to anyone else about it?"

"Just you. I was thinking about telling Jessie."

"If you trust her, you should. Be careful of strangers, though, or anyone who seems off to you. I want you safe." Marcia joined her at the window and slid her arms around her waist. Lexie leaned back into her chest. They stood that way, enjoying the closeness, and with a hum of contentment Marcia kissed the crown of her head. "Thank you, Lexie. I was touched by your actions at the bar function, how you made a statement by dancing with me. It reassured me you're invested in this relationship. And when I just appeared in your bedroom—well, that could have become ugly. Thank you for taking a chance with me and for believing in me." Marcia hugged her, feeling a sense of belonging and acceptance flow through her. "And I'm here for you as you navigate your own changes. That meteorite must have a unique composition to cause these types of changes in us."

"It must." Lexie turned and rested her hands on Marcia's forearms, squeezing them. "You're welcome. And you're right. I am serious about this. About you. I'll do whatever it takes to make you feel safe and loved."

Marcia's heart stuttered at that word. She wondered whether Lexie meant that literally. *Does she love me?* She heard a resounding yes echo through her mind. *I suppose if I tell myself over and over that she loves me, I'll believe it.* Nevertheless, Marcia needed Lexie to tell her. Although she felt the truth in her gut and saw it in Lexie's eyes, it wasn't enough.

Lexie gazed at her. "You're the only one who's inscribed her name on my heart, and I'm entrusting it to you."

Marcia kissed her, brushing their lips together before moving to kiss one corner of her mouth. Raising her head, Marcia grazed Lexie's closed eyes and forehead before making her way back to her mouth, exercising more control than she ever imagined she could by delivering light, chaste kisses. Lexie's soft sighs compelled her, though, and she kissed with more passion, fingers raking through her hair.

Before she lost all semblance of control, Marcia broke the kiss and hugged Lexie tight. "I should go," she whispered. She felt Lexie nod. "May I use your bathroom first?"

"Of course."

Walking into the master bath, Marcia used the bathroom and washed her hands. She splashed water on her face and braced her hands on the edge of the sink, trying to clear her mind of everything but Sammy. She looked at the mirror and saw Lexie in her bedroom, staring. Smiling at her, Marcia returned her focus to her own eyes. They were glowing bright violet. She pictured her daughter asleep in her bed, and her body began to vibrate. Distantly, she heard Lexie gasp her name. A moment later she stood at the head of Sammy's bed while her body finished materializing. She let out a breath and pulled the sheet over Sammy's shoulder before leaving the room, tired but happy. And on Sunday night she had no intention of allowing Lexie to leave her arms.

# Chapter Seventeen

*MONDAY, OCTOBER 16, 2017 6:03 P.M.*

*I'M HERE,* PATRICIA TEXTED, grinning when the door swung open a few moments later. She stepped inside and pulled Marcia in for a hug.

"It's so great to see you," Marcia said. "Let me take your coat."

Patricia tucked her gloves inside the coat pockets before taking it off, handing it over and unwrapping her scarf. Removing her wool hat, she fluffed her hair a bit before handing over the rest of her winter wear. "It's cold outside."

"Wimp. It's not that cold. It's October," Marcia teased as she led them into her den where a cheerful fire burned. "Come by the fire. Dinner should be ready in about thirty minutes."

"It being October means nothing. Remember the April blizzard? Now that the sun has set, the temperature's dropped to the forties. That's cold in my book," Patricia said, settling in to a comfortable leather armchair. She smiled as her gaze met large floor-to-ceiling bookshelves. Marcia loved books as much as she did, and they often traded tomes.

"You have a point." Marcia sank down on the loveseat, one leg curled beneath her.

"Anything new happening with your powers?"

"I appeared in Lexie's bedroom after the bar function Friday night, and I became invisible."

Patricia felt her stomach drop. "Oh, my God. How did that play out?"

"Unbelievably well," Marcia said, grinning. "Somehow she saw me and tackled me so I wouldn't leave. We talked. I confessed to the meteorite and my abilities. Turns out she'd figured it out."

"How?"

"She was at the resort the same night, and..." Marcia shrugged.

"Wait. Are you saying she saw the meteorite?"

"Not only did she see it, she took home some souvenirs, too."

Patricia sat back. "Does she have powers, too?" she whispered.

"Yes. And there's something else I should tell you since I'm tagging along to the party tomorrow night."

"What?"

"I'm pretty sure Kiernan has powers, too."

"Kiernan Connelly?" Patricia squeaked. *I'm surrounded by superheroes. Holy shit!*

Marcia hummed. "Remember when I went to that party with you a couple of months ago and Rudi freaked out?"

"Yes. I was so thankful to Kiernan for teasing her about it. Hold on. Are you telling me she knew you really popped in on Rudi?"

"I'm pretty sure. I mean, she didn't confirm anything, but I don't know. It felt like she knew. She found me in the bathroom to reassure me. Anyway, maybe we'll get a better idea when we see her. Also, I'd like to schedule some more trial runs soon to see if I can materialize fully in front of you again. Now that I've done it twice successfully, I want to get better at it."

"More than your head and glowing eyes would be an improvement," Patricia teased.

"No kidding."

Chuckling, Patricia sat back with a sigh, her body warming up. "Where's your lady love?"

"She's having a working dinner, and before you ask, Sammy's at her friend's house working on a science project."

"Right. Well, I'm looking forward to meeting her tomorrow." Noticing the dreamy smile on Marcia's face, Patricia chuckled. "You've got it bad."

"So bad," Marcia agreed, pink tingeing her cheeks. "How was the lecture last week?"

"Fantastic. You should've come with me."

"I'm sorry I couldn't make it. I do want to meet Thea. I feel like I already know her."

"Well, you'll meet her at the party tomorrow night. In a surprising twist, Kiernan was also at the lecture."

"Interesting." A timer chimed, and Marcia rose. "That's our cue."

Leaving the fire reluctantly, Patricia followed Marcia into the kitchen and moved around the familiar space, collecting utensils and napkins to set the table. Marcia set down bowls of salad before grabbing the dinner plates. As she filled them, she requested, "Can you grab the salad dressings from the fridge? I like the creamy Italian, and if you don't like that one, there are several others."

"Sure." After Patricia grabbed the dressings, she brought them and a basket of fresh artisan bread to the table. "I'm going to gain ten pounds just from this beautiful meal, and that's before I eat any of it."

"In that case, you might as well have some wine to wash everything down." Marcia filled two glasses with Prosecco and handed one to Patricia before holding hers up. "To friends. They are our lifelines, our confidants, our support. I'm so glad you're in my life."

"Me, too. You're my best friend," Patricia said with a soft voice. She took a sip of the wine and hummed.

"Are you sure Thea isn't your best friend?"

Patricia looked over at Marcia and smiled. "No one can replace you." She poured some dressing over her salad. "She is a friend, but she holds back a part of herself. She's experienced a lot of life changes lately—her job, her relationships, and she's in the middle of having a book published. Those types of changes will affect anyone. I think she wants to build our friendship slowly so it will last." She took a bite of her chicken piccata and groaned. "Besides, how could I give you up as my best friend when you're the best cook ever?"

"That I am," Marcia said. "Did you ever find out who she wrote the letters to?"

"I'm working on it."

"What are you planning for tomorrow?"

"Some touristy stuff with Thea. Her lecture series is over, so she'll be returning to Boston soon. I offered to take her around the city. Want to come?"

"That sounds enticing, but it'll be so cold."

"Oh, stop teasing me. You can use some of your expert cross questioning skills to find out who the mystery recipient of the letters is."

"That does sound promising. You know," Marcia said with a lilt in her voice, "you're single. She's single."

"I don't think she's into the fairer sex." Patricia ducked her head, eyes skittering around the room.

"I notice you aren't denying that you might be interested in her."

"That's quite a stretch, and it doesn't matter. She's my friend. My straight friend."

"You don't know that. She could be a friend with benefits." Marcia wiggled her eyebrows, and Patricia laughed. "You know, you can't just look at someone and know their sexuality."

"What, you haven't heard of gaydar?"

"Oh, please. Didn't you learn anything from Thea's class? Appearances can be deceiving. Perspectives can be manipulated. Until I told you about Lexie, didn't you believe I was only into men?"

"That's not a fair question. You said yourself that Lexie's an exception. Besides, if you were into girls when we were younger, you would've made a pass at me in college," Patricia joked.

"While you were swooning over every attractive female on campus? I think not." Marcia laughed at Patricia's expression of outrage. "Maybe I was attracted to other women, but they've never kept my attention. How could they after 'That Night' with Lexie?"

"I can hear the quotation marks surrounding those words."

"Capitalization."

"Right, and don't forget the bold and underline, too."

"Exactly." Marcia grinned. "So, are you going to spend some one-on-one time with Rudi while you're in town?"

"Probably. She was upset when I didn't the last time. She offered to make me dinner tonight, but that seemed to be inviting trouble."

"Or a night of passion." Marcia gave her a wicked smile.

"I don't think that's a great idea. She seems to be opening up to me more, and I'd rather concentrate on building a friendship right now."

"But there's a chance you might consider more at some point?"

"Anything's possible." Patricia was still attracted to Rudi. *Who knows what might happen in the future?* All she knew was that she was friends with some great ladies, excited to write her next book, and ready for her next adventure.

***

## KARINAN CYCLE 5 KATRINET 4

Lerzep, First Prince of the Katakitites and rebel leader turned secret agent, stood at attention while listening to Supreme Commander Flerg of the Katakitites Royal Fleet relay to the military advisers Ubel's progress. *As inept as always.* Still, Flerg had ordered Ubel to return with three human females who were affected by the manufactured meteorite within one sun cycle. That didn't give Lerzep or his followers much time to prepare, but they would be ready to sabotage his dear brother's plans. To Flerg, Ubel, and others who were part of this delusional quest to wrest control of the government through the use of the humans' new abilities, Lerzep was a high-ranking second cousin of the royals. In truth, his cousin was killed during the revolt, and Lerzep took his form to masquerade as a royal supporter.

It was ironic, he supposed, that he was seen as a supporter of his own family's defeated regime when he was one of the main instigators of the revolution. This was the only way to know what the royals were doing, though, and he would rather die fighting for a better future than remain a part of an outdated, draconian government. That meant treating all individuals with the same dignity, respect, and decency, regardless of sex or station. His own mother was treated as inferior, and her intellect was superior to most men.

"Gufel, you will be on duty tomorrow night once the humans are secured," Flerg said to Lerzep.

*Kiernan, Lexie, and Marcia.* He knew their names, even if Flerg did not bother to remember them. Bowing low, Lerzep said, "I will do as you command."

The meeting ended, and Lerzep left the compound to let the small band of rebels hidden several clandos away know the latest developments. He caught sight of his appearance in a reflective window as he left the compound and shivered. His body was strappy, defined muscles peeking through the slits in his scarlet uniform. That didn't bother him. It was the aquamarine color of his skin and the yellow swath of fur on his head that made his skin crawl. Quite unbecoming. He would be glad to be back in his own body with his dark blue skin and black ring of fur covering his ears—both features he inherited from his beautiful mother.

Lerzep bounded across the rocky ground, thankful this little moon had a breathable atmosphere, unlike the planet it circled. Once he arrived at the outcropping where his forces were hidden, he opened a small, temporary hole in the invisibility cloaking shield and entered the building, listening as the shield snapped back into place behind him.

In the barrack, a small squadron of officers carried out their duties. Each officer nodded to him as he passed by, a sign of respect he appreciated. Most did not realize he was a prince and heir apparent. He wasn't sure how they would react once they were told.

*That is not a matter to entertain right now*, he reminded himself. It was enough that they trusted him while believing him to be a relative of the ruling family. When he spoke to his mother yesterday, she seemed to believe the rebels would be happy to know he helped to orchestrate the coup. It would add stability to the government since a royal was instrumental in implementing the new ways. He hoped she was correct. He trusted her judgment, unlike most males of the royal line.

She was one of the few who knew his true identity. Not that he had to tell her. She was able to see through his disguise, much to Lerzep's amazement. *A mother always knows*, he mused. It would surprise the royals to learn his mother was not inferior, not weak, and not to be ignored. A vicious grin covered Lerzep's face. His dear brother would pay for the years of abuse he and their father rained on his mother. He would pay for the death of Lerzep's sister, too. Best of all, he would learn once and for all never to underestimate anyone who was different from him. *Appearances are deceiving*, Lerzep thought while peering in a mirror. He shuddered. As the Katakitites say, the warrior and the scholar seem the same until one speaks.

\*\*\*

### TUESDAY, OCTOBER 17, 2017 10:48 P.M.

Spotting Marcia and another woman near the front door of Palorma's, Patricia hurried over. Marcia wore a long chocolate skirt and green print blouse with matching wedge boots while her companion wore black slacks with a navy button-down shirt and high heels. They made a striking couple.

"Hey," Patricia said, leaning in to hug Marcia. "And you must be Lexie. It's a pleasure to meet you."

"The pleasure's all mine." Lexie lowered her voice. "I'm hoping you'll tell me some stories of when you two were in college. I'm convinced she did more than study all the time."

Chuckling, Patricia said, "You've got that right. This one was a magnet for trouble."

"Excuse me! I was the model student," Marcia said.

With a smirk, Patricia said to Lexie, "We'll talk." The hum of various conversations acted as a beacon, guiding Patricia, Marcia, and Lexie toward the back of the restaurant where the after-play party was in full swing. Although Patricia had attended several of these gatherings, the novelty hadn't worn off. She shot a grin at Marcia. "This will be great."

"I bet. What happened to Thea? I thought she was meeting you at your hotel," Marcia said.

"She decided to meet us here. You missed out today. Thea and Kiernan were looking pretty cozy. I started to feel like a third wheel." They weaved their way through the restaurant to the function room at the back.

"That makes sense since their auras are pink," Marcia said.

Following Marcia's eyes, Patricia saw Thea and Kiernan standing near the food table next to Rudi, who was acting as gregarious as ever. "What color's my aura?" Patricia asked.

"Yellow," Lexie said, and Patricia's mouth dropped open.

"You can see auras, too?"

"It's a recent development," Lexie said, scrunching her nose. Marcia's lovesick smile made Patricia chuckle.

*They're so cute together.* Patricia bet if she could see auras, theirs would be bright red. She led the way over, her heart fluttering when she saw Rudi's eyes light up in greeting. Patricia leaned in to give Thea a hug. "I'm so glad you decided to come. Thea, these are my friends, Marcia and Lexie." Marcia was supposed to play tourist with them earlier in the day, but she was called into court.

Thea stepped forward to give Marcia a hug. "Patricia's mentioned you enough times that I feel like I know you. And the physical changes—I have to say, I love it!" Thea held Marcia's shoulders, as she studied her hair and eyes.

"I agree," Lexie said, wrapping an arm around Marcia's waist and holding out a hand. "It's a pleasure to meet you, Thea."

Patricia snorted, placing a hand over her lips. *Jealous, much? As if she has to worry.* Patricia's eyes met Kiernan's sparkling blues. *She must have caught that, too.*

"It's good to see you again," Kiernan said to Marcia, squeezing her arm before turning to Lexie. "I'm Kiernan. It's lovely to meet you." To Patricia's surprise, Kiernan stepped forward to hug her. "I'm glad you're here," Kiernan said, and Patricia smiled.

The French restaurant was decorated with distressed wooden tables and wrought iron seats, and unlike many Manhattan restaurants, guests were not on top of each other. The hardwood floors and open kitchen format evoked a sense of space and familiarity Patricia enjoyed. She liked how the hanging light bulbs, white shelving with dishes stacked on them, and paintings of well-known French attractions created a welcoming atmosphere. Glimpsing some of the hors d'oeuvres, Patricia bit back a moan. They looked delicious.

"They are as tasty as they look," Kiernan whispered, delivering a conspiratorial wink that made Patricia giggle. "Come on. I'll check them out with you." Since Marcia, Lexie, and Thea were talking to Rudi, Patricia decided it was the perfect time to nab some delectable cuisine. Choosing a few appetizers, Patricia contemplated asking Kiernan about Thea. Did she know her before today? Why was she at Thea's lecture? Why did they look like a couple? A hand on her elbow turned her attention to Kiernan.

"Patricia, you can ask me questions. I know Thea cares about you, and although our acquaintance came through Rudi, I'm hoping you and I might become friends. What do you think?"

"I'd like that," Patricia said. *What did I do to attract so many strong, sharp women into my life?*

A loud shout rent the air, and Patricia turned toward her friends. She rushed back, confused at what she was seeing. A man pulled on Lexie's arm, a knife to her throat while another man thrust a blade at Marcia, who dodged out of the way. Patricia gasped, fear making it hard to breathe. Gathering her courage, she pressed her lips together and slammed her plate on Lexie's assailant, hitting him on the back of his head with enough force that he slumped over. Lexie stepped away, letting him fall to the ground.

Kiernan headed over to help Marcia, but she shouted, "Don't!"

"It's them!" Kiernan yelled. "They plan to kidnap us." She dodged a third assailant, using a platter full of food as a shield. The food fell on the floor, and her attacker slipped on the antipasta, hands and feet askew. If the situation weren't so serious, Patricia might have laughed.

Stepping in close to her assailant, Marcia pulled at the man's arm and turned into his body. She elbowed him in the face and pounded his hand onto the metal backing of a booth. The blade clattered to the floor. The man pulled out of her grip, but she turned to face him. Marcia's grim look communicated that these men were willing to do anything to capture them. Patricia could hear her heartbeat pounding in her ears.

Marcia, Kiernan, and Lexie stood in a small circle with their backs toward each other. A third man charged them, diving at Marcia with arms outstretched. Three sets of eyes flared, violet, gold, and silver energy beaming outward. Marcia held her arm aloft, a shimmering shield forming in front of them.

Time slowed down. Patricia found herself frozen, a mute witness. The world tremored at its edges. Rudi stood with eyes wide, mouth dropped open, and a finger pointed toward Marcia's blazing eyes. Thea's hand was reaching toward Kiernan, her body forming a barrier between her and the attacker Marcia had fended off. And to Patricia's horror, she could see the man she had attacked suspended in place inches behind Marcia, ready to grab her.

# Chapter Eighteen

## *TUESDAY, OCTOBER 17, 2017 11:02 P.M.*

KIERNAN FELT HER BODY freeze and watched as an energy shield shimmered in front of her. She stood with Marcia on one side and Lexie on the other, close enough that her elbows touched both of them. In front of her stood people in various poses. Some held food halfway to their mouths while others stared at them. Rudi looked like a cartoon character with her eyes bugged out, mouth dropped open, and finger pointing. Any amusement Kiernan felt was replaced with worry. They were in danger. Thoughts bombarded her, nipping at her mind like excited puppies.

<*"Flerg expects us to return within the next cakrae. We have to get them now."*>

<*"Why can't I move? What's happening? This is crazy."*>

<*"Who's the redhead? I've never seen her before."*>

<*"Watch out for that guy!"*>

Kiernan tried to refocus on the people attacking them. She heard another voice in her mind, one she recognized. <*"I can't hold them off much longer."*> Kiernan peered at Marcia, noticing how sallow her face appeared, as beads of perspiration dotted her hairline.

Kiernan could only see one of the three attackers—he was blocked by Thea, who stood in front of Kiernan. She could hear all their thoughts, though, and she knew they were close. Movement to Kiernan's right side caught her attention. Marcia's arm trembled. That was all the warning she got before time sped up once more.

Thea was pushed to the ground, and Kiernan kicked her attacker in the stomach as hard as she could before hands grabbed her from behind, the grip so strong she couldn't break free. Lexie pushed Marcia out of the way, and a high-pitched buzzing filled Kiernan's ears. A bright light seemed to surround her, and she closed her eyes. One moment she heard people yelling, and the next she heard nothing. Feeling herself freed, she stumbled to her knees, hands splayed on the ground. The uneven terrain clued her in that they were no longer in the restaurant. Opening her eyes, Kiernan tried to regulate her breathing. She sat up and looked around.

Their three attackers stood in human form on the far side of a cavernous room which seemed to be carved out of black rock with veins of gold, green, white, silver, and purple threading through it. The stone reminded her of the meteorite rocks she took with her from the resort. Sunlight filled the room from openings high in the wall, and flashes of green light came from some type of technology near where her captors stood. She could hear their thoughts overlapping their spoken words, and she had a hard time making sense of everything. It took her a few more moments to realize they were speaking a different language consisting of clicks and whistles. She was glad their thoughts translated somehow into English.

<*"I need to get to Flerg before he hears about what happened from these two parskan-headed puppets. I can make this seem like the mission was a success."*> More sounds floated through the air, and Kiernan watched one of them straighten and place his hands on his hips while answering with a series of hisses and squeaks. Kiernan figured that was the leader.

<*"Flerg will be upset that we didn't capture all three humans or the stones. I'm not getting executed for Ubel's mistakes."*>

<*"How dare Grak question my command. I'll break his neck with my bare hands."*> The leader—*that must be Ubel*—stepped forward, only to stop when the other man bowed low to the ground, speaking for several seconds. Whatever he said—*is that Grak?*—must have worked, since Ubel responded with an arrogant toss of his head before exiting the room.

<*"That was close. Next time Kafil suggests I volunteer for a career-making mission with him, I will punch him until his first row of teeth is no sharper than a rackteen's belly."*>

"Do you understand what they're saying?" Lexie asked. Kiernan peered to her right and saw Lexie next to her, a curtain of auburn curls hiding her face. "I've never heard their language before."

"I can't understand their language, but I can hear their thoughts. My brain is translating them." Kiernan kept her voice low. She had no idea how they were going to get out of this. She tried to ignore the fear struggling to climb up her throat and free itself in the form of a scream. The last thing they wanted was attention. Judging from their thoughts, their captors were desperate and ruthless. "They didn't succeed with their mission.

They wanted to get us and Marcia. And the meteorite stones."
After a moment, Kiernan added, "I saw how you pushed Marcia
out of the way. That was pretty gutsy."

Lexie shook her head, her curls sliding away to reveal an angry
expression. Her eyes glinted. "She seems to have the most
developed powers. I didn't want them to get her."

Kiernan hummed. "And you love her."

After a pregnant pause, Lexie sighed. "And I love her." She
moved into a seated position, resting her hands on her lap. "Do
you suppose they'd mind if we walked around?"

Lips twitching at Lexie's sarcastic tone, she answered, "I'd
rather not gain their attention. Maybe at some point they'll leave
the room. Do you think they work a nine-to-five shift?" They
grinned at each other for a moment before refocusing on the men
at the far end of the room. "I'll keep monitoring their thoughts.
Maybe I'll hear what their plans are. That's my power. What's
yours?"

"My senses are sharper. I can see and hear from far distances.
And I can see auras, not that I know what the colors mean."

Kiernan sat up, keeping an eye on their captors. "Any idea who
they are or where they took us?"

"No. All I know is that it's related to the meteorite. I can't
believe they attacked us in a restaurant. One moment we were
impersonating Charlie's Angels, and the next moment we're here.
Maybe I blacked out when I tackled that guy."

"I don't think so." Kiernan scanned the area in front of her.
Besides the two attackers, who were dressed in dark clothing, she
saw three others near the far wall, backs to them and heads bent
as they worked over flashing monitors. After listening to their
thoughts for a few minutes, she was able to piece together that
they were studying the results of portal usage, and that
Commander Flerg would be arriving in one katrinet for debriefing.
"They're saying something about a portal. That's how they got us
here. And one of them called us humans a few minutes ago."

Packed sand and small rocks covered the ground. The air was
sharp and cold, reminiscent of autumnal mornings. Although
natural light filtered through the cavern, shadows draped much of
the room, making it hard for Kiernan to determine if there was
more than one exit. The opening Ubel used to leave the cavern
was too close to their abductors to attempt an escape.

Lexie gasped, and her thoughts filled Kiernan's mind. <*"Oh, my God. They're aliens."*>

Eyebrows raised, Kiernan glanced at Lexie, following her horrified gaze to the other side of the room. One of the men at the monitor walked toward the side by some stacked canisters. The natural light hit his features, and Kiernan held back a scream. At least seven feet tall, he had pale, cornflower blue skin, beady black eyes, and no nose. His appearance was the composite of every science fiction story where the alien looked evil. When he turned to the side, Kiernan noticed how his steel gray uniform had slits in the sides of the legs and arms, and muscles bulged through them. His thighs, in particular, were long and defined, their thickness reminding her of grasshoppers. "No way can we outrun them."

"They look like they could tear our throats out with their teeth," Lexie whispered.

His sharp teeth caught the light, and Kiernan shuddered. "Shark's teeth. Hopefully, they don't view us as alien food delicacies. I can't imagine being eaten by them would bring any pleasure. Certainly not in the ways we'd like our special ladies to dine on us."

"I can't believe your mind went to sex."

Kiernan bit back a satisfied smile. "I always enjoyed gallows humor."

<*"They're conscious. It's time to find out what they can do."*>

"Here they come," Kiernan warned.

Ubel and another alien who was taller, broader, and covered with different-colored medals on his chest approached. His uniform was an emerald green, unlike the others in the room. They each held several small machines in what she figured were their hands, though they looked more like mini-octopuses with eight squiggly fingers covered by suctions. About ten feet from them the two aliens stopped, and Ubel entered a sequence into one of the machines he carried. An energy force field flickered. They stepped through the area, and he repeated the action, causing the energy shield to flicker once more. They stopped a few feet away from Kiernan and Lexie.

<*"Good thing we didn't try to walk around."*> Kiernan nodded, agreeing wholeheartedly with Lexie.

The one with the medals spoke first. "My name is Supreme Commander Flerg of the Katakitites Royal Fleet. If you cooperate, no harm will come to you. We are researching how the meteorite has affected you." His voice was translated through one of the devices he carried, each word delivered in a monotone string. Flerg's ears were erect and turned toward them, reacting to the sounds around them.

"Where are we? Why did you take us?" Lexie asked, swiping her hair out of her eyes. Kiernan's gut tightened. Lexie had blood and dirt caked on her right temple.

Ubel leaned in and swatted her on the side of the head, causing Lexie to gasp. She placed a hand on the wound, a rivulet of blood trickling between her fingers. "You have no right to address the commander, human," he shouted with a confusing Bostonian accent. Dressed in jeans, a navy-blue polo shirt, and boat shoes, he looked like a typical, forgettable male or a Sperry shoe model. "Tell him about your powers."

Lexie crossed her arms and stared at them, scowling. She looked fierce with the blood oozing down her face.

<*"So much for their cooperation. If Ubel weren't royalty, I'd execute him for this fiasco. He's failed at every stage of this operation."*> Flerg stared at them for another moment, before turning on the other device he held. It beeped, flashed, and buzzed before he extended it toward Kiernan, who cowered back. He ignored her, running the scanner from head to toe several times before tapping the buttons and staring at the screen. Flerg turned toward Lexie and repeated the process. He engaged in conversation with Ubel, ignoring them. They lowered the energy field and left the area, restoring it once they were clear. Kiernan heard his thoughts. <*"These readings confirm their exposure to the meteorite. Ubel said he wasn't able to determine their abilities. We may have to wait until we move to the main facility to scan their brains."*>

"They weren't able to figure out anything, yet," Kiernan told Lexie. "Are you okay?"

Lexie shifted to her. "Yeah. Just a slight headache. It will make a hell of a story once we get out of here."

"I like your attitude." They shared a grim smile. After several minutes, everyone left the room, an ominous clanging confirming that they were locked inside. The monitors were dark, and the natural light was fading. "It must be evening for them. I wonder whether they'll have a night shift." Kiernan looked behind them and saw three small cots attached to the wall. She gestured to them. "Looks like they planned to bring us here. Might as well use them." She rose, holding in a groan as her muscles screamed at her. She extended a hand toward Lexie to help her up. "Have a seat while I take a look at that energy field."

Kiernan walked toward where she remembered the shield to be and stopped about five feet from it when a high-pitched beeping began. She stepped back two feet, and the beeping stopped. She looked behind her shoulder and saw Lexie sitting on one of the cots, watching her.

"They have some type of proximity alarm in place. I suppose that's a good way to prevent us from walking into the energy field." Kiernan stepped forward again, and the alarm started its insistent beeping once more.

"What happens if you keep walking forward?" Lexie asked.

Kiernan took three more steps, but stopped as the beeping became louder and faster. "I'm thinking that means I'm getting closer to it." She tapped her foot on the ground. "I don't think I should get closer. I mean, who knows what will happen if I walk into it."

"Well, it's possible that you'll walk right through it."

"Or it might electrocute me like an electric fence."

"Right. Let me—" Lexie rose and crossed over to her. "I can see the wave currents of the energy field. It's about five feet in front of us."

Kiernan squatted and picked up some small pebbles. She tossed one, and the energy field emitted a short buzzing noise when the pebble hit it. "Well, there it is." She threw another pebble, harder this time, and watched it bounce back toward them. She tilted her head and pointed at it. "It's burnt."

"And still smoking. We're not going to get through there unless we find a way to turn it off," Lexie said, her shoulders slumped. She looked tired and in pain.

Kiernan sighed. "Let's get some sleep, and we'll figure this out tomorrow." They returned to the cots, each lying down on one.

<*"More comfortable than I thought they'd be."*> Kiernan had to agree with Lexie's thought. The cots were much too small for

these aliens. She supposed it could be for their offspring. Or maybe it was only the males who were so huge. She hoped never to find out.

When she woke up, the room was dark. She remained still, curled on her side, waiting for her eyes to adjust. Two plates of food and cups filled with a clear liquid had been placed on a low table near their cots.

<*"She's awake. Good."*> A light came on, illuminating an alien in a red uniform with several medals across his chest a few feet from them. He looked like a muscular exotic frog with a blond mohawk. Kiernan heard Lexie snort, and she looked over to see her sitting up. "Kiernan and Lexie, I mean you no harm. I am here to help you."

Kiernan propped herself against the rock wall. It took her a moment to realize he was speaking English, although he spoke in a slow monotone. "Who are you? How did you get through the energy field?"

The alien shifted from one foot to the other. "I am Lerzep. I have an energy modulator. They plan to move you in two days' time to their outpost. Once they do so, it will be hard for you to escape. I am part of the rebel group currently in control of our planet. Ubel is part of the royal family we deposed. We will help you escape tomorrow evening. Be ready."

"Why should we trust you?"

"What choice do you have? I will come for you tomorrow at this time." The light was extinguished, and Kiernan sat in the dark. She saw a flash of light at the far end of the room as a door opened and closed.

Lexie shifted beside her. "He's right. We have no choice but to trust him."

Kiernan sighed. "I know. How's your head?"

"Better. Sleep helped."

"Is it odd that their commander couldn't speak our language, but both Lerzep and Ubel could?"

"Maybe they studied our language." Lexie shrugged.

Kiernan shifted on her cot and stared through the darkness. "Is that food?"

"Looks like it, and I doubt they want to poison us. They want to use our powers somehow. I say we should keep up our strength as best we can. That means eat, drink, and rest," Lexie said, as she rose from her cot.

Kiernan followed Lexie to the table. She lifted the plate and sniffed. "I guess chicken is universal." It was a mixture of meat and something that looked like gruel. She looked in the cup. "As is water." She retreated to the cot with her meager meal, sitting down on the edge.

Lexie sat down next to her. "Okay, fearless leader. Eat up."

<*"Aren't you a barrel of laughs."*> Kiernan heard. She decided to try the drink first, pleased by the fresh taste. It was tangy and light, reminding her of flavored water.

"Not bad," Lexie said after taking her first bite of the food. "Edible."

"A ringing endorsement if I ever heard one." Kiernan tasted the bland food and sighed. It would do.

They ate together in silent companionship for several minutes before Lexie broke the silence. "I wonder how they'll explain what happened. The fight. Our disappearance."

"They'll figure something out," Kiernan said. She set her empty dishes down on the table and walked toward the back corner of their prison. A rudimentary wooden stool with a hole in the middle was positioned over a deep metal bowl. To the side were some broad leaves and a bowl of water with some fragrant herbs. The stool was high enough that Kiernan needed to climb up. Once seated, she pulled her dress over her hips and pushed her panties down. *Don't think about how this looks.* It was embarrassing, but necessary. Taking a quick peek toward Lexie, she was glad to see she had shifted so her back was toward Kiernan. Taking a deep breath, she allowed herself to empty her bladder. She used a leaf to wipe herself before pulling her panties up and smoothing her dress down. Once she finished, she hopped off the stool and dipped her hands in the bowl of herbs. She returned to the cot and she sat down with a sigh of relief. "Well, that could have been much worse."

Lexie chuckled. "My turn."

While Lexie mastered the stool, Kiernan lay down once more. She had no idea what to expect tomorrow. She was afraid. Her mind turned toward her new romance with Thea, and regret coursed through her. She should have reached out to her months ago.

Lexie's hand on her shoulder brought her out of her thoughts. "Don't worry. We'll get out of this." Lexie squeezed her shoulder before moving back to her cot. She wanted to believe Lexie's words. She needed to. With that last thought, Kiernan closed her eyes and let her body rest.

*** 

### TUESDAY, OCTOBER 17, 2017 11:02 P.M.

Marcia felt her energy reserves draining with each second. She knew she couldn't maintain the shield for much longer, and as soon as she lowered her arm, everyone would be able to move once more. She couldn't see the alien masquerading as Peter, but his two henchmen were close enough that she could see the determination in their eyes. She lowered her arm and felt herself thrown to the side. Twisting to see what was happening, she reached out, although she knew it was futile. Before her eyes, Lexie, Kiernan, and their three attackers disappeared through a bright beam of light. Loud clapping came from several people nearby, their smiling faces at odds with what occurred mere moments ago.

Patricia ran over to her and helped her up. "Are you okay?"

"Yes. Someone pushed me out of the way." Marcia listened to the conversations humming around them.

"That was Lexie." Patricia leaned in and whispered, "People think that was a skit or some type of preview for a new Broadway play."

Rudi sashayed toward them, still clapping. "Why didn't you tell me they were going to do that?"

Marcia and Patricia looked at each other before turning toward Rudi.

"Pardon?" Marcia asked.

"Why didn't you tell me your friends were going to give that performance? I must admit I'm hurt Kiernan didn't tell me, but I'm glad she has another job lined up. She was so upset she had nothing. I mean," she waved her hand, "she wouldn't admit it, but that's Kiernan for you. Anyway, is your other friend an actress, too?"

Patricia let out an unattractive guffaw, and Marcia elbowed her in the side. At Rudi's confused look, Marcia sighed. She couldn't deal with this amount of stupidity. They needed to figure out where Lexie and Kiernan were taken.

"I'm sorry, Rudi. That would've ruined the surprise." Patricia patted her arm. Thea joined them with a questioning look. "Rudi, we're going to get going."

Marcia was thankful. Patricia was always great at reading a situation. Marcia nodded, as did Thea.

"I'll call you tomorrow," Patricia said to Rudi, kissing her cheek.

"Very well. Good night. It was nice to meet you both. Those special effects were wonderful," she added, looking at Marcia. She pointed toward Marcia's eyes. "Those purple eyes are mesmerizing."

"Thanks." Marcia bit her lip to keep from saying more and took Patricia's arm. They moved toward the front of the restaurant, Thea following.

Once they were outside, Marcia turned toward her companions. "Thea, I'm sure you're confused as to where Kiernan went and why she didn't warn you beforehand." She considered several ways of sending Thea on her way, but she couldn't convince herself to lie.

"Please don't send me away," Thea said, an edge of desperation threading through her voice.

"Well, we can't talk here. We can return to my home or go to one of your hotel rooms." She raised an eyebrow, waiting for an answer.

"Is Sammy home?" Patricia asked.

"No. She's sleeping over at a friend's house."

"You were hoping to get lucky tonight, weren't you?" Patricia asked, wiggling her eyebrows.

Marcia grimaced, thinking of Lexie. She was scared for her.

Patricia gave her a quick hug. "I'm sorry, Marcia. That was thoughtless of me. Let's go to my hotel. It's close, and if anyone is looking for us, they'll have a harder time tracking us down."

Once they were safe inside Patricia's hotel room, Marcia sat down in a chair, head in her hands. She felt helpless. Her body was tired from the energy she exerted while fending off their attackers. She had been naïve to think she could protect anyone. *Not that I knew I could create an energy field. Or freeze time, for fuck's sake.* Not that it mattered. Her romanticized notions of what she could do with these powers meant nothing in the face of a real threat, not if she couldn't protect those she loved. She hadn't told Lexie how deep her feelings ran, but she was in love with the woman. The thought of losing her again tore at her heart.

"That wasn't a sneak preview of an upcoming show, was it?" Thea asked, her voice quiet. She was seated in a chair while Patricia perched on the edge of the bed.

Marcia looked up. Patricia had a question in her eyes, and Marcia debated what to do. With Thea's connection to Kiernan, this situation affected her as much as it did them. "No. That was an abduction attempt by some bad people. If it weren't for Lexie, I'd be with them. Our problem is that we don't know where they are."

"Can't you find out?" Patricia asked.

It took a second for Marcia to understand what she was asking, and her eyes flitted to Thea before addressing Patricia, weighing each word. "I can, but I have to rest for a bit before I try. My body needs to regenerate. I feel like I ran a marathon."

"You can trust Thea to keep our secrets," Patricia said.

Marcia chewed on her lip. "It's not that so much as not wanting to place her in danger."

Thea leaned forward. "I'm already involved. Kiernan—I know our relationship is new, but I care for her. I want to help."

Marcia could see the sincerity in Thea's brown eyes, and more than that, she could see her aura—a deep red. She nodded, sitting up and taking a deep breath. "I think tonight confirmed Kiernan's abilities," Marcia began, only to be interrupted by Patricia.

"Her eyes were glowing. So were Lexie's during the attack."

"And yours," Thea added.

"Yes. We all have something in common. We were at a spa for different reasons on a night when a meteorite hit the ground near it. I touched it, breathed in some chemicals, and took home some souvenirs. Kiernan and Lexie also took home some rocks which had splintered off it. Over time, we've all developed certain powers. I've changed the most, as you can see." Marcia waved in front of her body. "I've also developed abilities such as astral projecting, teleportation, and invisibility, among other things. I found out recently that Lexie's sensory perceptions have become much more developed. I'm not sure about Kiernan's abilities, but my guess is she can read minds. What I do know for certain…" Marcia stalled, not sure how to say the next part without sounding crazy.

"Is that those men who kidnapped Kiernan and Lexie are aliens," Patricia finished.

Marcia raised her eyebrows, and Patricia shrugged, a slight smirk on her face. Rolling her eyes, Marcia observed Thea as she digested what they told her.

"Okay. That's a heck of an origination story." Thea got up from her chair and paced the room while Marcia and Patricia sat without speaking, allowing her to think. She stopped in the middle of the room, panic in her voice. "Will they come back to get you?"

"I don't know. What I do know is that one of them knows where I live."

"You can stay here tonight while we figure out what to do."

Marcia smiled her gratitude. "I think after eating something I'll be strong enough to astral project. See where they are and that they're okay. Then we can make a plan on how to help them."

"Is there anyone else who can help?" Thea asked.

"No one I know," Marcia said, "but we're three intelligent women. I believe in us, and I believe in Lexie and Kiernan. We'll find a way."

"Does Rudi know?" Thea asked, turning toward Patricia.

Patricia chuckled and shook her head. "She wouldn't believe it. You saw how she reacted to the attack. She jumped on the first viable explanation. Let me call room service. Call me paranoid, but I'd rather reduce the chances of any more aliens coming after you by eating in the restaurant."

Marcia got up and hugged Patricia. "Don't be afraid. I don't think they'll risk another attack."

"Still…"

In answer, Marcia found the room service menu and wrote down what she wanted.

After they placed the order, Thea sat down next to Marcia on the couch. "Once we get them back, I'd love to ask some questions about your abilities."

Marcia patted her hand. "Patricia trusts you, and that's good enough for me. Besides, I'm sure Kiernan was going to tell you at some point. As for your questions...I would expect nothing less from the good professor." They all chuckled.

"Well, I am interested to know how you plan to contact them," Thea said, a gleam in her brown eyes.

"Astral projection. I won't be able to speak to them or hear what they're saying, but I'll be able to see where they are."

"Wild. I can't wait to see you do it. What about teleporting?" Thea asked, her eyes wide. She leaned forward, body coiled with anticipation, while Patricia shot an affectionate smile Thea's way from her position next to the window.

"I'd do that, but it takes too much energy. I'd end up trapped with them while I rested. Astral projecting doesn't take as much energy, and I can check things out before allowing anyone to see me. That way, if anyone is with them or it looks like they're being watched, I can remain undetectable."

"How do you know you'll be able to astral project to them? I mean, can you go anywhere or does distance not matter?"

Marcia nodded, a thoughtful look on her face. "Good question. I've visited Patricia in Boston and others in New York. I guess we'll find out soon enough."

They sat in silence as their plan acted as a balm, soothing the raw hurt they felt at the possibility of never seeing Kiernan and Lexie again. *Somehow, we'll get them back. We have to.* Marcia had so much more to share with Lexie. She wanted to introduce her to Sammy. Confess her feelings. Make love. Experience what life felt like, being loved by the passionate woman. How the mornings felt awakening to their legs tangled together.

Patricia's gentle voice stirred Marcia from her thoughts. "We'll get them back. You'll see." She shot a grateful smile at Patricia.

The food arrived, and they did their best to discuss light-hearted topics. Once they were finished, Marcia lay on the bed, taking slow, deep breaths to help her focus. She visualized Lexie's beautiful face, her eyes tracing every inch of the beloved visage. She kept an image in her mind of how she looked mere hours earlier. She felt her body begin to buzz, even as it sank further into the mattress. Eyes closed, Marcia felt her body tingling, vibrating, traveling. She would see where Lexie was in a matter of minutes. When she felt movement, she opened her eyes and peered into a large, dark area. She didn't see anyone or anything at first. No aliens. Nothing to hint at any type of video surveillance. No metal bars or alarms, either. It was a huge area. She moved past several blank monitors toward the back of the room.

As her eyes adjusted, she saw three small beds against the far wall. Movement on one of them brought a smile of relief. She glided closer, her body moving through a small table she hadn't noticed. *What a weird sensation.*

Lexie sat up straight, signaling she could feel Marcia in the room. An empty plate clattered to the ground. *At least they were fed.* They didn't seem to be hurt. She could see Kiernan speaking and pointing to her, but all she could hear was a low buzzing noise. Raising a finger, Marcia made sure she was covered in the mist that signified she was invisible and walked around the area, looking for exits. She stuck her head through a door and saw two guards leaning against the rock wall, speaking. Backing up, she crossed to the other side of the room and found another door. Walking through it, she saw it led to a long, dark tunnel. No guards were present. *This might be a viable escape route.*

Returning to Lexie and Kiernan, she made herself visible and watched Kiernan remove a small Sharpie marker from a hidden pocket before handing it to Lexie. *Wow! I guess actors really do carry them around all the time.* Excited they would be able to communicate, Marcia touched Lexie's arm. As soon as they made contact, Marcia felt an electric jolt. Even more surprising, she could feel the solidness of Lexie's bicep.

A moment later, a familiar hand cupped her jaw. Her eyes flew up to connect with stormy gray ones.

"You're a sight for sore eyes," Lexie said, her voice tremulous.

They stared at each other, relief overwhelming Marcia. She could hear Lexie's voice. "I hear you," she whispered in awe. Leaning forward, Marcia delivered a short but heartfelt kiss. "Tell me what you know."

"They plan to transfer us in two days. A rebel named Lerzep is going to help us escape tomorrow night. He said they took control of the planet from the royal family. Rest up and come back tomorrow night a little before this time."

Marcia nodded and blinked back some tears. She was so relieved. "I—"

Lexie stopped her with a finger to her lips. "Not until we're back and safe. It can wait until then."

Marcia sniffed back her emotions and nodded. She reached out and touched Kiernan's hand, feeling another pulse of energy. "Are you okay?"

Kiernan smiled. "Right as rain. Tell Thea."

"I will. She's with me and Patricia right now. I'll see you both tomorrow." Marcia stepped back, breaking her connection with both of them. She shot a smile at them before visualizing Patricia. When she felt the pull under her belly button, Marcia opened her eyes. She allowed her body to settle, the vibrations abating as her body solidified. Patricia and Thea stared at her.

"That was incredible," Thea murmured.

"Right?" Patricia said. "You disappeared."

Marcia sat up. "I made an unscheduled pit stop. It seems touching them provides me with a jolt of energy."

"From Lexie, no doubt."

Marcia chose to ignore Patricia's comment. "They're okay. They're being moved in two days, but a rebel leader came to them earlier and offered to help them escape tomorrow night. I'm going back then."

Patricia scoffed. "That sounds like the worst plan I've ever heard. How can we trust him? Where are they? How will they get back here? How will we stop this from happening again?" Patricia kept firing questions, her voice becoming more strident.

Marcia jumped off the bed and grabbed Patricia, hugging her. "I don't have the answers. I'm scared, too. But they're alive, and they have help. It sounds like there was some type of power grab, and the former rulers are trying to take control again. Somehow we're in the middle of all this." Marcia sat them down on the edge of the bed, rubbing Patricia's back as Thea sat on the other side of her. "Let's not borrow trouble. We'll get them back and find a way to make sure this doesn't happen again."

"Patricia, do you realize you're the nucleus of a group of extraordinary women?" Thea asked. "Marcia, Kiernan, me. And by association, Lexie. Even Rudi."

"Let's not go wild here," Marcia said. They chuckled.

"She really isn't what I expected," Thea said.

"Not the brightest bulb," Marcia agreed.

"Hey. She has her good points," Patricia defended. Marcia raised an eyebrow. "Don't give me that. She can be sweet, and she wouldn't be successful if she didn't have some good qualities. Besides you kept encouraging me to give her a chance."

Marcia smirked but let the subject drop.

Thea continued. "At any rate, what I'm pointing out is that you are part of a network, and we will support each other. Find a way. Believe in that."

Patricia nodded. "Okay. Thank you." She reached out and squeezed their hands. "You two are great friends."

"Well, this great friend is going to return to her hotel. Patricia, I'll call you tomorrow." Thea rose and retrieved her purse. "Marcia, it was great to meet you. Just think, one day we'll look back on today and reminisce about the small alien abduction attempt. Then we'll talk about a hundred other adventures we've shared."

They moved to the door, and Thea hugged them both before leaving. Patricia locked the door and leaned against it. Marcia could see the sarcastic remark formulating in her friend's mind, so it came as no surprise when a moment later Patricia said, "Want to watch a movie? *Close Encounters*? *War of the Worlds*? *Independence Day*?"

Shaking her head, Marcia threw an answer over her shoulder, as she made her way back to the bed. "Let's stick with a rom-com instead."

# Chapter Nineteen

*KARINAN CYCLE 5 KATRINET 4*

LERZEP STARED AT THE mirror, scrutinizing his disguise. Soon he would be able to revert back to his natural appearance. He could hardly wait. Part of being a skilled spy was not being recognized, not even by his relatives. The other royals didn't know the rebels possessed technology to alter their appearances. Unsurprising, since only royals controlled such advancements. Lerzep stole it, along with several other technological prizes, when he made the decision to remove his family from power. As the next in line, Lerzep had entertained the idea of biding his time and making substantial changes in policy once his parents died. Seeing so many of his people suffering under draconian measures convinced him not to wait. He begged his father to change, but he was adamant about keeping with tradition, regardless of how the majority of citizens struggled to exist. After much soul-searching, Lerzep decided to help the rebels.

The rebels consisted of a group of dissatisfied, brave people, many who were deserters of the royal military. They left after the last planetary raid of a neighboring civilization. The rebels didn't agree with the royals' decision to plunder other planets for no reason other than to become richer. Such actions flew in the face of their people's sacred tenets which spoke of making alliances with other civilizations to further knowledge, promote peace, and strengthen their ability to survive.

Once Lerzep made the decision to act against his family, he infiltrated his way into the rebel camp. It took much time and many tests, but finally the rebels trusted him. During the coup, clues were left to make it seem as if Lerzep was taken as a prisoner of war. In reality, he gave the information needed for the rebels to gain control of the government.

For the last few karinan cycles the rebels bided their time, gathering information and planning how to defeat the royals and their supporters once and for all. The time to act was tonight. Lerzep would lead his people to a better way of living. His part of the attack included helping the humans escape and delivering them to the portal, another technological advancement the royals believed only they controlled. While he helped the prisoners, the others on his team would subdue everyone working at the military installation, and the beta team would sweep the outer facilities for any other royal supporters.

Lerzep made his way to where the prisoners were being held. *Everyone should be in place.* He made his way inside the building, strolling up to the two guards standing in front of the prison door. They wore navy blue uniforms, signifying they were ensigns. Lerzep knew them both. They attended the military academy together, often competing at matches which tested their skills. Of course, they did not recognize him in his present state. What they would recognize was the color of his uniform and the medals he displayed. His appearance demanded respect. They snapped to attention when he stopped before them. "Flerg sent me to check on the prisoners. Did they feed?"

"Yes, Sir. They're sleeping."

Lerzep opened the door and peered toward the back of the room. Both females were supine, eyes closed and faces toward the back wall. He would have to wait until they were out of the building to determine whether they were abused. He was banking on the royals' mindset that the humans must be treated with gentle hands so as to optimize their chances of breeding future royals through them. He blanched at the thought. *No being should be treated this way.* Closing the door, Lerzep nodded. He turned away and swiped his hands away from his body twice, the signal for his team to move in.

Lerzep spun and hit the closer guard with both hands, boxing his ears. The guard squealed in pain. Three members of Lerzep's team arrived and used a zapping rod to render him and the second guard unconscious. Lerzep entered the room while his team dragged the unconscious guards inside.

The two females stood, waiting. He crossed the room and disengaged the energy force field, gesturing for them to follow. While they did, his men transferred the unconscious guards to the cots, their legs and heads hanging over as if they'd drunk too much pankah. His team tied the guards' arms and legs, and once they moved out of the area, he reactivated the energy shield. He signaled his team to proceed with the next phase of their operation and led the women to a side door, which he unlocked. They entered a long, narrow tunnel and stopped while he secured the door. Unlike in the prison, no light shone through the area. He stopped to turn on the luxfactorum he carried and looked back at the humans.

"Faex!" he swore under his breath, upset to see bruises on Lexie's face and a large scab on the side of her head. At least she seemed alert.

"Don't worry. It looks worse than it is. We're both okay," Kiernan said.

Reassured, Lerzep nodded. "This way." He hurried down the tunnel, glad to see both females were keeping pace. The tunnel was an old access route used by menial workers, and royals would never deign to use it. They turned the corner, and a translucent female head appeared in front of them, stopping their progress.

Lexie reached out and cupped the woman's cheek, causing the phantom to solidify. "We're okay. He's helping us."

The woman who materialized before them was dressed from head to toe in black. Her violet eyes glowed, offset by long, white tresses.

"I'm Marcia." She nodded to Lerzep in greeting.

From what Lerzep had read, Marcia was the most powerful of the three.

Before Lerzep could respond, Lexie said in a low voice, "Someone's coming."

"This way," Lerzep replied, leading them through a series of tunnels to an access panel. He input the code to unlock a metal door and jogged through it, leading the three women to hide behind an enormous air conditioner condenser unit. He crouched next to them. "My team will be here soon. We will bring you to an area where we can activate the portal to send you back."

"I can hear others' thoughts," Kiernan said. "Two guards are coming this way. They were ordered to check the perimeter due to two guards failing to check in. Are those the two you left in the prison?"

"Yes. How close are they?"

"I can see them," Lexie answered. "They're at the far end of the complex."

Lerzep peered into the darkness, but he couldn't see anyone. He waited for several cakrae, his eyes watering while he focused in the direction she pointed. Movement caught his attention—an enforcement squad. His team would be close behind, but he worried they would not arrive in time. A hand on his arm caught his attention. *Marcia.* Lexie and Kiernan each had a hand on one of Marcia's arms. Before he could ask what she was doing, their eyes began to glow in concert. Breathless, he could not believe what he was witnessing. He'd read the stories of people with extraordinary powers, but he'd never seen anything like this.

The air around them seemed to vibrate, and a fine white mist enshrouded them. The squad came closer, yet they continued moving without pause. The royals' military marched within three clarks of their position. Once they were out of sight, Marcia dropped her hand, and the mist dissipated.

"That was most impressive," Lerzep said. Several short bursts of light caught his attention, and he grinned. "My team is approaching." Once they arrived, Lerzep stood and demanded their report.

Greag, his first commander and oldest friend, stepped forward. His midnight blue skin and rich brown fur reminded Lerzep of the wild bercheks—wily, savage creatures on their home planet. Greag could be much the same during combat. "All military barracks are under our control, as is the royal residence. I will send this team to capture that squad," he said, pointing in the direction they marched. "The Royal Mother wishes to speak with you. Prince Ubel is demanding an audience."

Lerzep scoffed. "The royals can wait until tomorrow. I want a detailed report of all technology recovered and a summary of what they planned to do with the humans."

"Should we keep the humans here until after we have reviewed the reports?" Greag motioned to the three women.

Lerzep shook his head, puffing out his chest and resting his hands on his hips. "No. I refuse to take away their choices any longer. It's bad enough their bodies have been altered without their consent. They will return to Earth."

"As you wish. Let me send Alpha One with you for protection while we sweep the rest of the base." Greag bowed low before taking his leave.

Accepting the elite squad's help, Lerzep led everyone to the jump out point. Once they entered the small structure, he turned to the humans. "I apologize for your treatment at the hands of the Katakitites. We are not all barbarians. It is my hope that you will consider entering a peace accord with us."

"Oh, well, we can't really speak on behalf of Earth. We have no authority to represent our government," Marcia said.

"To me and my people, the three of you are the only humans we would trust with such a sacred bond. Even in the short time I have known you, I recognize your strength."

"He's sincere," Kiernan said to the other two women.

"I know. I can see his aura. I might not know what all the colors mean, but I'm a pretty good judge of character," Lexie said.

"I agree," Marcia said. "We are honored. Perhaps we can discuss your offer in greater detail once you have dealt with the people who were responsible for our abduction."

"Very well." He held out a small device. It was an oval blackish-brown metal with three buttons on one side. "I will be able to contact you using this device." He waved over one of his men. "He will treat your injuries, and then I will send you on your way. I will be in touch in two of your moon cycles, or what we call karinan cycles. By then my government will be put to rights, and I will make sure this type of treatment will not occur to other planet dwellers. I look forward to revisiting the possibility of building a lasting alliance with your world when we next speak."

With a nod, Lerzep stepped aside, watching as the medical tech cleaned and healed Lexie's wound by using the sanafactorem. Once Lexie was whole again, he gave permission to open the portal. The three females crossed over, and he closed his eyes, counting to sextorix. He needed to center himself before meeting with his people. The next few days were sure to be challenging. It was best to keep in mind all the good he would do not only for the Katakitites but for those who came in contact with them. He planned to elevate his people. Today was their first step on the ladder.

*** 

### WEDNESDAY, OCTOBER 18, 2017 12:17 A.M.

Patricia paced in her hotel room—four steps, turn, four steps, turn. Again and again. "What's taking them so long? Shouldn't we have heard something by now?"

"I'm sure they'll find us once they're back," Thea said from her curled up position on the small couch. She had a paperback book resting open on her lap, but it seemed to be more of a prop than a way to pass the time as they waited.

"Marcia's been gone for over an hour. How long does it take to free them and come home?"

"Patricia, you said it yourself. It's only been a little over an hour."

"How can you be so calm?" Patricia flopped down in a chair. "A thousand things could go wrong."

Thea gave her a look. "You saw what they could do when the three of them were together. Their abductors captured them through blind luck. With their collective powers, they'll find a way home, regardless of whether anyone else helps them. I believe in them."

"I do, too, but who knows what they're up against?"

"Bumbling aliens who underestimate our friends?"

A knock at the door pulled Patricia across the room. She opened it, expecting to see her friends. Instead, Rudi thrust a bouquet of flowers in her face. "I hope I'm not intruding," Rudi said, pulling Patricia into a hug, twirling her into the room, and closing the door before releasing her. "I was hoping to see you at the play or the after-play party tonight, but I realized we hadn't discussed it. So, I came to you." She gave a little bow. As Rudi straightened, her eyes focused on something behind Patricia. *Not something. Someone.* "Oh, hello, Thea. It's nice to see you again. I thought you'd be with Kiernan since she failed to show tonight, too."

"She had a prior commitment, so I'm spending time with Patricia."

"Oh? Does it have to do with that preview she was part of last night?"

"Sort of," Patricia said, placing the bouquet on a table before moving further into the room. "We're waiting for them to come by. I can call you tomorrow?"

A knock on the door stopped Patricia, and she returned to the door while muttering, "Grand Central Station. How can I help you?" Thea's chuckle made Patricia smirk. She opened the door, her smile widening when Kiernan, Marcia, and Lexie piled into the room. "Thank God! We were so worried." She closed the door and followed them, pulling Marcia into a tight hug.

"Why were you worried?" Rudi asked, her forehead furrowing.

"We made plans to get together earlier. I'm sorry we're so late," Kiernan said, reaching out to pull Thea into a long hug. "I'm sorry, Rudi," she added, turning to her. "I was going to contact you tomorrow. Thea extended her stay, but she needs to return to Massachusetts soon. I wanted to spend as much time with her as I could."

Rudi dismissed the explanation with a hand wave. "It's fine, Kiernan. I get it." She turned to Patricia. "When do you have to leave?"

"I can stay a few more days." She watched Rudi's face light up, and her traitorous heart sped up. *So, not over her.* Catching the smirk on Kiernan's face, she glared at her. *Not fair to read my mind.* An elegant shrug was all the response she received.

Although Patricia wanted to hear all the details, she didn't know how to get Rudi to leave. If she were honest with herself, she didn't want to. It would be so much easier if Rudi knew what happened, but she had no idea how she'd take the news.

"Maybe we should tell her?" Kiernan asked.

"Well, you know her best. Do you think she'll believe it?" Patricia asked. "And keep the news to herself?"

"She's our friend. Don't you think it's worth the risk?" Kiernan asked.

"If you trust her, I'm game," Marcia said. Lexie nodded.

"What are you talking about?" Rudi asked, her eyes jumping to each person.

"Darling, last night wasn't a preview for a new play," Kiernan said, sinking into the sofa next to Thea, who pulled her closer. "Three men tried to abduct us, and Marcia was able to escape."

"Thanks to Lexie pushing me out of the way," Marcia added. "We'll be talking about that later," she added, directing a dark look at Lexie.

"I'd do it a thousand times to keep you safe."

"Talk about romantic gestures," Patricia teased.

"I don't understand," Rudi said.

"I think this may take awhile. Let's order some food and drink," Patricia suggested.

"Great idea," Lexie said. "I'm famished."

"Didn't they feed you?" Patricia asked.

Lexie grimaced. "Yes, but it was some type of slop that was less than palatable."

Thoughts of how they were treated raced through Patricia's mind. It reminded her of the recent danger they faced and the uncertainty of the future.

"We're okay. No one will try to kidnap us again," Kiernan said, her eyes kind and voice soothing.

Patricia considered Kiernan's words and nodded. She was sure once she heard what happened, she'd understand why they seemed so confident. "Let me order the food." She ignored the hum of conversation while she placed the call, rejoining the rest once she finished.

"So, will someone please help me make sense of everything?" Rudi asked.

Marcia grinned. "Well, do we have a story for you..."

*** 

### SUNDAY, OCTOBER 22, 2017 8:47 A.M.

Waking up after an electrifying dream, Marcia puttered around the house, waiting for Sammy to wake up. She sat in her favorite chair, eyes flittering over the full bookshelves. Those books were filled with wisdom, and with her ability to remember everything, she could supplement what she remembered with so much more knowledge. Her sight turned inward, as she thought of Lexie. That woman was a revelation. Certainly not a one-book wonder. No, she was a series of novels, an endless stream of experiences Marcia wanted to read. *Yes, that's what I want. I want to be able to fill a bookcase with novels dedicated to Lexie—each book a study of one aspect of her personality—her thoughts, reactions, feelings, and background. Everything.*

She heard Sammy rustling in the kitchen for a few minutes before she entered the room, a granola bar in her hand. Marcia raised her eyebrows, as Sammy bent to deliver a kiss on her cheek.

"That's all you're having?"

With a giggle, Sammy said, "No. I'm gonna have some English muffins, too. They're toasting."

Nodding with approval, Marcia said, "Sit down, sweetie." Sammy sagged against her on the sofa, and Marcia stroked her hair while gathering her thoughts. "Sweetie, you know Lexie's coming over tonight, right?"

"I know, Mom. Do you still like her?"

*Well, that's pretty blunt.* Marcia liked that characteristic in Sammy, although in the past it had placed her in some uncomfortable situations. Having her ask in a stage whisper why the woman didn't wipe the ketchup off her face or what the yucky smell was after someone farted had mortified Marcia. Still, she hoped Sammy never stopped communicating in such a direct manner.

"I do. I care for her a great deal. I really want you to like her, Sammy. She wants to make me happy, and when I'm with her, I feel that." She took a deep breath and added, "I've fallen in love with her. I will do anything to make this relationship successful. I don't want to lose her."

Sammy was quiet, staring at her hands. "Do you love her more than you loved Daddy?"

Marcia firmed her lips together. The short answer was yes. She felt more alive than she ever felt with John. She'd loved him in her own way. He'd accepted all she was able to give him, and she gave him everything she could. Marcia couldn't tell Sammy any of that, though. She knew Sammy wouldn't understand.

"I loved Daddy very much. Those feelings were different, though. It's like comparing your closest friends, Rosie and Stephanie. They're two different people. Do you like them for the same reasons?"

Sammy played with Marcia's hair, focusing on her fingers as she sifted them through some white strands. "No. Rosie's crazy and loud, but Stephanie thinks more and is quieter." She shifted, allowing their eyes to connect. "I guess I can see what you're saying. So, Lexie isn't anything like Daddy?"

"They're alike in some important ways, but in other ways they aren't. I'd like you to give her a chance by getting to know her. Will you do that?"

"Yes. As long as she isn't like Peter." Sammy scrunched up her nose, and Marcia couldn't help but chuckle.

"They couldn't be more different."

"Does she know you love her?" Sammy asked in a soft voice.

"I haven't actually said the words, if that's what you mean. But that will happen soon enough. Sometimes, the words aren't so important as long as our actions show it. Watch her when we're together, and you'll see that she cares for me, too." She patted Sammy's arm. "You'll like her, Sammy. Just be open to it."

Sammy leaned over and hugged Marcia before jumping up. "I'm gonna go eat."

\*\*\*

Marcia allowed herself to get lost in research documents, notating relevant information for future use. She kept at it until she glanced up and noticed shadows creeping toward her, the afternoon gone. Lexie had offered to bring dinner, and although Marcia objected since she'd invited her over, Lexie had insisted that she knew a great Italian restaurant nearby. Getting up to change, her excitement built at the thought of seeing her again. They had spent the last few days catching up at work, and although they kept in touch, it wasn't the same.

Hearing the doorbell, Marcia called out to Sammy, "Can you get that? It's Lexie. I'll be right there." She looked at herself in the mirror one more time, noticing how she glowed. *I wonder if this is from the changes I've undergone or the anticipation of spending more time with Lexie.* She figured it might be both. Even her eyes blazed. The violet-colored irises were mere rims, swallowed by black pupils. She wondered whether they would light up the room if the lights were turned off. Flipping off the light, she turned back toward the mirror. *Holy kamole! It's like having a built-in night-light. I wonder if Lexie's eyes do the same thing.* She couldn't wait to find out.

Shaking off those thoughts she strode into the kitchen, where Lexie removed the food from a plastic bag while Sammy told her about a movie she watched the night before. Marcia leaned against the doorjamb, listening as Lexie asked questions.

Sammy was animated, loving how she was the focus of attention. "So, then the guy said, 'Just—uh, just go.' And the look on his face was so funny!"

Lexie chuckled, and Marcia wondered whether she was laughing at the movie or Sammy's description. Either way, Marcia loved how she was so responsive toward Sammy. *I love her.*

As if hearing her thoughts, Lexie looked up. "Well, hello there."

Marcia straightened and approached her. Not knowing how demonstrative Lexie was willing to be in front of Sammy, Marcia pulled her in for a quick hug and kissed her cheek. She stepped away, reminding herself to be a good host. "What would everyone like to drink?"

"Water," Sammy and Lexie said together. With a laugh, Marcia filled three glasses while Lexie removed the lids from the food.

"Mmm, those smell delicious," Marcia commented. She watched Lexie move around the kitchen as if it were her own. She seemed relaxed. Happy. Sammy continued to talk to her as if they'd known each other for years. *I'll have to thank her later.* It was obvious she'd taken Marcia's request to heart and was attempting to get to know Lexie.

Retrieving some plates, Marcia asked, "Who's getting what?"

"I'll have the chicken parm," Sammy piped up. Marcia raised an eyebrow at Lexie. "Is the shrimp scampi yours?" she asked, spotting the third entrée. It was baked eggplant, Marcia's favorite.

Lexie nodded, and Marcia hummed her approval. She transferred the salad into a dish so everyone could share and carried it and a bag of breadsticks into the dining room. Sammy followed with the other two plates, and Lexie grabbed the drinks. Lexie retreated to the kitchen, probably to get Marcia's dish, and Marcia followed her to get some napkins.

Marcia reached her side by the refrigerator. "Hi."

"Hello, yourself," Lexie said in a smoky voice.

Marcia's heart picked up speed, her eyes devouring every detail now that she could take a few moments to stare. Lexie wore black jeans that fit her like a glove, a caramel-colored silk button-down top, and black stilettos. Marcia stepped into her space, not wanting to waste the opportunity of a proper greeting. Their kiss was restrained—a necessity with Sammy in the next room—but intense. Marcia fought back a moan as she tasted Lexie's minty breath. She craved the physical connection.

"Mom, what's taking you so long?" Breaking off the kiss, Marcia spotted Sammy frozen in the doorway. "Uh…"

"Oh, honey! I'm so sorry. We're coming in right now." She glanced at Lexie, an apology on her tongue, and noticed her balled fists. *Is she angry with me? She must understand we can't just make out when Sammy is around.* Insecurity ate at Marcia.

She squeezed Lexie's bicep before turning away, hoping this wouldn't become a problem. Since Lexie had no children, it was possible she didn't understand how it changed, well, everything. Once they sat down to eat, Marcia hazarded a glance at Lexie, who shot her a small smile. Marcia exhaled. *Good.* Whatever that was about, Lexie wasn't angry with her. *I'll ask her later.*

Dinner was filled with conversation and laughter. It went better than Marcia had dared to hope. When Sammy left the room to bring their empty plates to the kitchen, Lexie turned to Marcia with an apologetic look on her face.

"I'm so sorry, Marcia. I should have waited until I knew Sammy wasn't around before kissing you. I guess I lost my head a bit."

Marcia's eyebrows shot up in surprise. "Lexie, that was as much me as you. I wanted to kiss you." She lowered her voice. "I want to do it again. And I intend to." She watched with satisfaction as Lexie swallowed.

Sammy reentered the room. "Mom, Rosie's dad is outside with her to pick me up. I won't be home until tomorrow afternoon." She grinned while raising an eyebrow before giving Marcia a hug and turning to Lexie. "It was nice to meet you. See you later." With a small wave, she was gone.

The click of door seemed to echo through the house, as Marcia realized she had Lexie all to herself until the next day. Turning toward her, Marcia gazed in her eyes. *I suppose that jumping in her lap wouldn't be the smoothest move. Better to start simple.*

"Would you care for some wine?" Marcia rose, making her way toward the kitchen.

"No."

Stopping short, Marcia turned toward her, a question forming on her lips.

"Come here," Lexie said, her voice throaty and compelling.

Marcia stalled for a moment, stunned by the raw hunger she could read in darkening eyes. She moved with quick strides and grasped Lexie's extended hands to pull her up. When Lexie's tongue touched her lips, Marcia felt a strong current of lust rise. She moaned, pulling Lexie forward by the back of her neck for a deeper kiss. Chills ran through her as their tongues tangled, and she licked the inside of Lexie's mouth with provocative strokes.

Fingers weaved through her hair while Lexie's lips slid across her cheek to whisper, "Take me to bed, Marcia."

Lexie tongued her ear, swirling around before nibbling the lobe. Marcia was a shuddering mess. Instead of releasing her, Lexie held her in a tight embrace, licking the shell of her ear and ripping a groan out of her. Marcia's knees nearly buckled, as heat filled her belly.

*What's all this newfound strength good for if not to whisk her off her feet?* Marcia picked her up, smiling at her squeak of surprise, and headed toward the stairs. She concentrated on not dropping her, which became much harder when Lexie wrapped her arms around her neck and began plying it with kisses. She placed Lexie back on her feet next to the bed and watched, spellbound, while Lexie undressed for her, dropping each garment on a nearby chair. Once she was nude, she stepped toward Marcia, a question in her eyes.

Marcia took her time to run her eyes over Lexie's toned body. She chewed on her bottom lip as she felt desire roll through her.

"I love you, Marcia."

The air sucked out of her. "You do?"

Lexie stepped closer. "I do, and we can do as much or as little as you want. I'm not going anywhere."

Transfixed by the luminescence of Lexie's eyes, silver rings reflecting the moon's glow, Marcia bridged the small gap between them and ran her hand down an upturned face. "I love you, too. So much."

"And is this what you want, Marcia?"

"Yes. I want this. I want you. No more waiting." Marcia had never felt so sure of anything. Their bond pulsed between them, and she saw the energy pulling them together. She refused to fight their connection any longer. Marcia leaned in and delivered a heated kiss. Shaking hands loosened Marcia's clothing, lips skating over her body as each barrier was removed. Once she was bare, Lexie took her hand and led her to the bed. They hugged, and the feeling of skin on skin made Marcia's blood burn.

"Lie down, my love. I want to explore you." The huskiness of Lexie's voice caused goosebumps to break out on Marcia's body. She was quick to lie down, not needing any more motivation than Lexie's obvious desire.

Once on the bed, Marcia watched Lexie climb over her on her hands and knees like a hungry cat, her ravenous expression and unhurried pace indicating she was going to take her time. She placed her hands on either side of Marcia's head, holding herself above her just high enough that their torsos didn't touch. Marcia could feel the heat of Lexie's body, and she felt her own body heating up in response.

Lexie lowered her face so that their lips brushed together as she spoke. "I've dreamt of making love with you, of erasing our first time and replacing it with the way you should be loved. Of touching you and making you mine. Do you want that, Marcia? Do you want me to touch you?"

"God, yes," Marcia declared, her voice hoarse, as she fought her inclination to grab Lexie and pull her against her body. Instead, Marcia gripped the sheets beneath her and whimpered when Lexie's hair tickled her collarbones. She arched her neck and closed her eyes, sinking in to the addictive feeling of Lexie's lips tasting her neck, chin, and, finally, lips. Marcia opened her mouth and rubbed her tongue against Lexie's dexterous one, loving the friction, the texture, the thoroughness of her kisses, and her obvious desire to find every one of Marcia's secrets and make them her own.

Marcia found herself in a haze of desire. Lexie explored her body, kissing every inch of her face and neck before lowering herself fully on Marcia and sliding down to straddle her waist. Groaning at the feeling of Lexie's arousal painting her stomach, Marcia tangled her hands in her hair. Lexie nipped at Marcia's collarbones, tonguing the indentations before leaning down to flick at one of her nipples. Marcia whimpered. Lexie was merciless, moving back and forth between breasts, sucking and flicking and licking and chewing until her nipples were tight and sensitive. Marcia could feel how much her responses were affecting Lexie. She cupped Lexie's ass and pulled her forward, her hands falling on Marcia's biceps as they flexed. Their eyes connected, and Lexie moaned breathlessly.

"Oh, Jesus. You feel incredible," Lexie muttered before she swooped in to deliver a devastating, forceful kiss. She moved back and forth over Marcia's flexing abs a few times, and Marcia starting moving Lexie against her in a rhythm, kneading Lexie's taut backside. Lexie tucked her face into the crook of Marcia's neck, her hips thrusting. With another thrust her movements became jerky, and with a strong shudder, she came, Marcia's name breathed in her ear.

Marcia wrapped Lexie in her arms, running one hand in soothing motions up and down her back, feeling the small tremors working their way through Lexie's body. She kissed Marcia's chest and stretched her arms and legs before lifting herself off Marcia and resting on her knees. She delivered a wide smile. "You are irresistible, but you got me distracted from my mission to taste every part of your body." She shook her finger at Marcia and sported a playful smirk. "No more distractions."

"I make no promises." Marcia giggled. She withstood Lexie's mock glare.

Lexie leaned in and licked every indentation between Marcia's ribs, the definition of her hipbones, and the spaces in between her abdominal muscles. "Ohh," Marcia breathed, wiggling a bit at the ticklish sensations.

"I taste good on you," Lexie said, and since Marcia found it hard to think coherently, she chose not to reply. Instead, she rested her hands on Lexie's shoulders and squeezed, earning a smirk.

Marcia found it hard to control herself as Lexie took her time learning her body. "Lexie," she whined. She kept dipping her tongue in Marcia's bellybutton, and it was driving her insane.

"Shh, love," Lexie responded, running her fingers over the back of Marcia's knees. After a few more minutes of torture, Lexie said, "Turn onto your stomach."

Quick to do as she wished, Marcia felt lips kiss down her spine, hands roaming over her back and settling on her hips. "Up," Lexie whispered, guiding Marcia onto her hands and knees. She felt Lexie settle herself underneath her before strong hands wrapped around her thighs.

Crying out when she felt Lexie's pouty lips capture her throbbing clitoris, Marcia did her best not to smother her, keeping her hips from grinding forward. That became infinitely harder when Lexie grabbed her ass and pulled her closer to her busy mouth.

"You taste delicious," Lexie murmured. She blew on Marcia's bundle of nerves before flicking it with her tongue and sucking harder. That's all it took for Marcia to fall over the edge with a guttural groan.

Marcia closed her eyes tightly, gasping as her body trembled, wave after wave of ecstasy flooding her system. Lexie kept massaging her clitoris with her lips and tongue, and Marcia nearly screamed when three fingers were thrust forcefully inside her. Lexie set a fast rhythm, demanding Marcia give her everything. Marcia held nothing back, trusting Lexie, trusting herself. Soon she felt her body succumbing to an even stronger orgasm, and Marcia moaned long and low.

"Lexie," she groaned, slowing her motions while Lexie lapped at her weeping center for several minutes.

"God, you taste divine. And your ass...I love every inch of you."

Laughing, Marcia looked through her legs, watching Lexie crawl out and plop next to her before she allowed herself to lie down on her stomach. She turned her head toward Lexie, and they shared a languid, loving kiss.

"You made me feel so good, Lexie." She wanted to say thank you, but she figured that would sound rather silly. Still, she felt so grateful. It was hard to believe that this magnificent, powerful woman loved her.

Lexie hummed. She ran her hand over Marcia's back, resting it at the base for a moment before caressing Marcia's backside. "You really do have a marvelous ass. So chiseled."

Shivering as Lexie's hands became more focused, Marcia leaned over and kissed her with focused intent. "Why don't you rest on top of me? I want to feel you." Lexie delivered a heated gaze before doing as suggested.

Marcia sighed, loving how Lexie's body sank into her, surrounded her—her back, her ass, her legs—like her favorite blanket. She could feel Lexie kissing the top of her shoulders, lightly massaging them with her hands. Marcia made herself relax, moaning at the sensations Lexie was creating. When she unclenched her muscles, she heard Lexie's breath catch.

"Marcia," she groaned. "God, that feels so good. Squeeze your ass together again."

Doing as requested, she let go when Lexie told her to and flexed when asked to do so again. It didn't take her long to realize that Lexie was riding her, and each time she flexed, she felt Lexie's entire body shudder. Lexie moved against her, establishing a rhythm that Marcia adopted, clenching and relaxing as Lexie grinded against her backside.

Lexie moaned. "Don't stop."

Marcia felt her own body reacting to their rhythm, clenching, and grinding. "Oh, Lexie, I'm gonna...I'm gonna come," Marcia said, trembling as she propped herself on her elbows to gain some leverage. Lexie's hands wrapped around her body and squeezed her breasts, as she bit down on Marcia's shoulder.

Marcia felt her body explode, pleasure overwhelming her. She could feel Lexie against her and knew she was climaxing, too. Their voices mingled, moans and sighs filling the air. With a large exhale, Marcia fell back down on the bed, and she hummed when she felt Lexie press into her, head resting in between Marcia's shoulder blades while they both caught their breath.

"Wow," Marcia muttered.

"Wow is right," Lexie murmured, delivering a sweet kiss on her shoulder, causing Marcia to smile sleepily.

"I don't think I can move," Marcia said.

"Me neither. Thankfully, you make a surprisingly comfortable pillow."

"Oh. Good." Marcia allowed herself to close her eyes, knowing she wouldn't wake up tomorrow resigned to the harsh truth that their lovemaking was a figment of her imagination, created with her dream lover. No, this time she knew that in the morning she would feel the warmth of Lexie's arms around her. This time she would wake up and find her dreams had come true.

# Chapter Twenty

THE LARGE LECTURE HALL was abuzz, the room filled to capacity. Kiernan realized she shouldn't be surprised. Patricia had told her how packed the classes were. No doubt since they were at B.U. where she had a following of loyal students, Thea's classes would always be well-attended. Patricia led them up the steps of the stadium seating to sit toward the back.

"What's the topic?" Kiernan asked once they were settled.

"No idea. She said it was a surprise, which is pretty usual for her."

Kiernan wondered whether Thea preferred to wait until the last minute to decide on the class content.

"She would've prepared for this for a while, though," Patricia continued. "She likes to think about the subject, really let it settle in her mind, before she writes anything out."

Everyone quieted down as Thea entered. Kiernan watched her stroll across the amphitheater, place her notes on a podium located at the front, and gaze around the room. As her eyes connected with various students, she nodded or smiled in greeting. When her eyes captured Kiernan's gaze, she heard her thoughts as clearly as if she were whispering the words in her ear. <*"Hello, lover. I can't wait to get you in my arms."*> Kiernan smirked at the sparkle in Thea's chocolate-colored eyes. They promised mischief. Hearing Patricia chuckle, she glanced over.

"This ought to be interesting," Patricia whispered.

Laughter brought Kiernan's eyes back to the front of the room. Thea was laughing. At first it was gentle and light, rolling across the air with an invitation. Thea's eyes crinkled, as she looked at everyone watching her. This seemed to feed her mirth. *What's making her laugh?* She didn't seem inclined to share the joke. Instead, her laughter became louder, more sustained. Tears began gathering in her eyes, and her hands rested on her hips as she leaned forward a bit. A giggle in the front started a wave of people giving in to the urge to join their voices. It didn't matter that they didn't know why Thea was laughing. She looked so happy, so carefree. People couldn't resist the compulsion to laugh, too.

Kiernan looked at Patricia, and they both burst out laughing. The crowd fed off each other, their voices surging across the room and bouncing off the walls. For several minutes Thea led the room's occupants with her laughter, but then a curious thing happened. The participants began to quiet down. The laughter turned to giggles and snickers, and people began taking deep breaths as they calmed down. Most people, Kiernan noticed, still sported huge smiles. Thea stood, smiling, quiet and calm while she swept her gaze across the room.

Finally, she spoke, "Good morning. My name is Thea Corelli, and in case you were unaware, this will not be a normal seminar."

People tittered at the pronouncement. Someone shouted out, "What was the joke?"

Thea raised an eyebrow. "You need a joke? Okay. What did Baby Corn say to Mama Corn?" She waited a beat. "Where's Pop Corn?" The way she delivered the punch line caused people to laugh once more. She grinned. "I believe that in order to discuss connecting with others, we need to connect." Thea waved her hand from left to right in an all-encompassing motion. "And you know one way to bring people together?"

"Laughter!" several people offered.

Thea nodded. "That's right. Laughter is a great ice breaker."

Kiernan's mind wandered to the last time they were able to spend time together a month ago. During the fall Thea came to New York several times, but with the acting classes Kiernan was teaching this semester, it was harder to find the time. Columbia was on spring break, and this was Thea's last class until the following Tuesday. They planned to spend the rest of the week together.

After class, Kiernan remained in her seat, listening to different conversations and watching Thea. She could see how happy teaching made her. It made her wonder whether she would ever consider teaching at Columbia or NYU or really anywhere in Manhattan. Kiernan had no doubt that Thea could secure a position in any of those institutions. But would Thea ever want to leave Massachusetts?

*Am I willing to leave New York?* It was a question Kiernan often visited. She wasn't sure, and it was that uncertainty which kept her from asking anything of Thea. She had no right to be so selfish. As it was, she'd been afraid to ask Thea to travel to

California with her to visit her father. She wanted to show Thea her childhood home, and she wanted her father to meet the woman who'd upended her world. They were leaving tomorrow night.

"Ready to go?" Patricia asked.

Kiernan looked up and saw her standing in the aisle. With a nod, she rose, and they made their way to the front of the room. Thea saw them, and her face brightened. Patricia hugged Thea before stepping aside, and Thea delivered a kiss on Kiernan's cheek with a soft greeting.

"Your class was wonderful. I'm glad I got to sit in," Kiernan said.

"Well, it's only fair since I sat in yours last month."

"Wait, how come I haven't been invited to go?" Patricia asked, indignation in her voice.

"It's an acting class," Kiernan said. "I don't think you'd find it interesting."

"Don't listen to her. It's fascinating," Thea said, pulling on her winter coat and gathering her things. "Let's go. I'll leave my car here. We can take the train to the North End and eat some of the best Italian you'll ever taste," Thea said. <*"That's not true, of course. You're the best-tasting Italian I've ever eaten."*>

Kiernan tripped, and Patricia's hand shot out to steady her while Thea choked back a laugh and Kiernan scowled.

"What did I miss?" Patricia asked, used to their wordless conversations.

"Nothing," Kiernan said, feeling her face heat up.

"Oh, it must have been good," Patricia crowed. "Look at your face."

A blast of cold air helped Kiernan cool down as they hurried down Commonwealth and stopped at the platform. She was glad to see a train coming toward them. The car was crowded, but they managed to find seats. They took their time over lunch.

Kiernan excused herself to use the restroom, wanting to freshen up. She stood in front of the mirror, touching up her makeup when Thea entered. Turning, Kiernan welcomed her kiss, taking her time to explore every inch of Thea's mouth. Her earlier comment had stirred Kiernan's blood, and she'd found it hard to push down the passion she felt every time she looked at Thea. It hadn't helped to hear Thea's constant mental monologue of all the things she intended to do to her once they arrived at her home. Thea had become quite good at sending mental snapshots, and each vision was sweet torture. Kiernan could see Thea's eyes slamming shut as her body arched during an orgasm, the sensuality so obvious in her rolling hips—each thrust long and slow. She saw Thea's lips spilling forth low-pitched sounds and her tongue licking her swollen lips. Kiernan groaned as their tongues explored together.

<*"Jesus Lesbian Christ! That's hot."*>

Kiernan broke the kiss with a small laugh, peering at Patricia, who was holding onto the doorknob, mouth dropped open.

"That must have been a great comment," Thea said with a smile.

"I'll have you know that my inner dialogue is pretty fierce," Patricia said with an indignant huff.

"I'm sure," Thea agreed.

"Anyway, sorry. I didn't mean to interrupt. I'm just gonna..." She pointed toward one of the stalls and made her way inside it.

Eyebrows raised, Kiernan smirked. She turned toward the mirror and applied her lipstick, watching Thea do the same. "See you at the table," Kiernan called. She clasped Thea's hand in hers and pulled her out of the room. "You are a trouble-maker."

"And you love it."

*And I love you*, Kiernan thought.

Thea stopped, and Kiernan barely managed to sidestep her. "What?"

Eyes wide, Thea broke into a wide smile. <*"I heard that. I love you, too."*>

It was Kiernan's turn for her eyes to widen. They reseated themselves at the table, grinning at each other like lovesick fools. Thea leaned in and covered her hand. "Can I tell you something?"

"You can tell me anything."

"Remember how I told you that I broke up with someone who moved to California?" Kiernan nodded. "I hadn't felt any inclination to try a long-distance relationship, never mind move with her across the country." She looked down at their hands, a slight blush covering her cheeks. When their eyes reconnected, Kiernan felt a surge of affection. She didn't know whether the emotion was from her or Thea, but it didn't matter. "I'd move with you. To you. For us. So, if you'll have us—me and Peanut—

that's something we can discuss. And it doesn't have to be anytime soon," she hurried on. "I just wanted to let you know."

Kiernan stared at her, allowing her words to sink in.

<*"Oh, my God. She isn't saying anything. I'm rushing her. What do I do?"*>

"Thea," Kiernan said, squeezing her hand to get her attention. "You're not rushing me. I want to plan a future with you. Whether that means I move here or you move to Manhattan, or we keep two homes and alternate depending on what projects we have, we'll work it out."

"You'd do that?"

"Of course. I love you, Thea."

"Shoot. I have the worst timing ever," Patricia complained, plopping into her seat.

Thea grinned. "It's okay." When Patricia looked at Kiernan, she nodded.

"Phew!" Patricia made a show of wiping her brow with her hand. "Twice in a row would tie my record."

"You have a record for interrupting important moments?" Thea asked.

"That's not much of a record," Kiernan mused, receiving an elbow in the side.

Patricia winked. "Really it was two times too many. Marcia and Lexie would give you a run for the title of hottest lesbian couple."

"I hear that title might belong to you and Rudi," Kiernan said. She covered her smirk with her glass, watching Patricia shift in her seat.

"Oh, um, we're not together. Not really. I mean, we're taking things one step at a time."

"But there's a possibility you might date her again?" Thea asked.

"Anything's possible," Patricia answered with a shrug.

"To possibilities," Kiernan raised her glass, waiting for Thea and Patricia to raise their glasses before taking a sip. She smiled, humming with pleasure as the taste of white wine filled her senses. She knew that whatever came next, she would enjoy experiencing it with such great women being a part of her life.

***

## KARINAN CYCLE 1 KATRINET 3

Ubel sat at the back of his cell, throwing small pebbles at the energy force field in a lackadaisical fashion. No one else was in the room, and no natural light streamed through the small slits high in the stone wall. He could hear dripping, although he was unable to determine from where the water was originating. The area was cold and damp.

He heard two guards talking the other day. Lerzep was in control of their planet, and he was restructuring their laws, making their people weaker by the day. He had even formed an accord with the humans, a peace treaty. To add insult to injury, he was allowing their mother to have input while Ubel rotted away on their moon, alone and forgotten.

Movement at the far end of the room caught Ubel's attention. He strained to hear anything, but all he could register was the sound of his own breathing. His eyes flicked across the expanse, waiting for several cakrae for any indication that someone else was close by. Blowing out a breath, Ubel tossed another pebble, expecting to see the shield shimmer when hit. He saw nothing.

Rising, Ubel made his way, one careful step at a time, to where the force field was positioned. He was surprised to not hear the alarm sound as he paced closer. If he touched an active force field, he would lose his hand. He turned, eyeing the area. During each meal, a guard watched him eat, retrieving the dirty utensils after Ubel finished. Nothing loose was in his living area. The bed was a wooden slab attached to the wall, and the thin fabric he used as a blanket was sewn down one side with a thin metal thread, also attached to the wall. He moved back to the force field which separated him from civilization and tilted his head, contemplating.

Gritting his teeth, Ubel inched his hand forward, holding his breath. Beads of sweat dotted his forehead, as he looked for any sign of energy waves, his ears swiveling. He saw nothing, heard nothing. He thrust his hand out and froze. He felt no pain. Shuffling forward, he passed the area and exhaled. Exhilaration filled him. *I'm free!* He ran to the door, checking to see how many guards were posted. He saw no one. Although he paused, uncertain as to whether he should trust his escape being this easy, he needed to take the chance.

He followed the corridors and found the exit without difficulty. Once outside, Ubel ran across the barren field to the outer perimeter. He hid behind a small utility shed, waiting for his breath to regulate. Once his breathing slowed, he left his hiding place and loped toward the shuttle yard. His heart was filled with savage joy. He would get off this moon and find his supporters. They would start again, rebuild and conquer. It would take time, but that didn't bother him. He turned between two rows of fighter shuttles and stopped short. Before him stood Lerzep, his mother, and several females dressed in military armor. He sneered.

"Ubel, right on time," Lerzep drawled. "We knew you would take any opportunity to leave your cell. Let me guess." He bared his sharp teeth. "You thought you could escape, round up some supporters, and reclaim the throne. That sound about right, dear brother?"

Ubel stood tall, waiting. He knew nothing good would come of this, but he refused to cower.

"You see, since you were in the line of succession, we could not execute you. Although most people support the changes we've made, some are still stuck in the past, wishing for the old ways. A dangerous, unstable royal escaping, however...that's a different story." Lerzep spread his arms wide. "We tried to take you in without bloodshed, but you resisted." He stared at Ubel. "Resist, Ubel. It's your last chance to escape."

Ubel charged forward, stopped in mid-stride by a blast of energy. He shrieked, the pain indescribable. With blurry eyes, he saw his mother holding her arms aloft, bright light streaming from her hands, and her face filled with sorrow. While he screamed, "No!" during the last moments of his royal life, his mother's voice answered him in his mind.

<"Yes.">

The End

# About Jazzy Mitchell

Jazzy Mitchell is the proud publisher of Launch Point Press and on the founding Board of Directors for OPUS Literary Alliance. Jazzy's the author of four other contemporary lesbian fiction novels: *Lost Treasures*—which received an Honorable Mention for the 2016 Rainbow Awards, *You Matter*, *Undertow*, and *Leveling Up*. Jazzy lives in Portland, Oregon, with her beloved wife, three vivacious children, and small in body but huge in spirit, five-pound puppy.

Connect with Jazzy

Facebook – JazzyMitchellauthor

Email –publisher@launchpointpress.com

Website – www.launchpointpress.com

## Note to Readers:

Thank you for reading a book from Launch Point Press. We have made every effort to edit this book. However, typos do slip in. If you find an error in the text or formatting, please email is at publisher@launchpointpress.com so the issue can be corrected.

We appreciate you as a reader and want to ensure you enjoy the reading process. We would like you to consider posting a review on your preferred media sites and/or your blog or website.

For more information on upcoming releases, author interviews, contests, giveaways and more, please sign up for our newsletter and visit us as at Launch Point Press: www.launchpointpress.com and "Like" us on Facebook: Launch Point Press.

Bright Blessings